A BLANKET FOR HER HEART

RC Bonitz

Cover Art: Evan Scheidegger

ISBN-13:978-1470117856
ISBN-10:1470117851

This book is dedicated to my dear friend Bobbie Griffith, my very first reader, editor and fan. My pen would long ago have gone still were it not for her.

And to my wonderful, loving family- My wife Karen and our children-Nancy, Sue, Lisa, Rob, and Amy

Also by RC Bonitz

A Little Bit of Blackmail

PROLOGUE

He checked into the old Victorian hotel, dragged the ancient ten-speed bike from the rack on the Toyota, and headed along the shore, away from town. The route was familiar, ridden many times with his wife long ago. Back then, only two or three boats rocked quietly in the harbor. Now there had to be three hundred, rivaling Newport just across the bay. Shops and restaurants, once part of a sleepy little town, thrived on the bustle of early season tourists.

He cleared the harbor and headed south over the sandy isthmus that held the island together. The land had a name he'd seen on maps, Conanicut Island, but he called the whole place Jamestown, after the town. Passing Fort Getty, he started up the long hill he hadn't seen since Carol died.

Proud of her riding, she'd always beaten him to the top, except once, that last time. He had teased her, laughing with victory. She had smiled and said it was just a fluke; she hadn't had her vitamins that day. A first warning, it had gone unrecognized.

That was a long time ago, before he met Ellie and before she dumped him last year. Inactive since then, the last of the climb he had to do on foot.

Back on the bike, he pedaled toward the lighthouse, up and down the rolling hills. The New England air was crisp, but warm enough, and the ancient bike rolled smoothly under one of those clear blue early June skies. Scrub trees and bushes lined the road and an old rock wall, nearly hidden in the undergrowth, followed the pavement, its neglected top missing stones.

The heaviness of his last few months returned with a sudden certainty the island was a lonely place to live, not at all as bright and open as he'd remembered it.

A bird high overhead caught his attention. An osprey or a hawk soaring, probably seeking prey. He caught his breath as it dove suddenly, flashing downward like a dart.

The bike lurched. His attention diverted, he had drifted into the ditch at the side of the road. Pulling hard to the left, he tried to recover, but the front wheel struck one large rock and then another. As if a spectator, he watched in disbelief as the wheel collapsed, pitching him forward, over the handlebars. The rocky ditch offered a hard greeting.

As his body registered pain, he lay unmoving, hoping someone would come by. But the road was devoid of homes or cars. He was alone.

Raw flesh against the rocks and pavement brought an involuntary cry as he struggled to get up. He lurched to his feet, his left arm crooked, panic clutching at his heart. Sliding his right arm below the left for support, he took a step and groaned in spite of himself.

A single driveway beckoned. It had to be followed, but its slippery, sloshing gravel made each step he took a grim adventure into pain. Finally, a house appeared deep in the woods, barely visible but a very welcome sight. Waves of pain ripped through the arm with each stumbling step, but he goaded himself onward.

"One more step, one more blasted step."

At last, the house. Thick shrubs shrouded the front, extending from the garage around to an L-shaped wing, a castle wall to block his entry. The garage was closed, no car in sight. Silence lay heavy in the air. He stared, numb, his mind uncomprehending. So much effort for nothing.

The deep roar of a motorcycle reached up from the road, unmistakable help gone by, a blow to his belly. Someone had to be home. Three steps toward the garage revealed a path, barely visible in the shrubs. He eased through, trying to avoid branches, and emerged in a sheltered courtyard.

~ ONE ~

First light formed leaf shadows on the cabinets as she entered the kitchen. Those big trees had been there for years, but they were old now, tall and thinned out, blocking less of the early morning sun. Winter sometimes seemed better, on sunny days when bright rays slid through barren branches to flood the breakfast table. Not always though. Not when winter's cold was dark and penetrating.

Bright and sunny, just comfortable, the day was starting well. She'd been up since three, reading and pacing, waiting for the light so she could start her day outside. Early was a pattern lately, into bed and out of it, bored to numbness when sleep was so elusive.

Her friend Molly thought it was time to see a doctor, but there was nothing a professional could say she didn't know already. Physically her health was perfect.

"I need a new bed, that's all," she told her friend. "Besides, I'm always thinking of what I'm going to do in the morning."

"What's so important?" Molly asked, and she offered the usual list of things.

That was what she did, things. This thing, that thing, nothing. Tend her garden, read Jane Austen or some travel book; wash the dishes, paint, or whatever. Granted, her paintings were beautiful and she did so many one always sat unfinished on the easel, but she hadn't sold any. Furniture restorations brought in some income, but she usually didn't do that many pieces.

Fifty-four years old and not counting, she lived like a hermit with few friends. She did know one neighbor, but she'd never married, and had always lived alone. Molly often told her she'd be happier if she did more with her life and she struggled with such thoughts these days.

She turned on the TV, hoping the movie channel might have something good.

Sly Stallone in his first *Rambo*. So stimulating. Thought provoking. Annoyed but too bored to care, she settled back in the sofa and within minutes the images barely touched her mind. By seven-thirty, she'd had enough and punched the off button with the remains of her wrist. Dry cereal and milk, half an orange, and coffee for breakfast; she dumped the dirty dishes in the sink twenty minutes later and abandoned the kitchen.

The patio garden looked like an impressionist's palette. Her one green thumb coaxed flowers to brilliant life year round. Indoors in winter of course, but she had plants ready to bloom as spring temperatures began. Each morning she spent two hours weeding and pruning, winding her fingers through the dirt to carefully arrange it to her whim. The stump of her left arm served as well as her right hand, caressing dirt and flowers with the same gentle touch. It was a touch returned by the earth, giving her the best hours of each day in quiet occupation of her mind. She put a dozen pansies in a juice glass and remembered she hadn't thanked Molly for picking up the flats this year.

After gardening, she returned rake and hoe to the garage and cleaned up at the slop sink in the corner. She wiped black dirt from her knees and delivered a good scrubbing to the right hand. A scrub brush screwed to the wall just above the sink did the job. Small stitch scars in her stump got an easy wipe. The skin was smooth and quite soft for all the abuse it got. Both hand and stump got a dose of hand cream, spread liberally, but only lightly rubbed. A wipe with the old towel she kept handy finished the job.

Lunch was the usual. Peanut butter and grape jam on white, red wine, and a handful of Lorna Doones. Sometimes it was cream cheese instead of peanut butter, chocolate chips instead of Lorna Doones, but that was about it as far as variety went. She took two glasses of merlot this time instead of one. That was not unusual lately.

Afterwards, she wrapped a dishtowel around the left arm and secured it with two rubber bands to wash the dishes.

"You'd be amazed what I can buy through the mail now, Hannah. Rubber bands, seeds, books, clothes, all sorts of things. You'd probably be selling things on a website these days yourself." She wiped the breakfast bowl with the left arm towel and set it on the drying rack. "Not like me though. I hate that ridiculous computer. Molly talked me into buying one, but I can barely turn it on right.

"I'm having trouble with that painting I've been working on too. It looks so bland, not even that maybe, so much as gray and dismal. I should probably trash the thing. You know what? I think I'm going to catch a little sun this afternoon."

It was one sided, this conversation with her dead grandmother, but quite all right. She knew it was imaginary, though sometimes it almost seemed she got an answer.

Her father got an occasional remark as well, but little more. It was Hannah she talked to, Hannah she often wished were truly at her side. Their chats had served to keep her company, at least until now. There was no one else to talk to most of the time.

Except Molly, or Grace, when one of them came around, which didn't seem to be that often lately. The house was still too, her world so very silent these last few months.

Dishes washed, towel removed, she headed for the bathroom, stripping off her pink tee shirt as she went. She dropped it in the hamper, brushed her teeth and hair, and relieved herself quickly. Then it was out to the patio, where she pulled one white lounge chair into place and stretched out to take the sun on her back. She'd heard all the cancer warnings, but never did the sun thing very long. Besides, everyone needed some vices in their life.

Face down on the lounge, wearing only shorts, she was drifting into sleep when something made a sound behind her. She turned. A man smiled weakly, then stared, eyes wide, as she dashed for the house.

"Please. I need help," he called as she slammed the door in his face.

Breathing hard, she crushed an ear against the heavy wooden door, trying to draw sound through it. There was only silence, a deafening unnerving lack of noise. She berated herself for being careless. In all her years of sunbathing, the crunching of tires on the gravel drive had given warning of someone coming. No one had ever caught her unexpectedly like that.

She ran to the bedroom and pulled on a sweatshirt, grabbed the phone, and dashed back to the hall. Windows open to catch the breeze had only screens to keep her safe. She heard a muffled sound and found him at a window, looking in.

"Go away," she shouted. "I called the police."

"Good."

Gray-faced, spotted with blood and clutching his left arm, he was clearly hurt.

"What do you want?" she demanded, berating herself as the words came out. He wanted help of course.

He stumbled to the lounge and eased down cautiously, mumbling something inaudible.

She keyed the phone then, for an ambulance and police, and cautiously opened the door.

"What happened to you?"

"I wrecked my bike."

"Are you all right?"

In response, he slumped further into the lounge.

Apprehensive, leaning against the front door with her hand on the knob, she studied him. He was about her age, tall, not fat, nice features, but too bloodied for further assessment. She heard the first siren approaching.

"You're bleeding on my furniture and now I have people coming here in droves. Why couldn't you have gone somewhere else?" she whispered softly.

She could have stepped out to help or comfort him, but she held tight to the door knob, just in case.

Tires sounded on the gravel as an ambulance rushed up to the house. One more look at him brought a sudden burst of sympathy and a memory, of a day long ago, of another accident. She wrapped her right hand around her left arm. Trembling, she turned to face more strangers.

"Through the bushes," she called from the walkway. A young man in his twenties and another, middle-aged, grabbed medical kits and followed her words. More sirens wailed as an emergency squad and two police cars arrived.

"What happened?" asked the young medic.

"He said he had a bike accident. I think he has a broken arm."

"Is he your husband? I'm sure he'll be okay," the young man said, giving her a reassuring smile.

"He just came and asked for help."

"That must be his bike on the road then."

A cop entered the patio, pulled out a notepad, and asked her name.

"Anne Hoskins," she replied brusquely and repeated what she'd told the EMT.

Answering innumerable questions, wishing for escape into the house, she winced as they moved the man to a stretcher. The cop roughly patted the man's pockets, looking for identification.

He found a wallet, withdrew a number of cards, and announced, "His name is Paul Breland. He's from Connecticut."

"You better give me his insurance card," said the medic. "He'll need it."

~ * ~

One by one, they started to leave, and she realized her body had calmed down. The trembling had been no surprise, but its sudden ending with strangers around was. No matter, she didn't need this. It was better that they went away and left her alone. Good riddance.

Yet when the last attendant climbed into the ambulance, and its flashing lights tore away, the very solitude she'd always sought was suddenly disconcerting.

Back on the patio, none of the white plastic furniture seemed to be in its usual place, but it was hard to be sure because nothing really had a usual place. Blood spots on the lounge cushion caught her eye and she was glad it was washable. The stains came off without much trouble and suddenly all sign of their presence had disappeared. It was an odd thought, so she buried it, just like the note of pity for the man.

Life worked better that way. All feeling in a deep hole, well hidden. She roamed the patio, aimlessly moving cushions and chairs, trying to put her thoughts in order. It was no good. One after another, fear, then anger, then an unknown exhilaration brought agitation, until the fear prevailed as it always did when the lid came off. At least the fear felt comfortable in a way. An old acquaintance, it was known and manageable. She picked up the phone and put it down, then finally dialed.

"Island Realtors."

"Molly, it's Anne."

"Hi! How's your day going?"

"Can you come here? I just had visitors. A whole crowd of people."

"Are you all right? What's going on?"

"Can you come?"

"Ten minutes."

She dropped the phone on the lounge and paced, trying to settle herself. How silly, to get so wound up about a bunch of people coming to her door.

Her mind changed direction then, to something easier to manage. The bike he rode should be retrieved. The man might come back for it someday. She would, were she him. It was likely still where he fell unless it had been stolen. She entered the house to find her old loafers that went on easily, then hurried back to the patio.

Walking down the drive, she moved slowly, deliberately placing each foot in front of the other. This wasn't a walk to enjoy, this path to the world. When her neighbor Betty came by they sometimes ran along the road, but that was different. She focused on Betty and the running, excluding all else, and that worked.

This walk was more the usual, done with anxiety, a tension that ate at her. It wasn't bad, not like years ago, but it was there, and she knew it was and still kept going.

She reached the road, but there was no bike, just a road, and the whole business seemed to be one of her dreams. A reflection a few yards away caught her eye. Gold-rimmed eyeglasses, twisted and bent, lay broken at the edge of the wild grass. She reached for them, sure they were his.

A car approached. Anxiety surged in her belly and she turned to study the stone wall buried in the brush. Another car appeared as she started back to the drive. Stupid, she didn't have to avoid being seen like this. Impulsively, she made no attempt to hide her arm. The car passed and she started up the drive without breaking stride.

"That wasn't so bad, Hannah. At least I found his glasses. It wasn't a dream."

With the glasses safely stashed in her studio, it was time to change. She found bra and tee shirt and a better pair of shorts in her bedroom chest and dressed again, this time taking care. Running a comb through her short, wavy hair, she decided Molly would want coffee. She always did. Pacing the kitchen, she watched the black liquid drip into the glass pot and the numbers slowly flip by on the old digital clock. Finally, a car sounded in the gravel.

~ * ~

Molly embraced her, then stood back and stared. A friend of many years, still attractive, she was two years younger than Anne, and like Anne unattached. In her case, that was unusual.

"You look calm enough. What happened?"

Anne launched into the story of the injured man and the police and ambulance crews. "Wasn't that something?" she concluded.

"I don't know. Are you all right?"

"It's almost as if I didn't want them to leave," Anne whispered.

"Were they nice to you?"

"They were busy with that man. They practically ignored me. I mean, I didn't want them here, but when they left I felt... I don't know."

"Nobody made a fuss?"

Anne's face went hot, knowing exactly what Molly meant. Her left arm was something she did her best not to discuss.

"I can't believe I didn't want them to leave."

"Maybe you just wanted someone to talk to."

"You think I'm lonely? I'm very comfortable with my life. You know that."

As soon as the words were out the skin of her arms prickled. She was accustomed to being alone was what it was, but not quite as satisfied with her existence as she had been once.

"What about the guy?"

"What about him? I didn't even talk to him except to find out he was hurt."

"I wonder how he's doing."

"Why do you care?"

"Because he was here and you helped him. Aren't you curious?"

"Not in the least."

"I don't believe you."

Typical Molly, thinking she was so smart sometimes. "I'm mixed up, that's all. Those people didn't bother me very much."

"You sound surprised. You've been up to Providence to see Dan and Grace twice this past month. Don't you think there might be a trend there?"

"What? That I like going out now? Dan had work for me. It was strictly business."

"Yes, but you don't usually go to their shop."

"Well, I did this month. It was nothing special." She shook her head, reassuring herself.

She wandered outside again when Molly left, mulling over her unruly thoughts. Clothes stayed on this time and the day played in her mind and wouldn't let go. Molly's comments and her reactions were all a jumble. She hadn't mentioned the glasses. They were in the studio, on the shelf beneath her palette. If Molly had asked why she had them she would have had no answer, but Molly never got the chance.

The stranger was a bit intriguing. Paul Breland? In great pain clearly, yet still strong enough to find help for himself, a stoic apparently. His hands and legs and even his face had been one big bloody mess, but he never complained.

Trying to picture his face without the blood didn't work and the best she could do was guess at the color of his hair. Black, or was there a little gray around the edges? Was he a neighbor? Betty was the only one she knew.

Connecticut, the cop said, of course. She wondered if Mister Breland was married with ten kids, and envied Molly's nerve again. Molly went after what she wanted and could probably get Paul Breland, ten kids or not. Maybe not for long, Molly never kept her men very long, but she'd be happy for a while. A burst of anger startled Anne. Was she jealous? Of Molly with her men? How ridiculous was that?

Her missing left hand was not a problem when it came to function. There was very little she couldn't do, but that wasn't all of it. It was people, how they looked at her, or offered assistance as if she were helpless, or avoided her eyes. Staring, gaping people whispering behind her back as if they knew her secret. Whispering and laughing and turning their backs on her like they did in high school. Staying home was easier, and she'd kept to herself so long strangers were quite alarming.

She went out, but only at certain times and to certain places. A run with Betty twice a week was fine. Molly thought going to Dan's antique shop in Providence was a change but it wasn't. He and Grace were like family. She visited them occasionally and didn't mind because there was parking behind their shop and a back door and never anyone to see her.

Life was mostly good the way it was. Unencumbered, she could do what she wanted when she wanted. Still, now and again, there had been dreams of men, and marriage, and children. Even one man who'd been real, except she'd been a fool and that had been a fiasco. Dreams passed, but this injured visitor may have started one of those 'again' times and with a difference now. All those people and that man on her patio, they'd been real, and she didn't feel like herself.

~ * ~

She rose early the next morning to work on Dan's cabinet. The garage had been built for two cars, but she had one, an old Ford, rarely used. She'd walled in half the space and converted it to a workshop. An old-fashioned radio console, partially restored, stood on a low table in the center of the shop. There was one coat of polyurethane on the body of the cabinet and the doors were ready to be done.

But the day was too pleasant to be wasted, so she threw open the window and door to capture the warm sunlight, then began her work. She would rather have finished the piece in French polish, but Dan insisted it wasn't valuable enough to make the effort. It would get quite a bit of polishing before she finished nonetheless.

With the cabinet by the open door, she used an orbital sander fitted with extremely fine paper and then shifted to hand work. There was no confusion in the effort and that was a fine thing at this moment in her life. Completely absorbed, she was about to start the last section when crunching gravel announced a visitor. Not expecting anyone, she locked the door and peered out anxiously.

It was a strange car, carrying two people, but she couldn't identify them through the glass. A hurried call to Molly's office reached the answering machine, so she left a quick cry for help and hung up. Then she shook herself. All right, she wasn't a baby, and besides, who would bother to come up the long driveway after her? Who even knew she lived alone? She picked up a hammer and faced the window. Act your age, she told herself, trembling just a bit.

The car stopped. A man and a woman emerged. It was the man from the accident, with his arm in a sling.

~ TWO ~

A fog of light seemed to fill his eyes as he came awake. Intelligence returned, and he hurt. All over, everywhere.

"Hi Dad."

He turned to see his eldest daughter sitting in a chair beside his bed. A hospital bed.

"Hi Jane," he said matter-of-fact, glancing somewhat carefully at his surroundings.

"What happened to you?"

He told her the story; of the bird, the deserted road and the woman. Jane asked who she was and where it happened, but he still felt somewhat groggy, grew frustrated, and gave up.

"What were you doing all the way up here?"

"Your Mom and I used to ride our bikes in Jamestown."

She looked surprised at the reference to her mother. He realized there hadn't been much mention of Carol in recent years. He swore silently, remembering the screw up at the end.

"I talked to the doctors. You have a broken arm. You'll be in a cast for a while," Jane said.

"You've told Scott and Helen?"

"Yes. Your other children will be calling."

"Nobody has to call."

Paul thought about the bird, and the woman, and the gravel driveway to her house. None of it was clear. The woman seemed to be a phantom, an elusive face in a shroud of pain. Was he full of drugs? No, the pain was there, lurking, just waiting for him to move. He shifted his body a tiny bit and learned exactly how much good some drugs might do.

"I'm tired."

"Rest then. I'll be here," Jane whispered.

~ * ~

The following day she brought fresh clothes to take him home. He was sitting on the edge of the bed, ready to go, when she arrived.

"You certainly look better than you did yesterday. I'll help you dress."

"No thanks, I live alone remember? I need to be able to care for myself."

"That's ridiculous. You'll stay with us," she told him, but he gave her a hard stare. "I know, you want to go home."

"Wait out in the hall would you? I'll give a shout if I need help getting dressed. By the way, I want to stop and thank that woman. Do you mind?"

"No, of course not. Do you remember where she lives?"

"How can I forget?"

~ * ~

He directed her over the bridge and onto the small streets of Jamestown and eventually to the gravel drive.

"This is it."

"You were lucky she was near the road when you fell," Jane said, as she headed the car into the woods.

"I walked up the drive."

"All this way with your arm such a mess? Good Lord, Dad."

"I was a little fuzzy when I reached the house." He grinned at the awe in her voice.

"This driveway has to be hundreds of feet long."

"I'd guess about three hundred, yeah."

She parked near a garage. He got out of the car and led her through thick shrubbery to a terrace. That much he remembered.

He took in the flowers surrounding the patio, all colors, all kinds, blooming everywhere, and the row of bushes he'd been so concerned about yesterday. A wall of shrubbery, strong and seemingly impenetrable, secure against intruders.

"It's like a greenhouse," Jane said.

"All I remember is how glad I was to find someone here."

Standing in the center of the patio, surveying the place, he remembered it, sort of.

Two chaise lounges, a table, and chairs with brightly colored cushions filled the space near a carved Spanish-style front door. The door was attached to a two-story structure that seemed to be the original house. A stone chimney, cracked clapboards, and thick paint on the window frames suggested considerable age. To the right, a one-floor section included the garage. A more modern wing, with high roof, large windows, and two skylights, made an 'L' from the left end of the original house.

Paul knocked on the door and then wandered over to the large windows. Shading his eyes, he peeked through the glass.

"She's a painter. There's an easel and some paintings in there."

"Maybe her husband paints. Don't be so nosy."

"No harm done," he said in a tone that rejected her admonition.

The door swung open and a woman stood there, framed against the darkness of the interior. She wore a plain white tee shirt and paint-streaked blue jeans. Her beautiful blue eyes and long dark lashes struck Paul like an arrow to the heart.

"Hello," she said. "You're the man from the accident."

"I wanted to thank you for your help yesterday," he croaked, amazed to think he hadn't seen how beautiful she was the other day.

She wasn't twenty, but her body could be, and her eyes, those long lashed eyes, riveted him in place.

"Anyone would have done it," she said, giving Jane a nervous look as if she were afraid the newcomer might bite.

"This is my daughter, Jane Carson."

The woman nodded and Jane added her thanks too.

"You're welcome," she said, and lapsed into silence.

Her short dark hair, sprinkled with flecks of gray, had a slight curl to it. Paul stared, captivated, then abruptly turned away to avoid embarrassing himself.

He caught Jane smiling at his reaction and felt a touch of heat rise in his face.

"I'm sorry," he said in his normal voice. "I don't know your name. I'm Paul Breland."

"My name is Anne Hoskins. I know yours from the accident." She hesitated, then added, "The policeman told me."

He nodded, feeling unbelievably fidgety. "Nice to meet you officially. Thanks again."

"You're welcome."

"We're on our way home, but I wanted to thank you first."

"That's very nice. Thank you." She paused, and her face changed just a touch, a bit of concern showing in her eyes. "Is your arm broken?"

"It's not a bad break."

"That's good. I'm glad."

"Thanks." Feeling mindlessly stupid, struggling to say something intelligent, he glanced around. "Your flowers are beautiful. I don't know how I didn't notice the other day."

Her face reddened and she did a little half bob of her head. "You didn't?"

"To be honest, I didn't notice much of anything. I was just so relieved to see you."

"Relieved?"

He wondered why Ms. Hoskins seemed so nervous, the way she answered, but he went right on.

"Sure. I thought maybe there was no one here, but there you were, sunbathing." He stopped, remembering something else he'd forgotten. "I'm sorry. If I had known. You know..."

The woman shook her head. "It doesn't matter. You couldn't have done anything else." She glanced at Jane, who looked confused. "I was sunbathing when he came. You know."

She displayed a shy smile and a touch of red in her cheeks and Paul thought Jane understood. At least he didn't have to explain and neither did Ms. Hoskins and he was glad of that.

"I expect it's normally very private here," Jane said.

"I hear the cars coming. The gravel makes noise."

Jane smiled and got a small one in return.

"Are you an artist?" Paul asked, pointing to the large windows.

"It's just a hobby."

"That looks like a regular studio."

Anne Hoskins smiled with more confidence than he'd seen in her so far. "It is."

"Do you paint a lot?"

"Yes."

Paul was no expert or critic, but he had some nice paintings in his house and he liked art. "Do you mind if I peek?"

"From here? Go ahead."

She looked from him to Jane and away again, almost like an animal in a trap. Paul hesitated, wondering what to do, but he walked to the window and looked in anyway, tossing caution aside.

"You did all those canvases?"

"Yes."

"I like art," he said quietly.

"That's nice."

Nice? He was being as sweet as he could and she was not reacting, not the way he would have liked her to at least. She looked like she wished she were anywhere but there.

He studied her a second longer, decided she was shy, that was all. What to say next. The sound of crunching from that gravel on her drive put an end to his frustration for the moment. She glanced at him, her expression an apology, and excused herself to greet this new arrival.

Jane grinned at him like a Cheshire cat. He had flipped over this woman and she knew it. He gave her a wink.

A car door slammed and a voice said, "Are you okay? What happened?"

Paul couldn't hear Anne's reply, but seconds later she returned, trailing behind a blonde full figured woman in a tan suit and ruffled red blouse.

"Hello," the woman said, with one of those "I just love you so, so much," sweet smiles that Paul always thought were completely phony.

"Hi." He stared at her for a second.

This woman was the antithesis of their hostess. She was pretty and worked at it, but there were miles on her Anne Hoskins didn't have. And there was that fake smile.

"Molly, meet Mister Breland and his daughter Jane. This is my friend, Molly Wagner."

"Nice to meet you," Molly said, her eyes on Paul.

He acknowledged the greeting with a nod, and Jane gave her a polite, "Nice to meet you too."

Watching her, Paul thought Jane could have said, "Drop dead," and Ms. Wagner wouldn't have noticed. She was a flirt and had her eye on him. He almost laughed, but kept his expression as staid and polite as he could.

"What brings you here?" Molly asked.

"They came to thank me for helping yesterday," Anne said.

"Oh, that's nice. How's your shoulder?" Molly continued.

"It's my arm. Not bad. I'm on pain killers."

"That doesn't look like any cast I've ever seen. Can you move your arm?"

"It's temporary, until the swelling goes down."

"You certainly collected enough scrapes and bruises, poor thing."

"I slid along the ditch when I went down," Paul said, and Anne gave a small shudder. Sweet of her, he thought, and somehow that did not surprise him.

He caught Anne's eye and got a fleeting, enigmatic smile, wondered if she were uncomfortable or maybe even a little confused by what was going on. Her friend was trying to interest him without a doubt, and had to have done this in front of her before? Or maybe not?

"Have you seen Anne's paintings?" Molly continued.

"I beg your pardon?"

"She's an excellent artist, you know."

"We know," Jane replied.

Noticing the look of panic on Anne's face, Paul nodded, though he couldn't really guess how excellent Anne Hoskins might be.

At that, Anne started to interrupt, but Molly kept going. "Anne, why don't you show him?"

Anne glared at her and hesitated. Her friend moved closer to Paul, as though she were going to take his good arm and lead him into the house.

"That's okay. We hardly know each other," he said, determined to let Anne off the hook.

"It's time for us to go, Dad," Jane added.

She started for the driveway with Anne hurrying to lead the way. Paul had no choice but to hang back with Molly, who had taken his arm and was in no hurry.

"Do you live around here?" she asked.

"No, in Connecticut."

"You didn't ride a bike all the way from there, did you?"

"I drove up."

"Is your car still here?"

"Yes. We'll have to see if that hotel in town will let us pick it up in a week or so," Jane said.

"You can leave it here, Anne won't mind," Molly said, without blinking an eye.

Anne agreed, but it was politeness speaking, Paul believed. Her face suggested her friend's offer wasn't quite welcome.

"There's room in the driveway," Molly added.

It didn't matter if Anne disliked the idea. She intrigued him. He wouldn't let the opportunity slide by.

"Thanks. That would be great. We'll bring it over when we leave."

"I don't think so, Dad. You've had anesthesia. No driving yet."

"I'll drive it for you," Molly said.

"Thank you," Jane said, obviously happy for that offer at least.

"Are you coming along Anne?" Paul said hopefully.

"No thank you. I'll wait here."

~ * ~

They were heading for I-95 by way of Route 3, near the town of Kingston. He hadn't said a word since leaving Anne's house.

"You're plotting something, I can tell," Jane said.

Paul broke into a smile. "That woman should have herself a dog. A big black, mean dog for protection out there in the boondocks."

Jane laughed. "I don't see her with a dog like that. She'd have a cocker spaniel or a little poodle, a dog to keep her company and cuddle with when she got lonely."

"You think she lives alone?" he asked.

"I wouldn't be surprised. Her house and friend, it just feels like that to me. I think Molly came to help her when we showed up."

He stared at the road again. Anne Hoskins had looked nervous. If she had a man in her life, she probably would have called him. "I don't know. You might be right."

"I think you hope I am. You like her."

"She's a nice woman."

Jane laughed softly. "Pretty, you mean. Don't kid me."

He ignored the tease. "She's talented too. I only saw a few of her paintings through the window, but they're beautiful."

"She seemed a little nervous about something."

"Yes, shy I think," Paul said.

"You don't know that. We're complete strangers to her though, so maybe. Did you notice her hand yesterday?"

"No. I hurt too much after the accident."

"What about that? Does it bother you?"

"Her hand? Why should it bother me? When you get past thirty we all have wounds. Hers is just there for all to see."

Unlike his.

His vision seemed to dim, the way it did sometimes when he went into himself. There were scars and there were scars, and he had plenty of his own. He would not screw things up again.

He sat back in the seat and closed his eyes, trying to let his breathing settle down. He used to think he was having a heart attack when the pressure in his chest grew tight, but he'd come to know it was only the aching grief. Only, that was a laugh. At least doctors could treat a heart attack if it didn't kill him. Nothing could take away this pain. He had thought Ellie would, but she hadn't, not even close.

Ellie. He had wanted her to be so right, but she wasn't. They'd met about three years ago. He'd been lonely and she seemed to be the one he needed. Wrong. He'd been blind, but his kids had pegged her from the start. A gold-digger, that's what Jane had called her.

His radar was normally pretty good when it came to spotting phonies. He never trusted women who seemed too sweet, too interested, too enamored of his charms. Crap, his charms were about as shiny as a worn out piece of sandpaper. Ellie had been enamored though, or so it had seemed. Very much like Anne's friend with her smiles and gushing conversation.

He almost laughed aloud thinking about her and Anne Hoskins. Anne reminded him of Carol. Quiet, friendly, genuine. She wasn't as brusque as Carol had been when he met her, but Anne had something he couldn't put his finger on. Carol did too, in the beginning. He'd figured her out eventually.

In Carol it had been the sweetness, the love in her eyes for everyone she knew. His breath caught. Anne might have that too? Her eyes were beautiful, stunning, magical. Filled with love? He tried to clear his head. He was attributing Carol's magic to Anne. That was stupid. Anne was a mystery to him. He didn't know a thing about her. But she was magical. A beautiful, single, magical mystery woman. And he had a chance to see her again. He laughed.

Jane laughed too.

"What?" he asked.

"You think you have this Anne all figured out."

He didn't reply, just grinned. His children thought they knew him so well. The only thing he knew was he wanted to see the lady again. Wanted to look into those beautiful blue eyes again.

~ THREE ~

His Toyota sat under her big maple tree, inanimate and benign, but there. She liked order, and her own routines, and now that car was there, bringing only one certainty- his eventual return.

Last month the contractor spreading new gravel had damaged that beautiful tree. He'd hit it with his tractor and ignored her shouts until the gravel she threw hit him in the back. She amazed herself that day, and remembered it with pride. The last of the gravel went down with rake and shovel, by her, wearing the stupid prosthesis of course. It took forever, but she still felt pleased with herself for the whole business.

Molly had parked his car so close to the tree it might have scraped it too, but no, it was fine. Bird droppings violated the hood, but that was fine too. Better the birds than a dent and accident reports.

The house was as silent as a hole in the ground. The contrast was startling, people and voices and faces on the patio, this man and his daughter here, and all of them gone again. Two days she never imagined, and then it ended, all the excitement gone. She shook herself. He'd come back for his car.

Molly made an appearance Monday with her usual groceries, and more.

"What's in the other bag?" she asked.

Molly smiled. "Makeup. A little perfume too."

"What for?"

"You. Sit down and I'll show you how to put it on."

She frowned. "You know I don't use any of that."

"Listen, the man's coming back? You need to be ready."

"What for?"

The question was rhetorical; she didn't need Molly's answer. It was only her annoyance speaking. Who said she needed makeup? And why? She disliked Molly's assumption. Assumptions. That he liked her and that she wanted him. Those two for starters. Suddenly her hands felt warm and damp.

"Anne, you know what I mean. The man likes you."

"I'm an old maid. That's silly."

"You're not old. He paid no attention to me. It's you, my girl."

"You sound like he's going to ask me for a date or something. He was just being polite."

"To me. He positively gushed over you."

"Men don't gush!"

"Anne, I only saw him for a minute, but when he looked at you- believe me, he was gushing. It's a great chance. You want to knock his socks off when he comes."

"No I don't," Anne hissed as a knot twisted in her stomach.

Molly ignored her. "It's some of my extra makeup that I thought might look good on you. I'll show you what to do."

Typical Molly, in her face as usual, but she had no desire to start a fight just then. Not with her brain spinning as it was. She couldn't get her head around the idea. Paul Breland gushing over her?

Good grief, she was over fifty and missing a hand. Her life had a pattern, a routine she didn't know how to change. It had to be a mistake, Molly was wrong.

"Molly, I'm not interested in this. Why would I want to seduce him?"

That got her a grin from Molly. "Seduce? Your word, not mine, love."

"That's what you're talking about. Make myself up to trap him."

"Don't worry. The man likes you and he's coming back. You want to look your best when he does, don't you? Nobody's talking seduction."

"I don't see the difference, and besides, I don't care if he likes me. Older men like eighteen year old blondes, not old maids like me."

Molly stared at her, apparently considering the remark. "You've got a point, but only if they fit the stereotype. He likes you, believe me."

"He probably found out I have some money and thinks he's going to cheat me."

"Oh stop. He's a nice guy."

"We have no way of knowing that."

Molly sighed. "Actually, I could Google him and find out." She grinned. "Maybe he has a record. He's a serial killer who goes after old maids for their money."

"Now you're being silly."

"Listen, I'll take a look and see what I find. In the meantime, have some fun with him."

"No thank you," Anne said, trying for angry, but having a hard time breathing properly.

Why did she feel so anxious? Paul Breland wasn't a serial killer. That much she was almost sure of.

"Well then, we'll forget the makeup. As long as you're clear about him, of course."

"I am," she said, but with a gnawing thorn beneath the words.

Clarity would be nice on the subject of Mister Breland, but trying to forget the man was like holding up her hand to stop the waves on the beach.

Molly's sarcasm she did not need either. And makeup that she would not use. There had never been a reason for it in her life and there was no need now. Molly was a dear, but a know-it-all at times and this was one of those occasions.

Anne sent her home unhappy, which happened rarely, but she felt incapable of placating her friend at the moment.

A white vase stood on the Shaker table in the hall, filled with pink roses. The vase was solid, sturdy, not her style, a gift from Grace and she cherished it accordingly. She'd actually grown fond of it. The roses had come a few days before Paul's arrival, a not infrequent gift from Molly. She liked roses. Anne did too, but had none in the garden. The Japanese beetles devoured them unless she used chemicals and she wouldn't. The other flowers did well enough on their own. Absently, she ran a finger along the vase and brushed against a rose petal.

A friend since high school, Molly always helped. She did the shopping and whatever else wanted doing in the outside world. Grace though, she was Anne's second mother. Anne loved her as she'd loved her grandmother. Not quite the same way perhaps, but nearly as much.

Molly handled the mundane and simple sort of secrets, the ones that sisters shared, but it was Grace she needed this time. All-the-answers-Molly she'd had enough of at the moment. It was calm advice she wanted and Grace was the one for that.

Dan answered at the shop and said they were busy.

"All right. It's not important," Anne said.

"I'll have her call you back."

"All right," she said again, but it wasn't.

"I'm not upset," she insisted when they called back minutes later, Grace on the main phone and Dan on the extension in the storeroom.

Dan laughed. "Sure. That's why you sounded like a dead rat on the phone."

The words drew a "Dan, for goodness sake!" from Grace, but she continued asking questions.

How was she to tell Grace why she called? Anne liked her life, didn't want it disrupted, but there she was, a mess over a thing that might never be.

He'd take his car and go away and it would all be over. She'd be glad of that, and yet her pulse took off for the ceiling at the idea.

Grace was so pleased to hear of Mister Breland you'd think she was about to marry the man. She didn't argue with her as she had with Molly. Grace just said not to worry and let things happen as they would. It sounded so easy when Grace said it. Everything would be fine.

Anne believed her, perhaps because she wanted to, or had great faith in Grace, or was simply tired of second guessing herself. She hadn't asked anyone's advice twenty years ago when she jumped off a cliff all on her own and made such a mess of things.

All right, she'd take Grace's advice. When he returned, she'd see what he wanted to do. If he elected to see the paintings, she'd let him. If he took his car and went away, she wouldn't get upset.

But she was upset. He represented something. An opportunity for excitement, for the life she'd let pass by, for love she never thought she'd have. Molly was right. He seemed to be a very sweet man and he was interested in her. A storm of curiosity seized her heart. She wanted him to want to see her paintings.

~ * ~

She made an early breakfast and followed it by her usual dressing in slop clothes to pull weeds when the beds dried a little after last night's rain. Not too much though, damp soft ground made for easy work. Next came a shower and better clothes before choosing the first activity of the day.

The old black chair Dan gave her to repair awaited attention, but she disliked the ugly thing and dawdled over it. It could wait another day before she did anything with it.

She started a new canvas, but the brush made choices of its own and the result left her unhappy again. It wasn't the first painting she'd discarded, but nothing went right the next two days.

She stumbled on a familiar trail behind the house and gave her ankle a painful twist. It wasn't serious though, just sore. She had to remember everything would work out just fine, whatever happened with Paul Breland.

~ * ~

Molly's call started with the usual "Hi. How are you?" but grew serious very quickly. It was plain she and Anne had been thinking the same thoughts since meeting Mister Breland.

"Have you heard from our accident victim?"

"No, not a word."

"Well, don't worry. He'll call."

"I should hope so. He's going to need his car."

"You want the makeup?"

There was something extra in Molly's tone, subtle annoyance perhaps. Anne wasn't sure.

"No. I told you. Just forget it."

"Anne, he's not going to bite you. Look at me. How many men have I had in my life? I've survived."

More orders she didn't want, and she snapped out a reply. "I was there Molly. I held your hand through the hard times, remember?"

"Okay, okay. But remember, he prefers you. He'll be calling soon. Let me know if you want a chaperone."

"Did you Google him?"

"I did a quick look. You can't imagine how many Paul Brelands' there are. It's going to take a while."

"Well, I don't need a chaperone, so do that instead if you want to help."

Molly didn't actually seem upset, but she had to be hurt. That stupid crack about being there, and the man preferred Anne to her? Everything had an edge suddenly, small and sharp. Edges could hurt and she wanted no part of that.

~ * ~

Every time she stepped outside his Toyota sat there, under the maple tree, bird droppings and all. She cleaned it for him, darned if she knew why. Finally, he called to say they'd come for it, he and his daughter. When he asked her out to lunch it was a shock, the wrong thing of all he might have said. She couldn't do that. Not with him or anyone.

Trembling suddenly, she offered lunch at the house instead and he accepted. She was just trying to be polite, wasn't she? Oh my, she was on a road to somewhere.

She bustled about the house the next morning, cleaning, rearranging, polishing, and worrying. It had all been done yesterday, but she did it again, needing something to burn energy, to calm her heart. By eleven, she was looking for non-existent dirt and the clock told her it was well past time to stop. After one final inspection, she dashed for the shower. The house would have to do.

It was only when she thought of what to wear that reality found her at last. She'd been pretending all week. A very nice man would arrive soon and Molly said he liked her.

She wanted him to. He wasn't like the carpenter who built her studio addition—the guy she threw herself at twenty years ago. The guy she'd imagined wanted her, except it turned out he had a wife—after she'd made a horrendous fool of herself.

Paul was sweet, interested in her as a person, as an artist. And he was better looking, even if he was older. What would it be like to have sex with him? Maybe she should be utterly impractical again. She'd gotten a taste of life with the carpenter before the truth came out. She'd survived.

Why not another little snack? Dear God, at least Molly always thought she was into something permanent. Sex snacks, what was happening to her?

She pawed through the closet to find her best skirt and newest blouse. Her dressiest outfit, but completely out of date now, both should have been replaced some time ago. She plopped down on the edge of the bed and stared at the mirror behind the door, a bone in the pit of her stomach suddenly. Oh my, she looked awful.

Nothing but tired old clothes to wear, a sunburned face, and hair in a mess. Not a good time to finally care how she looked. She had a nice life, just the way she wanted it, but here she was going crazy over a man. She scowled at the face looking back at her. Now she'd decided to want him? Oh brother. She should have used the makeup when she had the chance.

She pulled Grandma Hannah's fancy silver hairbrush through one last time as tires sounded in the gravel, did another look in the mirror, excited this time, smacked a smile on her face, and hurried out to greet them.

"I heard your car. Please come in."

"Thanks for the invitation," Paul responded. He offered his hand and she gave hers in return. He squeezed gently. A tingle began at her fingers and raced up her arm. Oh my, that was not good. She'd never felt that with the carpenter.

"It's my pleasure," she replied and realized she was wearing a silly schoolgirl smile. Once she knew it was there, it was engraved for the duration. She said hello to his daughter and Jane looked amused. Laughing at her? Oh well, the young woman was polite enough.

"It's good to see you," he said.

"Me too," she said, and felt like a country bumpkin.

He asked if she'd done any painting since last week and she told him she had, but it wasn't very good. She opened the door and he was inside, his feet on her hall floor, his daughter beside him. An easy thing after all. The house hadn't collapsed. She was still alive.

He hesitated in front of her studio as if he wanted to go in.

"Could I see your paintings? I'll be careful."

Careful with your thoughts? Careful with your words? That was all that mattered. But even though she hadn't actually said he could go in, he was standing in the doorway, studying the stacks of paintings lining the walls.

"How do you choose titles for them?" he asked.

"They don't have titles."

"None of them?"

"None of them."

He nodded as if in simple acknowledgment, and then added another question.

"Where do you get your inspiration?"

"It just comes."

He was in the studio now; how had that happened? Drifting slowly to the first row of stacked paintings, he studied the one in front. She caught herself smoothing her skirt. Be still hand, be still!

Silently, he moved to the next pile, looking only at the top painting. The next was based on flowers, size exaggerated, colors brilliant, as she liked them. That one she did two years ago. He stopped again and nodded again and moved on.

A lighthouse scene, done long ago, more realism than her recent work. He turned as though to speak, said nothing and continued. He studied a fourth, silent again and moved on once more. A touch to her arm. She turned; it was Jane with a smile and a whisper.

"He likes them."

As if he'd heard, he said. "They're beautiful. You're very good."

His approval brought her pleasure, one brief fleeting instant and no more. What did he know of art? And what did she care for his opinion anyway? A stranger, off the street, a lover imagined ever so briefly, but still unknown. She was a fool. If this was what it was to have a man around she didn't need a bit of it.

Her heart pounded with hot emotion. Who was he to keep her in suspense, to judge her? And she'd allowed him to, silly fool.

Oblivious, smiling happily, he asked if he could see her other work as well.

"Lunch is ready. We'll eat first." A pathetic answer that was, but she didn't know what else to do. Why was she so angry?

~ * ~

It felt strange to have a man at her kitchen table. Dan had been there many times, but that was like having her father across from her. Not quite, as Dan brought easy conversation and laughter. She would certainly welcome his presence at this moment.

Paul's face came alive when their eyes met and she tried to return his smile, but she had to struggle not to look away. Her eyes seemed to lock on his firm chin and that touch of gray in his dark hair. The soft bronze color of his face suggested long hours in the sun. He had the look of an athlete, though there was more than a little softening around the edges.

When Jane put a glass in the sink, Anne's blissful contemplation ended with a furtive look to see if she'd missed anything. Paul seemed unaware of her distraction, thank goodness. She offered ice cream for dessert and he accepted with a twinkle in his eye.

"I love ice cream. Any flavor, any kind," he said, and she laughed, thinking *me too*, as a tingle of something ran up her back.

"Excuse me. Do you mind if I look at your paintings again while you two chat?" Jane asked. She caught Anne's eye and smiled.

Anne gave her a "Certainly," in reply. The approval was instinctive, but she would have preferred to keep Jane in the kitchen by Paul's side. Talking was so much easier in a threesome.

In spite of herself, Anne shivered with excitement as Jane left the room. She got a split second to relish that before Paul commented on her kitchen cabinets. The ones on the outside walls were see-through cabinets, with glass doors and small windows in the back that gave a view of the outside world through stacked glasses and dishware.

"They're beautiful, but they must let in the winter cold," he said.

"Not really. They're that modern glass, so they insulate very well," she replied with delight.

Cabinets and glass doors! He was as awkward as she felt!

He threw a sweeping glance around the kitchen, slow enough to take in everything.

"Who did your decorating?"

"No one. I did it."

A slow smile spread across his face. "You're a no one?"

"What?"

He shook his head, still smiling. "I'm sorry. That was too good to pass up. You said no one did it and then said you did it."

"Well, I did."

"I got it. You did a beautiful job."

"It was fun to do. I enjoyed picking the colors and the designs."

"That's another career you could make a living at, I think. You could start by doing my house."

His eyes were twinkling and she didn't know how to answer him. He was laughing at her, or with her, she didn't know. But there was no way she was going to traipse in and out of his house to decorate it, not even if he lived next door.

"No thank you. I have enough to do right now."

He nodded and shook his head. "Of course. Me and my kidding around. I mean, you did a great job on your kitchen. And you probably could make a career of it. I just... I'm sorry about the teasing."

"That's all right," she said, wondering at the expression on his face. He seemed upset.

"Tell me about yourself," he said softly.

"There's not much to tell."

"Pick something. Anything."

He didn't sound demanding, but the words were a request that wanted answers. She felt her back go up. Her life was her own, no one else's. It had always been that way, even as a child. No one knew about her mother's drinking in the beginning. And no one knew about it from her. Not until the accident.

"I hate to watch television," she said, "but I do a lot. It's a terrible waste of time."

"I know. I'm the same way, but I get addicted."

"What do you watch?" she asked and relaxed. Her important secrets could stay secret today.

They told each other odd pieces of information about themselves, asked and answered mundane questions, until Jane returned to announce their departure time had arrived.

At this news Paul groaned, then gave Anne a sweet smile and said, "I had a wonderful time. I'd like to come again and buy you lunch this time."

"No, thanks," she said, but realizing how he might interpret the refusal, she continued, "I'd love to have you come here again."

"You're on. I'm supposed to come up soon to swap this temporary thing on my arm for a hard cast. May I call you then?"

"Yes," she said, hardly believing what had happened. He wanted to see her, and once again, she'd invited him for lunch. The contortions of her brain were baffling.

Lord Molly, I think I've caught an express train!

~ FOUR~

The clerk hadn't shown up again and Molly had to cover the phones at Island Realty. Third time in the last two weeks. That was it, she'd tell her boss to fire the kid's irresponsible butt.

It was a quiet day and after she wrote the note to George she sat back and mused about Anne. The silly thing was starting to sound like her. What would her friend do with a man in her life at long last? This one was a dandy. Yesterday he told Anne he was a grandfather six times. A retired engineer and a widower. At least she got the married question answered. Probably never asked though. A grandfather!

Molly sighed. She'd have to check the guy out before they got too serious. On the other hand, Anne wouldn't take advice on this, so it probably wouldn't matter if he were a serial killer. Anne could be so stubborn when she got going on something.

She turned on her computer and was typing "Paul Breland" into Google search when a silver Mercedes pulled into the parking lot. A man stepped out, studied the office briefly, and then strode lazily to the door. She'd told George a dozen times to get the crummy building painted, but he hadn't bothered, as usual. The guy came in anyway.

He had a sour look on his face, and his shirt was wrinkled like he'd been out in the heat all day, but a smile might make him good looking. The car and clothes were first class. His white hair and smooth tan fit an older, well-tended face. She guessed at mid-fifties.

She got up from the cluttered desk and presented her best hundred-dollar smile.

"Good afternoon. You look like you've been in and out of properties all morning," she said sweetly.

A flash of appreciation appeared on his face and the surly look evaporated.

"I'm about ready to quit, but I'm in a hurry. Is there anything worth looking at in this hick town?"

Arrogant jerk, she thought, but she held the smile. "That depends on what you want."

He grinned. "Is there much available in a place like this?"

"The only properties around here belong to hicks waiting for city folk to pay top dollar," she replied amiably.

He blinked, then broke into a grin. "Ah, I see. Do you know any of them?"

"I know just about everyone on the island. What are you looking for?"

"What about in Newport? I see you advertise business as well as residential. I need both."

"I don't know everyone in Newport, but I'll get you what you want."

He smiled broadly and offered his hand. "You're okay. Graham White. I want a house around here and gallery space in Newport, downtown."

She smiled back. "Molly Wagner, at your service."

~ * ~

She showed him an old house, beautifully restored, but he called it dull. Inspired, she took him to a contemporary place on a bluff overlooking the East Channel. It had been redone in a modern European style and he loved it. He didn't even blink at the nine-hundred-thousand dollar price, simply told her to bid six-hundred.

She gave him the business listings for Newport and he studied them while she typed up the offer. When she finished, he had a list of places to look at and they headed for Newport in the Mercedes.

By dinnertime, she'd learned a good deal of his life story. He was in the middle of a divorce, moving his life and business away from his soon-to-be ex. No children at least. He invited her out for a drink and a bite, and she concluded he wasn't such a bad guy. Good looking and interesting. Still, she sent him back to his motel after dinner. Not because she was shy or prudish, but because it was good for business. Best to let him think there was a possibility, but keep him at a distance. She was good at that. But, if she decided she liked him he might be allowed a little leeway.

Anne thought she was blasé about men, but that was wrong, flat wrong. When they left she cried, but she always knew the next guy would be the right one. The keeper. At least, she used to be sure, but lately there weren't many next guys to think about. Not the quality type, and her standards for those were a good deal higher than they once were. "Happily ever after" was a concern that hadn't been there for a long time and she was surprised to find it in her thoughts as she studied Graham White.

~ FIVE ~

She had a knot in her stomach as she started breakfast. Nerves and excitement, no doubt about that. Paul was coming again and he'd be there with her in a couple of hours, without his daughter, and no Molly either.

Her friend had offered to come, "to smooth things out."

Molly had made her promise to call when he was coming, but she hadn't. She did buy a new jumper, yellow, and was wearing it without a blouse or tee shirt. She tried a bra without the straps, and then abandoned that idea, convinced it wouldn't stay in place. An ordinary bra wouldn't do; the straps would show. Then again, the arm would best be hidden in long sleeves. Bravado, courage, whatever the reason, bra and sleeves were forsaken in favor of the jumper alone.

Normally, her clothing was chosen for comfort. Not this time. The jumper had turned out to be a pinch small, but she studied it in the mirror fifteen ways from Sunday and decided it would be fine.

She couldn't believe she was doing this. A man she did not need, but here she was, acting like a schoolgirl. Sure, he was a very nice man and she liked him, but that seemed a poor reason to fuss when you'd lived alone so many years.

As the knot in her stomach twisted tighter reality hit. She was all dressed up to seduce him! Oh, that word again. She'd gone crazy. If she decided to have sex with him it wasn't going to be the stupid way she'd gone after that carpenter. Al Vargas had been an animal. Naïve as she'd been, all she'd seen was how handsome he was. Things were different now. If she did decide to sleep with Paul Breland, and she wasn't sure she would, there would be romance first. She should change or put on a shirt.

That thought flashed through her mind as gravel crunched under fast moving tires outside. Sucking in a deep breath, she smoothed the jumper and strode out to meet the man.

~ * ~

Three times he'd approached the house, and the thick gravel and green-shrouded patio were familiar now. Parking under her maple tree, he took a white rose from the seat and stepped out. The rose was probably a dumb idea, what with her being a gardener, but he could think of nothing else to bring. Jewelry or clothes were too intimate at this point, her taste in books unknown. Somehow, he didn't see her liking candy. He could have brought wine, but he wasn't sure she liked that either.

His breath caught when she appeared through the hedges.

Man, she was pretty.

Never having dated a woman in her own home, he wasn't entirely sure how to proceed. A restaurant or movie would have been easier to start. There was that bedroom down the hall and the absence of another person in the house. He had to be careful. He'd made enough mistakes with Carol and Ellie. He had to get this right.

"Just a token," he said, offering the rose.

"Thank you very much. Come in." She accepted the rose as if it were a precious thing.

Her yellow outfit drew his eye, and a scent of lilac reached him. Had he underestimated her? From the first, she'd seemed unlikely to fall into bed right off and that actually pleased him. Not that he'd turn down an invitation. Into bed right off was there, at least a bit, but he was looking for more.

Anne was getting to him. It wasn't the jumper, that just fit her body very nicely. He hadn't had sex on the mind very much these last few months. The family claimed he'd been depressed since Ellie left. They must have been right, because sex was there today, in spades. Wearing brand new slacks and shirt from L. L. Bean, he was glad the pants were the loose fit kind.

Anne offered a cheerful smile and he was suddenly reduced to clichés.

"You look very nice today," he said.

"Thank you. You do too."

"I have to thank L. L. Bean for that."

She laughed. "I prefer Land's End."

The vase she found for the rose seemed to need attention. She washed it, dried it, found a spot, washed it again, polished it with a paper towel and filled it with water before inserting the rose. She smiled and relief flooded through him to see she liked it. Wine next time though.

"I've been looking forward to this," he said, in his best casual.

Color rose in her neck and she almost dropped the vase. "What do you think?" she asked, holding it out for his inspection.

"Maybe you should paint it. Have you done anything new since last time?"

"I haven't touched a brush since you were here the other day."

"Oh. Well, there are some I haven't seen yet."

"Let's do something else. A walk?"

He nodded and saw tension leave her face. Walking worked for him too. Outdoors, less personal, that was good for now. The paintings deserved another look, but another day would be just fine. They were great, but more than anything they gave him something to talk about with her.

~ * ~

The kitchen door opened to a small, clear yard in the back, dirt and fine sparse grass. A large oak towered over the house, and brush and saplings started where the thin grass ended.

"Let's go this way," she said, and set off along a well-worn trail into the brush.

She strode along quickly, which was not her normal thing, but she felt him behind her and just knew his eyes were on her body, on the yellow jumper that felt like it was climbing up her legs. The bare shoulders and tight fit were too much for her comfort. If only she'd worn something else.

"That big oak must be eighty feet tall," she said. "I love it, but it's hard for the smaller trees to grow in its shadow. There's a big maple by your car that does the same thing. Did you notice? Mushrooms like it here. The ground is usually damp close to the house, so I get a good crop every year unless there's a drought. The hardest thing is to hang my bird feeders. The bottom branches are so high, you know?

"Do you feed the birds at home? I have all different kinds of feeders, even one for squirrels. Most people hate them, but if you have the right feeders, they're not a problem. They deserve to live too, don't you think?"

She kept going, taking short quick breaths, rattling on so fast she lost track of what she was saying. He tried to make adequate replies, but she could tell he had no idea what she was talking about. That was fine because it was nothing but anxious babble anyway. Still, he listened as if botany were the love of his life, which was very sweet.

Back in the kitchen, she pulled food from the refrigerator and set it on the table. She had a yellow tablecloth with blue napkins set out, and was using her grandmother's plated tableware for the occasion. The décor was as perfect as she could make it, the color coordination a result of repeated experiments.

When he offered to help, she said, "That's all right. Everything's ready. How was the drive up?"

"Not bad. There wasn't much traffic."

"Oh."

The hum of the refrigerator filled the room before he spoke again. "I'm sorry I barged in on you the day I got hurt. I wasn't doing very well."

"That's all right. I wasn't very helpful, locking the door in your face the way I did."

"I scared you though, and you did help."

She shrugged. "You were in trouble. I had to."

He moved his broken arm a bit, a tiny gesture. "You know, it was almost worth getting this."

Heat rushed to her cheeks. Tongue tied for the moment, she couldn't find a word to say.

He continued quickly, "I mean, it gave me the chance to meet you."

It was definitely a compliment, awkwardly given, but an approach of sorts. Her heart began to pound, but she made a cautious reply.

"That's very nice. Thank you."

He tried again. "Do you live alone here?"

"Yes."

"It's a nice house. Who takes care of it for you?"

"I do."

"Really? The old part must take a lot of work."

Did he think she was helpless just because she had one hand? She tried to bite back a surge of annoyance, but it crept into her words.

"I take care of everything. I also restore furniture and do the garden. Last month I did the driveway."

The tone she used showed her irritation, but he didn't apologize, couldn't really, she supposed. Not without admitting he considered her a cripple, which sent a wave of nausea into her belly. Was he like everybody else? She struggled to hold back the rush of disappointment that gripped her with the thought.

"Tell me about the furniture," he said, looking rather sheepish.

Long practice took over. She fought back the emotions that threatened to rip through her and shrugged as if nothing he'd said meant anything at all.

"I restore antiques for friends who pay me a ridiculous amount of money to do it."

"You must do good work."

"That's what they say, but I still think they pay too much."

"Are you working on anything now?"

"A radio console. It's almost finished. And a chair I haven't started yet."

She pressed a loaf of dark bread against the cutting board with her left arm and began to slice it with a long knife.

"Are you sure I can't help?"

Don't push it, she thought grimly. "That's all right. You're my guest."

"How about doing a movie or a show sometime?"

"No thanks," she replied, quite abruptly. Then, wanting a diversion before she said something she'd regret, "You were in a lot of pain when you came that day. I don't know how you walked all the way up the driveway."

"I'm a tough old coot," he said with a sweet grin.

"You don't look so old."

"I'll be fifty-six in February."

"That isn't old."

"It's getting there. I'd like to be as young as you again."

"I'm almost as old as you are."

"Well then, you're a very beautiful almost as old as I am," he said chuckling softly.

She picked up two glasses, set them on the table, and realized she'd held them with the rims squeezed between her fingers. He might be squeamish about that. She hurriedly wiped them with a napkin.

"I'm sorry. Is that all right?"

"Sure," he said, a puzzled frown on his face.

He probably never noticed the fingers in the glass routine. Why was this so difficult? She was second guessing herself, holding back her emotions. Feeling defensive for no reason at all. The man was just trying to make conversation.

"Have you always lived here?"

"I lived with my parents until my father died."

"Oh. I'm sorry."

She pulled a plate from a cabinet. "It was a long time ago. He had a heart attack. It was an easy death, as deaths go." She squeezed the pickle jar between her body and arm and twisted the top off.

"You're pretty good at that."

"You learn."

"Oh," he said, looking chagrinned.

She speared a pickle as if it were a snake, then smiled. He wasn't a jerk, he was trying. Maybe if she talked about her missing hand a little he'd relax. Perhaps he would, but it wasn't up to her to fix his embarrassment. She had enough trouble with her own feelings.

"It was a car accident," she said, the words brittle.

"Oh, I'm sorry," he said again.

"That's all right," she said, but didn't mean it. Would he get that from her tone?

Sitting at the table, she lapsed into silence. He started to talk about moving back to his own house after recuperating with Jane and her family. She asked where he lived and what kind of house he had and that took them through the meal comfortably. She allowed him to help clean the kitchen and then he excused himself to use the bathroom.

She was staring out the window when he returned. Startled, she did a little hitch and he apologized for being so quiet.

Slipping a cup into the dishwasher, she said, "It wasn't you. I was thinking of my grandmother."

"Oh. She's not still alive is she?"

"Physically no, but to me she is. I mean it seems that way sometimes."

Heat returned to her cheeks along with a sheepish smile. She couldn't tell him how alive Hannah seemed. He'd think she was crazy.

"I know what you mean. I used to talk to my wife sometimes. Right after, you know."

"What happened to her?"

"Cancer."

She studied his face and saw him flush. "You still love her."

"Ellie used to say that."

"Who's Ellie?"

"She was my girlfriend for a while. We broke up last year." He frowned, apparently not liking the conversation very much. "What about your grandmother? Were you talking to her just now?"

He sounded as if that were the most natural thing in the world. A tingle ran up her back. Maybe she was crazy, but if she were, then he was too.

"I was wondering what she'd think about you being here."

"That generation would probably be horrified that we're alone in your house."

She laughed aloud. "Not Hannah. Nothing fazed her. She left England to get rich. Married a man she met before she left and dragged him along with her."

"Did they have a good marriage?"

"Absolutely. They had two boys and a girl. She was very special to me."

"Which one was your parent?"

"The girl, Jean. We didn't get along."

"Oh."

"You and Hannah would like each other."

"I'm glad. She sounds a bit formidable." That got him a nod and another smile.

He was the first man she'd ever dressed up for. The first she'd thought about that way. Except for Vargas the carpenter of course. She'd been such a fool, walking around with her shirt half open until he'd reacted and she'd given herself to him.

Desperate, that's what she'd been. Hearing Molly's sexy stories had made her feel like an idiot that she was still a virgin at the age of thirty-five. Well she wasn't a virgin now, but she hoped not all men were like Vargas. Yuck.

Funny, she hadn't thought about that recently, hardly ever did for that matter, but Paul had brought it all back. She could tell herself she wasn't interested in him at all, say she just met the man and had no idea what she wanted with him if anything, but her body and the morning's agitated preparations told a different tale. Would this time be different? A spurt of excitement flooded her body.

She mentioned a movie she liked and he replied and that was where the conversation went.

"Did you see...?"

"Oh, yes, wasn't it great?"

"I didn't think..." he started, and she interrupted.

"Oh, I have the movie channel."

Movies got them into music, and more to talk about. They both liked classical and jazz. He liked the early jazz players though, while she was a fan of the latest. He didn't even know Diana Krall, and that to her seemed quite impossible.

Why didn't he make a pass? If one were to believe Molly, she should have been ravished by now. It was a silly thought, of course, Molly always exaggerated. Still, he could at least make an attempt, do something in that direction.

It was late afternoon and he said he'd had a wonderful time and would like to come again. She answered yes to that, no hesitation, and they made another date.

~ SIX ~

She turned to the house after he left, walking slowly. The visit had been wonderful, though sometimes it'd been hard to find words when it was her turn to speak. He'd tried to entertain her, but obviously struggled too. It felt nice not being alone in that, a thing they had in common. A minor point to most people perhaps, but to her, the touch of any connection was a treasure. And was that ever a surprise. Was she falling in love with him or with anybody who'd talk to her?

The house seemed oddly quiet, empty as never before. The radio offered no help, nor did the television, and she stepped out to wander the woods. Birds scattered from the feeders as she left the kitchen.

"Hello girls. Don't be frightened. I'll be gone in a minute." She laughed with a new thought. "I'd better start calling you girls and boys. We have a man to think about now."

A nuthatch returned, recognizing her apparently. That pleased her. A light wind from the East carried sounds of surf, just a quarter mile behind her home. Normally, she noted the weather and the birds and paid close attention to details, but this time Paul occupied her mind.

He liked her, she liked him. They could become friends or even lovers. But eventually he'd want to go out, would insist on it certainly.

She dreaded the thought. The facts were simple, her feelings as uncertain as the future. Did she want a man coming to see her, dropping in all the time? He'd be back Tuesday for another visit. He'd be there in the house with her, just them, and he liked her. Sex sometimes—that would be a part of it. What would it be like with him? She'd heard enough of Molly's lurid stories to know Vargas had practically raped her. Paul was gentle and kind. It had to be better with him.

Sex meant complications galore though. Unless she kept it to a one night stand. Somehow, that seemed unlikely. Her palms turned a little sweaty and she shivered with nerves. What if he wanted more? To stay with her. Forever. That couldn't happen to her. She couldn't let herself think that was even possible. She'd have to live a normal life to keep a man like him. Be a normal woman. Go out and go places with him.

She shook off the reverie she was in. It was so silly to think that way, but there she was, putting herself in fairyland. She needed to get her head on straight before she opened her blouse in front of him. Or wore that yellow jumper again.

Wanting someone to talk to, she called Grace. Dan answered the phone. "Hey Annie, how are you? I have another project for you. I'll bring it down tomorrow."

"I'm still working on your radio cabinet and the chair you gave me."

"That's okay. It's a good piece. Victorian music cabinet. Some idiot painted it, but when you get done it'll be real nice."

"All right, but it'll take me a while."

He said hold on and she waited for Grace to reach the phone. Her friend's antique shop was nothing particularly fancy to see, but Dan did handle high quality items when he found them. Those he sold to selected customers, regulars for many years. The shop sat in a dying strip mall and the old couple should have moved long ago, but Dan procrastinated endlessly.

"I know everybody here. We're all right for a while yet," he'd say, and that would be the end of it for another six months.

"Hello dear," Grace said. "How was your date?"

"Not a date, Grace. He came for a visit and it was very nice."

"I'm glad. What do you think of him? Is he a nice man? How old is he?"

"He's sweet. I like him."

"That's good. Is he handsome? What's his name again? Do you think he'll come see you again? Have you made a date?"

"He's coming Tuesday. Paul, Paul Breland."

"Tuesday? Oh, that's nice. Was that his idea or yours?"

"His."

"Are you pleased? I'm sure you are, or you wouldn't have a date. Would you?"

Anne sucked in a breath. Did she really want to get into a long discussion about the crazy ideas floating around in her head? Paul might not even want to have sex, or be with her after he got to know her better. "I do like him, Grace. He's very sweet."

"You be careful, Annie. You hardly know this guy," Dan said suddenly.

"Daniel Sinnis, have you been listening in?" Grace cried. "Hang up Daniel. This is women's business."

"Remember, watch your step," said the old man, and he was gone.

"I'm sorry, Anne. He's an old fool."

"It's all right. He means well, and I suppose he's right, but I'm sure Paul is a good man. "

"Well, I would say you shouldn't worry too much. That would be my thought."

"I'll try. Will you be coming down with Dan tomorrow?"

"He forgot. He's going to an estate sale. I'll call when we can come."

She put down the phone wearing a smile. She'd known them thirty odd years and would worry if their needling stopped one day. They treated her like the daughter they never had. Dan was seventy-five, Grace a bit younger. They still ran their antique shop as they always had, with the exception of large heavy items, no longer bought because they were too hard to manage now.

She'd have to get working on that chair and radio cabinet. The last thing she needed was another piece of furniture to restore, but she did want to see them, and if they didn't drop by in the next few days maybe she'd take a ride to their shop.

Molly arrived for dinner at seven after a late invitation.

"Well, he certainly stayed a long time. What did you do all day?" she asked.

"He left a while ago. I had things to do."

"Oh," Molly said, and paused, staring at Anne, obviously waiting to hear more. When she offered nothing, Molly continued, "Well, how did it go? Is he coming back again?"

"Next week."

"Tell me everything. Did you get your new clothes in time?"

"Yes, almost."

"What does that mean?"

"I bought a yellow jumper and it was too tight. I won't wear it again."

"You're too conservative. You have to push yourself out there if you want something to happen."

"I'm all right the way I am. He's coming back and that's enough."

"He won't if you don't try to interest him."

"Stop, please! I knew you'd be like this. I can't be the way you are."

"Who said you should be? I'm just telling you the best thing to do if you want him."

Anne shook her head. "All right, I'm sorry, but you have to listen. I'm not sure what I want. He comes and he's sweet and I like him and that's all I need right now."

"He'll stop coming, I'm telling you. He will."

"Then that's what he'll do."

Clearly frustrated, Molly studied her and finally smiled. "You're different over this. No more my quiet friend. Okay, you're forgiven. What did you do with the man all day?"

"Never mind, I'm forgiven. Just be quiet and I'll tell you."

"Talk then."

She did, describing the walk they took, the snug fit of the jumper, the lunch and talk of family and interests.

"You like the same music? That's good," Molly said.

Anne's heart eased and her breath seemed to flow like a whisper again. "We like to walk too. I know more about sports than he does though."

"Did he say he likes to walk?"

"Not in so many words, but it was nice."

"What about friends and family?"

"He said something about a man named Ben. He talked about his kids and grandkids. He's very proud of them."

"He's supposed to be."

"I know, but not everyone does what they're supposed to."

"That's very nice, but hey, you need a Romeo, not Father Time."

"I'm not young either, Molly. He's perfect for me."

"No, no, no. Nobody's perfect, especially a man. Watch out for that idea."

Why did this kind of conversation always tie her in a knot? Anne groaned.

"You know what I mean. Age-wise, that's all."

"And you know what I mean. I always thought they were perfect when I first met them."

"You're starting again."

"What?"

"Telling me what to do. Miss Know-It-All."

"Wow, you are touchy tonight."

"Molly, I don't want advice, from you or anyone, telling me what to do as if there were nothing to this. I mean I do need help, sometimes."

"You're confusing me."

"That's because I'm confused. I don't know, maybe it's a time to take a chance."

~ SEVEN ~

She'd talked to the birds, Miss Nuthatch and Mister Finch, thought of Paul, called Grace again, and thought more of him. Molly visited for dinner that once, and then again, and they spoke of him. And he was going to return this morning, after confirming with a call last night.

She tended to last minute cleaning and then began to dress, taking as long as the cleaning had taken. The yellow jumper stayed in the closet, replaced by three new outfits more to her liking. She picked one of the sundresses, rose with faint white flecks like tiny flower petals, and knew Hannah would agree it was pretty. A better fit too.

She'd accepted Grace's thought to ride the wave, deciding nothing for the moment. Yet, she had to make some decisions, and apparently had already. She'd never fussed so much about getting dressed before.

Still, early Monday morning she'd voiced her concerns to Hannah. Concerns she hadn't shared with the others.

"Grace made it sound so easy. Relax and everything will be fine. I'm trying, but he asked about my hand already. My friends never asked like that. Molly knew more than I did from the beginning. I remember not being able to get out of the car and the doctor's face when he examined my hand. That was all, until Molly said Mother was so drunk she didn't know I was caught under the car. I told Grace myself when I was ready. I am not ready to tell Paul."

That had been her low point and for the rest of the day she'd hidden from Molly, avoided calls, dwelt on the worst of possibilities. Not only would he want details of her life, he'd expect her to go out immediately, and probably a lot.

The black mood had passed by evening, replaced by an inexplicable optimism that carried forward to the morning. Everything would be fine, just take it easy, she told herself.

Grace had said it. He'd be good for her. A warm little ripple flooded her body at the thought. A very sweet feeling. All she had to do was hang on to the idea. Right? He was a special man and he liked her.

She slipped into the new sundress. Molly was on her way. She'd wear makeup too, which got her a leering grin from

Molly when she made the announcement over their most recent dinner. It would be the first time for that since high school.

There was only one problem this morning. Molly had promised to show up at eleven to help with the makeup, but she was late. Paul would arrive at twelve. Always punctual Molly was late on purpose, had to be. She was probably betting Anne wouldn't turn her away in front of Paul. She'd lose that bet today.

Eleven-thirty came before Molly rolled in. "Sorry, business. Let's get to work."

Multiple varieties of powder, lipstick and other sundries poured from the makeup bag she'd brought.

"All kinds I've used over the years." She chose lipstick, powder, eye shadow, and applied them with elaborate care, then shook her head.

"These are wrong on you. Wash it off. We'll try again."

At five to twelve, she was making a third attempt. "That looks good. Take a peek in the mirror."

Anne stared, uncertain. "It's too much. This isn't me. Take some of it away."

"Can't, unless we start over. You look beautiful. That's the combination."

"I don't know what to say."

Molly had made her a new woman, striking but completely unfamiliar.

"Don't say anything. Let me show you how to do it yourself."

"Not now, he'll be here any minute. We have to clean up."

Anne started a mad scramble, dumping everything back in Molly's bag except the items she'd keep. She dashed for the bedroom with those and hurried back to find Molly carefully, deliberately, tying up the makeup bag. Grinning.

"You planned to be here when he came," Anne said.

"I won't stay long. I just want to say hello."

"One hello and then leave us alone."

"My, we are certainly sure of ourselves today."

"Molly, please. You've been telling me to put myself out there. How can I with you here?"

Molly laughed. "Okay, okay. I'll leave right after lunch."

"No! Go now. Please."

"You'll be glad if I stay. Conversation is easier with three."

"Never mind. Put these things in your car. My kitchen looks like a beauty parlor."

As Anne prompted Molly rather emphatically toward her new metallic green Buick, Paul's Toyota pulled up the drive and stopped.

He slid out of the car with a bottle of wine and another single rose. His face wore a look of surprise, dismay in fact, and Anne knew for sure he was reacting to Molly's presence.

"Paul, you remember Molly?" Anne said, barely able to keep from snapping out the words,

"Good to see you again," he said.

"Me too," Molly replied. "How was the drive?"

"Easy. No problems."

"How long will you be staying?" she asked offhandedly as she unlocked her car.

"Staying? That's up to Anne."

Molly nodded and climbed in. "I'll call you, Anne. Maybe we can do dinner tonight, okay?"

"Fine," Anne said without pleasure.

Somehow, Molly's comment seemed odd, a dismissal of Paul, a demand.

"I'll see you later."

As Molly eased the Buick down the drive, Anne stared after it, her arms crossed in front of her. That was enough of Molly for the day. Yet, still she clutched herself. She turned to Paul.

"Do you always come with a rose, Mister Breland?"

"Always."

"Ah, you're a romantic." Anne attempted a smile, but her face felt like a contorted mask.

"Are you okay?"

She nodded. "It's just strange to be here like this, watching her leave." The whole time with Molly had been strange, with Molly's snide remarks and her own prickling at her friend.

"With me you mean?"

"No, I don't know." His question assumed too much, correctly, but too quickly. Molly was the one she shared feelings with, not strangers like him. What had happened to her loyalty? Her stomach tensed.

His next question was mundane, as if he knew the last had been out of line. "How long have you known each other?"

"We met in high school."

"Were you in the same class?"

"She was a year behind me. When I left school, she visited me at home."

His blank face said he didn't understand. She hesitated, but the obligation to explain was strong. It didn't matter. It seemed like a hundred years ago. Why did she need secrets now? Her mother was a drunk. Big deal.

She choked back the bile that rose in her throat and said instead, "My mother rarely welcomed visitors. Molly came anyway, until she went off and got married, of course."

"She moved away?"

"Yes. It was ten years before she came back. By that time I was living here."

"Did you move in here right after high school?"

"After my father died. I wanted my own home." She paused, as she digested an odd thought. "I used to do a lot of things, but it was easier then. I guess I just gradually stopped going out."

Gradually grew dependent on Molly? A spurt of goose bumps caught her by surprise.

He glanced at her stump and quickly looked away. "You never go out then?"

"I do some things. My friends Dan and Grace own an antique shop in Providence. I drive up there sometimes."

~ * ~

He waited, wanting more, feeling too much the intruder already. She seemed logical and level-headed most of the time, but did things that struck him as inconsistent. Topless sun bathing, didn't go out but did. How did she do one and not the other?

He muddled about the contradictions, but that didn't bother him much. He could muddle when he wanted to and he wanted to over her. It was those eyes. She had beautiful eyes. Looked stunning today too.

And she was so vulnerable. He liked that about her. Not the hiding bit though. She'd be going places with him soon enough. An optimist, that was him, at least about some things, the kind that he could fix. This time he'd get it right.

"She's a nice friend for you," he said, for lack of something better.

"More like a sister."

"You seem very different."

"We complement each other. Sisters can be different, you know."

You're not sisters though, he thought, and stopped, not sure he should go there.

"Of course. By the way, you said you don't go out much, but how about lunch next time? We could find a cozy restaurant in Newport."

"We'll see. Would you like to take a walk after lunch?" she asked as they ambled into the house.

"I'd really like to see your paintings. Would you mind?"

"All right," she said, looking anything but pleased at the prospect.

Apparently, planning a lunch out wasn't her favorite thing and showing off her paintings was hardly any better. He was certainly finding her touchy points. Not scoring any though, that was sure.

"What do you think about when you paint?" he asked as he sat at the table and she set a sandwich and beer in front of him.

Sitting across from him with her own lunch, she said, "I don't know. It's sort of a letting go thing. If I worry about what I'm doing, it doesn't work."

"How do you start? You must have an idea," he said, between bites of ham and Swiss.

"I see something beautiful and I start. That's all."

"So you do pretty paintings then?" She frowned, but he continued. "That didn't sound right. I meant you don't do any of those extreme things, black and dark or strange looking? You try to capture beauty."

That got him a civil nod. Of course, she'd already said as much. He was making progress, maybe?

"Who's your favorite artist?" he asked.

"I don't have one."

"I like Rembrandt. No one captured the personality of the subject the way he did. His subjects are alive."

"I've only seen his paintings in books. My work is colorful, bright, and a little bit abstract. I don't like dark portraits."

"His aren't dark. You should see his paintings. Full size, so you can see the facial expressions. I'll take you to a museum one day."

"Maybe sometime," she said quietly, but the expression on her face begged him to back off.

He groaned to himself. He'd blown it again.

After they ate, he followed her to the studio and studied her paintings. That was easier than making conversation about her life, but relief turned to doubt as he examined one painting, then another, and the frown never left her face. What was bothering her?

He turned with a smile. "You really are good."

"Are you an artist?" she demanded, then seemed to cringe as if she regretted the remark.

He shook his head. "I just know what I like. Most of these are bright and cheerful, but what about this one?" He held up a dark painting done on a deep blue background.

"I don't like that one." She took it from him and set it down facing the wall.

"It's different from your others. Sort of angry looking."

"I like the light ones better." She moved to the other side of the room and he followed.

He picked up a painting; white background like a snow-covered field, a portion of rail fence sheltering a delicate red rose.

"Can I buy this one?"

"You can have it."

"That wouldn't be right. Let me buy it."

"They aren't for sale. A gift. That's the only way you can have it."

"Then I thank you very much and I accept."

He took her hand as though to shake it, then turned it palm down and kissed it. When he straightened there was color in her cheeks. "It's beautiful. You're sure I can have it?"

"Yes," she said, but there was a look in her eyes and he knew, just knew, he'd chosen a favorite.

He stared at the painting and gave it a name in his head. The Lonely Rose. Could he give it back or would that upset her more? No, the deed was done, too late to go back now.

"Lunch again soon?" he asked, as he placed the painting near the doorway. He was careful doing it, respecting its value. She seemed pleased at that, and at his question. He began to breathe again.

"Here? When?" she asked.

"Here if you'd like. Friday?"

"All right."

He smiled. "Maybe I should commission you to do a painting of me."

"I'd be happy to, but no commission please."

"That wouldn't be right. Give it some thought. Could we do a drawing for each of my kids?"

"That wouldn't take long."

He smiled. Progress, at least a little bit. He'd make this work out right.

When he carried his gift to the car, slammed the trunk lid and turned, she was behind him, close.

"I wish I could use both arms right now to give you a hug," he whispered.

She answered with a shy smile, so he drew her to him and gently caressed her lips. She stepped back, looking flustered, but didn't turn away. He touched her hand and let his fingers slide away as she stepped back further.

"I, uh, that sort of caught me by surprise," he said.

She nodded, her face flushed, and blinked.

"But I liked it," he said softly.

She hesitated, then nodded. "I did too."

He almost reached out to touch her again, but as if she'd read his mind, she shook her head.

"Friday then?" he whispered.

~ * ~

She watched him drive away, then turned and entered the house. He had kissed her. And her knees had turned to jelly when he did. Did she want him to touch her, to make love to her? Yes. No, she barely knew him. She was making a fool of herself again. A ridiculous fifty-four year old woman who should know better. But her body tingled even now.

~ EIGHT ~

He was ten minutes late to Kelly's Kitchen, the regular lunch hangout for he and his friends. Seated, the others were talking with menus untouched on the table. The waitress was a small blonde woman he'd never seen before. Mary never offered menus. They didn't use them, but she wasn't there and the blonde would learn.

"He's not coming, I tell you. It's his turn to buy. He'll have some excuse," Ben was saying in a stage whisper that reached across the restaurant.

"Are you saying he's tight?" Jack asked in the same tone.

"He makes Jack Benny look like a spendthrift," Ben said as Paul took a chair.

"Hey Marty, what do you say we find a better place than this? They let all kinds of people in here," Paul said.

"Hey Bud, what's with the sling? You get mugged or something?" Jack asked.

"I punched a guy six-foot-seven and broke my arm."

"Is it bad?" asked Ben.

"No, they call it a clean break."

"How'd you do it?" asked Marty.

"Riding my bike in Rhode Island. Trying to bird watch at the same time."

"Good thing your head hit the ground first," Ben said with a grin.

"Will it heal up right?" asked Jack.

"It should be okay. I go back up in a week for a checkup."

"To Rhode Island? For that?" Marty asked.

Paul shrugged. "Yeah."

"You can't get looked at here? What's the big deal?" Ben asked.

"Nothing special. They set it."

"So?"

"It's a boat or a dame. Those are the only reasons he'd drive all the way up there to do that," said Marty.

"He's got a boat. It must be a woman." Jack grinned.

"A lot you know. His boat is old. Maybe he has his eye on a new one. A nice new forty footer, Paul?" Ben asked.

"All right you guys. Knock it off," Paul said, carefully turning his attention to the menu.

"Look at this," said Ben. "He's trying to find something called 'My Usual.' Gentlemen, I think it's a woman we're dealing with here."

Silence followed that pronouncement as they waited for a response.

"Cat got your tongue?" Jack asked.

"You're right, Ben. It has to be a woman. If it was a boat he'd be telling us all about it," Marty added.

"You guys are worse than an old ladies sewing circle," Paul said, laughing.

"C'mon, give, who is she? A twenty year old blonde I bet," said Ben.

"Actually, she's twenty-two and a red head. Makes Meg Ryan look homely."

"Oh sure. She must be desperate to fall for an old fart like you," said Marty.

"Look who's talking."

"Listen, after thirty years with the same woman I'm just glad I'm still alive."

"Well don't get all excited. The lady is in her fifties and we just met."

"Be careful. You don't remember "Honey-Do-Lists" and day long shopping trips? You know she'll hate the boat on general principles," said Ben.

"We'll see," Paul said, grinning.

"Bad answer. He's lost guys. She's got him," said Jack.

~ * ~

Ben followed Paul back to the house. They were old friends, and along with Ben's wife, Hazel, they had been a regular foursome when Carol still lived.

"When are you going back up there?" asked Ben.

"Friday."

"You serious about this?"

Paul laughed. "Damned if I know. I think so, but we'll see."

Ben nodded. "I'll tell Hazel. What's the lady's name?"

"Anne Hoskins."

"She lives in Providence? Newport?"

"A place called Jamestown Island."

"I know where that is. Nice place."

"Yeah."

Ben went silent, studied him, then asked, "What's she like?"

"Pretty nice."

"Hey, you gotta give me something to tell Hazel. I'll catch the devil if I don't have more than that for her."

Paul laughed. "She has beautiful eyes, nice body, nice smile. Mid fifties. She's quiet and refined. A very nice person. Hazel will like her."

"Good. She divorced?"

"Nope, never married."

"How did you find somebody like that? You sure there's no secret there?"

"She has one hand."

"Oh." Silence.

"It may be a while before you meet her. She tends to hide out."

"You're not going to disappear again, are you?"

"Disappear?"

"Yeah. You know, Ellie stayed away from us. Kept you away too."

"That was different Ben. She thought you guys didn't like her."

"We didn't when she started that crap."

"She thought you resented her for taking Carol's place."

"Imagination. She wasn't much like us, but it was okay until she pulled you away."

"Well, I'll be going to Rhode Island a lot, but I don't figure to be gone forever."

~ * ~

He walked two and a half miles that afternoon, hard and fast, pushing the pace. No reason for it, he just felt good. Sometimes he noted his surroundings, because he chose to, or less often, something caught his eye. Not today though. He was focused in on Anne and nothing else.

Hopefully, when the arm was better, he could take her sailing. To a movie or to lunch in a cozy little place dark with atmosphere to hide in if she wanted.

Romeo he needed advice from, or Sir Lancelot, or the guy with the big nose, Casanova. They'd have good tips on romance. Carol did too, a long time back. Not flowers or candy, she taught him that. He laughed, remembering candle-lit breakfasts, love notes in the coffee canister. She showed him how, stuffing a note into the peanut butter jar the first time. Not practical, but certainly memorable.

"My dear Miss Hoskins, how shall I entertain you? Will I get the boot if you find me at the peanut butter jar?"

He was playing with ideas when Ben's reaction to her hand hit home. "Oh," and silence, nothing more. Awkward, like his own reaction when he tried to talk to her. She must get that a lot. No wonder she stayed home.

Confidence deserted him. What if she'd never go to lunch in Newport or in Boston? He'd hate to stay at home forever, but to give up on her now was impossible. More than conscience, his heart would not allow it. He couldn't wait to hold her in his arms, to run his fingers through her hair, to feel her bare skin against his own. To make love to her.

There had to be a way to get her out in the world. He let out a long breath. This time he'd get it right. An idea formed in his head, a plan for the next visit.

~ * ~

He was one day early, by design. The unexpected was required if he were right. She lived an entirely predictable existence, and that had to change. In his best white shirt, with a new bow tie to fit the role of the day, he knocked at ten to twelve.

"Come in," she called from behind the door, but he waited for it to open. "Grace? What's wrong?" The door swung wide and she stared. "What are you doing here?"

"I'm a day early. I couldn't wait."

"Oh my. Dan and Grace are coming. You're supposed to come tomorrow. They're bringing lunch."

He forced a smile. "That's okay, I wanted to meet them. Come with me." He led her, awkwardly resisting, to the car and opened the rear door. "I can't lift this cooler alone."

"What are you doing?"

He grinned and slid the cooler to her hand. "No more questions. I had a plan for today, but we'll change it."

"Why are you wearing a tie?"

"It's my waiter's uniform. Andre's Restaurant. We come to you." She stared, looking baffled, and he smiled again. "Andre the Waiter, that's me. I brought a restaurant to you."

"Paul, I --,"

"Nope, Andre, remember?"

"You're confusing me. What about Dan and Grace?"

"We're good. I brought food enough for a crowd. We'll need more good silverware though. I only brought enough for two."

"They're bringing MacDonald's."

"Never mind," he said, and lifted the top of the cooler.

Shrimp salad and cream of broccoli soup in Tupperware were the first to be taken out, hints of things to come.

A dirt spattered white van rolled up the drive and parked behind his car, effectively ensuring it couldn't be moved. He gave the faces behind the windshield a quick glance. They seemed as elderly as the vehicle, but that observation he kept to himself.

An argument was underway, the woman gesturing, the man scowling at Paul. When the doors opened, the couple spilled out onto the drive, and came at him as if they were about to go to war. Longtime smile lines marked their faces, but they were dead serious and the old man hefted a tire iron like a war club. He was a bit thick around the waist, the woman a little plump as well, and both were gray, with thinning hair. The old man stared at him, at the bow tie, and Paul saw the questions in his eyes.

"Paul Breland, Mister Sinnis. I'm afraid I barged in uninvited."

The old man studied the face before him and his harsh expression relaxed.

"Are you Anne's new friend?" the woman asked.

"That's me. I assume you're Grace?"

"Oh yes, certainly. How did you know?"

"She told me you were coming."

"See Dan, I told you it was him. Put that tool away."

Dan gave him the once over, apparently assessing whether he could be trusted. The old couple seemed to feel responsible for Anne, judging by their behavior.

"What have you got there?" Dan asked, indicating the tablecloth in Paul's hand.

"I had a surprise for her today, but I got surprised. I'm about to set the table for lunch."

"We brought MacDonald's, but only for three," Grace said.

"Where's Anne?" asked Dan.

"Getting some silverware. I brought a fancy lunch."

"She's not much for fancy. Plain as a plank for the most part."

"I'm sorry we spoiled your surprise. That's very sweet." Grace gave him a warm smile.

Paul grinned. "I was hoping she'd feel the same."

"I'm sure she does."

Clutching a handful of tableware, Anne rushed out to the cars. "It looks like you've met already. I'm sorry about this. We're all mixed up."

"Never mind, Annie. We'll make us a party today," Dan said, and then to Paul, "You going to be a few minutes with that cooler?"

"Not long. A couple."

"Okay. Annie, you leave that stuff to them and give me a hand. I have that cabinet for you. Let's get it into the shop."

"Your hamburgers are getting cold."

"We can't eat until the table's set, Gracie. You help him while Annie and I do this."

Anne looked lost, but offered Grace the silverware and followed the old man.

"That man! He could sit down and relax for one minute," Grace said, attacking Paul's cooler with gusto. "Ah, this must be soup. Anne doesn't cook much, you know. What's this, shrimp?"

"No, that's chicken."

She studied his face. "You like our Anne?"

"I do, yes."

"That's good, I think I like you. Dan thinks you're okay too, so far. Don't make us out to be wrong."

He smiled. "I wouldn't hurt her."

"Dan would have used that tire iron on you if you'd been a burglar."

He laughed then. "I thought he was going to for a minute."

She nodded. "I think we're going to be friends. Where did you get this beautiful lace tablecloth?"

"It was my wife's favorite."

She nodded again, approving the use of it for her Anne. "I'll arrange your food. You go see that cabinet my husband is showing off."

"You're sure?"

"Yes, I'll be fine. Go."

The garage door was open, and an elderly faded blue Ford, circa 1985, sat in the bay on the right. The space on the left had been walled in. He stepped through an ordinary door, perhaps a tad wider than the usual, and into a neatly organized workshop.

The gray painted floor was spotless, as was the small platform in the center of the space. An exhaust fan filled the top of a rear window, a workbench lined the wall that divided the shop from the garage, and a space heater hung suspended from the ceiling in the back corner. A broken chair sat on the platform next to a partially dismantled cabinet and Anne was examining another piece, obviously new to her, near the door. Orangey yellow, dinged and chipped, the thing was a monstrosity to Paul's way of thinking.

"Isn't that something?" asked Dan.

"Yes," he said, unable to come up with a compliment that wouldn't choke him.

Anne laughed. "It's a disaster Paul, but it has potential."

"You don't see it, do you? You gotta know this stuff. If some idiot fool hadn't painted it, fixing it would be easy. Just one drawer falling apart is all," Dan said, looking very intense.

"And a split in that front leg Dan," Anne said.

"Oh sure, but that's all. It's a valuable piece. English Victorian music cabinet and when you have someone like Anne to work on it, well that's the whole thing."

"You're going to fix that? Make it like new again?" Paul asked dubiously.

"Are you serious?" Dan said. "She'll make it like newly restored. Beautiful. Look at the lines on it. The style. Did you ever see such a beautiful leg?"

Paul smiled at the question, seeing multiple ways to answer. Dan noted his expression and laughed. "On a piece of furniture I mean."

"I can't say I've noticed, Dan. On a piece of furniture."

Grace called, announcing lunch. Only two plates were set at the patio table. "All right now sit you two. The hamburgers are in the kitchen, Dan."

"Whoa," Paul said. "You're not going to split us up?"

"He'll survive. This was your party."

"But I barged in! Please, let's eat together. There's plenty of food."

Dan hesitated, and Anne pulled his arm. "Stay Dan, sit."

The moment was awkward and Grace seemed uncertain, but she shrugged.

"All right then, you had your chance." She leaned close to Paul and whispered, "Next time, bring a waiter."

~ NINE ~

Lunch was surreal, an Alice in Wonderland party. Paul was in dress shirt, bow tie and creases, the others casual, even sloppy in jeans and old clothes. The table setting added to the image, with soup and salads in fine china, burgers in their paper wraps, all carefully set out on Carol's lace tablecloth.

No Queen of Hearts, but Dan could have been the Mad Hatter, extolling Anne's virtues without pause. Anne could have played Alice, the innocent among them.

"Annie's the best restorer in New England. Self taught too. Take a good look at that kitchen table she did," said the old man for the third time.

"Dan please," Anne said, rising from the table.

Grace reached out to restrain her. "Daniel Sinnis, you just close your mouth."

"What? What did I say so bad?"

"You have far too much to say. Apologize to Anne."

"She don't mind, Gracie. Do you Annie?" asked the old man, but a look at Anne drew a frown. "I'm just proud of her, Paul. That's all. I'm sorry, Annie. I guess I talk too much."

"Dan, you are precious," Anne replied.

The old man grinned. "I know. I hear that all the time, don't I, Gracie?"

"You need a gag, but that won't work. Find something else to talk about, you old fool."

Briefly uncomfortable with their exchange, Paul soon found himself amused. They seemed unperturbed by the scrapping between them, the barbs having had no effect as far as Paul could see. Dan asked about his arm in a matter of fact fashion, his wife's criticism apparently accepted without rancor or embarrassment.

~ * ~

Afterward, when Grace and Dan had gone, Anne was not extravagant with words. Dan's repeated boosting of her stock, and Paul's attempt to bring a restaurant to her home, even Grace's help with Dan ate at her.

Everything they said and did implied she was helpless. Was that new, or had it been there all along? Why hadn't she noticed before? Molly did it too, fussing about the makeup and telling her what to do. Why? Did she encourage that attitude in people? No, of course not, how silly.

"They talk too much, that's all," she said aloud.

"What?" Paul asked.

"Sorry, nothing. Never mind."

"It was a nice lunch, wasn't it?"

"I felt like a child with boasting parents. The village idiot."

"You're talking about Dan? He doesn't mean anything by it. He wanted me to know how special you are. They both did."

"I know."

"I like him, both of them in fact. You have great friends."

She sighed. "I know that. That's why it's hard. I don't know what to feel."

"That's easy. Be pleased. I'm betting I have their approval."

"Of what?"

"Of us. Of me as your friend," he said, his eyes twinkling.

"I suppose you're right. I just wish he wouldn't boast like that."

A great weight settled in her chest and she almost cried with the sense of shame that took hold in her head. She was a grown woman after all, why did everyone think she was so helpless?

"Paul, would you mind very much just going home?"

"Now? We've had no time alone."

"I know. I don't think I can take that right now."

"Did I do something?"

"No, no, it's me. Come again next week."

"In a few days. I'll call you."

"I'm sorry."

~ * ~

He packed the remains of lunch all in a heap in the cooler as if he was running away or she was chasing him with a whip. She knew better though; saw his concern and efforts to oblige. That was her impression at least and she was pleased to think it of him, were it not for the other.

Grace and Dan, always helpful, always caring, as if she were a child. Why hadn't she noticed that before? She sighed. After such a lunch, the last thing she wanted was an afternoon of romance.

She couldn't avoid that one question. Was she responsible for their attitudes? How could she be certain? She would have to change, but how? Feeling a chill, dark and painful, she entered the studio seeking some distraction.

Pleasantly comfortable, with its pale white walls, the paint stained smock on the coat tree in the corner amidst her paintings, the room did not warm her. She slipped into the smock and stood before the easel, blankly staring, lacking inspiration. A gritty black smudge on the smock stole her eye and she looked again, then pulled it off and sniffed. It needed a wash. The paint stains wouldn't come out, hadn't in years, but ordinary dirt would. It had always been that way, like so much in her life. So much of it ingrained, locked to this house and choices she'd made. Only ordinary daily details changed.

She hadn't dealt with Paul's coming unannounced and trying to pretend they were at a restaurant. What made him think she needed to play games like that? Or wanted to? And bringing enough food to serve a crowd, all fancy as a surprise. He might have found the house standing empty. Of course, he knew there was little chance of that. Was he trying to make a point of it? Did the man think she stayed home like an orphan?

He didn't know she'd been born a Boston girl, grew up in Jamaica Plain and Cambridge. He should know the places Hannah had taken her when she was young. New York and Providence, those had been the special trips. Those days were so wonderful. When Hannah took her to Sardis, which was Hannah's favorite, and the jazz clubs. The Metropole, Birdland and others. Hannah had gotten autographs and introductions to the famous for her. She had enjoyed that life once, and could again if she chose to. That was all it took. Her decision. No one needed to fuss over her like they did.

~ * ~

He was a little disappointed with the day, but meeting the Sinnises' had been great. Dan, menacing, hefting his tire iron, was quite the sight, a bit comical until he got close. There was no doubt he would have used the weapon and most likely with good effect. Gruff as he was, he was eloquent about Anne, and clearly a softie about her.

Grace seemed to be a total ditz initially, but showed real tenderness toward everybody, including him. Taken together, they were quite a pair. The first time the old man said "Aw Gracie," he'd almost laughed, but the sweetness of the man was obviously not weakness.

Molly was another story, one he'd have to work at. Anne's best friend, yet clearly prepared to pursue him if he encouraged her. She was a bit like Ellie. Ellie was more refined, in appearance at least, classy New England, a bit sparse and dour on occasion, but an elegant dresser. Her pursuit had been more zealous than Molly's and she made sure she caught him.

Anne though, what a puzzle. She hated going out, hid her hand, but seemed to have a good life. She was bright, talented, and able to generate great loyalty from friends. All good qualities to be sure, but if he were to be honest with himself, none of that mattered very much. It was her eyes, blue and deep, beautiful and bewitching. They stole his mind and stole his heart, and he loved every glance she sent his way. And he would help her.

Dan and Grace seemed to communicate without words. He wished he could read Anne's thoughts equally as well. Why she sent him home was a puzzle. He chuckled. Next time he'd do things better. At home, he was on the Internet in minutes, searching the Yellow pages in the Newport area.

~ TEN ~

Not having found a suitable gallery on the first go-round, Graham again dragged her all over Newport, and she felt like she'd just run a marathon and come in last. The man wanted an in-town location, but his grand choices were selling for at least a million dollars and that was way more than he'd consider. A smaller place she offered he rejected out-of-hand. She agreed he needed to be at the center of things, but given what he wanted to spend a lease would be his only option. But not for him, thank you. Just find something in the center for two hundred thousand or so. Anything large would suit him, even if it needed work.

"You'll never get it, not at that price," she said, and the man just smiled.

He was stubborn about the house too. As she expected, the agent laughed at his bid and wouldn't even make a counter offer until she pushed quite hard.

"Come on Molly," he said. "You really want a counter? All right. Tell your buyer the best we can do is drop it from nine-hundred-thousand to eight-hundred-ninety. I won't even mention your six hundred to my owner. Tell your guy to get real."

She didn't argue; he was right. Frank Kleticka was a good agent, a straight shooter. Graham blithely raised the bid by twenty thousand. She tried to explain the asking price was about right, and persuade him to offer at least fifty more if he were going to do anything. She was beginning to worry because Graham was being so ridiculous. She offered to show him other houses, but that went nowhere.

"One deal at a time," he said.

The man began to look like he could step into the shoes of P. T. Barnum, but when business was over for the day he treated her like royalty.

He returned to New York for a couple of days and she was at loose ends for the first time in years. A call to Anne brought a dinner invitation, which she accepted. Sometimes Anne's tales of wildlife in her yard and furniture repairs were tiring, but this time it was Paul, and only Paul, Anne talked about.

Her one mention of Graham produced nothing more than a pleasant, "Oh, is he nice?"

"I'm not sure. I think so."

"Well, be careful. I know that much about Paul at least."

"We should Google both of them."

"I thought you were going to do that, about Paul I mean?" Anne asked casually.

"I started to the other day, but I was interrupted. You've got a computer, you can do it."

"You know I'm not good with computers."

"Oh right, I forgot. You just don't want to know if he has secrets." Molly found an open bottle of merlot in Anne's pantry cabinet and poured two glasses. "Have you gotten past paintings and families yet?"

She was annoyed, but tried to hide it. It was the innocence and excitement in Anne, irritating because her own had faded away in failed loves and broken dreams so long ago.

"We talk about lots of things. He's very sweet."

"Has he kissed you again?"

"No."

"Well?"

"Dan and Grace were here the last time. That's all. He's been a perfect gentleman," Anne said, and a rose appeared in each cheek.

"He sounds slow to me."

"Molly, I like the way he is. Would you get some fish sticks out of the freezer please?"

"You have some out already."

"Oh, sorry."

"You sure he's coming again?"

"He said he'd call. You seem awful testy. Are you mad about something?"

Molly laughed. "I told you it's you he likes. Besides, I have Graham now."

"That man you just met. Be careful," Anne said. She had the fish sticks in the broiler and tore open a package of frozen vegetables. "Would you get another pot out please?"

"You've got peas and spinach in pots and now you're starting on string beans? How many veggies are you cooking?"

"Oh, sorry. We have enough don't we."

"You better take it easy. You've already made up your mind this Paul is fabulous, but you barely know him."

Anne gave her a quizzical look. "Just a minute ago you thought he was slow."

"I'm having second thoughts."

"Well, I like him and he likes me. I'm just not sure of me at the moment. I'm excited and I'm scared."

"Of what?"

"A man in my life. Romance, sex, who knows. I'm afraid it will happen and afraid it won't."

Molly choked back the response that started in her head. Anne was a grown woman. What was the big deal? She sighed. Anne might be naive and kidding herself, but that was better than what she was doing, playing Graham like a fish, baiting him with sex and hoping, what- that he'd marry her? Fall in love with her? Suddenly she wanted to be home, alone.

"You're a little premature. The next time he comes, you'll decide you don't like him. Some guys are hard to get rid of you know," she said as pleasantly as she could.

"That won't happen. It's me I'm worried about. He wants things from me and I don't know if I can do them."

"Like what?"

"He already wanted me to go out with him to who knows where."

"That's going to be hard. You'll probably turn into a sex fiend though, and a world traveler," Molly snapped.

Anne nodded, but said nothing, and Molly was sure she'd offended her. She felt crummy and didn't like it. Anne and her guy were a mirror, she and Graham the reflection, and the comparison didn't feel all that good.

Anne finally asked about Graham and she related the facts, but it was clear her friend was just being polite because the usual questions about her love life didn't come. Suddenly, she wished Graham would love her and it wasn't a child's birthday wish, but an ache in her soul.

Anne really hadn't asked dumb questions since they were young. The ones she asked now were the tough ones, like are you sleeping with him? Why? What's going on with his divorce? That last one she didn't have an answer to and she wished she did.

It was time to change the subject. "Stop worrying. I'll Google Paul for you. He might turn out to be a monster and you'll want to get rid of him."

"Paul is not a monster."

"I'll bet there's some kind of dirt he hasn't mentioned." Molly patted Anne's arm. "I'm kidding. Relax."

~ * ~

Dark house, dark life, Molly thought late that night at home. "Why do I do this?" she asked the world aloud. "There's nothing wrong with Anne. It's me. I'm cheap and stupid. Graham White can find himself another agent."

She wouldn't have challenged Anne if she hadn't been jealous. It was her life that needed help. Anne usually listened and made her feel better. They had talked a lot when Tom left all those years ago. That breakup may have been the hardest, but Graham was the hardest starting out. She never wondered about the others, was always sure each guy was perfect, the love of her life.

She should have suspected they weren't, at least a little. Anne was confused. In the beginning, Molly hadn't expected anything but a bit of fun with Graham, yet here she was with a pile of conflicting feelings staring her in the face. Maybe she was just getting old, horrible thought.

~ * ~

Graham's return was almost furtive. At least it seemed so, since she expected a call as soon as he got in. It came a day later instead and she did her best to keep the agitation out of her voice.

"I've been looking for an apartment," he said. "I gave up on the house. Didn't want to upset you."

"I'm sure we can find something less pricey."

"Not anymore. My wife wants to bankrupt me. I can't even get into my gallery until everything's settled."

"What are you going to do?" Not only had the commission on the house gone down the drain, it sounded like a new gallery was heading the same way.

"I'm not broke. The problem is my stock. I expected to use what I had on hand to open the Newport gallery. Now she's got it all tied up in legal mumbo-jumbo."

"So, have you found something?"

"No. I'm still in the hotel."

She stared out the window, blind to the traffic and the tourists meandering by. She might as well offer. With her commissions gone, what could she lose, other than a few tears someday.

"Why don't you stay with me for a while? I have a couple of spare bedrooms."

"You're sure? That's very generous."

"I'm sure. Come to the office and I'll show you where I live."

"I can be there in an hour."

"I'll be here."

"Dinner tonight? On me."

"Okay." She was glad he added that. He could also have said he was pleased to move in with her and he hoped she wasn't upset about the commissions. "Darn, I knew this would happen," she told the dead phone, and slapped it down on the desk.

~ ELEVEN ~

Wrapped in the sheet, tossing and turning the last hour, she gave up on sleep and let yesterday play through her mind again, wishing Hannah had real words to offer her.

"You probably know all about Paul, Grandmother. I just wish I could hear your opinion of all this."

She turned on the light and fluffed the pillow and stared up at the ceiling. Who would have thought? After all these years, this wonderful man just turned up and wanted to be with her. Love wasn't a word she'd use, not for him or for herself. Wanted to get to know her. That was quite enough at the moment.

"You're surprised?"

"Of course. I'm an old maid with one hand."

"You make it seem a curse. There is nothing wrong with you."

"You're talking to me. I'm so glad."

"It's your doing, child."

"I'm not a child anymore."

"To me you are, dear."

"I'm sorry I'm such a disappointment to you."

"Who said such a thing? That is not my view at all."

"You were so brave and I'm such a coward. I've spent my life hiding."

"You are wrong, dear. I am not in the least disappointed. You've done the best you could."

"Not enough. I want more now."

"Fine. That's good, is it not?"

"I don't know. I'm afraid. What will happen to me? To him?"

"You'll decide that."

"Are you real?"

"To your mind I am."

"Why does he come to me? What does he think?"

"He could say he loves you, if he wished to."

"You mean he doesn't? He does like me though. Right?"

"You know he does."

"What am I going to do? I like to be with him, but he won't be satisfied if there's nothing more than that."

"That is true. He relishes the world you fear."

"How can I do this then?"

"You know what must be done."

Suddenly awake, the light still on, she was alone. The clock display read four-eighteen a.m. "Hannah?"

Night silence answered. A dream, that she recalled, but of what? It was Paul. He liked her. That wasn't news. The question was what to do? Was there an answer in the dream?

Hannah, do you haunt me now? You were here, I felt you by my side.

Ever rational, she knew she'd been dreaming. And yet it seemed almost true, with Hannah offering real solutions to her doubts. She wanted to sleep again, to bring Hannah back, but consciousness held tight. She crawled from the bed and made a pot of tea to drink in gloomy silence, in the living room, before the dark TV.

The dream returned, in pieces, little clips of film at a time, until most of it had been recalled. And yet, there were no answers, except that she should see to herself. That she knew already. It had been a dream, that was all.

He'd come without an invitation, to bring exotic food and wine, and why? To impress her, or perhaps to be romantic. Either purpose spoke to what he was thinking. He wanted her. A man wanted to be with her. For sex? Was he that hard up? What else could he want? She didn't say the word she knew applied. To say it meant it had to be dealt with, his feeling and her own as well. He excited her, thrilled her heart with possibilities, and scared her half to death. Nothing would be free. Sex, or changes in the life she'd lived so long in this house. If he were to keep coming to her, she had to decide what she wanted. So she began, as the clock moved and dawn approached.

Life had already been altered, simply by his being there. Small changes so far, but made without the sort of effort she feared. She dressed for him, even bought new clothes for him. So, what came next? Sex. A simple question, do it or not, have it or not. The question was- could she have sex with him and not change her life? No, not entirely, but how much would have to change; that was what she didn't know. She wanted him though. A sense of urgency was growing in her, pushing forward, threatening to take her by storm. One day soon she just might throw herself at him, just like she did with the carpenter. She had to keep her head straight. If she could.

He had to be better than the carpenter. Women would all be divorced if every man were like him.

So, it was time to risk, and maybe if he were satisfied in the sex, and she liked it, perhaps that would be enough and nothing else would have to change.

Settled for the moment, she switched off the light. It was five forty-three, but she'd sleep a while beyond the daylight. Except Paul's face appeared before her and his body without clothes and her imagination began to play.

~ * ~

The house was quiet, as always lately, but for him there was a spark, a joy he hadn't known in many days. He raided the refrigerator, inventoried vegetables and meat, and decided to make a stew. Carol would have laughed.

"It's summer you goof, time for salad and burgers."

It didn't matter, never had. He chose food regardless of the season. Stew now would be good, take an hour to make and he'd use up all the groceries. He'd have to go shopping then soon.

That had been his life the last ten years. Keep busy, keep active, keep the memory away. The meddling idiots. Except when he first met Ellie, There had been respite then, for a while, but it hadn't lasted long.

He walked to the store when the weather allowed. It was good exercise, but more, it used time. Fifteen minutes in the car, or near an hour walking. It was too soon for a new bike. The broken arm of course. He went through the classifieds, made a few calls to find a decent bike. Not that a new one was out of the question. He could easily afford one. It was just, well, there could be a bargain that would suit him. If not, it was something else to do.

Retired four years, the television, bad as it was, drew him each morning, a hypnotic trap that drained away his life one moment at a time. He griped at himself for watching, and on occasion left it off, but it was always there, tempting.

He'd been a wise investor, or lucky some might say, but did pick his stocks based on market potential. Google early, among others, and he was wise enough to hold them long enough. He didn't need to work.

Life was pretty good, really. Lunch with the guys each week, fishing and sailing in the summer. He liked his skin now, more than in his youth. Always different, he was never the typical American male. He played tennis as a kid, hated baseball. Getting drunk and loud parties in college, sex with any woman willing, none of that appealed to him. In those days different was supposed to be everybody's thing, but different was disaster in reality, even then.

Different didn't matter any longer, but when Ellie left some ancient wound yawned open. And Carol's death, he'd had no choice in that thanks to his own stupidity. That was another whole story, full of pain, full of rage and desperation, blast the stupid government. He'd never let that go, no way.

He groaned. What was Anne about? She seemed to fear something. It had to be sex, though the hand was a possibility too. He wanted sex, but not without her heart. Anne Hoskins was beautiful. And vulnerable. He liked her a ton.

~ * ~

At a little after nine, as she was starting breakfast the next morning, he called.

"It's me. How are you today?"

"Fine, thank you," she said, wondering why he was calling.

"I thought I'd follow up on getting together. Is tomorrow good for you?"

"Tomorrow?" Not next week? Oh my! "Yes, that would be fine."

"Noon this time?"

"Oh, certainly. Will you have lunch? I mean I'll fix it."

He laughed. "I have a plan. Don't fix anything."

"You're not bringing all that food again are you?"

"Don't worry. I learned my lesson last time."

"Good."

"Tomorrow then. Twelve o'clock. Tell Molly you want to be alone."

"Paul, what are you doing?"

"Promise."

"All right. I'll call her."

"Good. See you tomorrow."

~ * ~

Her heart beat slow and steady this time, despite his secrecy, and she even took a breath or two while she dressed. Picking one of the new skirts she'd bought, the blue one, she laid it out on the bed, added an ivory white sheer top, and stood back to study the combination.

Sliding into the clothes, she did her own makeup for the second time. She'd made a first attempt last night and liked the result, so today it took less effort. In her predawn sleeplessness she'd made a decision. Tomorrow might be different, with worry back and uncertainty as well, but today she'd go for the moon.

He was a sweet man trying to be romantic and she liked his attention. They might never go out, and he might stop visiting her and that would be hard, but she'd survive. She loved the way he treated her, the little things he tried to do, the big things too. Why not make love with him?

The teapot was whistling when the phone rang. She shut off the stove and picked up the phone.

"Hi," Molly said. "Are you busy?"

"Not at the moment. I'm waiting for Paul."

"Good. He can answer some questions when he comes then."

"What kind of questions? Why?"

"Remember I said I was going to Google these guys? Well, I need more information. There are hundreds of Paul Brelands and I don't know which one I'm checking out."

"Molly! This is so silly."

"Never mind, it's serious. I'm finding everything from some inventor who's probably worth millions to a guy who tried to kill his wife. Some live in other countries, so I can eliminate them, but I don't know enough about your Paul to figure out which one he is."

"Why are you making such a big thing about this? Are you checking out Graham too?" Anne asked, her head starting to pound a little. She didn't need protection. It was that child thing again with Molly; take care of the helpless one.

Molly gave her a sardonic laugh. "I searched for him, yes. Google found millions of Graham Whites. It would take me a lifetime to go through the listings."

Anne felt her tension ease. "So, it's easy to check out Paul?"

"Easier. But I don't know enough about him. Like what company he worked for, when was he born, does he have any other family, did he ever live anywhere else?"

"I'm not going to cross examine him, Molly. He's a good man, that's all that matters."

"Just be subtle about it; a few questions at a time. Some of these guys are rich and at least one is a murderer."

"I'm sure Paul is neither," Anne said, but of course Paul didn't work, so maybe he had money. "How do you find out all this stuff?"

"Anything that's in the media can be picked up in the search."

"So, if he never got his name in the papers, you'll never find him listed?"

"Probably."

Anne laughed. "This is so silly."

Molly sighed. "Maybe, but it's got me hooked now. I feel like a detective, Sherlock Molly, hot on the trail. Listen, just ask Paul a few questions, will you?"

"Very few. Now, I have to get ready for him. Bye."

"Remember, sexy gets the man."

"Bye Molly," Anne said, and hung up.

She was crouching at the edge of the garden, picking flowers, when he entered the patio.

"Good morning. I decided to add a little color to the table today."

"I think I won't bring flowers anymore," he said, indicating the rose in his hand.

"I have another vase and please do."

"Right, it's a tradition."

She laughed. "That's wonderful. Thank you. Would you like coffee?"

"Sounds good. You look ravishing today," he said suddenly. "Absolutely stunning."

A touch of panic came with a flush to her cheeks, but she stifled it. "No woman my age is ravishing. That's for twenty-year-olds."

"Not so. You're more beautiful than any twenty-year-old I've ever met."

"Paul, stop!" She started for the door, clutching the flowers, embarrassed by the flaming compliment. He was being romantic, just what she wanted, but it felt undeserved.

With him close behind she led the way, suddenly very conscious of her body. The blue skirt swayed with her hips and he had to be watching it float from side to side. She desperately wanted another way to move her legs, to still her hips and the dumb skirt. Warmth blossomed in her cheeks as they entered the kitchen.

"Would you get the milk out of the fridge?" The words came out tight and strained. She couldn't face him.

"Sure," he said, and moved around the island to the refrigerator. She poured coffee, added milk and stirred, still managing to keep her back to him. Her heart grew quieter and breath returned.

"Well, where is your mysterious surprise?" she asked.

"Surprises." He held up the lovely shopping bag he was carrying, its handles adorned with ribbons.

"Is that food again?" she asked, almost sure it wasn't, but if it wasn't food it had to be a gift and suddenly she wondered just how extravagant he'd been.

"Let's not worry about lunch, not yet at least. I just brought some things I hope you'll like." He set the bag on the kitchen table and stepped back, his eyes smiling.

He looked so handsome.

"Go to it," he said. "It's nothing fancy."

She peeked over the top of the bag. Books, big ones, and small ones in paperback. She began to lift them out.

"I didn't know what you like or what you have, so I brought a bunch. Anything you have already you can donate to a library."

She turned each book in her hand to read the titles. John Adams by David McCullogh, Barbara Kingsolver's Prodigal Summer, Toni Andrew's Cry Mercy, and more.

"These aren't current books?"

"No. Some were mine, others I got in a used book store. I bought some I've read and liked."

"What's this one, Cry Mercy?"

He gave her a sheepish smile. "A thriller with a little sci-fi twist to it."

She nodded, a warm feeling rising in her belly. He liked all kinds of books. Something else they had in common.

"Thank you Paul. What a thoughtful gift. I don't think I've read any of these."

She drew out the last book and the bag fell over. Inside was one more thing, tall and thin. She lifted it out. A menu, from a restaurant in Jamestown.

"I thought we could order lunch today. Sort of like take out?" he said tentatively.

"You'll have to pick it up then."

"We'll have it delivered."

She had no idea why, but the warmth was gone, replaced by a twist of tension. Silly, there was no reason to be upset. She nodded.

"What did you do yesterday? Any new paintings?" he asked.

I thought about you constantly, and dreamed about you at night! I couldn't paint because I couldn't concentrate.

She kept the thought in her head. "I worked on the furniture. The radio cabinet is almost finished, and I'm ready to start the other one."

"Sounds like a busy day. Can I see what you did on the furniture?"

"All right. You go first." She'd had enough of him walking behind her.

The old console still sat in the center of the workshop. The doors lay on a bench against the wall with clamps attached along the edges. A smell of turpentine hung in the air. He offered to help, telling her he was a fast learner.

She hesitated, uneasy with the question. He knew she was a professional. Was it because she was a woman, or the other thing, her hand? She restrained an instinctive, angry retort, unwilling to challenge him. Then it struck her that he might simply be seeking another way to be with her.

"I suppose you could do some polishing. Let me think about it." She told herself he might damage the pieces, but there was more. Each piece of furniture felt like her creation, just like the paintings. They arrived damaged and worn, incomplete, unwanted. Finished, they were perfect, ready to resume their proper place in the world. She wasn't sure she wanted to share that with him. Even a little bit.

"A penny for your thoughts," he said, his eyes twinkling.

"I'm thinking about lunch. Are you hungry?"

"Sure, let's order." He ran his fingers over the top of the console. "You do beautiful work."

"Thank you," she said, but the compliment left a spike of tension in her belly. Again. What was wrong with her? Why was she so on edge?

They returned to the kitchen and reviewed the menu. He called in their orders and turned back to Anne.

"Thirty minutes."

"You have time then. It's only ten minutes to town."

"It's being delivered," he said softly.

"Oh." she nodded, wondering if that was part of his secret and why it made her feel so twitchy. He liked secrets. Which brought back Molly's phone call.

"Have you always lived in Connecticut?"

"No."

All right, she'd surprised him with the change of subject. She could try again, with a little subtlety this time.

"It's a pretty state."

"Unless you live in one of the cities."

"You don't?"

"No."

"Where then?"

"Branford."

"Where's that?"

"It's a town this side of New Haven."

"Where did you live before?"

"New York."

"In the country too?"

"Near Manhattan."

"Oh."

She felt like a fool, questioning him like this, just because Molly practically demanded it. Like a mouse in a trap of her own making, stuck on this string of questions leading nowhere. He obviously didn't want to talk about himself, probably preferred to talk about the two of them, but how could she get them to another topic. She picked up one of the books he'd brought and asked if he'd read it. Of course, he'd said he read them all, but maybe he hadn't.

"I love her writing," he said.

"I read the book about the Confederate wife. That was good too," she said, and then she heard it.

A noisy car coming up the drive.

The car she never saw, only the thin young woman who apparently drove it. She met them on the patio, wearing a yellow dress and apron combination typical of a waitress in a fairly upscale restaurant.

"Mister Breland?" the young woman asked.

"Yes. You're Elaine? Is everything all set?"

"Yes sir. If you'll both sit, I'll get started. Hello, ma'am. Will we be using this plastic table?"

Anne stared in silence as the young woman set the table, including silver, wine glasses and cloth napkins.

"Will you have red or white, miss?" the woman asked.

"I...I'll have white."

"Yes Ma'am," said Elaine and disappeared through the hedges, heading out to her car.

Anne's heart pounded, her breath came in shallow, almost silent gasps. This was wrong, bad, a testament to helplessness again, a sign of what he thought of her.

"What is this Paul? What are you doing?"

"It's a special lunch. Restaurant service with all the trimmings—just for you."

"This must be costing you a fortune." Stupid thing to say. She had to tell him what she felt.

He laughed. "A King's ransom, entirely appropriate for a beautiful Princess."

"Stop that. This isn't takeout. It's a catered lunch. Send her away."

"It's all arranged. We're indulging today."

"Paul, please. This is ridiculous. A waste of good money."

He stared, looked serious, almost angry. "It's supposed to be expensive. Even so, it's not that much."

"I won't eat anything."

He hesitated, studied her face, looking uncertain.

She trembled as waves of feeling roiled up in her throat and nearly made her gag. This was all so wrong. He was treating her like a helpless baby, just like everyone else did. He wouldn't have done this if she'd agreed to go out with him. It was Molly and Grace and Dan all over again. He thought she was a twit. He pitied her.

"Look, I paid a deposit. There's no reason not to enjoy it."

"I can't. It's too much."

"Anne, what's wrong? This is my gift to you. I can't always bring a rose."

She shivered. The woman returned with the wine and stood watching, obviously having heard them. Not meeting his eyes, or the woman's, Anne dashed into the house.

~ * ~

A single bird called from the woods, a chirp, nuthatch, or something else small. The woman cleared her throat, but Paul ignored her, waiting for a sign from the house. The bird twittered again, twice, three times.

"Uh, Mister Breland, what should I do?"

He turned to see the woman, standing with the wine in hand, trying not to look concerned, but failing.

"I guess we call it off. One eighty, right?" he said, and started counting out twenty dollar bills.

The woman nodded, watching him count the money. "I'm sorry your lady got upset. Maybe another time will be better."

"I won't try this again. Thank you. I'll help you load your car."

"It's nothing but the table settings and glasses so far. I've got them. Do you want the food, or should I take it somewhere?"

"I'll keep the wine. Is there a soup kitchen in town?"

"There's one in Newport."

"Drop the food off there."

She nodded, handed him the wine bottles, smiled, and was gone in a minute.

He turned to the front door and called. "She's gone, Anne."

The birds were quiet this time. He called again, waited, then turned away.

~ TWELVE ~

Anne stood in the studio, at her easel, in the tattered old smock, painting away. Rain beat against the skylights, making a drumming sound she barely noticed. The small canvas on the easel was becoming a disaster. It didn't matter. She had done a dozen or so the last couple of days, all dark and muddy looking.

A rap on the window produced one very quick spin around, and an even faster change in her expression. Molly, not Paul. Anne gave her a head nod, permission to come in, and went back to painting.

"Geez, hi Molly. It's good to see you," Molly said, shaking raindrops from her hair.

"What does that mean?" Anne snapped.

"You know. You looked as if I were an ogre, showing my face at your window. Are you expecting Paul?"

"No."

Molly sniffed. "You're a happy soul today. How are you?"

"Fine."

"Fine is usually a nice word. That sounds like a 'drop dead' to me."

Anne kept moving the brush, slashing with it, slapping down a dash of dark blue paint.

"Hey, mad lady. How about putting down that brush and talking to me?"

"We can talk while I paint."

"Oh sure. Just the way we are right now. What did he do to you?"

"It doesn't matter. It's over."

"Really? That was fast. A couple of days ago you were in heaven. Now it doesn't matter?"

"He won't come back." The brush went down, not cleaned at all, just dumped on her palette, a sacrilege normally. She wished Molly would go away and let her be. Didn't matter? Who was she kidding? Anne stole a look at her friend. Certainly not her.

"Are you going to tell me what happened?"

Anne told it then, about the catered lunch with waitress.

"Okay, I'm impressed. A nice romantic lunch sounds good. What went wrong?"

"It was terrible."

"What was? Something about your hand? Did the girl say something?"

"It was a trick to make me go out with him."

Because he cared, and thought she couldn't help herself, and she'd been so stupid.

"How did he do that?"

"He didn't do anything. I made him cancel the whole thing."

"Oh, he must have liked that a lot. So, he got mad?" Molly asked, wearing a puzzled frown.

"No. I don't know."

Anne stopped, seeing reproof in Molly's expression. It was veiled, but it was there and Anne knew why. She'd been a dope, had known that since Paul left. That was what the dark new paintings were about. Stubbornly, she started again.

"Surprises I do not need. A catered lunch. So much money and for what? A treat he called it. My eye. I don't need a restaurant here or anywhere else. He was manipulating and scheming as if I were an idiot, trying to get me to go out with him."

She was on a roll now, all of the frustration and recriminations boiling in her belly. He felt sorry for her too. The thought had hit her right after he left and had shocked her. Was that what the helplessness was about? Everybody pitied her, even Dan and Grace?

"What?" Molly asked, staring at her.

"Nothing. Why are you looking at me that way?"

"You're upset."

How do you ask someone if they feel sorry for you? She couldn't. If Molly did, and Paul, and the Sinnises', it was all her own fault. She would have to change everyone. She had to change herself.

Frowning, Molly spoke again. "Did you tell him all this stuff about his schemes and whatever?"

"No. I went inside and made peanut butter sandwiches. When I went out again there were just empty chairs, and the bare table, no woman and no Paul."

"Oh, dandy. He hasn't called?"

"No."

"Oh, dandy," Molly said again.

Anne started then, her face twisting six different ways at once, but she settled on bored indifference. It was either that or her tears would drown them both.

"It's done Molly. I knew it wouldn't last."

"Don't be a drama queen. The man was upset and left in a huff. You have to look at it from his point of view."

She'd been ready to kill Paul, but now the truth felt like a vise around her chest. She couldn't stand it if he pitied her.

"It was my fault, mine."

"Well, that's a good thing. You can apologize and everything will be fine."

Anne glanced up at her. "You really think he'll get over it?"

"How do I know? I can't read his mind."

Anne's stomach twisted with pain. If only she could ask Molly about the pity thing, but Molly surely felt it too. Why else would she take care of Anne the way she did? Everybody took care of her. And she let them do it too, hiding in the house the way she did. Fixing that was her job, no one else's. She had to take charge from now on.

"You better cool it if you want to see him. Don't go giving him motives he didn't have," Molly was saying.

"You're the one who tells me not to trust a man."

"And I have all the answers? Hah. By the way, did you find out anything about him?"

"Did I ask subtle questions, you mean."

"Did you?"

"Molly, stop with that. Please. That's the least of my worries."

~ THIRTEEN ~

He was ticked, but her call fixed that right up. It was a surprise, very nice since he expected nothing from her. He'd hoped she'd calm down, but in his own mind there was doubt enough to discourage him. There was nothing like a little reassureance. He wouldn't quit on her now.

Anxiety he'd expected, possibly some annoyance, but her walkout had surprised him. Made him mad as blue blazes too. After all, the luncheon had been a major effort on his part. He'd made dozens of calls to restaurants to work out all the details, and then Anne walked off in a stew.

The luncheon was his gemstone, a great idea he thought. Good food, nice service, romantic, the best they could do at home. Well almost. He did try to find a guitar or fiddle player, but had no luck with that on short notice. One guy was a possible for next time, but that wouldn't happen now.

He'd thought about her hand, figured she might be agitated with the stranger serving them, but that was necessary, the whole point if they were ever to escape the house. The question of surprise he'd considered quite a bit, and then decided it was needed. If she'd known his plan he believed she would have refused and then how could he have done it? So, he'd kept it to himself. Bad choice. She made that very clear on the phone.

She started awkwardly, half apology, half feeling him out. "I called because of what happened the other day. We seem to have had a misunderstanding," she said, when he answered.

Guarded, he replied in kind. "I suppose we did."

"You didn't say goodbye."

"I was afraid I'd start a fight."

"I'm sorry if I ruined your surprise. I'm not good with surprises."

"I should have let you know beforehand. It just seemed like a fun idea."

"I hope you didn't waste any money."

"That's okay. The girl was happy."

"You paid her?"

"Sure. We had a deal."

"Oh my. Was it a lot of money?"

"Not bad."

"I don't know what to say."

"Next time I'll ask first."

"You want to do that again?"

"You don't want me to? Was there something else you didn't like about it? Beside the surprise I mean?"

"Why do you want to do that? We don't need to," she said, ignoring his question.

"I thought you'd enjoy it. It would be fun, like going to a regular restaurant."

He waited for a response, but it didn't come.

"Would you tell me what happened?" he asked, knowing he should know her answer, but in reality he wasn't quite ready to entirely make peace about the thing. A fancy lunch on her patio still would be a great idea as far as he was concerned.

She hesitated, then said softly, "I'd just prefer you didn't do that again."

He didn't answer, and finally, she added, "It's pressure. I don't like it."

"I don't get that."

"You want me to go out." Her words were clipped and deliberate.

"I wanted to have a fun lunch."

"But you want me to go out with you. You ask every time you come."

"Sure, but what does that have to do with this?"

"It felt like you were pushing me. You think I'm a helpless coward."

"Hey, I didn't mean it that way. It's like an alternative, you know? Different and exciting. Romantic if you really want to know."

"But it must be expensive."

Why was she hammering on that? It was only money.

"That's the point. A ham sandwich isn't very special. I wanted to give you a treat, still do as a matter of fact."

"That's all of it? You don't mind if we don't go out?"

"Not at all," he said, the lie coming out without a hitch.

"I don't know if I believe you."

He sighed then, wishing they could back up a bit and stop. She needed an answer though, and it had to be truth.

"Anne, you're right. I wonder about going out, hope you will join me one day. But that has nothing to do with this. Well, I suppose it does in a way. If we were going out, I wouldn't have come up with this idea, but this was for fun all by itself. The future's later, not to worry about, not now. I just want to have fun with you."

"We can do that without expensive lunches."

"Giving you a treat is special for me. You have to tell me how I can do that."

"Just by coming to see me."

"That's all?"

"You sound disappointed."

"No, it's okay. How about I pick up some deli sandwiches somewhere and come tomorrow?"

She said all right and they were done for the moment and that was okay. He would have liked a different result, but she was still talking to him. Better, they understood a little more about each other.

He relaxed when she hung up, but there was no comfy warm feeling rolling through his body. It seemed his optimism was a bit overdone. She was brave enough to confront him, even comfortable making an apology. But, would she ever leave that house?

An enigma, that's what she was. Sometimes he felt more than a little frustrated dealing with her. Why he tolerated that was not at all clear. He was too old to be infatuated, or was he?

His son Scott called. "Where've you been the last few days? I tried to call you."

"Visiting a friend."

Scott laughed. "Janey said you have a girlfriend in Rhode Island. Is that who we're talking about?"

"That's where I've been."

"I hear she's a babe."

Paul didn't reply. A babe was not the way he wanted to speak of Anne.

Scott hesitated and then went on. "Janey likes her, says she's a nice lady."

"Your sister has good judgment."

"Jeez, Pop, loosen up. You must be real serious about this woman."

"Yeah, I am." He said it easily, but with a little bit of surprise, or maybe it was uncertainty.

"Jane said she hangs close to home all the time. Are we going to meet her one of these days?"

"Of course. Sure."

"Great. Is she a sailor? Maybe we can do a day on the boat?"

"Are you looking to go sailing?" Paul asked, his tone teasing. "Is that why you called?"

"I thought you'd never ask. With that busted arm, you'll need me and Maggie to sail the boat for you."

"That'll be the day," Paul said, but Scott was right. He couldn't sail without them at the moment. "How's Saturday for you?"

"Good. What about your lady? Will she come?"

"Not this time."

Was he chasing a dream? Hanging on to a hope that would never happen? The thought wasn't new. It had even niggled at him while he was with Ellie. He could have quit before she did, should have, came quite close a number of times, but always delayed. The why of it escaped him then, and continued to. Perhaps he simply tolerated unhappiness far more than most people would. Or maybe he had a need to make things right. A stab of pain hit him then, along with the memory of Carol's death. That sure didn't go right.

Anne's life hadn't changed in thirty years or more as far as he could tell. He marveled at his conceit, thinking he could change her with a couple of books and a catered lunch. For the first time, he wondered if she could ever change, and he didn't like that thought. There were certainly other women he could find to make a life with. But it was Anne he wanted. She'd come around. She had to.

~ * ~

He showed up with sandwiches in a bag the next day, just a wee bit early, eleven thirty instead of twelve as they'd agreed. The house was locked up tight, but he could hear, faintly, singing from the back. He parked himself on the patio and unpacked the lunch, then got up and stared into the studio. Canvases lay piled in the corner, but nothing else seemed to have changed. The tune stopped and he sat again, then stood and walked out to the drive.

Noting a spot of peeling paint on the door of the garage, he examined the place, mentally noting where repairs were needed. The back of the house remained off limits this time to be sure he didn't find her in a compromising position. All he needed was to see her through an open bedroom window as she dressed, and be seen himself.

No, the front and sides of the garage and house would get a good going over. The back he'd check out later. He'd offer to help with painting and repairs when the cast was off his arm. The old place could use a bit of attention.

A door slammed inside and he began to whistle. Not being very skilled at that art, and knowing little more than the first line of most songs, he began with *She'll be Coming 'Round the Mountain*.

There was no response from the house. He switched to *Jingle Bells*, and whistled louder.

"Paul, is that you?" she cried from somewhere deep within the house.

"It's me!" he shouted.

"You're early!"

"I know."

"Give me a minute."

"No problem, take your time," he said, picturing her sliding into panties and bra. "Take your time."

The image evaporated in seconds, as she appeared, fully clothed and breathless, carrying a pair of shoes in her hand. She sat on the lounge and slipped them on, then stood to face him, smoothing a pale green skirt with an inadvertent motion.

"I didn't expect you so soon. Wasn't it twelve?"

He grinned. "I'm way early."

A rush of crimson rose in her face. "That seems to be a habit with you."

"I'm usually late," he said, shaking his head.

"Oh," she said, and the crimson deepened.

"Lunch, madam, no choices today. Subway specials, with all the fixing's. I did bring wine though, and ice cream. Red and white for the wine, maple walnut or raspberry for the other."

Her mouth turned up in a tentative smile and he was sure she feared upsetting him as she had the other day.

"I thought there were no choices."

"I can't resist. It's my weakness."

"Well, it all sounds wonderful."

"I'm glad you like it."

"Thank you, Paul. This is very nice."

He laughed. "Don't get too excited, it's only Subway."

"I wasn't referring to the quality of the food. It's sweet of you to do this my way today."

"It's what we agreed on. That makes it best."

The smile she offered was shy, deferential, a thank you without words. "I suppose we need to talk about some things."

"No rush, we're good right now."

She ignored that. "You do want me to go out with you."

"Is that a question? I do, sure."

"I'll try. Some things yes, I can do them without much trouble, others like restaurants, no."

He opened his mouth to speak, but she continued. "If we pick and choose I'll be fine. We have to go slowly. I don't know why I'm this way, but I am, and you have to be patient with me."

He wanted to say to her what she'd said to him, 'I don't know if I believe you,' but wisely let that go.

"That's good with me. Someday we'll figure out what you fear, or whatever, and we'll go everywhere."

"That's a bit extreme. It may never happen, you know. If it does, it may take a lifetime to achieve."

He grinned at that. "Did someone say that was too long?"

She smiled, looking determined. "I'm going to change, I promise. I have an idea. I run with my neighbor Betty Miller. We go on the street. I've never had a problem with it, but I've only been with her. We could try that today."

"Make it a walk instead of a run and you're on," he replied.

~ * ~

Heading south along the road, they covered a mile before turning back. A light breeze, sunlit trees and flowers were wonderful, with all the issues settled for the moment, even if she was slightly anxious with him at her side. They were deep in conversation when a jogger appeared and waved.

"Who's that?" Paul asked.

"That's Betty. My neighbor I told you about. I'm embarrassed. I haven't run with her since I met you." She returned the wave.

Betty stared at Paul as she neared, as if trying to place him in the recesses of her memory. She gave him an almost imperceptible nod and spoke to Anne.

"I almost didn't recognize you. You're never out here except with me."

"I know. Betty, this is Paul Breland. Paul, this is my friend, Betty Miller."

"Nice to meet you," he said.

"How do. Are you the guy that wrecked his bike?"

"The one and only."

"Looks like that arm took the brunt of it."

"Yeah, pain galore, but it's nothing to worry about." Paul smiled.

"How are you?" Anne asked.

"Okay. Bill booked us into a cottage in New Hampshire last week. Today's my first day out since we came back. I tried to call you, but I guess you were out walking."

"I'm sorry. Should we run tomorrow?"

"Sure. In the morning?"

"All right. I'll be in."

"Nice meeting you," she said lightly, and jogged off with another wave.

"Same here," Paul called to her retreating back.

"I feel terrible. The last time I talked to her she was upset about her marriage. I should have called, but I've been so busy," Anne said.

"She went off for a week with Bill, who I gather is her husband?"

"Unfortunately, yes. She wasn't very happy about going."

~ FOURTEEN ~

Anne said she was in a rut, a stick in the mud. He could have told her everybody was some way or the other. His rut was broader than hers, and ran in more directions, but it was still a rut in its own way. He felt like she was the break in time for him and he was the same for her. He had to remember that and tell her. It might help.

He had dinner with Ben and Hazel. It was nice to be with great friends who went back to the early days. Carol had been Hazel's friend and Paul met Ben through her. They'd kept him going when Carol died, even through their own grief. When he called for help, or even when he should have but didn't, they were there.

Paul remarked the point on one occasion and Hazel had told him Carol made her promise to watch out for him.

"You think I'd bother otherwise?" she'd added, smart-alec as always.

She was shorter than Carol had been, about five three, and tending toward plump. Dark hair with some gray in it, and a sparkle in her eyes, especially when she looked at Ben. Except when she got mad at him. Then she'd get a mighty steely look. But usually it was the sparkle.

"A whole month I haven't seen you. Ben said you have a new woman in your life," said Hazel.

"Ben's a big mouth. He's probably told you all there is to know about her already," Paul said.

"Of course, he's a good husband. But like the rest of you, he doesn't remember a darn thing." Ben rolled his eyes at that and she continued, "So, I want to hear about her from you. What's she like?"

"I don't have much to tell you yet."

"Ben said she's a recluse?"

"Not really. Sort of."

"That's clear as mud. Which is it?"

"She's a recluse in some ways, not in others."

"That's still mud. Do you know what you're getting into?"

"Actually Hazel, not entirely."

She looked at her husband and shook her head. "Is it me, or is he waffling all over the place?"

"Label him 'the great equivocator,'" said Ben. "The man doesn't know if he's coming or going."

That was the beginning. They kept at Paul, good heartedly, with questions and needling, for a good hour.

Paul described Anne's physical appearance, what he knew of her life, and what they had done together thus far. All reports produced some form of nonsensical ribbing from the two of them, but they did get to the point at times. More often than Paul needed in fact. When he described his luncheon arrangements and Anne's reaction, Hazel laughed.

"You are a little ham-handed at times, Mister Breland," she said.

"I thought I was being romantic."

"Well, it sounds like you missed something. A signal, something she said?"

"I don't know. Maybe."

"It's the little things that make the difference, don't you know?"

"Like what?"

"Pearl earrings are good," said Ben.

"She doesn't wear jewelry."

"Candy then."

"She's not much for sweets. And don't tell me flowers. She has a yard full of them and I bring a rose each time I go. Used to anyway."

"I thought you didn't know her very well," said Ben.

"Those things I know."

"Are you in love?" asked Hazel.

"It sure sounds like it to me," said Ben.

That was the question Paul had been playing with, darn near from the beginning. Actually, he'd been mulling and considering and pondering constantly.

"It begins to seem I'm headed that way, doesn't it?"

"Quite a bit that way, I'd say." Hazel laughed.

That turned out to be the message of the evening, all clarified, and neatly wrapped for further action. He could always count on Ben and Hazel.

He rang Anne the next night at seven, got a breathless answer on the third ring, as if she'd just made a dash from the bathroom. Exercising his newly learned finesse, he made no stupid comments.

"Hi. It's me. How was your day?"

"Paul? I'm fine. What's wrong?"

"I miss you. I wanted to hear your voice."

"I thought something had happened."

"No. I'm just a lonely man who knows a beautiful woman in Rhode Island and misses her a ton."

"Oh," she said. "What's gotten into you?"

"Like I said, thinking about you. What are you doing right this minute?"

"I finished dinner, and I'm about to read a book."

"What book?"

"Prodigal Summer."

"That's one I gave you, right? Do you like it?"

"I just started it."

"I'll expect a full report," he said, with a smile in his voice he hoped she could hear.

Her response was simple, but the tone uncertain, as if she wondered what he'd had to drink. "What are you doing?"

"Indulging in a glass of wine and fanciful thoughts about you."

"Paul, please stop that!"

"Thoughts of a rather intimate nature," he continued, pushing.

She went silent. Perhaps he'd overdone it, again.

"Did I embarrass you?"

"No. Yes," she said too quickly.

"I'm sorry. Just trying to be funny. Tell me about your day."

"Only if you behave yourself."

"I won't embarrass you again. Promise."

She hesitated, and he wondered if he'd lost her. "All right then," she said. "I talked to Grace this afternoon, and I finished the radio cabinet."

"I'll bet it looks great."

"It's nice."

"Listen, how about I come see you tomorrow?"

"You were just here."

"Is that a no?"

"No, not at all. It's just that you've been coming so much and it's such a long drive. Don't you need a day to rest?"

He laughed silently at that, believing he knew her thought. "And I'm overwhelming you?"

She didn't answer. His words could be taken as an insult, or pure arrogance on his part. Dumb. But she didn't take offense, thank goodness.

"To tell the truth, you are a bit of a tornado."

"Never. Not me. What about tomorrow? Would you like a break?"

"Yes, and Molly will be here. Friday's good though. You're not going to do lunch again I hope. I'll fix it."

"Okay, lunch is on you then. I have something else in mind."

"No more surprises. Please, Paul."

"Okay, I've learned my lesson. This isn't the same. I have things to discuss with you, that's all."

"What things?"

"When I see you."

~ FIFTEEN ~

She'd lied about Molly coming Thursday. He'd been there too much, too fast. She needed a break, a chance to consider what she was doing. Molly wasn't coming at all, but a phone call would rectify that quickly if she needed her.

She called her, not with an invitation, but a need to talk. Molly laughed when she filled her in, said it was obvious what the man wanted, but Graham was taking her to dinner and could she call back when she got home?

"Of course," Anne said, but her chest constricted and she hung up quickly, cutting off Molly's breezy, "Great hon, talk to you later."

The clock said Grace and Dan were probably driving home, but she tried them anyway and as expected, there was no answer at the house or at the shop. They hated cell phones, so she was out of luck there.

She had no clue why she had such an urge to talk. Was she playing helpless again? She wasn't asking anyone to do anything for her. This business of changing oneself was tricky.

Being alone was nothing new and besides, there was always Hannah to talk to, and anyway, she'd made up her mind. Maybe. If only he'd stop this secrets thing. Why couldn't he say what he was thinking? He was terrible with secrets, teasing her all the time. Didn't keep them very long though, so that was good. Silly.

It could be about her hand, or going out, or even having sex. She couldn't imagine he'd bring that up so formally, after giving her a day's warning?

"That thing I wanted to tell you? Let's get laid." He wouldn't say anything like that, she hoped. Not that she'd object to that necessarily. It was just the way of it, not a bit of romance if he did it that way. It had to be about going out. Oh hell.

She looked at the clock. Eight-forty. If only Molly would call. But of course she was probably still all wrapped up with Graham.

Darn it, she'd been alone long enough. How amazing that one new person could affect her life so much. Just meeting Paul had changed everything. When had she ever lied to Molly before? And seeing herself in a new way, through everyone else's eyes? That was a bummer. Well, sort of.

It was time, she would be with Paul. Sex would be all right, and that would definitely change everything. She needed to do that, take charge of her life, take care of herself from now on. Wasn't that what she'd decided? Never mind calling friends every time she had a decision to make or felt scared or lonely. That had to stop too, but that part would be difficult.

Molly appeared for breakfast in the morning, bright and cheerful, like she was whenever she'd had a good time with a man. Probably slept with her new guy, but Anne didn't ask, wouldn't give her the satisfaction of talking about it.

"Any news yet?" Molly asked.

"He's coming tomorrow. I won't know until then."

"I think the pot's about to boil,"

"What?"

"You know. He's ready to commit himself. Move in or have sex or whatever."

"I won't marry him. It's too soon."

"Who said marry? He'll want sex. Why should he marry again?"

"Because he's a good man."

Molly sighed. "You're impossible."

"So are you. How can you be so sure?"

"That he wants sex? You know that's what men want."

"You're wrong about him. He hasn't even made half a pass."

"Then what's his secret? He's gay? He's going to dump you? Fat chance on both counts."

"He's not gay." Anne would not believe that about him, but the dumping? The thought of that made her stomach feel like it was full of frightened butterflies. "Don't talk about that."

Molly nodded, sympathetic, as she had been other times, mostly when Anne was young and incredibly naive.

It made her blood boil today. "Did you sleep with Graham?" she said abruptly.

"What does that have to do with anything? As a matter of fact yes, if you really want to know."

"Why?"

"Why not? I like a little fun and I like the man," Molly snapped. "What's going on here? You're in a great mood."

"I'm sorry Molly. I'm all worked up I suppose. I made up my mind to sleep with Paul and try to go out, and now he may be coming to say goodbye."

"You're going to sleep with him?"

"Yes."

"Really? Just like that?"

"No, I've been thinking about it."

Molly shook her head. "You look pretty forlorn for a woman in love. Relax, you'll be looking back and laughing in a few days."

"Let's move the calendar up then."

"I have an easier way. Listen, he's not going to dump you. He'd have done that on the phone. No way the man would drive two hours if that was all he wanted." She grinned. "Right? You know I'm right."

"I don't know."

"Yeah, I saw your face change. You eased right up when I said that."

"All right, so that makes sense. Now what?"

"Okay. Have you really decided to sleep with the man?"

"Yes."

"Good. Why?"

"Men like sex, right? And I like him. I'll probably never get another chance again."

Molly wagged a finger at her. "Keep going. You're just beginning."

"All right. I want him. I like him. When he's not here, I don't know what to do with myself anymore. That's dumb, but the house feels empty without him."

"You're in love, my friend. In love for sure."

"Stop saying that. I just want sex."

"Why?"

"Because he turns me on," Anne said, heat rising in her cheeks.

"Sounds good to me."

"I'm nervous, Molly. How should I tell him?"

"The same way you did it with that carpenter guy. Nothing's changed in that department lately."

"That went so fast I don't even remember how it happened." Anne did though. She just didn't want to remember how she'd paraded around half naked in front of the man. All because he'd been kind to her that day when she bandaged his injured hand.

Molly grinned again. "Now you're in my area of expertise. It's very simple. Prepare your bedroom for a little romance. Put a touch of perfume around, light a candle."

Anne nodded.

"Just let him know you're interested. You can figure that out."

"I'll drag him in there then," Anne said, giggling.

Dead serious, Molly said, "Wear your sexiest clothes, and fall all over his slightest signs of interest. He'll know."

Anne sighed. She could open her blouse too, like she did with the carpenter. "All right, thanks."

"That's all? You don't want more details?"

"I have done it before you know. Besides, you told me all your stories years ago."

"You remember? For crying out loud, we were just kids."

"Not quite. You described almost every affair you ever had. You used to titillate me with the details."

"You recognized that?"

"Of course. You liked to see my reaction, at least until I got over being shocked."

"Why did you let me do it?"

It was Anne's turn to grin. "Because I liked to hear it all."

"I knew that."

"I used your descriptions in imaginary affairs of my own, all those lurid little details."

"No kidding. You still surprise me sometimes."

"You aren't telling stories anymore."

"No, I guess not. Besides, since Jim split, these last three years there's been nothing."

"After him I thought you'd never get involved again."

"I know. It's funny, I'm much more blasé about Graham than I was with Jim or Tom. I don't think he's the "right one" or anything like that. It's just fun. Take it or leave it."

Anne blinked. Molly had always been frenetic about her men, when they were all shiny new at least. Apparently her face showed her surprise because Molly blushed, "Don't look like that. It's no big deal."

Anne giggled. "We're both going crazy at once."

"Or maybe getting sane at last. Me anyway. By the way. You should ask him more of those subtle questions."

"Molly!""

"Hey, it's not over right? You need to know if the man has secrets he's not telling you."

Anne stared at her, then shook her head. "I'm sure he doesn't, not dark ones anyway."

~ SIXTEEN ~

The blue skirt seemed to seek her hand as she reached into the closet. She took a deep breath and draped it over her arm, then caressed the fabric and held it up to the light. It was perfect for today.

Slipping it on, she turned before the mirror, watching the effect. As before, it swayed with her hips and the soft cloth clung. The blouse she had on was open at the neck, and not so near the neck. Her heart fluttering, she hoped Molly was right about his intentions.

"Well, here we go," she told the figure in the mirror.

He arrived by ten forty-five, his secret spread across his face in a grin, the fact of it at least.

"Good morning," he said, offering another rose.

"Good morning to you," she replied, her best smile on display.

"You look beautiful today."

"Thank you. You look nice too. I like your shirt. Is it new?"

"Fresh from the wrapper."

"That's nice."

Her blood was rushing in her head. He smelled of cologne and man and she felt an amazing urge to reach out and touch him everywhere. Instead, she offered coffee and he accepted and she served it right away.

"I want to..." she started.

"I came to..." he began, at precisely the same instant.

She tipped her head to one side and gave him a smile. "You first.'

"That's all right, you go."

He laughed then, that wonderful laugh of his. Easy, unconcerned, a happy laugh, she loved the sound of it. He'd laughed before, but this was different. She was just sure it was happier.

"I was about to say I want to hear your secret. I don't want to wait," she said.

"That's easy. Maybe you should sit down. No, I'd rather have you standing up I think."

She didn't know why it mattered, but she stood. He took a deep breath. "I wanted to tell you that I love you."

"Oh," she said, and stopped, deflated. He said nothing more and she finally said, "I'm glad. I think I love you too."

"You're not pleased?"

"Oh yes, I am, definitely."

"What's wrong then?"

"Wrong? Nothing, not a thing."

"You seem disappointed. You think you love me?"

"I'm not disappointed, Paul. I just thought you loved me all along. I mean, I'm surprised that you announced it like this."

"Were you expecting a marriage proposal?"

"I just didn't know what you'd say. I guess I half thought you might ask."

"Ah, and what would you have said?"

"I would have said 'no'. For now."

"Because you're not sure you love me?"

"It's just too soon for marriage."

At this point, she was lost. What next? Did she tell him her thinking or wait for him? It seemed he wasn't finished. She couldn't just say she was ready to sleep with him, or should she? He kept talking.

"I love you, Anne. I want us to be together. We don't need to marry, but I want us to be a team."

"A team? You mean lovers?"

He nodded, looking expectant but uncertain.

"All right." There, she'd said it! It was official.

He looked startled. "All right?"

"Yes, all right."

He grinned and took her in his arm, the one that worked, and kissed her. A kiss she would never forget, and she returned it, or tried her best. He laughed!

"What?" she asked, horrified at his reaction.

"I had this whole speech planned, all my arguments marshaled to convince you. I don't know what to say now."

"Oh. Well, I don't think I can help with that."

"Maybe we don't need to talk?"

She smiled at him, warmth flooding her cheeks. "I suppose we can wait on that."

Were those words truly coming from her mouth? How flippant she'd become, so easy this romance was. Almost laughing, thinking she'd been silly to worry so, suddenly she reverted to panic. Everything was in danger now, every single thing in her existence. She wished Molly was with her. Hell no she didn't, she could handle this.

He didn't crow over her agreement, but he was obviously pleased. He was a good man. She'd be fine.

But then, "I can't believe I'm doing this," she said, the words popping out with no thought behind them.

"You're very brave," he said.

She laughed with relief. "I'm a coward. I'm terribly nervous."

"Anne, I want to make love to you. I think you're very special."

"Mmm. That sounds interesting."

He touched a finger to her cheek. "Do I hear a yes in that?"

She blushed more then, but managed a definite nod.

"I love you, Anne Hoskins. You just made my day, my entire year!" He kissed her, delicately, and then like a mad man, sweeping his tongue across her lips.

She met his tongue with hers and her body turned to fire. He slipped his hand slowly up her back, kissed her again, longer this time, then again. This was it. No turning back after this.

"I think...."

Smiling, he put a finger to her lips. "I think it's time to find the bedroom."

Butterflies fluttered in her stomach, but she was absolutely determined, and shaking, not sure why. It was fear or excitement, or both at once, but she would not stop, would not let her courage slip away. She had gone twenty years without sex and it hadn't been so great back then, but she had to try with Paul.

The scent of burning candle filled her bedroom. Molly's idea of course, and now she felt embarrassed, but he paid no attention. The new blouse knotted in her fingers, and she turned to find him waiting, naked. He reached out to help her and she could not look at him.

"I'll do it," she said, and quickly finished. Her skirt and panties fell to the floor in a jumble of blue and pink, and she trembled as he touched her shoulder. "I'm sorry. I'm just nervous."

"Me too," he said softly.

"You've been married."

"It's my first time with you. So I'm a little edgy too."

That was so sweet! He reached out and drew her tight against him, and his touch went through her, hot and sharp, like fire.

"Are you okay?"

A question, her choice to say stop or go. That was very sweet, but she had chosen.

"You decide," she whispered.

He didn't answer, simply drew her to the bed. She stood, awkward like a fool, until he gently pushed her to a sitting position and sat down next to her, naked, both of them.

"You're beautiful." She started to protest, but he touched a finger to her lips. "No argument. Remember, I'm deciding things here."

He eased her back and leaned over, gently running his fingers over the contours of her face, talking, talking, all the time. "Have I told you how much I love you? I want to explore every bit of you. You're so beautiful."

He caressed with words, making them a mantra. His touch, and words, and the sight of him embarrassed her, but he was tender and passionate and her body was going crazy. Feeling held her now, no thoughts, only touch and fire and heat. Her skin tingled with every caress, and still his fingers moved gently, and she wanted him, oh yes she wanted him. Uncertainty was nothing but a ghost now, a vapor floating in the wind.

~ * ~

"Don't move," she whispered as he began to lift up.

He ran his fingers through her hair, sweet and gentle. "I couldn't even if I wanted to. I'm all done for now." He kissed her, stirring the embers again.

"I like the way you feel. The way I feel. Don't go away," she told him dreamily.

"I'm not too heavy?"

"You weigh a ton, but I don't care."

"Have I told you that I love you?"

"A thousand times."

"That's not enough." He kissed her again and rolled to one side, then made a slow swirl on her belly with his fingers. "Are you happy?"

"I feel delicious."

"So, it's likely we might try this again sometime?" he asked with a knowing grin.

She poked him, then rolled over and locked her lips on his, then found his tongue with her own and played a bit before she answered.

"I think that might be possible."

He sat up and slipped a hand along her arm. "There's a hickey on your neck."

"We'll have to take a picture of it. My first hickey."

He laughed and headed for the bathroom. "Don't go away."

She ran her fingers along the sheet where his body had been, relishing the wonder of what she'd just done. Sure her chances were long gone, it all seemed unreal. That carpenter had been an animal. Not Paul, Molly's descriptions of good sex weren't even close.

She hugged herself with the sheer pleasure of the moment. Life was wonderful, he was wonderful and the bed was wonderful and she liked it! She had doubted him and doubted herself and been blissfully wrong! She'd made a major change in this poor life she had, and it was quite the best thing she'd ever done.

He was back quickly and plopped down beside her, still naked, still smiling. He was so handsome!

"A dollar for your thoughts," he said.

"I'm very, very happy."

"Very, very good, I'm glad. If I were younger I'd say let's do it again, but the best I can do is say, kiss me woman, I love you."

She complied happily and they were soon caressing again, except this time she returned the favor, feeling far less awkward. "I thought the best you could do was a kiss."

He grinned. "I lied. It must have something to do with you."

She laughed and snuggled close and he ran his hand through her hair.

"How did you come to this so soon?"

"What?"

"Agreeing to make love?"

"I didn't want you to give up on me. Molly said you'd lose interest and go away."

He kissed the tip of her nose. "Well, you've got me for life now. You made sure of that today."

It was over then, the mood was gone. For life? Just because of sex? He couldn't mean it. She could not believe that was all there was to it. It just wasn't right, it couldn't be.

"What's wrong? What did I say?" he asked.

"Nothing. I just thought of something."

"What Anne? What is it?"

"I don't believe you. Sex isn't everything, it can't be."

He looked confused. "I don't get it."

She sighed. She had to say it all, in the open, and be done. She hated this, after such a sweet time.

"You'll want other things from me besides sex. You know you will."

"Ah, I see. Like having catered lunches. Or going out together. That's the rub, right?"

She nodded and after one more kiss, he kept going. "Forget that. Nothing is a lock. We'll do things when we're ready, both of us."

"What things?"

"Anything we want to do."

"Suppose I don't want to do anything at all?"

"Suppose you do? You decided to do this, right? Look how much you liked it."

"This was different."

"Okay."

"Okay? That's all you're going to say?"

"I love you. That's all I'm going to say. Besides, you said you want to change."

"I know," she groaned.

"So, what's the problem then?"

"I don't know."

~ SEVENTEEN ~

He held her off, trying to retain the morning magic, but she needed resolution. Always in a routine, taking easy time with each decision, she'd always had a clear direction, and with it, comfort, especially when she had advice from Grace or Molly. Except now she'd decide things on her own. Nobody was going to take care of her anymore. Well, she could chat with them a little, she didn't have to stop that completely.

They walked the woods, meandered through lunch, playfully, teasingly, and she relished all of it but that, the uncertainty. At two, he made another overture for bed, but she objected. The time for standing up had come.

"Paul, I need to talk about everything. I have to know what you're thinking. Beyond the sex I mean."

He settled his chair against the kitchen wall. "What would you like to know?"

"About you. What you want from me. You know."

"Going out?"

"Yes."

He studied a fingertip, tapped it against his thumb, then nodded. "I think we have to go places, but it doesn't have to happen quickly. Wait, don't get upset. Let me say the rest." He paused until she settled again, and then continued. "You go out on a limited basis now. We can figure out what else we can do easily, and do those things too. Maybe we can lick the fear a little at a time." He waited, studying her face.

She heard only that he wanted to go out and she'd have to go with him. Her stomach jumped; she fought it, wanting none of it, but wanting to agree. "I don't think I'm afraid. I don't know what it is." The words almost came out with tears, but she would not give way.

"All right. We won't do more than you can handle, I promise. We'll visit your friends, just as you do now, but more often. You can manage that?"

"Dan and Grace? Of course."

"Molly? At her house?"

She giggled nervously. "I've only been there a few times."

"Won't she let you in?"

"Of course, silly, but it's been a long time since I've been there."

"Can you do that?"

"I think so. Sure."

"Good, then you can check to see if she's keeping the place up to date."

She gave him a quizzical look.

He laughed. "Listen, if you haven't been there for a while you'll notice things she misses every day."

"Oh, of course."

"Where else are you comfortable?"

"That's all. Nowhere."

He gave a tiny shake of his head, but stopped instantly and smiled. "What's the standard? How about private places, with no people or just a few?"

Her heart sank. He was trying to make her feel good, make it all seem easy. He felt sorry for her again? Or was he just kind? "Like what?"

"A beach, early in the morning? You walk your road with Betty, right? We could do that and go further."

She shivered. Could it really be that simple? "I'll try. I'll try to go out alone sometimes, walking, you know."

"Good."

"You have to be patient."

His eyes took on a devilish twinkle. "I can't think of anyone I'd rather be patient with."

"Don't tease now, please."

"I believe in you Anne. You can do it, I know it."

"You scare me with your optimism. You're like a truck, racing down a hill at top speed. All I can do is get out of the way. I have to."

"I'll keep the brakes on. I promise."

"I used to go everywhere before. I bought this house, did my own shopping, everything."

"What happened?"

"I don't know. I just stopped."

He nodded, waiting for her to talk.

"It was people. It became too hard to face them all the time, to see the looks, hear the whispers behind my back." She sighed, remembering. "It started in high school, right after the accident. My friends all knew what happened. About my mother being drunk."

"I get that."

"I'm glad you understand. I'll do my best."

He hugged her then, one handed. "This blasted arm, I wish I could give you a real hug."

He stayed for dinner, after loving her again, late that afternoon, and night had fallen when the Toyota rolled down the drive. She stared after him, and then trudged back into the house. Black silence greeted her, save the candle on the table in the kitchen. It had been romantic, the two of them talking in the flickering light, but now it was a lonely sight, one single candle flame in darkness. She reached for the phone.

"Molly, talk to me."

"Anne? What's wrong? You sound awful."

"I'm lonely. Can we talk?"

"Of course."

"Your man isn't there? Graham?"

"He's in New York. Some problems with the divorce. He'll be back tomorrow."

"I don't know how you do it. How you've done it all these years."

"Done what? What's going on with you?"

"I miss Paul."

"Now I've heard everything. Wait a minute. Did you sleep with him today?"

"You shouldn't ask me that."

"Yeah, right. And now you're madly in love."

"Don't make fun of me. Now I understand what you went through. I always thought I did, but I was wrong. I'm sorry."

"What the devil does that mean?"

"Paul just left and I can't stand it. The house is like a cave. I want him back this minute. I never knew what that felt like. It's awful."

Molly laughed. "You obviously had a good day then."

"It was wonderful and I hated to see him leave."

"Then why did you let him?"

"He had to go home. It was late and he had a two hour drive."

"You didn't ask him to stay over? You could have, you know."

"I couldn't do that," she said, knowing she very well could. And now that Molly had mentioned it, she definitely would next time.

"Don't be ridiculous. Ask him to move in with you."

"Do you think he'd do it?"

"Of course he will. Why not?"

"Listen, I need to do more than I do now. I want to get used to going out. Can I come over one day?"

"Where? My house?"

"Yes."

"Sure. Come for lunch if you want, or coffee or whatever. Wow, you've really taken the plunge. What else does he have you doing?"

"We're going to do what I'm comfortable with. Slowly."

"How about a dinner with Graham? I'd like you to meet him."

She felt a touch of anxiety then, which she rapidly dismissed. She'd met other beaus of Molly's, so why not this one? "Let me talk to Paul. Maybe we can do it together."

"Your house or mine?"

"Mine." No equivocation, no chance for counter opinion. "Mine," snapped out again. Was she backing down already?

"Okay. Call me when you've consulted the Master."

"Don't call him that. He's not my boss."

"Girl, you're in love now? That makes him your Lord and Master. Ta, ta. Talk to you tomorrow."

"Wait a minute. Don't say that. Why did you say that?"

"I'm teasing, Anne. He has you doing new things, that's all. I'm teasing."

"You're sure? That's all?"

"That's all."

"All right then. Good night."

Meandering through the house, room by room, absently, her mind saw only Paul. She stopped in the shop, stared at the radio cabinet, finished now, beside the new piece Dan had just brought her. She turned on the fan and started working, stopping only well beyond midnight.

~ EIGHTEEN ~

They opened at nine, but it was only quarter to and Dan had already parked behind the shop. Fresh scratches and dents on the steel door were a sure sign someone had tried to break in during the night.

Inside, the counter looked oddly different as Grace drew near the front of the shop. Then the rest of the store came into view and she understood.

The cash register was gone, but that was the least of it. The front door hung ajar. Lamps, tables, and collectibles were scattered in disarray, many of them smashed, or broken. The old glass case near the counter lay shattered, the silver taken, all except one spoon, now bent. The decorative little picket fence around Dan's special chair was in a heap with other wreckage.

"You sons-of-," Dan started and threw her a sharp glance. He grimaced and went to his knees in the mess. "Call the cops, Gracie. Call the damn cops."

Her favorite table, just plain pine, was in the pile, but it was the Louis XIV chair that worried her. Dan called it their retirement chair, assuming it would bring a hefty bit of cash when that day came. Only if he sold it of course, and she knew better. The man loved that old thing and he'd keep it 'til he died. Would have. She made the call, then shouted at Dan to leave everything in place until the police came.

She wandered aimlessly through the shop, checking other damage, seeking order in the chaos. Finally, she pulled out the "Sales" notebook they kept behind the counter and turned to the blank back page. Pen in hand, she studied the broken items, trying to identify each piece and find some normalcy in the list she began to create. Some items she knew the prices of, such as the pine table. Others would need Dan's attention, but it was his chair, and only that, she knew he cared about. He was on the floor, picking out pieces of splintered leg, a broken arm, a sliver of the seat fabric, and piling them neatly to one side. She called Anne.

~ * ~

The morning began with questions for Anne. In front of her closet, sliding hangers back and forth, taking them out and putting them back. She couldn't find an outfit for the day. It was all different now. Paul was and she was and the house was, and everything should be right when he came. She donned paint spattered shorts and a button down shirt for the moment, delaying. Later, she'd decide what to wear then.

Lamps in their place for years suddenly weren't right, the couch pillows were suddenly the wrong color, and she found dust everywhere.

"I should have redecorated years ago," she said aloud, grimacing at faded living room drapes. "I need to get a bedroom ready, Hannah. I'm going to do it. No marriage, but a live in lover. Can you imagine? Me!"

She opened the door to one of the spare bedrooms and sighed. Unused except for random storage, it badly needed attention. Two windows, long unwashed, let hazy sunlight filter through. She shut the door decisively, and turned to her bedroom. How silly to think of giving him a separate room! He was her lover now.

The four-poster they made love in yesterday would be fine, but the décor was totally feminine and she wondered what he'd think. A man certainly wouldn't want to live in a room like that, but how to change it was the question. The pink trim around the canopy could be removed, and a new bedspread, less feminine, might be good. He was unlikely to appreciate sleeping under pink roses. Grace's phone call interrupted.

"Grace. How are you? I'm sorry I haven't called, but I've been so busy. How's Dan?"

"That's why I called, dear. The shop was vandalized last night. They smashed the Louis chair to pieces."

"Oh my. You've had that as long as I've known you."

"It's just junk now. They broke the legs and cut the fabric. Can you imagine anyone doing that? Some people do such horrible things."

"Can I help? What can I do?"

"Thank you dear, I hoped you'd say that. Could you come up today? It would be a great help for Dan to have you here."

"I have to wait for Paul. He's coming in about an hour. Is it all right if he comes with me?"

"Of course, dear. He can help too, if he wants to."

"What about the chair? I'll repair it."

"The wood is in splinters. And the fabric is ruined. You can't even sew it up. You can't buy that fabric anymore, you know. At least I don't think so. Do you? I'm sure you can't. It's very old."

"Let me try. I'll take it back with me."

"We'll see. I'll tell Dan you're coming."

~ * ~

What to wear for Paul suddenly mattered very little. Her hair was fine with a quick comb through, but she added makeup, hastily. The house would have to wait. She grabbed jeans and a decent blouse, the Velcro wrap sneakers; and dressed quickly; expecting Grace would need physical help at the shop.

It took a second to whip the flowery blue towels off the bathroom rack and sling older, plain ones over the bar in their place. That much she did to prepare for Paul. She had a lunch packed and the old Ford out and waiting when he parked under the maple.

"Good morning my love," he said, and kissed her. "What's with the car?"

"Dan and Grace had a break-in last night. They need me."

"In their shop? Are they okay?" he asked, reaching into his car for the sunglasses he'd dumped on the dash.

"Their antique chair was destroyed. A valuable Louis XIV piece."

"You want to take my car?" he asked, with a dubious look at her ancient Ford.

"No, I know where we're going."

He was with her and she was ready and that felt right. If Grace and Dan needed her she would be there for them, no matter what, but Paul was coming too.

"What do they want you to do?"

"I don't know. Maybe just hold their hands. We're family you know."

"Really? I didn't."

"Not by blood. It's just they are for me and I am for them. Grace has a sister, but she's no help, and the only other relative they have is the sister's daughter."

"Sounds like they're not very close."

"They are with the daughter, not her mother. Dan likes hard working, responsible people. Millie is, Claire isn't."

"Millie's the daughter? Will she be there?"

"I don't know."

It was near eleven when they arrived. Dan was at the back, in the office space, going through appraisals and purchase records, dragging. Grace sat on the floor, gathering wreckage and sorting it, trying to identify small items that might otherwise be missed. Hunched over, randomly picking at broken pieces, she smiled at the sight of Anne and struggled to her feet.

"Thank you for coming."

"Never mind," Anne said. "How's Dan?"

"Very upset. He pretends he's not, but this is hard for him."

Anne nodded. "Let Paul help you. I'll see about him."

Grace patted her and turned to Paul. "Hello dear. Thank you for coming."

"How are you?"

"I don't know. I really don't. Look." She held up a shattered leg of a chair. "Dan always called it "Louie," like it was a real person. It's just junk now. They even cut the fabric. Can you imagine anyone doing that? For no reason at all. A beautiful old chair like that. Some people are just terrible. They do such awful things."

"Maybe Anne can fix it."

She sighed. "It wouldn't have much value anymore. Besides, I doubt it can be fixed. No dear, that would be nice, but it wouldn't work."

"Everything will be okay, Grace. Come on, let's go back to the office."

"Thank you, dear. I'm glad you're here. I think you're very good for our Anne. Are you both serious?"

He smiled, "About as serious as we can be."

"Oh, that's nice. I'm very glad. Dan will be pleased too."

~ * ~

"Morning Annie. Nice day isn't it," Dan said quietly.

She planted a kiss on his forehead. "Not so very nice at all. Are you all right?"

"Yeah, I'm okay. Louie isn't and the shop isn't, but I am."

"What are you doing?"

"Trying to figure how much we've lost."

"Maybe I can fix some of it for you."

"Thanks. I might call you on some of it if the insurance isn't enough. The worst is Louie. I hate losing that chair." He sighed. "I really never planned to sell it, you know. It was the having of it that counted. Dan Sinnis, owner of a genuine seventeenth century chair. Former owner now."

"I could kill those people."

"Annie, my girl, I'm surprised. I didn't think you had it in you."

"I have my secrets, Dan, even some I'm just learning about. I'll make Louie as good as new. You just turn him over to me for a while."

"Can't Annie. The value is gone. I have to go through the insurance."

"Well, give it to me after they're done."

"They'll own it then. That's the way it works. They buy the junk and pay you part of the value."

"Then tell them I'll buy the junk."

"What are you buying?" Paul asked, as he and Grace joined them.

"I'm going to fix Louie."

Grace patted her arm. "Don't waste your time, dear. It's hopeless."

"I'm sure I can do it. Promise me you'll tell the insurance company I want the pieces."

"Oh, I wish you could, but it's so far gone. It would need new legs and fabric and you can't buy such old things anymore, dear. At least I don't think so."

"Let her try. We'll come for it when you've settled with the insurance," Paul said.

"I'll let you know. Thanks for even trying," Dan said. The resignation in his voice made it clear he was simply humoring Anne.

"What are you going to do?" Paul asked.

"You mean will we retire? No. We should have moved before, but now we'll do it right away."

"Are you up to that?" Anne asked.

"We'll hire someone to do the heavy work," Grace said, smiling at her husband.

"Moving all this will be a huge job," Paul said.

Dan grinned at his wife. "Tell the man about moss and rolling stones, Gracie. But let's have a kiss first and don't look so glum. We're not dead yet."

"What can we do?" Paul asked.

"When we get the new shop. You can come help us paint and set up. That would be very nice," Grace said.

~ * ~

"They're really something aren't they? As old as they are, and attacked like that, and they're planning their next move. Courage and determination in capital letters," Paul said on the way home.

"I know. They leave me feeling inadequate. Dan goes through life so easily, bouncing off the rocks and shoals and emerging just a little wet. I feel shamed by the two of them. I should have done so much more over the years."

"You did the best you could and you're doing your best now. For crying out loud, you're taking on a world that scared you all those years."

She squeezed his arm. "We haven't done a thing yet. We'll see how well I do."

"You were great with them today."

"I've been there before, remember?" She hesitated for a second, then plunged ahead. "Speaking of changes. It's been a long day. Would you like to spend the night at my house?"

He grinned at that. "Such an invitation. Are you kidding?"

"We could make it permanent," she said, and held her breath.

He reached over and touched a finger to her cheek. "I'd like that."

"Not *permanent* permanent. Not yet."

"I know, sort of permanent."

She laughed. "Do you have any idea what I mean?"

"Sure. You might kick me out someday."

~ NINETEEN ~

Anne was gone from the bed when he woke up at seven. He slipped into his pants and headed for the kitchen, and there she stood, at the door, sipping coffee.

"Good morning love," he said, and she turned, smiling that stunning smile that blew him away. He could take her back to bed in a second dressed the way she was, in faded blue cotton shorts and a very open blouse.

"Good morning sleepy head," she said softly.

"How did you like a stranger in your bed?"

"I had a rather unpleasant rendezvous with that plaster thing on your arm, but other than that, it was very nice."

"You must be a sound sleeper then, that's good. How long have you been up?"

"Since five. I did a little painting while you slept."

"Such industry. I may have trouble keeping up with you."

She laughed. "I wouldn't worry. You're strong enough. I'm glad I didn't wake you. I was concerned about that."

"About what?"

"I get up at odd hours and go to bed quite late at times. I was afraid I wouldn't be able to with you here."

"Oh, well, that has to change. When you're up you have to wake me so I can be with you."

She stared at him, her eyes a bit uncertain. He laughed and saw the laugh come to her face. "You scared me for a minute. I thought you were serious."

"That's my wacky sense of humor. You'll see a lot of that. What are we going to do today? Besides make love, of course."

She shook her head. "You choose. Anything but love making."

It was his turn to be surprised, but she grinned and said, "Ha, I can be wacky too."

"Oh brother, we're in trouble." He poured coffee from the pot she'd made. "How about a tour of my new abode?"

"You've seen most of it already."

"Not all of it. It's an interesting house. Did you buy it this way?"

"I built the studio and remodeled the kitchen. The rest is as I bought it, except for painting of course."

"How old is the original section?"

"Eighteen thirty-four. The kitchen was originally a kitchen and living room."

"You did a nice job with the remodeling. What about the second floor?"

"I never use it."

"Really? What's up there?"

"Three tiny rooms of odds and ends, antiques that were in the house when I moved in."

"Like what?"

"Lots of things. An Edison phonograph, the one with cylinders instead of records."

"Can I have a look?"

"All right." She led the way up and fumbled with the door at the top of the stairs. "This knob slips."

"I assume you don't close the door when you're up here." That was supposed to be funny, but she didn't laugh.

The door swung open, squeaking at the disturbance. Stale air slid down the stairs, giving a warning of what to expect as he moved up to the door. Faded Victorian wallpaper, dust coated Tiffany lamps, and heavy velvet draperies filled his view.

"This looks as if it's been abandoned for a hundred years."

"It was like this when I moved in. The downstairs bedrooms were built around nineteen thirty. I think these rooms were closed up then."

"Incredible. I'll bet Dan would love to spend a few days in here. Why don't you do something with it?"

She shrugged. "I wouldn't use it and it would be more space to clean."

She showed him the Edison phonograph and stood by quietly while he wandered through the rooms examining the old furnishings. He followed her back downstairs, puzzled by her attitude about the space. She seemed detached somehow, totally uninterested, an odd thing for someone who enjoyed restoring old stuff.

The thought departed, driven off by the blouse she had on. He suggested a bit of bed time, but she laughed.

"Is this the way it is with men? Sex all the time?"

"As often as can be, my love."

"I see. You may wear me out."

"Is that a no?"

"I feel like I'm on my honeymoon, so I guess it's yes. That's what you do on honeymoons, right?"

"And ever after."

"Don't tease. You will wear me out."

He grinned and kissed her, and opened the blouse another button. "I'll try not to. In the future."

~ * ~

An hour later, he dressed and prepared to leave. They had decided he'd go home for clothes and personal effects. He asked her to go with him and got a definite but hesitant refusal.

"I'm not a disappointment to you, am I? It's more than I can do right now. Do you mind?"

Not at all, he told her and that was true. He would have been surprised if she'd agreed. His friends met for lunch this day, so perhaps he'd join them. His plan to stay with Anne would earn some needling, but that was okay. At least they'd know he wouldn't be there next time and probably for some time in the future. He'd give his kids the news as well.

"How long will you be gone?" Anne asked.

"Five or six hours, I think."

"So long? Be quick. Be careful driving though." He laughed and she blushed. "I sound like an old mother hen. I'm sorry."

"Don't, I like it. That's the sound of love."

"Well, good. Be careful first, but be quick as well. Maybe I'll attack you when you come back."

He kissed her then, and once again. "Forget caution then."

"Don't say that. Be careful, please, or I'll withdraw my offer."

"Then expect me in a week."

"Oh you." She smiled.

He knew she hated to see him go and the thing was, he felt the same. New love did that to you somehow. It made you fear the loss of the one who loved you. Maybe that was it. When you loved for some time fear faded and you grew comfortable unless some event unsheathed the fear again. That thought brought him back to Carol. It had been that way with her. He had reached that point of comfort, enjoyed her and his life, and then one day the fear came back. In spades, doubled and redoubled. He shivered at the memory.

Morbid thoughts. He discarded them, and focused on the blouse Anne wore this morning. She was a wonder to him. He'd enjoy giving the guys his news. Nothing they could say would matter- he'd have the last laugh.

At home, he packed a suitcase, extra glasses, the book he'd been reading, and finally headed back to Anne's, detouring to Kelly's first. Late again, his buddies were preoccupied with the Yankees' latest win over Boston. A dirty thing, according to Ben.

"It was a stupid call, I tell you. The ump should have called interference for crying out loud, not a home run!" Ben cried hoarsely.

"The fan never touched it," said Marty, equally emphatic.

"Ah, baloney. Wilson woulda had it if he didn't."

"Hey, Paul, did you see it? Settle this will you?" Jack said.

"Didn't see it guys. Sorry."

"Geez, what's with you? I thought you were a Yankee fan," said Marty.

"I didn't see the game. If it was against the Sox, the call had to be right." He leered at Ben.

"Where you been lately? You missed last week," Ben said.

"Rhode Island, and I have some news."

"Uh oh. You broke up with the dame?" asked Marty.

"He's too happy. He's getting married again," said Ben.

"Marriage doesn't make you happy. Not at this point in life. He's moving in with her, right Paul?" said Jack.

"Moved. Officially, as of today."

"What are you doing here then?" Ben asked. "Come back to say goodbye?"

"Not goodbye, at least not for good. I'll be back, but I am moving in with her."

"Are we going to meet this dame sometime?" asked Marty.

"I'll bring her around one of these days."

He didn't like that question much. Anne's situation was not one he wanted to discuss. Introductions could wait until she was getting out like everybody else.

"You got a phone number for us up there? Just in case one of us dies or something?" asked Ben, with some annoyance in his voice.

"I'll keep in touch, Ben."

"Hazel won't like it if you don't."

"What's her name?" asked Marty.

"Anne Hoskins."

"I like the name. You got a good one this time?" asked Jack.

He did a double take on that, never thinking Jack paid much attention to Ellie. Apparently they all had, just like Ben.

"She is, Jack, no doubt about it. You'll see when you meet her."

~ * ~

He was back by six. The house was quiet, so he dumped his stuff in the hall and scooted out the kitchen door, figuring she was walking in the woods.

"Anne, I'm back," he shouted and listened for an answer.

Nothing. He wasn't too surprised by that. She might be playing with him, teasing him like she had the other day. He started along her favorite path, the central one, so he could cover ground quicker. Called again, and then again, and vainly waited for the sound of her response. After five minutes at a dogtrot, he'd covered all the paths. She wasn't there.

Concerned, he searched the house, room by room. The place looked normal, not the least disturbed. The kitchen was clean, her obsession that was. On the platform in the shop, the new cabinet sat with the drawers removed. Clearly, she'd been working on it.

She might be out with that friend of hers, that Betty. He grabbed his keys and headed out in the car. A van zipped by at the end of the drive and he stopped to check for other traffic. And there it was, the old blue Ford, unmistakable, coming from the South end of the island, not the North. North was town and Molly, and Betty's house too. Where had she been to the South?

The wheels spun gravel as he threw the car into reverse and backed his way up the long drive. She followed in the Ford, laughing through the windshield as he careened from side to side.

"You are a crazy man, backing up so fast. You're lucky you didn't hit a tree!"

"You make me crazy! Where were you?"

"I went to the beach and the lighthouse. What are you so mad about?"

"I got home and you weren't here. I spent the last half hour searching for you."

"I decided to go out, like we agreed I should. I've never been to the lighthouse before."

"You scared me half to death."

"Didn't you see the car was gone?"

"I never thought to check for that."

"Well, it's your own fault then." She said it with a lilt, a touch of laughing at him.

Anger flew away and he kissed her, hot and hard. "You scared me woman. Leave a note next time."

"I don't know. I might. How was your trip?"

"Okay. Ben's mad. He thinks I'm gone for good."

"That sounds like he's jealous."

"No. It's just that we've been friends a long time, and he and Hazel felt I dumped them when I met Ellie. In a way I did. He thinks this is more of the same."

"Will you go to see them occasionally?"

"More than that, I think. I'll want to take you with me, once we've licked your fear."

She went quiet then, but nodded. "All right. After that."

"How was your lighthouse tour?"

"I didn't do much. I stayed in the car mostly, except when there was no one else around."

"Next time then."

~ TWENTY ~

There was so much to consider. Paul was so funny about her drive to the beach. Mad as could be, but proud of her. It was a nice thing to see, the pride, and his concern as well. All for her. Molly worried, and Grace too, but this was different, with the pleasure in his eyes.

Paul just didn't understand. She would do what he wanted, this going places. She'd made a decision all those years ago, to stay alone and private, and now she'd made a new one. That was the whole thing in a nutshell.

People would be stupid though, not changed at all because she was. She simply wouldn't let them bother her. She wouldn't dwell on that, didn't want to worry anymore.

The phone rang. Molly's voice. "Anne, are you sitting down?"

"No. Should I?"

"You won't believe it. I got a letter today from Tom."

"Tom who?"

"Carrera. The guy we thought was dying? Remember?"

"The one who sent that awful letter? He's alive? What happened to him?"

"He wants to see me."

"I hope you told him off."

Molly should of course. One of those rotten men she always found, telling her to get checked for VD, as if he had something awful and would die from it. Molly cried many tears over that man. That had to be twenty years ago or more.

"I can't. I don't know where he is. I'll have to wait until he contacts me."

"Well, tell him off then. How can he contact you?"

"He sent a letter to the house. I haven't moved in a long time. Good grief, I just realized, he kept my address all that time! He wrote to Molly Simmons. That's who I was back then."

"What about Graham?"

"I wish I knew if he felt something for me. Just so I'd know where we might be going."

"I thought you said you learned your lesson. No more men?"

"Right. I won't stay home, that's all. I'll spend my time at Graham's gallery when I'm not in the office. I can't believe he's come back. Tom, I mean. Didn't you think he died?"

"Yes."

"I have to run. See you later," Molly said.

Poor Molly. The very idea that the jerk still cared about her was enough to cause her trouble. That had been her problem from the start. A man liked her and she was done, hooked. Silly, that was what it was. Anne couldn't believe a woman would fall in love with someone just because of that.

Paul smiled when she told him. "A lot of people do that, men and women both."

"Really? That's a recipe for disaster, don't you think?"

He grinned. "Maybe, but I think I did that with Ellie. When I met my wife too, I suspect."

"You liked them because they liked you? That was all?"

"No, but I think you have to feel someone's affection for you to fall in love. Would you like someone if they didn't like you?"

"But Molly always falls for someone just because he likes her and it always ends in disaster."

"I'll bet there's more to it than that."

She sighed. "I suppose, but she has no idea what and neither do I."

"That troubles you?"

"Absolutely. What secrets don't I know about myself? How do I know we won't end up hating each other someday?"

"We don't. We do our best, that's all."

"That's depressing. Listen, Molly and I talked about having a dinner. Us, and she and her Graham."

"Great. Have you ever had a dinner as a couple?"

"No, and I don't think I want to. Not if you're going to make it a training exercise."

"A what?"

"I don't care if I never did it before. It will be fun, that's all."

"That's what I meant. What's wrong with what I said?"

She grimaced. "It sounded like you thought it would be an educational event. Teach the dummy something new."

"Anne! I don't know what to say. I didn't mean to sound that way."

"Well you do, all the time. We spent a good part of the morning picking places to go. Safe and easy sites to visit, just for little old recluse me."

"We were just making plans. I thought that was the idea."

She sighed. "I know, but it doesn't come out that way. I feel like I'm a child and you're my overprotective parent. Ugh."

"I don't mean it that way."

"I suppose. I'm sorry Paul. I'm just touchy, I guess."

He smiled. "No problem. What do you think? I like this dinner idea. Where are we having it?"

"Here," she said, and wanted to crawl into a hole.

This was so stupid. They'd been together a week and it was kisses and differences from day one. Another body in her bed, waking her with snores, soft at least and not too often. That was just plain revolutionary. That and the loving. It was sex of course, but much more, a gift of his heart every time, and she'd be deliciously content, except for this stupid business of going somewhere. If only he didn't care about that.

Having company for dinner would give him something to think about. Unless Molly cancelled now that Tom was back on the scene.

"I don't know if we'll do it though. Graham may be history."

"Well, she can bring the other guy then."

"Don't be facetious. She wouldn't do that."

He smiled. "We'll just have to confirm the seating arrangements before I start cooking."

"You?"

"Hey, I'm pretty good in the kitchen."

"I'll help then."

"That isn't necessary, I can handle it."

"What about your broken arm? I'm the one who knows how to work with one hand."

"Yeah, okay, we'll do it together."

He took on the dinner planning though, and sat down to make up a menu and shopping list. Anne started some advance cleaning, but the first time she turned on the old vacuum cleaner it gave off an acrid smell.

"The motor's burned out," he said.

"I know that. Would you pick one up this morning?"

"Why don't you come with me and get one you like? They've got eight million kinds to choose from now."

It was the same issue he kept raising and she hated it. They'd made a plan, made lists of places she agreed to go to. Shopping wasn't one of them, not yet. Her irritation should have been obvious, but he didn't wait for an answer.

"I'll get some bagels for breakfast too. How about coming with me? We can have coffee and bagels at the store and then buy a vacuum."

"No thank you."

"We can go together. I don't want to leave you alone."

"Why? I'll be fine. It's nothing new."

"That's the point. Will you go to the beach while I'm gone?"

"I have no idea."

"Okay then. I won't be long."

She put away the bowls and spoons she'd set out for breakfast. "We could take our own coffee, and eat the bagels in the car." She had no idea why she said that, but she'd be all right in the car. At least she'd try. He probably planned it all out again.

"I thought you didn't want to come."

"I won't go into the store. I'll stay in the car."

"Deal, that's good."

"I have to get some shoes on."

She stole a peek at him from the corner of her eye as they drove to town. Lips set in a hard line, hands clenched in his lap, he looked positively grim. The man had to be as nervous as she was. Good,_served him right.

"Where are we going?" she asked.

"Standard Market. They have a small lunch counter in their bakery section. I want to get some fancy bread too."

She didn't respond. He turned in at the store and found a parking spot in front of the entrance.

"I'll be right back."

"Don't be long."

"Five minutes."

He was almost as good as his word. Ten minutes later, he appeared, talking and laughing with a pretty young brunette. Her stomach clenched and she groaned. She couldn't be jealous, could she?

"Who was that?" she asked, when he slid into the car.

"A young lady who heard me talking to myself. I didn't like the bread selection and she said there's a real bakery about a half mile from here."

"You don't even know her. She may not know what she's talking about."

"We'll find out soon enough, won't we? Let's have our bagels and then go bakery hunting."

Anne selected a bagel and took a bite. "So, we're off to another store now," she mumbled between chews.

"That's the plan. I can take you home and come back again if you like," he said easily.

"No, it's all right." No way she would quit now. The car was fine, almost as private as her house. Almost.

Their bagels were down to a bite or two when a car horn sounded behind them. Paul glanced out the window and shook his head at the other driver.

"What's that?" she asked.

"Somebody wants our parking space."

"I'm done eating. I can drive."

"No need. There are other spaces."

The horn sounded again. Paul waved his hand in front of his window and continued eating.

"Please Paul, let's leave." She hadn't bargained for something like this.

He took a last bite of bagel and started the car. "Okay. This guy will have a fit if we don't move."

Another car cut in front of them to take the space as they backed out. The first driver blasted his horn at the intruder as Paul pulled away.

"Poetic justice. I love it." He laughed.

"That wasn't nice. He was waiting for that spot."

"Now he'll have to walk a little. There are plenty of other spaces."

"Were we in a handicapped space?"

"No, and he isn't driving a handicapped van," he said with a grin.

"You're mean."

"No way. We bought our bagels in the store. We had every right to eat there without being harassed. He got what he deserved."

"You're funny. Righteous indignation personified."

"That's me. What kind of bread do you want?" he asked, as the Toyota eased to a stop at the bakery.

"Make it a surprise. Something special."

"You got it."

She watched him go with mixed emotions, knowing he was happy, her stomach still twitching with anxiety. He might be happy because she'd come along this morning. Anne wasn't certain if he'd been mad back there at the market, or was having fun with that other driver, but he obviously felt very confident about himself. If only she could match him in that.

She was sitting quietly when he returned. He handed her a small end piece of dark bread from one of the bags.

"I used to buy fresh bread for my mother and eat the end slices on the way home. Try a piece. They call it Black Forest bread," he said.

She bit and chewed slowly, savoring the taste. "Freshly sliced?"

"Hot off the slicing machine," he said, stuffing the other end piece into his mouth.

The bread was delicious beyond reason, as was his smile, and there was nothing quite like the warmth she felt at the moment. She realized he'd been entirely fair at the market, of course, and she now felt safe, knowing the other driver had received his just deserts. She hoped the guy had to walk a mile.

In fact, their expedition was turning out to be very pleasant. She decided to try more excursions than what they'd originally planned, though she'd choose just where and when. There was a lot she could do, if she made the choices. She touched his cheek and laughed.

"I think I love you."

"You're not sure?"

"It's that righteous indignation I'm concerned about."

"Ah, well that's genetic. Nothing I can do about it."

She laughed again. "You've never told me much about your childhood. What was it like?"

He shook his head. "I try to forget. I know you really can't, but I try."

"Was it that bad?"

"I was micro-managed seven days a week, twenty-four hours a day. My mother was all over me like glue, and stuck to everything I did, everything I said."

"I don't understand that. Did she spend all her time watching you?"

"I used to think so. She nitpicked everything I did. Or didn't do."

"What about your father?"

"He wasn't as bad, but he backed her up. I hate critics. That was what she was, a critic, and I never, ever, got a good review."

"I'm sorry."

He shook his head. "It wasn't that bad."

"It sounds pretty awful."

"I got out as soon as I could, just like you. I could have been a delinquent, but I knew I'd never get away with anything." He paused. "I just realized that's an old fashioned word. Now kids are 'emotionally disabled', or something."

"It sounds like you had good reason to be."

"I don't know. Enough of that. There must be something better to talk about."

His tone seemed light, but the story saddened her. "Tell me about your sailing."

He talked about his boat and his racing experiences, taking each of her "Reallys," and "That's amazings," as spurs to further stories. As they neared home, he stopped.

"That's enough about me. You must be bored."

"Not at all. The sailing sounds like fun."

"It is. You'll have to go with me sometime."

"I don't know if I can do that," she said, and groaned inwardly. Again, there it was again; time to go out somewhere, and she came up with an automatic no. Here she just concluded she could do all sorts of things and she was running away again.

"Handling the boat might be tricky at first, but we'll manage," he said, and she was confused. She worried about the going out and he had something else in mind.

Her stupid arm, that was it! She could have kicked him then, but he went on, casually oblivious.

"We can go to my yacht club in the morning. On a weekday, with light wind, you'll get small waves and a nice ride. And there won't be many people around."

"Just a few I suppose." The sarcasm was lost on him, or ignored in a welter of detailed explanation.

"Just the launch attendant when we get there. Maybe a member or two on their way out to their boats, but we'll only see them for a couple of minutes."

"But you think I can survive on your boat?"

That got her a funny look and she could tell he recognized he'd made a faux pas. "I'm sorry if I upset you. I was all involved in talking you into going. I wanted to reassure you."

The man looked positively crestfallen. She couldn't stay mad. "All right then. I'll try it, but not right away."

Her breathing slowed again, but she felt quite sure she could erupt in a second.

He turned his attention back to the road. She hadn't mentioned the vacuum again and she wondered if he'd forgotten, but at the house, as she picked up the bread and stepped from the car, he remained behind the wheel.

"How long will you be gone? Should I have lunch ready when you get back?" she asked.

"I don't know. Probably."

"Don't spend a lot of time shopping, Paul. I don't care what kind you get."

"They come with all kinds of features these days. You're sure you don't have a preference?"

"Get one like the old one. Nothing fancy."

He nodded and drove off and she stood watching for a moment. She was sure he felt pleased that she went for coffee with him, but if only the silly vacuum hadn't broken this particular morning. She missed him already. How could that be? This was a most amazing business, this falling in love. Maybe in another week, or a month, or two, she'd go shopping with him and it would all be easy.

He returned with a Hoover, the most basic model, and laughed about it. "You wouldn't believe how hard it was to find one without all the do-dads."

"You didn't have to do that."

He set the box on the floor. "I tried to get one as close as I could to your old one. Just give me a few minutes and I'll have it all assembled."

"That's all right, I'll do it."

He stepped back and watched silently as she tore apart the box. He seemed confused. Had she insulted him somehow? Apparently she was expected to let him put the vacuum together for her? She'd always done everything herself, so why should she stop?

The box open, she began to pull out parts.

"Your daughter Helen called while you were gone. She's very sweet. We had a nice chat, all about you and your bad points."

"Uh oh, I don't think I like that."

She laughed. "I didn't learn any dirty secrets. She wanted to know if you'd made plans for your family get-together."

"Damn, I forgot all about it."

"What is it? She didn't explain."

"The kids all come to visit. It's like a three or four day family reunion kind of thing."

"You do it every summer?" For three days? He'd leave her then to visit with his family?

"I'll have to spend some time at home when they come."

She hesitated, a surge of sudden emptiness dragging at her heart. She wouldn't see him for a week or more if he had to get ready for their visit. Before doubts assailed her, she blurted, "You could invite them here."

"That's a great idea. I will. Are you an impulsive person?" he asked abruptly.

"I never thought so, but I seem to be lately." What had she done? Impulsive, yes, oh my. Well, she'd survive their visit somehow.

"I'm starting to get that impression too. I like it."

"I think you're impulsive, too."

"I like to think of it as being decisive. When an opportunity presents itself I move fast." He grinned.

"I like that in a person. Now, how about getting me some tools from the shop?" She said this without thinking, then instantly wondered if she'd upset him, wondered why she said it so abruptly. He wasn't her messenger boy.

"I'll put it together for you. You don't need to anymore."

"I like mechanical things. I'll do it."

He looked exasperated, as if she should know he wanted to do it, or perhaps only men did such things.

"My arm isn't a problem. I can do it," he said softly.

"It's not hard. You get the tools."

He stared, a scowl starting on his face, then turned, and headed for her shop without another word.

She groaned, but he'd already turned his back. Was she being obnoxious? What was wrong with her?

"Well, you can turn the screwdriver and I'll hold the wrench then. How's that?" she called after him.

"Dumb. I'll get the tools," he said over his shoulder. There was no laughter in his voice.

She watched him stalk from the room, her heart suddenly heavy in her chest. Why was she so stubborn?

He started advance preparations for the next day's dinner that afternoon, making lists and polishing her unused silver. She hesitated, picked up a knife, and put it down again. Would he be mad if she offered to do the polishing? That she couldn't predict, so she went off to dust the living room.

Their own dinner for the evening was to be at five, prepared by Paul as well. As she poured the wine, she noted his struggle to maneuver spinach, rice and pork chops around the kitchen.

"Would you like some help?" she asked before she thought, then held her breath, awaiting his response.

"Sure. Thanks. If you'd grab a fork and spear the chops, I'll trim the fat."

She stood next to him with a fork jammed into the chop as he worked. Suddenly he moved so they touched. Startled, she glanced up at him. He was smiling.

"You smell grand. The aroma of soap, I think."

"You really know how to compliment a woman. Soap! That's certainly original. Not very romantic, but definitely original." She stuck the fork in the next chop. "Come on, finish this. I'm hungry."

He put the chops in the broiler, then rinsed the spinach in a mixing bowl.

"What are you doing?" she asked, as he took her largest frying pan out of a cabinet.

"You'll see. Have you got a lid for this?"

"In the back of the cabinet." He seemed happy. Maybe he liked to be in charge? Was that why he'd wanted to set up the new vacuum? She had a lot to learn about him.

He dripped a little oil in the frying pan, turned up the heat, and added the wet spinach.

"Take your seat, Madame. Tonight's dinner will be ready in a minute," he said, and a few seconds later he turned off the stove and began to plate the food.

"You know," she said over dinner. "I wish I'd met you thirty years ago."

"If we'd met thirty years ago we would have had a problem. I was happily married at the time."

"Twenty years ago? No, ten years ago would have been better."

"Twenty years ago my wife was still alive."

"I know. That's why I said ten."

He stared at her, silent, blank.

"Did I say something wrong?" she asked.

His eyes had gone dark with pain so deep she felt it spear right through her. What was that about? She was afraid to ask.

"No. I'm just tired, I guess," he said, a little too casually.

She didn't have the heart to push him. If he still loved his wife that much, what could he feel for her? A spark of fear stabbed her heart, but she pushed it down. This wasn't the time to question his love.

"You need real exercise to get your blood going. Tomorrow we'll take a long walk."

He smiled. "Make it a short walk and you're on."

"Lazy bones. My garden needs attention. Once we're done eating would you like to sit on the patio while I work on it?"

"Smart aleck. I can pull weeds."

There was a slight breeze when she stepped outside, but on the patio, behind the bushes, the air lay still and hot, the sun a bright orange ball through the branches. She waved a can of bug spray at him.

"The mosquitoes will be out tonight," she said, as she sprayed her arm and legs.

"Good idea. Would you spray my back?"

He turned and she began spraying in a wide circular motion, suddenly feeling very tiny as he filled the space in front of her. His shoulders seemed a mile wide, blocking her view, dwarfing her. She wondered what would happen if she touched him, so she did, running her fingers up to his shoulder.

"Mmm, nice. Would you like me to return the favor?" he asked, and she knew he was thinking they'd end up in bed.

"No thanks. I want to stay out here for a while. That can be for later."

"Sounds like a plan."

"Think of it as an excuse. I just wanted to touch your back."

He laughed. "And here I was getting my hopes up. Doggone."

She handed him the can and held her hand out with a laugh. "I know. You've been so deprived lately." After she said it, she wondered if he'd be upset. Maybe he wasn't satisfied with her. He seemed happy. Why did she worry so much? Dopey. She wouldn't, at least not right now.

The spray felt cool as he did her hand and then moved it up and down her back. No one had ever done that for her before. The spray on her shirt felt wonderful, so cool, and so caring.

He worked at her side pulling weeds and telling stories until only the quarter moon glistened softly on their faces.

"I'm ready for a glass of wine," she said, brushing dirt from her hand and knees. "How about you?"

"I'll be delighted to join you," he said, with mock formality.

He put the tools away while she went into the house. She was back before he finished, with the wine on a tray.

She sat silently, staring up at the stars. The stillness of the night took her, and then the night insects and the occasional passing of a car on the road. Dampness settled in and the warm summer night began to chill.

"Anne," he said softly, almost whispering.

She turned. "I'm sorry. I almost forgot you were here."

"You seemed to be off in another world."

"I was listening to the night. It's full of lovely sounds you don't hear in the daytime. Listen."

"I know. I was listening too."

They fell silent again. Crickets called, but the staccato chorus of cicadas claimed the night. An owl hooted occasionally.

"What's that faint rushing sound in the distance?" he asked.

"That's waves breaking on the shore. You can hear them sometimes, on the quiet nights."

"I thought you were staring at the stars."

"I was. I look at them and wonder what they see." She gave him a sheepish smile, embarrassed by the admission.

"What do you mean?"

"Look to the East. Those stars can see London and Paris. They look down on a woman in Piccadilly or Montmarte. I can be carrying a book or a shopping bag and can visit the markets with her." She smiled. "That's how I travel the world. I can go anywhere the stars can see."

"What's your favorite place?"

"Paris. My grandmother used to fascinate me with stories of her trips. She went there a dozen times at least. She stayed in a grand hotel on her first trip, but in the end, she went to a boarding house in Montmarte."

"Why did she do that?"

"She wanted to live like a Parisian. By that time she spoke fluent French and knew people in the city."

"She must have been a special lady."

She laughed. "For a poor English farm girl, she turned out to be quite cosmopolitan. I think she even met Manet once. So, when I look at the stars sometimes I pretend they see her, still enjoying the life over there."

"We should go someday."

"I couldn't. I just couldn't," she said, and came to her feet in a strange kind of panic. She didn't have to go, did she? "I'm going in."

He followed her. "Are you going to bed?"

"Yes," she said, and stepped into the bathroom. "I need a shower first."

He stood for a moment, left behind, and she closed the door in front of him. Her heart was pounding. Paris and the bakery and the beach, all together, and not, all the same and not.

Her breathing had quieted when she opened the door again. He stood there waiting, in shorts, ready for bed.

She said, "I'm going to sleep," and stepped into the hall.

"Are you okay?"

She hesitated and studied him, deciding finally that something had to be said.

"I'm just a little melancholy, I guess. Hannah's adventures often do that to me. If I had half her courage, I'd do some of the things she did, but I don't."

Blowing him a kiss, she headed for the bedroom, trying to avoid the predictable reassurance he'd surely offer. She was not wonderful. Ridiculous, she couldn't even go into a store with him.

He slid into bed and nuzzled her neck. "You have plenty of courage, love. Look what you're doing with me."

"Paul, thank you, but I don't want to talk about it right now."

"Okay, I'll shut up. I just want you to know that everything will work out for us. I don't want you to worry."

She turned to face him and smiled ruefully. "All right. Just kiss me now, and whisper all those romantic things you said this morning."

An hour later he was asleep, his face soft against the pillow. She remained awake, contented and loving him. Funny, he was like a Peter Pan, soaring in the clouds, and she was Wendy of course. A crazy, silly new world she'd fallen into, with this joy of living, and fear as well. Weird, she felt wild tonight. When was the last time she felt so free?

How could he be so sure of her? Courage? She'd never thought herself brave, quite the contrary. Optimistic yes, but only sometimes. With her luck, Captain Hook would show up and ruin everything. Why was she so negative lately? Scared. Oh yes, she was scared. This was different though, entirely new. It felt like someone could steal the magic and she'd come crashing to the ground. Wendy would forget how to fly.

She shivered. Eleven o'clock and he lay curled up like a baby. She touched his face and he grimaced in his sleep. She'd talk to him in the morning, tell him how she felt. Then it dawned on her- normally she'd plan to talk to Molly.

Sleep finally came, but at three she woke up and Captain Hook was back.

~ TWENTY-ONE ~

There was no help for it. Anne was right, of course. The louse had dumped her all those years ago and she shouldn't even talk to him, but the man could answer a few questions. Like why he ran out on her, and where he'd been all these years. And why in the world he came back. The ass. He was a handsome guy back then, with those deep black eyes and muscles, boy, did he have muscles.

She wouldn't see him; that was all. She was sick of men who walked away, not just with their bones, no, even that wasn't so bad. It was the feelings, all the sweet times gone. Molly hated being alone. A warm touch, the hugs and stroking, those were what she missed. Tom Carrera had been exceptional at making her feel good. Then he sent that stupid letter from Singapore, or someplace. No one else ever made her feel as bad as that. He could disappear again quite nicely. She didn't need his answers anymore.

Graham would be at his new gallery early this morning. He had a meeting with the guy who was getting the place in shape for him before they left for New York. Graham had this silly idea that only New York artists could paint worth a darn. So, they'd be off to find some art to hang on the walls.

Half way through breakfast, the doorbell rang and it all went out the window. There was Tom, older, almost bald, and a lot thinner than she remembered, but there was no question-it was him, come to catch her early in the morning. Same silly grin he had before, like he was embarrassed, or something.

"Hello Molly," he said. "I wondered if you still lived here. You're not in the book anymore."

"Yes, I am. It's Wagner now."

"You're married."

"Used to be, no more. I thought you were dead."

"No. Not me. You look great Molly, just like I remembered you."

"Sure. Twenty-eight year old kid, just like you. What do you want?"

His face took on a serious look. "I wondered how you were doing, so I came to see."

"That's all? After all these years and that stupid letter? That's a little nervy."

He shrugged. "You needed more than a come and go sailor, only in your life on rare occasions. I figured it was best."

"What? That I should think I was dying of some terrible disease you gave me? That was a rotten trick."

"A dumb thing, a coward's thing. I know that. It wouldn't have worked though, between us, not then. You wanted someone here with you. You would have wanted another guy one day, when I was at sea. It would have been a mess."

"It would have? I suppose you stayed on the ship when you hit port?"

"That too. It was best. You married up eventually. Found a Mister Wagner."

"Yeah, I was stupid. A couple of months later and it lasted just about that long. He reminded me of you, the jerk." He didn't need to know Henry Wagner came later, much later.

"Oh," he said, and took a breath. "What about now? Are you seeing someone?"

That was the big question of course, and it stopped her for a second. Was she seeing Graham? She didn't even know, but it didn't matter. Not a bit. Tom Carrera she knew once, but this was a stranger she was talking to. The lie came easily, surprised her.

"I'm engaged to a real sweet guy."

"Oh," he said, disappointment showing on his face.

She forced her emotions into a quiet calm and kept her face expressionless. He'd had his chance.

"Well, congratulations then. It was nice to see you again," he finally said.

"Same here," she replied, surprised to realize that was true. True, but enough. "Take care of yourself."

"You too." He turned away with a wave. He looked old. Balding and tired, and she wondered about his health.

"Are you still shipping out?" she called.

He turned and smiled. "I've signed up as mate on a tourist boat up in Maine. Never out of sight of land. Day sails, you know."

"Good luck."

He waved and walked away.

She warmed coffee in the microwave and rushed through the rest of her now cold eggs, worrying all the while if she should tell Graham. He knew not a thing of Tom so far. Why should he? Graham was, after all, just a little fun.

Hot and muggy, the air in New York felt like a soggy blanket, but Graham didn't seem to notice. On the third floor and climbing without a break, he clearly knew where to go in the dumpy building. She'd almost call the place a slum, but that was her suburban eye, she decided. The place wasn't terrible. By city standards, it was probably just an ordinary walk-up apartment. Their second stop today and she pitied Graham. The first guy they visited as much as told him to drop dead. He'd shrugged off the insult, saying the fellow always had an exaggerated opinion of his artistic ability.

Graham was not doing very well at all collecting the art he needed. These people had their work in New York galleries and viewed Newport as the hinterlands. He had visited twelve artists last week and came away with six paintings. She'd taken today off to come with him, thinking it would be interesting and exciting, and also to keep him company. And, after Tom Carrera's unexpected visit it was just as well to be away in case the man made a second attempt to drop in on her.

Interesting New York was, but exciting? She'd had more fun staring out the window at a bird feeder at home.

She hadn't mentioned Tom, wouldn't ever see him again, so why bother. She and Graham didn't share all their little secrets.

He knocked on a door on the fourth floor and she got quite a surprise when it opened. Max Reineke did not live in poverty. He had a loft, with high ceilings, wide-open space, and beautiful furnishings. The man liked wood. There was one stuffed chair in the place. All the color came from massive paintings hung along the walls and used as room dividers. Anne would have a field day with the furniture, but the paintings would leave her cold.

The man used deep somber colors, depressing looking to Molly's mind, but powerful none-the-less.

Max Reineke looked about forty-five, with a hard chiseled face and dissipated eyes that undressed her before Graham made introductions. The man thought he had her pegged, no doubt thanks to the outfit she had on, which was designed to keep Graham interested, not the likes of him. But the man made her feel cheap. That had happened a few times lately and she didn't know what to do about it. Yeah right, she was kidding herself. She always dressed this way. She should buy herself some new clothes, the frumpy kind Anne wore. Mister Reineke was a jerk.

Graham introduced her as his fiancée. She started, threw him an astonished glance. Where had that come from? She played along, but couldn't believe her ears. Reineke offered congratulations with a smirk and she had the distinct impression he had recognized the lie. Some fancy explanations were going to be needed when she and Graham got out of there, and she wasn't the least bit sure she wanted to hear them, whatever they were. The man could not be serious.

Graham came away happy after a few minutes discussion with Reineke. The man agreed to provide paintings for Newport as long as Graham arranged for continued gallery space in New York. Graham promised to set him up with one of his friends and they left with three of Reineke's smaller paintings in the back of the car.

"What was that about?" she asked, as they crept through downtown traffic.

"My fiancée? Max is a letch. I wanted to make sure he left you alone."

"Oh, well thank you. That was very nice." Not bad, a bit of a surprise. Graham seemed to have more caring in his bones than she'd expected. His next comment took the shine off though.

"I wanted to keep his attention on business. We would have been there all day if he thought he had a chance with you."

"Oh."

He smiled. "Disappointed?"

"I would have dealt with him."

"That I know. I meant the fiancée thing. You're not into that, are you? I figure you're like me."

"Meaning what?"

"You know. No illusions, no promises. I like you and I figure we're both in this for a good time."

"Yeah, you're every man, aren't you? A roll in the hay is all you want."

"Hey, I didn't say that. I said I like you. I just figured we both have a few miles on us and don't need more pain. I don't anyway."

She hesitated at that, trying to decide what she felt. Just friends, but going to bed together. Nothing more. He was right, that was their game. What the heck, maybe it was better that way.

"Okay, no promises, no plans. That was how we started, right?"

"I thought so."

"Let's keep it that way."

"Okay, good." He went silent for a moment, blew the horn as a taxi cut him off, and then said quietly, "My first wife left me because she wanted kids."

"You didn't?"

"I did back then. No such luck though."

"I should have been your first wife. I never wanted any."

"Oh."

The day was all business after that. They made four more stops, but signed only one artist. She asked what he'd do next and he said his New York contacts were exhausted.

"I'll check art schools and clubs in Rhode Island now. It won't be easy though. My time needs to be spent on the gallery so I can open before the tourists leave for the winter."

"I'll help with that. What do you need done?"

"I've got a good carpenter doing the construction, but I'm doing all the painting."

"The sophisticated New York art dealer does his own house painting?"

He laughed. "I enjoy it. I even have my own coveralls."

"Well, I've painted my share of walls, so I guess I can help."

"What about your friend who did that painting in your living room? You think she'd give me some of her work?"

"You think she's good enough?"

"Yeah. She has a nice touch."

"She never exhibits anything."

"You think we could persuade her?"

"She can be stubborn, especially if you push too much. You better leave her to me for a while."

"There's not much time. I can't open a half empty gallery."

"I know, but let me feel her out."

The next afternoon she stopped to see Anne. No one answered the door. The house seemed deserted, so she went in. The kitchen looked like assorted hoboes had dropped in for a free meal, and that was worrisome, given Anne's finicky neatness about her kitchen. Paul's clothes lay scattered around with hers as though they'd left in a hurry. The Ford sat in the garage, but Paul's car was gone and that she didn't like. He often went out, but where was Anne? Imagination allowed all possibilities, not all of them good.

Her Google search had turned up one Paul Breland who'd been arrested for attempted murder and she had yet to confirm this Paul wasn't the same guy.

Anne wasn't walking in the woods either. Once that was verified, there were few other options to Molly's way of thinking. She left a note on the kitchen table and stopped at Betty's on the way home. Knowing nothing, Betty couldn't help. Molly swore. Anne hadn't questioned Paul, not the way she asked her to at least. She'd do it now or Molly would give her the devil next time she saw her.

Anne called about fifteen minutes after she got home.

"Paul and I went to the beach and up to see Grace. I would have called you, but we've just been so busy."

"You've been to the beach? All day?"

"No, just this morning. It's part of our plan."

"What plan?"

"To get out of the house. We're doing things I can manage. The beach is beautiful in the morning light."

"Jeez, a beach is about as public as you can get! You're right. You're doing it, just as you said you would."

Anne laughed. "We go to the Lighthouse. Hardly anyone goes there, especially early."

"That's still amazing. Maybe we should go up to Boston or something. I guess not though. Paul will help you with that."

"We'll all go soon. Come with us, Molly."

"Three's a crowd. You don't need me."

"Molly!"

"Hey, it's all right. I bet I got busy whenever I found a new man. You should have said something." Molly laughed at herself then. "You know what? I just reached the point where I thought I knew everything and now I feel like a dunce. Of course it's Paul you'll do this with. If you were going to go out with me we would have years ago."

"You make me feel terrible. I love Paul. I can't be the old me anymore."

"That's what I'm asking for, aren't I? Good solid Anne, always there, never changing. Sounds pretty selfish. How did we get into this conversation?"

"You're not selfish. I love you, you dope. We're sisters and always will be." Anne stopped then, when Molly laughed.

"Thanks hon, I needed that. I guess I'm learning a few things about myself these days. You too. You're pretty amazing, you know that? Paul pegged you right from the beginning. Tell him I said he was right, will you?"

"You tell him. Why don't you come over tomorrow?"

Molly laughed again, louder this time. "Guess who's going to help paint walls tomorrow? Who doesn't have time for whom? Hey, the man asked about your paintings. He likes the one I have in my living room."

"I assume we're talking about Graham? What happened to the letter writer?"

"He's history."

"Good."

"Yeah, but you know the best thing? I didn't go into a tizzy over him like I usually do. And I'm not in one over Graham either. Life goes on and I'll survive. Isn't that neat?"

"I'm glad Molly," Anne said softly.

"Listen, I was worried about you today when you weren't there. I want some history about Paul."

"What for?"

"I told you I was going to Google him? I can't narrow the search without the information I asked you to get."

"Molly. Don't be ridiculous."

"Hey, humor me. I worry about you. What do you know about him?"

"I know his name," Anne said flippantly.

"Funnee. And he's about fifty and he lives in Connecticut. What else? Make with the latest."

Anne groaned. "He used to live in New York. He's a retired engineer. And a widower."

"His wife's name?"

"Carol. She died of cancer."

"Great. Now, that wasn't so hard was it?"

"You're a pest, you know that?"

Molly could hear the laughter in her voice. "Okay. Enough about Mister Breland for now. Keep digging."

"Oh stop. Paul's a good man."

"Yeah, and my mother wore army boots. What about your paintings? Can I tell Graham you'll put some in his gallery?"

"I have to think about it."

"I can't wait to see them on display. I'll tell everybody I know the artist."

"I didn't say yes."

"I know. He could talk to you about it over dinner."

"When you come here? I suppose."

~ * ~

Molly searched through the back closet for clothes to wear painting. An old sweater and grungy skirt were in there somewhere, but it had been a while since she'd used them. The New York outfit almost got demoted to take their place, but she found the old things in a pile on the floor and New York was rescued for the moment. The wardrobe would change thanks to the meeting with Mister Reineke. Never again would the word cheap apply, never again would she dress that way.

The old clothes needed a run through the washer, but Graham was waiting to leave. She shook out the skirt and sweater, picked off some dust balls, and stepped into them.

"Coming Graham," she called. "I just have to comb my hair." Actually, she wanted a spray or two of cologne on the ratty old sweater before she faced him.

He grinned when he saw her.

"Well, well. I'll bet you don't wear that outfit very often."

"Never in public. You're the first person who's ever seen me dressed this way."

His grin faded to a soft smile. "That's quite a compliment."

Suddenly she felt warm all over. "Let's go paint." A compliment? The thought would never have occurred to her, but in a way, he might be right. On the other hand, perhaps she just didn't care if she impressed anyone anymore. Or, on the other *other* hand, maybe she was just beginning to see things with a new eye. And anyway, he was pleased she let him see her with her hair down so to speak and that sent a tiny tingle up her back.

He seemed happy as they painted, relaxed and pleasant, not the hard driving New Yorker she met that day at the office. There was the question of Anne's paintings. She told him they might be available, but he wondered about the timing since he wanted them framed for the opening. He announced he'd call Anne himself.

"I can't wait for the dinner."

"There's time yet. I begin to think you are an impatient man, Mister White."

He grinned. "You're getting to know me too well. At least you think you are."

"Am I wrong?"

"No, but that only pertains to business. I don't like loose ends. Talking to your friend on the phone first would be a plus of course."

"Of course. You'll get a head-start that way."

He nodded and she sighed for no reason. Stupid, the word popped into her head. Was she worried? Jealous? How ridiculous was that.

"You seem a little subdued this morning. Something upset you?"

Her roller stopped halfway up the wall and she stared at him, all laughter gone. He had her pegged. She did feel different today, but his dealings with Anne had nothing to do with it. Actually, whether Anne agreed to exhibit had barely concerned her in the ruminations of the last couple of days. It had all been Anne, tasteful Anne, and Miss Molly Wagner, the cheap trash. Crap, was that really what she was? She threw a glance at Graham. He was studying the wall where he'd been painting.

Graham's concern was sweet and she liked it. He really was a nice man. Maybe too nice. Too close. She had no desire to end up with another stupid Singapore letter. She thanked him for asking, told him no, she was just a little pensive. He was getting to be a real person, this Mister White.

~ TWENTY-TWO ~

She called Anne to introduce Graham and see about the paintings, to no avail. Anne said the paintings could be discussed over dinner and that was the end of that. She suggested they didn't need to arrive early because Paul said he'd do the whole meal.

Back in her house later, she wondered if the two men would like each other. Graham was a New Yorker, an art expert, and Paul seemed to be a meat and potatoes guy. He was intelligent enough apparently, but Graham was another cut above and that might make for an awkward evening. Why in the world was she worrying? It was Anne's party, not hers.

Her stomach roiling with frustration, she turned on her laptop and Googled Paul again. She scanned the first page of listings, then the second and the third. Nobody that sounded like Anne's Paul. At the rate she was going she'd be reading web pages for a solid week.

She almost gave up, but tried one more page of listings. There it was, the one about the murderer.

Excited, she clicked on the listing. It referred to a newspaper article from the New York Times files. She'd found it before, but hadn't read beyond the headline since she'd known so little about Paul. She read it this time. Dated ten years ago, the article was from an inside page of the Times. The man it described sounded like he could be Anne's Paul. She shivered and read on. The man had lived in New York, his wife's name had been Carol, and he'd been arrested for trying to kill her. It had to be Anne's Paul.

Anne would never believe it. What was she going to do? She picked up the phone and called the gallery.

"You don't know for sure it's him?" Graham said.

"Not absolutely, but I think he's the same guy."

"We'll see what happens tonight. I'll handle it. Just follow my lead."

~ * ~

Anne's stomach twitched as she prepared for the evening. Paul had surprised her with a brand new basic black sheath and a beautiful pearl necklace that must have cost him a lot of money. She was thrilled that he'd been so thoughtful and, even more impressive, had gotten her size right. She slipped into the dress, arranged the pearls around her neck, and turned before the mirror in the bedroom. Was she overdressed? Running a finger along the pearls, she laughed. Molly would dress up for Graham, no need to worry about that.

What a turn her life had taken these last few weeks. Luck, that's what it was, new and good and wonderful. She wandered into the kitchen, cautiously, to check on Paul's success with his one handed cooking. Cautiously because he had shooed her out not thirty minutes ago.

He stood stock still when he laid eyes on her. "Hi beautiful," he said softly.

Her heart surged and that felt wonderful. How often did a pounding heart feel so exciting? "Hi."

"Our guests should be here any minute."

She glanced at the clock and gave him a wry smile. "If Molly has anything to say about it they will be."

He nodded and began to emulate her trick with the wine bottle he was holding, tucking it under his arm and clamping down while he tried to turn the corkscrew with his good hand. He grimaced. The bottle turned.

"Would you like a little help?" she asked, lowering her eyes demurely.

"Oh, I can do it," he said. "But if it would make you feel better, please pitch right in."

She sent him a smirk and reached for the bottle. He brushed her cheek with a kiss as the door reverberated with the sound of the knocker.

"Hi sweetie, I hope we're not late. It's been a busy day," Molly said cheerily as Anne opened the door.

Graham gave Anne a dazzling smile while Molly did the introductions.

"I'm delighted to meet you, Miss Hoskins. Molly's told me a great deal about you." Graham spoke softly, but his diction was precise, oozing politeness. He offered his hand, almost tentatively, as if he didn't want to offend her in some way.

Anne gave him a perfunctory shake. "I'm pleased to meet you. Come in."

"That dress is new isn't it?" Molly said, not exactly sounding happy.

"Paul bought it for me. The pearls too. Wasn't that nice?"

"He has excellent taste in clothing and in women," Graham said with a charming smile.

Molly seemed to be trying to keep a bland expression on her face, but wasn't succeeding very well. Anne realized she had dressed conservatively, in a plain purple dress and little jewelry, and was probably upset by Anne's appearance. Anne offered her a wry smile and sighed to herself. She should have told Molly what she'd be wearing.

Anne led them past the darkened studio and into the kitchen.

"That was her studio, but we'll see it later," Molly said, as she trailed along down the hall.

Graham threw a quick glance into the darkness. "May I see some of your paintings after dinner?"

"Certainly, but come meet Paul," Anne said, with nary a glance at Molly. If Mister White was here just to see her paintings, it was going to be a long evening.

Paul wore dressy Khaki pants, blue oxford shirt with open neck, and a charcoal blazer that hung over the back of a chair at the moment. It was an outfit Anne had heard Molly disdainfully describe as "the Yacht Club getup." One of Anne's aprons draped around his neck marred the image, but he didn't seem to notice. He greeted Graham with a firm handshake and offered wine as if he'd known him for a hundred years.

Anne felt a touch of pride watching him with Graham. She realized nothing seemed to fluster Paul Breland. Relaxed, that was him.

Candles lit the table. Cloth napkins lay rolled into silver rings and a fine set of silverware marked each place.

Molly stared, obviously surprised at the display. Anne noted her expression. "That's my Grandmother's good silver."

"You've never brought it out before," Molly said, fingering a delicate spoon.

Anne shrugged. "Paul was going to drive home to get some from his house until I remembered I had this."

"It's a beautiful set. I hope you have it well insured," Graham said, with another broad smile for Anne.

"She has a silver platter too," Molly added, flashing Graham a look of annoyance.

Anne wondered at Molly's irritation. Graham was being kind, could that be it? Or was it that she didn't look her best tonight? Which was odd. Molly usually looked fabulous and she certainly had plenty of beautiful jewelry she could have chosen from.

"She has a number of silver platters, and I better start getting some of them on the table," Paul said with a laugh.

The platters and serving dishes appeared bearing roast pork and potatoes, bowls of carrots and beans and creamed onions, Greek salad and fresh wheat bread. Graham appeared quite pleased with the meal, but Molly seemed upset with him again.

What was that about? He was clearly enjoying himself, and he and Paul appeared to be getting along just fine.

Concerned, Anne thought to draw Molly to a private place for a second, but Molly turned and smiled at her and she gave up worrying. Molly was a big girl. Whatever was bothering her couldn't be too important. Anne picked up a piece of the bread Paul had made a special trip to their new bakery for.

As the dinner went along, Graham kept directing his comments to her. He freely offered his opinions and life story while Paul kept the food and drink flowing. The man loved Manhattan, but said his wife's lawyer was trying to steal everything he owned. It was time to reduce overhead, in a place where he could still make a decent living doing what he knew best- promoting new artists. At least that was his version of things, the one Molly must have heard already. Paul had a secret smile on his face, probably wondering what the ex-wife would say about him.

"New York is quite the place. Center of the world and all that," Graham said suddenly. "Did you ever live there, Anne?"

"No, I grew up in Boston."

"What about you, Paul?"

"I lived there for a while."

"In the city?"

"No. New Rochelle."

"Nice town," Graham said.

Suddenly they were talking about her studio. Anne usually hated to talk about her art, but Graham seemed oblivious, patiently trying to draw her out. Her reaction surprised her. She felt no heat, no desire to argue or disappear, and that was just fine. He seemed kind and somehow trustworthy, a man who would not be brutal about her poor efforts.

"I've seen the two paintings you gave Molly. They're quite good, quite good indeed. I'd very much like to put some of your work in my new gallery," said Graham.

"Wouldn't that be wonderful, Anne? People would see what you've done," Molly added, looking decidedly happier than she did when she first arrived.

Anne shook her head. "I don't care about that. I did them for me."

"Ah, but Molly's right. They'll sell quite well," Graham said.

"You've only seen the ones Molly has."

"I'm sure they will unless you've suddenly collapsed as an artist, or gone to a radical style. Molly tells me you haven't, so I think I know what I'm talking about. Why don't you let me put one or two up for sale and we'll see what happens?"

"Try it, Anne? It would be fun, make you a professional artist," Paul said with his best beguiling smile.

"I'm glad you all like my paintings, but I'm not thrilled about the whole idea."

"Many new artists are reluctant to show initially," Graham said quickly.

Anne stared at him as if he'd just told a fairy tale, but then she relaxed. His words were very reassuring.

"Why don't you do it? Your paintings are so wonderful. Just think, they could end up in some grand home in Newport or Boston!" Molly said.

Anne grimaced. "Stop Molly, you're too much." She turned to Paul. "You think I should?"

"People should see your paintings." He turned to Graham. "What does she have to do? What would the arrangements be?"

"My commission is thirty percent, plus the cost of the frames. You get the rest," Graham said. "I'll do the framing and set the prices where I think they belong."

"No long term commitments?"

"None." He grinned at Anne. "Of course if you start to sell like hotcakes, a formal agreement would be nice."

"It sounds easy enough," Paul said smiling.

"I'll think about it."

"I'll be opening in two weeks," Graham said.

"We'll see."

"Graham has brought a bunch of paintings from New York. He gets down there quite often. How about you Paul? Do you go back?" Molly asked.

"No."

"You don't miss it? When did you leave?" Graham asked, with a quick look at Molly.

"It's been ten years," Paul said, glancing from one to the other.

"Was that when your wife died?" Molly asked innocently.

Anne stared at her. Questions about Paul's background, what was she doing? The two of them.

Paul nodded, his face set suddenly.

"Can we show Graham some of your paintings now?" Molly asked brightly.

"All right," Anne said, her stomach tightening with nervous tension. Molly was up to something and Graham was in on the act, she was almost sure. And Paul looked unhappy.

Graham scanned the studio as he entered. "You have a very good work space. Very professional."

"Thank you."

"Excellent, excellent," he said, slowly walking through the room. When he had thoroughly perused the space, he turned to Anne, and fixed her with a look so intense her stomach tensed into a knot.

"What are you staring at?"

"You. Your paintings are quite beautiful, typically female, but they also show great power. There isn't a thing frilly or cute about them. The beauty is in the forms, the bold design, and the colors. They're strong. You have the same look about you."

The pronouncement was made in a very businesslike, unemotional manner, but how could he dare to be so personal? Then she realized he was trying to explain why the paintings were good. Anne nodded and began to pay close attention to his observations.

Graham kept talking while he studied paintings and began to organize them by some logic of his own.

Paul left the room to get more coffee.

Suddenly, Graham grabbed Anne's arm. "There's something you should know," he said quietly, glancing toward the hall.

"What?" she asked, shocked by the intimacy of his behavior.

"Molly's done some research on the Internet. We think your Paul's a murderer."

Anne stared at him, opened her mouth, and closed it. That was so insane she had no words to respond.

"It's true Anne," Molly hissed. "The guy I found lived in New Rochelle ten years ago. He was arrested for attempted murder of his wife, a woman named Carol. It was in the New York Times."

Her heart thudding with sudden confusion, Anne stared at her. This couldn't be—it was crazy, ridiculous, a mistake.

"Not Paul," she gasped.

Molly nodded emphatically. "Paul Breland. He was forty five years old. The same age your Paul would have been."

~ * ~

Paul heard whispers as he approached the studio with a tray of steaming coffee cups balanced on his one good hand. He couldn't tell what they were saying, but because they spoke so softly he felt his stomach tighten. Curiosity aroused, he eased closer to the studio, hugging the wall.

"You have to kick him out of here," Graham was saying.

"Or else you have to leave," Molly hissed. "You can stay at my house until he goes away."

"I don't believe this," Anne said. "You're wrong about...."

"It was in the New York Times, Anne. He tried to kill his wife," Molly said.

Paul swore. More busybody meddlers. His heart began to pound. He set the tray down on the hall table before he dropped it.

"Not Paul," he heard Anne gasp.

"Paul Breland. He was forty-five years old. The same age your Paul would have been," Molly said.

The blood began to roar through his head and his broken arm spasmed as his fists clenched. But, struggling for control, he paid no attention to the pain. This couldn't be happening again. It was different, but the same, another meddler interfering. Carol all over again, for no blasted reason but Molly making herself important. He ground his teeth, trying to be calm, trying to figure out what to do. He had to stop this, right now. Had to shut her up, her and Graham. He stepped into the studio.

"Are you having fun?"

They turned as one and stared at him. He had eyes only for Anne. She looked as if someone had hit her with a baseball bat.

"You've seen the Times article," he said in a flat voice.

"It was you?" Anne whispered.

"In that article? Yes."

"You tried to kill your wife?"

"No."

"But you were arrested," Molly said.

"Yes."

"What happened?" Graham asked.

"They dropped the charges."

"Why?" Anne whispered.

"It's a long story."

~ * ~

She stared at him, waiting, but he looked grim, a scowl etched deep across his forehead. He said nothing.

"Paul?" she asked

"This isn't the time."

"We need an explanation," Molly snapped.

Paul spiked a glance in her direction. "Anne does. You don't."

"We all do. You can't be left alone with Anne without a satisfactory answer," Graham said sharply.

"She's perfectly safe."

"We'll be the judge of that."

Anne felt faint. She had to sit down, had to find a seat. Brushing past Paul, she darted into the kitchen and slumped down in the nearest chair.

"Are you all right?" he asked, following her.

He seemed to loom over her, but she couldn't turn her eyes away from his. Paul a murderer? An almost murderer? What was the difference, he'd been caught, been stopped before he killed his wife? The wife who died of cancer? Had that been a lie?

Cancer? Had he tried a mercy killing? That thought stopped her churning insides. She saw it in his eyes then. He knew what she was thinking.

"Did she ask you to?" she blurted.

"It's a long story," he said, stone-faced, his eyes hard.

"That's not good enough," Graham said, coming into the room with Molly behind him.

Ignoring Graham, his eyes still locked on Anne, he shook his head.

She couldn't make sense of the swirling emotions clashing in her heart. He looked so hard, so fierce, so unlike the tender man who'd made love to her. A murderer? Not Paul, he couldn't be. But why wouldn't he explain himself? She darted a glance at Molly. She looked confused, even frightened. They were afraid to leave her alone with Paul. She shivered, turned back to him, couldn't think, couldn't speak at all.

"I'll stay at the hotel in town tonight if you want. We'll talk in the morning," he said. His voice was softer, almost gentle and she met his eyes again. There was something there besides the anger.

"Forget that," Graham snapped. "You could come back and break in any time you wanted to."

"We should call the police," Molly said.

For an instant Anne thought she saw a look of panic on Paul's face, but then it was gone, if it had ever been there. He was trembling, as if he were fighting for control.

"You two can stay the night with her, if that would make you feel better." He sent Molly a smirk. "She'd be safe that way, as long as you don't forget what you're here for."

"What's that supposed to mean?" Graham huffed.

"Do I need to spell it out? Molly knows what I mean, don't you Molly?"

Anne shivered as a cold chill ran up her back. "Please stop. This was supposed to be a nice evening."

"Yeah," Paul said, glaring at Graham. He swung his gaze back to Anne. "I'll collect my things and go. But I'm coming back tomorrow to talk to you. Just you."

Her heart settled then, almost in an instant as she stared up at his face. She'd been right before. There was pain and something else? Fear? Not fear *fear*, not the kind that meant he'd run, or thought he'd be locked up, or anything like that. Pleading, that was it. He was afraid she'd turn him away.

"Don't go, you don't have to."

"Anne!" Molly snapped.

Forcing a smile, Anne turned to face her. "If he wanted to kill me, he had plenty of opportunities already."

"You can't let him stay here," Graham pontificated.

"I can and I will. You and Molly go home and leave us alone now."

"Anne. He was arrested for trying to kill his wife," Molly cried, desperation in her voice.

Anne turned back to Paul. Her heart warmed at the relief in his face. Her sweet, easy Paul was back. He would tell his story, to her and only her. She had an almost overwhelming urge to kiss him, but would wait until they were alone.

"He's innocent. You guys should leave now."

"Anne," Molly started.

"No more. Go home."

"We'll call every hour," Molly insisted.

"The phone will be disconnected."

Anne had to physically shoo them out the door, but she was finally alone with Paul. He stood loading the dishwasher when she returned to the kitchen. Face gray, his eyes almost sunken, he looked drained. He picked up the dishtowel and wiped his hands.

"You're supposed to wash up first," she said automatically.

No laugh, no wisecrack, he simply nodded.

"What happened tonight?"

"You saw, you heard."

"No, I mean, what's this all about?"

"It's about nightmares and death and people who meddle," he said bitterly.

She reached her hand out to touch his face and he kissed it.

"And it's about you."

"Tell me," she whispered, awed by the grief in his voice.

He drew in a breath and put on a forced smile. "I left the coffee in the hall. You want a cup?"

"I don't care."

He gently brushed her cheek and stepped past her, returning seconds later with two cups. He handed her one and gestured to a chair.

"Let's sit down."

She did not know why, but she wanted to stand, so she shook her head and leaned against the wall. He took the chair she'd been sprawled in not so long ago.

She waited, then finally sipped the coffee.

"This goes back a long way," he said, so softly she almost couldn't hear his words.

"Your wife had cancer?"

"I told you that I guess? It started in her lungs. It went fast. By the time we found out, it had already spread. They treated her, but it was too late."

He paused, staring at his coffee cup, his face calm for the moment. "It was too late," he said again, almost inaudibly, and then shook himself and smiled up at her.

It was the saddest smile she'd ever seen. Her heart clutched at the pain in his expression.

"I knew I was going to lose her. She knew it too." A tear formed at the corner of his eye, but he ignored it. "She was so brave. She told me to marry again."

"But you still love her," Anne whispered.

He went on as if she hadn't spoken. "We did all the usual things. Got Hospice involved. Told the kids. Told her mom, who was still alive."

He took another sip of coffee, stood and walked to the window. Staring at the trees outside, he didn't move, didn't say a word. Anne waited. Finally he spoke.

"Carol wanted to die at home. I told Hospice to send a nurse instead of putting her in a facility. The end was close, we both knew it. The cancer had gone to her bones and the pain was terrible."

"I thought Hospice did things about that. Gave pain pills or something."

He looked up at her, the fire back in his eyes. "That's the idea, isn't it? They sent us this sweet little nurse who bustled around, fluffing pillows, all that stuff. A meddler, just like those two."

"Who?"

"Molly and Graham," he growled, then shook his head and returned to the table. "I can't talk about this now. I'll get a motel room."

He left the dishwasher wide-open and didn't bother with his things. Anne tried to stop him, but he just barged out the door and left. She turned back to the kitchen, gave a cursory glance around the messy room, and gave up on it for the night. Housekeeping didn't matter at the moment.

She couldn't seem to think straight. Paul was innocent, wasn't he? He had to be. But Molly considered him dangerous and Molly had much more experience with men than she did.

She locked the front door, checked the back, and headed for her bedroom.

His shirt hung from the doorknob, sloppy man. She rebuked herself. The shirt was the only thing of his that was out of place. It wasn't fair to pick on him just because Molly thought she knew everything. He said it was all a mistake or something. He was honest. He even admitted the article was about him.

She sighed. Paul couldn't be a con-man, could he? People like that were supposed to be very good at fooling women. Had she been a fool? It couldn't be.

She turned down the sheets. The house was so quiet, so empty without him. She wanted to slide into bed and feel him beside her, cuddling up close. Feel the warmth of his body, the gentle way he caressed her. It wasn't just the sex, it was everything. The way he smiled when he looked at her. The way he teased with that impish grin on his face. He had told the truth. He'd come back tomorrow and explain.

She began to go through everything that happened, trying to recall his exact words. Molly's insistence that he was dangerous kept obscuring her memory. Stupid Molly. Everything had been going so well until she brought up that horrible newspaper report. There had to be a way to find out the truth. If only his wife were still alive. There was that other woman though, that Ellie he talked about. He hadn't really explained why they broke up. If only she had a last name for her. Paul had never mentioned that either.

Anne sighed again and curled up into a fetal position. Paul would explain everything in the morning. Now she had to sleep.

~ TWENTY-THREE ~

She lay spooned around Paul, with her hand around his waist. The heat of his body against her belly was wonderful. She felt safe and warm, and then she woke up completely. She was clutching a pillow. Puzzled for a moment, she remembered the night before. Molly and Graham and their suspicions. The phone was ringing. She groaned and threw a glance at the clock. Eight thirteen? Who was calling so early?

"What?" she barked into the receiver.

"You're okay?" Molly asked.

Anne shook herself, groaned. "Molly, stop will you. I'm fine."

"Where is he? In the shower?"

"For your information, he stayed in town."

"He's not there? Good, I'm coming over."

"I don't want you here. He's coming back this morning to explain everything."

Molly snorted. "And you'll believe every word he says."

"I don't know what I'll believe. I don't know what he's going to tell me. But I don't want you here when he arrives."

"You shouldn't be alone with him."

"Molly, I am hanging on by the skin of my teeth. Just leave it alone for now," Anne said, and slammed down the phone.

She trembled as a flood of conflicting emotions swept over her. She never treated Molly that way, but Molly was the enemy now. And where was Paul? Would he even come back today, or was he so upset about last night that he'd leave her? It almost didn't matter if he was a murderer, but even as she realized that she knew she had to calm down and think. Where was he? She needed an explanation.

Slipping off the bed, she opened the dresser, selected a pair of panties and stepped into them, added shorts and a tee and headed for the bathroom. Ten minutes later she stood in the kitchen, staring at the mess, trying to decide where to start. The mess was good. It gave her something to work on, something to think about besides Paul.

It didn't take long to fill the dishwasher, and then she started hand washing the platters and pots and pans. She checked the tablecloth for spills and shook out crumbs before folding and putting it away. When a knock came at the front door, she sucked in a deep breath and opened it, praying it wasn't Molly.

He looked bedraggled, gray in the face, and weary, as if he hadn't slept all night.

"Hi."

The urge to kiss him was so strong she almost stood on tiptoes to do it. She didn't. They had to talk. He had to explain first. She had to keep her mind clear.

"Come in. Have you had breakfast?"

He shook his head.

"Would you like eggs or pancakes?"

"Coffee, I need coffee. You choose on the rest," he said as he followed her into the kitchen.

He served himself, reaching out to find a mug and fill it with coffee. He took a sip. "Are we going to be alone?"

She shivered at the question. Normally, she wouldn't have given it a second thought, but after last night?

He noticed apparently and smiled. "I meant is Molly going to bust in here soon?"

"No."

He took another sip of coffee and nodded. "You need some answers. I'll try to get through everything."

"There's no hurry," she lied.

"You might want to sit down. This will take a while."

Anne shook her head. He looked so tired, so defeated. "You want to wait? Do it another day?"

"You have to hear it sometime." He sighed. "Carol asked me to kill her one day. I thought she was a little crazy with the pain, but then she asked again and then again. What was the point, she'd say. I didn't have an answer. Not 'til later, the third time she asked."

He got to his feet and began to pace the kitchen. "You'd think, after ten years, it would get easier."

She nodded silently, then shook her head, not sure how to respond.

He drew a breath and went on, not looking at her. "We really talked that third time. How to do it, when to do it, what to tell the kids. I tried so hard to talk her out of it and she finally began to listen. I told her I was selfish. I wanted every single second I could have with her. Told her I didn't want to go to jail, and besides who would be there for the kids if I did."

Anne felt tears begin to stream down her face. She rubbed them away.

"She smiled at me then, a crooked smile, that's all she could manage anymore, and I knew she'd changed her mind." Not for you, you jerk," she whispered, "for the kids.""

Paul touched Anne's cheek and then the tip of her nose, his face a mask of pain. "I told her I'd force that nurse to get her some more meds and I kissed her and told her I loved her. And then the cops charged in."

"What?"

"That sweet little nurse liked to listen at doors. She also had selective hearing and a dramatic imagination. She was crazy."

"She called the police?"

"Among other things. I explained what happened and then she really went to town. She told them I'd convinced Carol I should kill her to end her pain. That I'd assured her no one would ever know the truth. That we'd made detailed plans to do it that day."

"What happened?"

"They ignored Carol's protests and left her to the mercy of that witch for the next four hours. They dragged me off to jail. Which I resisted, so that made it worse."

"You must have been out of your mind."

He shook his head. "I couldn't stop thinking of Carol. What it must have been like for her."

"Alone with that nurse? What happened?"

"I used my one phone call to reach Jane. Told her to grab her brother and get over to the house and get that blasted woman out of there, stay with their mom."

"And they did?"

He shook his head. "The house was empty."

"What?"

"The idiot had Carol dragged off to the hospital, claimed she was going critical."

"How could that happen?"

"That's another story. The woman was nuts."

"Didn't the Hospice people know that?"

"It turned out she was a new employee. They hadn't checked her references. She had no business working with dying people."

Anne shook her head. "What happened to your wife? Did you take her home?"

"Death doesn't wait for bureaucracy," he whispered.

"She died?"

"In the blasted hospital she hated. Alone. While they had me in front of a judge, with a prosecutor who thought he had the case to make him famous."

"Where were your children?"

"Jane was chasing after the medical people. Scott and Helen were in the courtroom, trying to get me out so we could take her home," he said, his voice hoarse.

"Oh Paul," she said, and stood to wrap her arms about him.

He kissed the top of her head and ran a finger through her hair. "I sued their butts off. The county, that blasted woman, Hospice, all of them."

"So, they let you go." She kissed him.

"I couldn't hold her hand when she died."

Anne could see he was fighting back tears, even after all this time. She laid her head against his chest and hugged him tight, until he began to stroke her hair.

Leaning back then, smiling, she asked, "And what was going on last night? About me I mean?"

He stared at her as if he didn't understand the question, then nodded. "I was afraid I'd lose you. It felt like Molly was that crazy nurse all over again, telling tales about me."

She remembered something else. "You must have been horrified when she mentioned calling the police?"

Having seen the panic in his eyes, she could only imagine what he'd been feeling. She reached up on her tiptoes and kissed him gently.

He seemed not to notice. "I envisioned court orders forcing me to stay away from you." He paused, then went on, his voice harsh. "I would have ignored them. In case you were wondering."

She kissed him again, her tongue probing this time.

He matched her kiss and they stood together, locked in each other's arms until he asked, "We're okay then? Not scared of me or anything?"

~ * ~

She glanced at the clock in the kitchen. They'd slept after making love and it was almost two o'clock. Her heart warmed with the memory. He'd been so upset he hadn't wanted to at first, but she'd seduced him, for real this time, and she'd loved every minute of it. She turned on the radio, found a classical station playing soft music, and swirled around the kitchen in a haze of quiet contentment.

The sound of the shower reached her. It was a good time to call Molly, before Paul came into the kitchen and had to listen as she argued for him.

"Hi," she said when Molly picked up.

"You turned off the phone. I've been trying to call you."

"I'm fine Molly. Paul explained everything."

"And you believe him of course," Molly snapped sarcastically.

"He admitted the article was about him while you were here last night. Remember? And yes, I believe him."

"What's the story then?"

Anne paused, considering.

"I don't think I should tell you. Not without his permission anyway."

"Come on."

"No. It was very painful for him. When he says it's all right, then."

"You're not going to tell me?"

"Just one thing. He sued everybody involved and won. That's all."

"So, he was the victim of some big evil conspiracy?"

"He'll tell you when he's ready. He's getting out of the shower now. I'm fine, that's all. I'll talk to you later."

Anne dropped the phone on the counter and stared out the window. Her life was changing so fast. Was she going to lose Molly in all this? Refusing to tell her something, she'd never done that before. And Molly sounded so snippy. She turned. Paul stood by the table, watching her.

"Thanks," he said quietly. "I won't tell her about Carol, but you can. She probably won't leave you alone until she hears it all."

Later, sunlight streaming into the garden as they weeded together, she asked, "What should I do about Graham?"

"He's a con-man."

"He was very sweet until, well..."

"He's a jerk."

She stared at him then, amazed at the possibility that occurred to her. "Are you mad about the Times article or jealous?"

"Why would I be jealous?" he asked, yanking a weed out of the ground, avoiding her eyes.

"You are jealous," she said, incredulous.

"He was trying to seduce you."

"Well, so what? A little flattery feels nice sometimes." She laughed. "You're silly. He's no threat to you. He just wants my paintings."

"I suppose."

She nodded. "You haven't forgiven him either, have you?"

"No, but don't let that get in the way."

"You still think I should let him sell my paintings?"

He shrugged. "You're a very good artist. Take advantage of his interest."

"You still don't like him though."

"Liking has no bearing on it. He knows his stuff. Go for it."

"All right. I'm going to do it."

"Good."

She pulled a weed and moved to his side, making sure their hips touched. He glanced up at her and winked. She touched his hair, smoothed down an unruly strand and melted into happiness. He was a good man and he was her man. She still had things to master and to learn, but she would with him at her side.

"Let's go to his gallery. It'll be part of my program. You know, getting out."

He sent her a startled look.

"I'll be in Newport, on the street and in his shop," she added.

"You'll wander around the city?"

"Not that much. Just, we could go and see the place."

"Yes, and the door will close and you'll be alone with people you know. That's not much different from an early morning walk on the beach."

"I'm not ready for more than that," she said, shocked at his insensitivity. He was supposed to be encouraging, wasn't he? "Maybe I'll go to the beach again before I do anything else."

He nodded. "The gallery or a restaurant after that?"

"Maybe. Now kiss me, silly."

He grinned. "I have to teach you a few things yet. One is, you never call a man silly. That's a gross insult."

"Really? What should I call you then, a fool?"

"That's a little better. We can be jerks, that's best."

"All right then. Kiss me, you jerk."

~ * ~

The following morning she left the bed as a lightening sky set the stage for the sun's appearance. Dressed in robe and pajamas, filling the coffee maker, she wished the first sunlight could reach the tree shrouded kitchen windows. She hadn't seen a sunrise all summer. With a laugh, she realized today would be the change of that if she kept to her plan.

Today would be the day. Leaving early, she'd stay long enough to meet someone. Lots of people if she were going to change herself.

Lots of people. The thought stuck in her head, hammering, pervasive. Yet, despite the anxiety she felt, there was a touch of anticipation too. She'd take her paints. Who knew, she might meet no one. Paul wouldn't like that. She laughed, thinking she could tell him she met scads of people even if she didn't.

A lie. It surprised her, how easy it came. Her mother used to do that with Father, about the booze, always. He did as well, she was sure. The woman, whoever she was, the one he claimed he didn't have when Mother challenged him.

A lie to Paul was not the thing. Not like this, important, outright. No, whatever happened, he'd hear it all. There might be July tourists, but the beach didn't get much play, so who knew, perhaps she'd just paint. Why not?

She took one more sip of her coffee and hurried to dress. Paul slept on, curled like a baby in the rumpled bed. "I love you, you silly. Graham White! Oh my! He's no competition for you, my love."

Lacking portable easel and travel box, she grabbed plastic bags from the kitchen and feverishly stuffed them with paint tubes and brushes. She dumped the dregs of coffee and hurried to the car. It struggled to life, protesting the early morning disruption of its rest.

"Come on. Come on," she said, as if it were alive. "Hurry up. The sun will be up any minute."

The engine coughed, then caught and ran unevenly. It stalled. "Come on now, cooperate." She started it again, then backed out and left the garage open as she headed down the drive. A left turn took her toward the lighthouse and a few minutes later the shoreline came in sight.

The limb of the sun was just peeking above the horizon, and color blossomed in the sky over a deserted beach. She couldn't remember the last time she watched a summer sunrise. Light and color filled her soul with golden liquid warmth. She hugged herself as the light danced in front of her, trimming the clouds with golden edges that faded to white cotton as sunrise became morning.

She ignored her paints. This was to see and feel, to savor like fine chocolate or good wine.

She strolled the beach, talking to herself, squishing the sand in her toes, relishing the roar of surf and cries of birds wheeling and diving. A tinge of melancholy struck her with the thought of so many lost years. That had been her choice though. It hadn't been squandered, was in fact quite satisfactory in its way. She'd seen the news and happiness seemed a rare commodity to her way of thinking.

Two figures appeared in the distance, moving along the beach. A man and a woman, heavy-set, jogging slowly in the shallow water. She watched them approach and continued walking, fascinated by their obvious effort. Were they trying to lose weight? She wondered if they were as unhappy with themselves as she had been sometimes. She smiled as they passed and smiled inside, feeling a unique kinship, a first in her experience. Savoring the sentiment, she turned back to the car, pleased that she'd come here and succeeded. Instead of the car, she turned to the lighthouse, determined to find other early morning walkers.

Molly's Buick was rolling down the drive when she returned home. Anne stopped to let her pass, then started up, knowing from the frantic hand signals behind the Buick's windshield Molly would turn around and follow.

Paul stood in front of the garage when she pulled up, his face set in those hard lines she'd seen two nights ago. She stared at him, wondering if they had tried to kill each other while she was gone. He didn't appear bloody or bruised, but judging by the look on his face, Molly hadn't come to make peace.

"Where were you? I show up and find the garage door wide open and Paul claiming he has no idea where you are. You scared the wits out of me!" Molly cried as she brought the Buick to a stop.

Anne laughed. "I went to the beach." She grinned at Paul. "I met people, a half dozen at least. I was going to paint, but I just wandered around instead." She turned back to Molly. "I didn't expect you this morning."

"I have a new listing to check out. I brought donuts and coffee, but the coffee's cold by now. You went to the beach? When, in the middle of the night?"

"No, I wanted to see the sun come up. You're a grump this morning!"

"You had me worried! Your car is gone and the garage is open. What do you expect?"

While Molly ranted, Paul simply stared at her.

Anne watched his face. Something had happened with Molly while she was gone. He smiled for her, but only briefly. His eyes were dark with anger. She had to fix this, get them back to being civil with each other.

"Sit down, Molly. I need a donut or I'll die of starvation. Tell me about your new listing."

"It's a half mile up the road. You know the big A-frame they built two years ago? They're moving to Texas. What do you mean, you met enough people?"

"That's a nice house. I wouldn't mind living there. The windows on the A-frame side would give good light for a studio."

Molly shook her head. "They want a million for it, but it only has an acre of land." She threw a cautious glance at Paul, hesitated, and said, "Speaking of studios, what about your paintings?"

"What about them?"

"You do remember Graham wants to represent you?"

"I can't make up my mind. I think I'll keep them."

"He'll be disappointed."

"He'll survive," Paul growled.

Molly looked away, avoiding his eyes. "Would you hold off on a final decision? For me?"

Anne shrugged. "For you, all right, but don't get your hopes up."

"Okay. Now, what about the beach?"

"I went there to see people and stayed until I did."

"Are you going to tell us about it?"

"No. It's complicated, but I actually enjoyed myself." And Paul deserved to hear first.

"Good," Paul said. "Think you're ready for lunch now?"

"It's barely ten-thirty," Molly cried.

"Yes, tomorrow, or the day after." Anne watched Paul's face for reaction, but he just smiled. "Is that all right?"

"Absolutely."

"What are you talking about?" Molly demanded, looking annoyed.

"Going out to lunch," Paul said.

"In a restaurant? Really?"

"Yes." Anne hesitated. Paul looked a little more relaxed than he had when she first drove in, but should she try to get them talking about Molly's accusations? She shivered. It was probably not the best time, but she could do one thing that might change the situation. "I'm going to give you a painting for Graham."

"Oh, that's good. He'll be pleased."

"It was Paul's thought. He's been urging me to go ahead."

Molly's smile turned a bit crooked, a bit forced Anne thought, but she turned to acknowledge Paul.

"That's wonderful, thank you."

Paul nodded silently.

After watching Molly drive off, she slipped her arm inside of his as they turned toward the house. "What happened while I was gone?"

He bent his head and kissed her. "Nice try. Nice work too."

"What?"

"Giving me credit for offering Graham a painting. And the visit to the beach."

She poked him in the ribs. "You didn't answer my question."

"Determined aren't you? She showed up about ten minutes before you got home. Freaked when I said you were gone. Practically accused me of murdering you."

"Oh dear, I'm sorry."

"She took off, either to look for you or get away from me. Whipped out her cell phone as she got in the car. I'm surprised the cops haven't come roaring up the drive."

Anne sighed. "What am I going to do? She's acting crazy. She doesn't mean it."

He touched a finger to her cheek. "Talk to her. I'll come too if you want."

"I couldn't put you through that," she whispered, picturing Molly tearing into him as he relived the pain of Carol's death again. "Let's go inside. I'm going to call her right now."

"You want me to take off so you can see her here?"

She stuck her chin out provocatively, giggling a little. "She's going to meet me at the beach. And bring lunch for both of us."

"No fast food. Make her stop at the market and get you something good."

"I will. And a couple of beers. Or a bottle of expensive wine."

He kissed her, his eyes crinkling at the corners. "I'm glad you're on my side."

~ * ~

"We're meeting for lunch today. One o'clock at the lighthouse. You're buying," Anne said, as soon as Molly answered her cell.

"What? Why?"

"I won't have the most important people in my life at each other's throats. Bring a good lunch. I'm hungry. Not fast food either. And a bottle of wine."

"I...."

"Good wine, a white. I'll bring glasses and a cloth. We're eating on the beach"

Paul grinned at her as she hung up.

"Now I need a snack to hold me over," she said triumphantly. "And I want the rest of the story."

"The what?"

"The rest. How you got out of jail, the lawsuit, all of that. Before I meet Molly."

~ * ~

She parked the Ford at five to one, got out and set up a tablecloth on the sand. Two fishermen a good way down the beach caught her eye. As one of them made a cast, her pony tail flew wide. The other person was shorter, smaller, and Anne wondered whether she was seeing two women or a mother and child.

"Well, you're certainly bossy today," Molly said behind her.

She turned with a grin. "Never mind. Sit down and listen."

"You're going to give me Paul's version of things?"

"Just listen, please." She began as Paul had, with the discovery of Carol's cancer. Between bites of shrimp and macaroni salad, and sips of an excellent Sauvignon Blanc, she related the story of Paul's arrest and Carol's death, cutting Molly off every time she tried to interrupt.

"He was in jail two days. They wouldn't give him bail until his wife died and even then he almost missed the funeral," Anne said.

Molly stared out at the breakers. Frowning for the moment, she silently refilled her glass.

"Paul sued everybody. He hired an investigator and discovered the Hospice people should have known that nurse was crazy. They had a report from another family, but ignored it, supposedly because they were short of nurses. That was after Paul's lawyer subpoenaed their records."

"So he sued and won?"

"Yes. Hospice had to pay and so did the county. They knew they didn't have a real case, but they went ahead anyway."

"I can't believe that part."

"Paul has all the paperwork from the court and everything. He'll let you read it if you'd like to."

"Have you seen it?"

"No. He has it at home."

"Tell him you want to see it. You can't just take his word for this."

"Molly, you had to see his face when he talked about it."

"He could be a very good actor."

Anne groaned. "He wasn't acting. If you want to see the paperwork, ask him for it."

Molly sighed. "I will. How much money did he get?"

"Almost a million dollars."

"He really got his pound of flesh."

"You could say that, but it was a poor bargain."

"You believe all this. Con-men are good liars you know."

Blood surged into Anne's face. She struggled to control her temper. "First he's a murderer and now he's a con-man? What's next Molly? A rapist? Kidnapper? You owe him an apology."

Molly stared at her and sighed. "What's happening to us? We never argue."

Anne suddenly noticed the waves crashing on the beach and the smell of dead weed on the sand, the smell of the sea. They never argued before Paul. Before she began to change.

"I don't know. It's not a big deal. Everybody argues sometime."

Molly gave her a wry smile. "I hate apologizing. How about I give him a bottle of wine, or scotch or something?"

"Just tell him you made a mistake."

"Booze is easier."

"Chianti then. A good one."

"I still want to see the proof."

~ TWENTY-FOUR ~

She woke up early with a tense knot in her stomach, unable to sleep any longer. Getting out of bed without waking Paul was a new skill, but she managed it quite well. Minutes later, she was dressed and outside. Cool damp air met her at the door, but she didn't need a sweater. She headed off through the woods, walking fast. Wet brush, heavy with morning dew, soaked her sneakers. The walking didn't help.

A small trickle of a stream wandered along the back border of the property, separating her land from the rest of the world. She plopped down on a flat rock, took off the wet sneakers, and stuck her feet in the water. The sudden chill grabbed her attention momentarily, but she couldn't escape the day ahead. There was a world across that bit of water she didn't want to face, but today at noon she would. She couldn't stay home anymore. Returning to her old life wasn't going to work.

Paul had been nothing but supportive, but she'd only done the easy trips so far. The quiet beach, so empty, with just a few people there. Not everyone sent her the averted glances or embarrassed smiles when they saw her empty arm, but in a crowd some would. She hated that, yet here she was having promised to go out to lunch with him. Paul was patient, but he wouldn't wait forever.

She wiped her feet and slipped the sneakers on. The return to the house went slowly, a stall forever were it up to her. He had finished breakfast when she got there, nine o'clock come and gone.

"Where have you been?" he asked.

"Out walking."

"Everything okay?"

"Yes." She poured a glass of juice and dropped bread into the toaster. "I've been wondering if I should wear my prosthesis. If we go to an air conditioned restaurant I can wear long sleeves over it."

"I'm sure the restaurants around here are air conditioned."

Big help that was. "Should I wear it?"

"You should do whatever's most comfortable for you."

"It's as comfortable to wear it as to leave it off."

"I meant emotionally, not physically."

She made a face. That was what she wanted his help with, the emotional side of it. Oblivious, that was him.

"We have those two places I checked out. Angelo's, and Fletcher's English Pub. Fletcher's was less crowded when we drove by, judging by the parking lot. We'll go there," he said.

"Angelo's looked dark and private."

"Probably, but we'll go to Fletcher's."

"All right," she said, growing more nervous, but not prepared to argue. "What should I wear?"

"Slacks or a skirt will be fine. You can wear one of my shirts if you don't have a long sleeved blouse."

"I have one or two, thanks."

She picked out a pair of slacks and a blouse Molly had bought her recently. Her wardrobe was limited and even included clothes from her high school days, unused in many years. Maybe it was time to get rid of them, along with some of the memories she still carried around like an old sack. She'd spent only a couple of weeks in school after the arm healed. People had tried to be nice, but their sympathy and stares and whispers behind her back had been too much. Whispers she could hear, about the accident and her drunken mother and her arm. She'd hated it.

When she dropped out, her parents were upset, but she would not go back. What a miserable time that was. She sighed. Ancient history. She wanted long sleeves today. No prosthesis.

Fletcher's was small, rustic, with dim lighting and empty tables, and a popcorn machine jammed into one corner. Antique license plates adorned the ceiling. A waiter dropped a bowl of popcorn and two menus in front of them and the next thing Anne knew she was slipping popcorn into her mouth.

They ordered beer. She tried to focus on the menu as Paul selected chowder and a burger. She gave up and ordered the same.

"How are we doing?"

"All right I suppose," she said, pretending to be calm.

"I knew you'd be okay."

"Paul, we just got here."

He nodded. "Sorry. What do you think might happen?"

"What do you mean?"

"Do you know what you're afraid of? Specifically, I mean."

"Don't ask me that. Look at the old license plates on the ceiling. There's one from nineteen thirty-six."

He glanced around the room. "Nineteen thirty-two and from Iowa no less. I wonder how that got here."

"There's a Massachusetts nineteen twenty-seven plate. I think that's the oldest one they have."

"That's just because you found it. I haven't given up yet."

She laughed, suddenly feeling happy. "I like this place. It's Victorian, with that stained glass window by the bar and the spittoons in the corners."

"I bet they stole that window from a church."

The waiter set his tray on the next table. "Two chowders, two burgers. Anything else I can get you?"

"Do you usually serve the soup with the main course?" Paul asked.

"No sir. The chef was a little too fast for me today. Would you like me to take the burgers back?"

She touched Paul's hand. A confrontation was the last thing she wanted just then.

"Never mind. We'll eat them together," he said.

The waiter smiled and departed before Paul could change his mind.

"Thank you," she said softly, and started on her burger.

"I wouldn't have pushed it. I just wanted him to know he should pay more attention."

"Let's forget it. What should we do later?"

He smiled. "How about trying a movie or sailing?"

"Not today please. Maybe I'll go sailing with you someday."

"My arm is pretty well healed. We can go whenever you're ready."

"Right now, I want to eat, so no more conversation for a while please."

He grinned at her and spooned some soup into his mouth.

Despite her admonition, they ate and chatted until she felt nature calling. "I need to use the ladies room."

She glanced around, searching the room for she knew not what. Drawing in a deep breath, she stood and began to move her legs, feeling as if she were in a cloud, floating, vulnerable, unable to feel the floor.

As she threaded her way between the tables, a man suddenly stood up in front of her.

Instinctively, both arms went out to avoid crashing into him, her purse swinging wildly, almost hitting the man's back. Her heart seemed to jump from her chest and she fought to breathe. Steady, hold on, don't move, they won't notice you, she told herself. Breathe, just breathe.

The rest of his party stood as he counted out cash for the bill. Stomach churning, she stood there while the family, if that was what they were, collected themselves and finally left. Then she scooted to the ladies room, almost running. Stupid people. Totally impolite. They'd ignored her, as if she weren't even there. Thank goodness for that, actually.

Dreading the walk back to the table, she washed and re-washed her hand, fussed with her hair, wiped off her lipstick, applied it again, all to delay. If they both had cell phones, she would have called and told Paul to meet her at the car. But she didn't have one, so she sucked in a breath and started back to the table.

Deep in conversation, or into their menus, new patrons had arrived. They ignored her and she could breathe again by the time she reached Paul. She could be pleased that the stupid man didn't notice her. He and his family had to have known she was there, but impolite, not a one had moved or acknowledged her presence. She could be invisible, or at least not notable, and so too was her hand. A revelation, that.

Paul gave her a smile. "I thought you got lost. I ordered coffee and carrot cake for us."

She nodded, and he took her hand in his and stroked her fingers as the waiter walked by.

"I'm glad we did this today. I know it's hard for you. I love you."

"I love you, too," she replied. She felt calmer, the panic just a little nudge now. "I wouldn't do this every day of the week, but it's not terrible."

"I'm glad. I hoped you'd enjoy it."

"It isn't fun exactly, but it hasn't been overwhelming."

"Good. We'll have to celebrate when we get home."

"Celebrations can wait until outings like this are easy. I'm not exactly happy, relaxed, or romantic right now." Was that all he could think of?

"I'm sorry. I guess I'm carried away with my own excitement. What do you want to do?"

"I'm undecided between taking a nap and settling down on the patio with a good book," she said, oozing sarcasm.

"It's been harder than I thought, hasn't it?"

"It's no cause for celebrating."

"Okay. I'm glad you tried. Next time will be better."

He took a last gulp of coffee and signaled for the bill. They stood to leave, and he slid his hand around her stump as they walked to the door. That was nice, but it didn't make up for anything. Next time would be better? Pushy man.

~ TWENTY-FIVE ~

Insensitive, selfish man. She labeled him so despite his gesture, but dropped the harsh opinion by the time they reached home, concluding finally that men were just different, since he'd otherwise been sweet all day. With that change came another, pride in her accomplishment, pleasure even, remembering their quest to find the oldest license plate.

The next day she decided to go somewhere again.

"We could go see Graham's gallery and leave him a painting," he said.

"You're all right with that?"

He shrugged. "You said Molly owes me a bottle of booze. I'll forgive Graham if he sells your paintings."

She snuggled against his chest. "Should we go this morning?"

"You really mean it?"

"There's always a first time."

"You'll be glad you did."

"I think I've heard that before. I'll give you one thing, you're persistent. A bad influence too, Mister Breland."

"Corrupting you all over the place, I know." He brushed his lips against her hair. "How many paintings should we take him?"

"I said it. One."

"You're amazing."

"Why? I just made up my mind to do it and I will."

Paul found a place to park a block from the gallery. A long block. He turned off the engine and sat for a moment, watching her.

"Ready?"

She glanced around, feeling a ball of tension in her stomach. A couple their age walked by, the woman talking, the man ignoring her. A young couple, obviously lovers, passed in the opposite direction.

Anne opened the door and slid out of the car, forcing a smile for Paul's benefit. Preoccupied with getting her painting out of the back seat, he missed it.

"Let me carry it," she said, and grabbed the painting from him, holding it in front of her stump. All right, so she looked ridiculous holding it that way. She switched to holding it like anyone else would. Who cared if anyone noticed.

He slipped his arm around her waist and squeezed. "Love you," he whispered.

She felt disappointed with the gallery, expecting she knew not what. Larger than she'd imagined, ornately decorated, it was close to the Newport waterfront attractions. Two paintings hung in prominent positions near the entrance and others occupied the outer walls, but much of the space remained barren.

Graham glanced up as they entered and did a double take. Excitement flared in his eyes for a second, but quickly gave way to a look of suspicion directed at Paul.

"Thought we'd stop in to see the place," Paul said amiably.

"Great. Welcome," Graham said, still regarding Paul with hooded eyes. He seemed to make a decision, then turned to Anne with a smile. "Let me show you the gallery."

He began to guide her past the art, making comments about the other artists.

Silently, as if he were completely unconcerned, Paul followed.

"Many of these people do mediocre work, my dear. Once I'm fully established here, I'll be replacing them with artists like yourself, talented people whose work will one day be recognized."

She stared at him then, wondering if he was just out and out arrogant or strictly a con-man as Paul had labeled him. Inclined to believe the former, she wondered what he really thought of her paintings.

Paul reacted with a scowl when she glanced at him, but Graham went right on, as if he'd said nothing more than 'How are you today?'

"There's a good deal of blank wall here yet. How many paintings will you give me?"

"Just this one."

"Oh, I thought you'd decided to offer your work. I think you'll have great success."

"I know, you've said that."

"Your paintings could bring you a good deal of money."

"How much?" Paul asked.

"Three thousand, I'd say for this one."

"That seems like a lot," Anne said, staring at the painting.

"That isn't expensive at all. When you're established we'll charge considerably more. What are you working on at the moment?"

"I haven't painted much recently. Nothing serious anyway."

"I'd like to see anything you do. Even sketches can be valuable."

"Well, when I finish something."

"People will buy your paintings, Anne. Your style and skill and subject matter are all excellent, especially in this market. Once you have a name, they'll sell very well. You want to be ready to take advantage of that."

"Thank you, no. I just wanted to see if one painting would sell," Anne said.

Graham wrapped an arm around her shoulders and smiled. "You can be a very prominent artist one day. You'll see. I know my business."

She twisted away. "We have to go now. I'll be in touch."

~ * ~

Dan's battered van, passenger door ajar, sat parked in front of the open garage as Paul halted the Toyota in the gravel. The old man emerged from the garage and stood, hands on hips, waiting as they climbed from the car.

"Thought I missed you this morning. Out to the beach again?"

"Newport," Paul said.

"Hey great. Annie, you're getting to be a world traveler. Good, good."

"Not quite Dan, but thanks for the thought."

"What's in Newport? A fun trip?"

"We took one of her paintings to a gallery over there," Paul said. "Molly's friend is going to sell it."

"That Graham guy? You think that girl will settle down this time?"

Anne shrugged. "I don't know Dan. I don't know what they're doing."

"Well, I hope she finally has a good guy. Hey, I brought Louie down. Cost me a buck to buy it back, so you better fix it." He grinned, and then went on. "Big investment right? The insurance guy laughed when I told him you'd fix it. Said if you do, he wants to meet you."

"I will," she said quietly. "Where is it?"

"One box inside, in the back corner, one still in the van. I'll get it."

"We'll put them right in the shop," Anne said and drew keys from her purse.

Paul waited for Dan, unable to help. Both boxes were heavy and awkward for a man barely recovered from a broken arm. By the time Dan transferred the second box from van to shop, Anne was pulling parts from the first one. Junk it all seemed to Paul, but she was excited, and smashed legs and arms were soon piled on the bench.

"You'll need to replace these legs," Dan said, picking up a splintered piece.

"No. I can fix it."

"It's got a million jagged ends," Paul said.

"I can fix it," she said again.

"I don't see how," he insisted.

As though dealing with a child, she sighed. "I'll chip away the ragged ends until I can get the pieces in a box the same length as the good leg. Then I'll glue and wedge them in the box until the glue dries. Then I'll inject epoxy to fill the gaps. After that, I'll drill a long hole in the end and insert a metal rod for strength. And then I'll refinish the surface."

"Wouldn't new legs be easier?" Dan asked. "I'll pay for them."

"It's not the money. There won't be any substitute legs or arms on this chair." Her eyes met Dan's surprised stare, then quickly returned to the wreckage.

He carefully placed the damaged leg on the bench. "Let me pay for your time at least."

"No, Dan. I said I'd fix it and I will. But you can't pay me. It's a gift. It's the least I can do."

The old man planted a loud kiss on her cheek. "You are a doll, my girl. Does this young fellow understand how lucky he is?"

She grinned. "I doubt it."

"What was that? Young fellow? Who's lucky?" asked Paul, with a smile of his own.

"Time for me to go. Gracie probably figures I ran off with some young blonde." The old man grinned at Paul. "I know, fat chance. See you two."

~ * ~

With Dan gone, he offered to help with Louie.

"I can do some of what you described. The finishing may take skill, but some of the other stuff doesn't."

"I know. I appreciate the offer."

"But you'd rather do it alone."

"I suppose you can help a little."

"What are you going to do about Graham?"

"Nothing. I've done it."

"He's not going to be happy with only one painting."

She gave him a quizzical look. "It doesn't matter. That's all I'm going to give him. He owes you an apology and he didn't say a word today."

"The man's embarrassed."

"I think he's listening to Molly. They still think they're right about you."

"Their loss," Paul said cryptically.

Anne shook her head. "It's not right. Molly's being a pain for no reason. I told her to apologize, but she's stubborn."

He nodded, but said nothing. She was sure he felt insulted, sure Molly's attitude bothered him, but he was being amazingly patient about it and she felt bad for him. And annoyed with Molly. She'd call her tomorrow and give her the devil.

"So, are you going to start on the chair today?"

Anne laughed. He was so sweet, letting her friend's crappy attitude go and worrying about what she was doing. "We'll start now. I need a sturdy box to hold the pieces securely in place. You can help with that.

With Paul beside her, she started on the damaged legs. Trimming and matching broken ends occupied the rest of that day and most of the next. They carefully scratched away ragged tips of broken ends, tried the fit and repeated the process until pieces could be brought together with some degree of overlap and matching. He built the box and wedges she asked for and they made the first attempt to glue up a leg the next morning. As soon as the pieces were in the box with wedges set, she picked up another leg.

"We need a break," he said.

"We're doing fine."

"No, we're not. We worked until nine o'clock last night. What's the hurry?"

She played with the pieces of a second leg, pressing one part down on the bench and twisting another piece to fit them together.

He took her hand and held it. "Enough. I want to go to a movie. Or out to lunch. Or both."

She tried to pull away. "Let go."

"Anne, what's wrong here? What's the big rush?"

She stopped pulling and he relaxed. She stroked the broken leg with her stub, in a slow, silent caress.

"What is it?" he asked.

"I want to fix it."

"That's great, but you don't have to kill yourself over it. I don't understand the hurry."

She placed the leg on the table and crossed her arms. "I want it back together, that's all."

He wrapped her in a hug. "We'll do it. That first leg is the test. If we save that one, we can save the rest."

She leaned against his chest and silently hugged him in return, her breathing almost even.

"Your fix is going to work. You'll see. But let's give that glue a chance to dry and take a break before we do more."

"What do you want to do?"

"A movie? I'll call and see what's playing."

"I have a better idea. Let's try to find a place that sells really old upholstery fabric."

"We're supposed to be leaving the chair alone for a while."

"I know, but we won't be physically working on it. I wonder how to find a place like that."

"You don't want to know."

"Why? Where?"

"Boston, I expect. There can't be many restorers around here. If we leave now we can have a late lunch in the city and be back before dark."

"Boston? You want me to walk around in a city?"

"It's your idea. That's where I'd go."

"All right then, if you say so."

"Are you sure you're up to it?"

She smiled and cocked her head, like a small child trying to charm a parent, which was what she intended to do.

"I think so. Won't that be special? My first trip to Boston."

"This is not good," he said.

"Why not? It's what you want me to do isn't it?"

"Yes, but not because you're going crazy over a chair."

"I'm not crazy. It's a compromise."

"You won't get scared will you? There won't be any place to run to."

"Paul, I'm not a baby."

"I know. I worry about you, that's all."

"You're afraid I'll quit, that I'll stay home and hide again." A headshake was his only reply and she went on, feeling a touch of triumph, "You have a lot to learn about me, my love."

~ TWENTY-SIX ~

Boston grew ever nearer, and he kept glancing over at her, worried, she could tell.

"Relax Paul. I'll be all right."

"Unclench your hand then, before you get a cramp."

He was right. Her knuckles were bone white, the skin stretched tight. She straightened her fingers, flexed them a bit.

"So I'm a little anxious. I'll be fine."

She had no reason to challenge him really, but he worried too much, about her anyway. It annoyed her sometimes, but she knew it meant he cared. Her friends all worried too darn much, but with him it was different. Much more intense, more personal?

He didn't understand. She wasn't sick, just unaccustomed to going out. More comfortable with friends than strangers. She could do what she wanted, always had really. Boston was just another adjustment in her new life.

She'd lived there once, in Jamaica Plain. They had family there, on her father's side. Not Mother, her family came from Providence. She had to be dead of the drink by now. So stupid. Seventy-eight now if she were still alive. Such a waste.

Paul said he knew where to find some antique shops, but he wanted her to see the sights, like a tourist, as if she'd never left the house when she was young.

Her memories didn't need to be revisited. He said Quincy Market was the place to go, but Hannah had taken her to the docks, wharves she called them, all those years ago and Anne wasn't interested in some yuppie version. Back then they had reminded Hannah of the Liverpool streets she worked as a wagon driver of all things. Anne preferred to remember them that way, thank you.

Paul found a shop and then a parking lot and they had to walk a bit. That was quite all right, she was ready.

"Just take it easy and ignore people. They'll ignore you," he said.

"I'm fine." Why couldn't he get that through his head?

"You can do this. Just tell yourself these people can all drop dead."

"That isn't nice."

"So? Use what works. They're all rotten people, dirty no good so-and-so's and I have a gun to shoot them if they laugh."

"Don't tease about killing people," she whispered.

"Crap. Sorry," he said, a scowl creasing his forehead.

She touched his hand. "I'm sorry. I know you didn't mean anything by that."

"Yeah, but I'm labeled now. Every time someone mentions killing you're going to look at me."

She poked his arm, trying for levity. "No, I'm going to think of Molly and get mad."

He gave her one of his silly grins. "Great idea."

Her heart melted and she laughed as he turned her toward a shop. Burnham's Antiques.

"See, we found one, and you're all in one piece," he said and he was right. They'd walked a good block and a half and she felt no tension at all. She'd even been calm when they left the car, until he brought up the subject of walking. And killing.

"You wouldn't do anything if someone laughed, would you?"

"I might snarl, but I wouldn't commit violence." He hesitated and then smiling, added, "Not unless thoroughly provoked."

She liked his teasing. This would be a fine Boston day with him beside her. "You are a darling man."

"I keep telling you that."

They visited other shops and made inquiries, and came away with the names of two restorers. One old man invited her to visit his shop when they called. Carl Traeger his name was, and he made himself quite helpful, even selling her, at a reasonable price, a piece of old fabric for Louie's seat and back, then directing her to a supplier who sold truly antique items. Mister Traeger seemed impressed with what she was trying to do and approved her methods. She couldn't help giving Paul a triumphant grin.

"The man said I can do it," she told him.

"Are you surprised?"

"No, why?"

"Well, you've sounded so sure you'd fix the old thing, I just thought you never had a doubt."

She laughed. "I'm still not completely certain."

"You sure fooled me."

"I guess I'm good at that. It's almost three o'clock. Shall we go home now?"

He cocked his head at her, looking very serious. "Wouldn't you like to check out the old neighborhood?"

She didn't like the question. He'd asked before and she'd refused him once. They'd done enough for one day. "I like my memories as they are."

"You just want to go home?"

"Yes please."

~ TWENTY-SEVEN ~

Paul still thought they could have done more in the city, she could tell that from his frowning face. She felt her temper rise for a moment, but the joy of the day overrode the blip of irritation and she relished her success. Even the two skateboarding boys who almost bowled her over on Boylston Street had left her laughing. Success in dealing with the busy streets, approval of her plans for Louie by the experts, everything warmed her soul. It had been a good day.

When they reached home, she dashed to the workshop to match Mister Traeger's bit of fabric against Louie's original material.

"Look how close the color is," she cried.

"That's good," he said, but then suggested the chair should wait until they completed the music cabinet. The latter had been languishing half finished in the corner. She brushed the words aside, but he persisted. "Dan's waiting for that, not the chair."

"He wants Louie back. Besides, I might buy the cabinet for myself."

"The cabinet is business, regardless. You should get it done."

"You are so bossy," she snapped, but conceded the point. "Are you going to help?"

"We're near the end, aren't we? I don't have the skill for finishing."

"I'll show you."

~ * ~

A week later, she had talked Paul through the restoration of the cabinet and joined his efforts on the French polish, with the repeated hand rubbing that finish required. He griped about his aching wrists and elbows, having done far more polishing than he deemed necessary, but the wood glowed as only fine cabinetry could.

"I'll buy it for you," he said with a grin.

"That isn't right. You did a lot of the work."

"Makes no difference."

~ * ~

They met Dan at the shop to make the deal. Anne had bought her restorations before and the old man always played with her about it. He couldn't pay full price for such poor work, the piece was still extremely valuable, such threats and more he spouted with great seriousness.

Warned, Paul played along, and laughing, Dan said, "What am I going to do with these two, Gracie? She has him in the game now."

"You could make it a gift," Grace said.

"Just what I need, a helpful woman. How's a hundred plus Anne's bill sound?" the old man said to Paul.

"Aren't you giving it to us at that price?"

"My final offer, take it or leave it."

Anne laughed. "It's a deal."

"One condition. We'll be down your way this week. I want to see it."

"Certainly," Anne said. "What's down our way?"

"Wickford. We're leasing a new shop there. We start Wednesday."

"You're going ahead with a move?" Paul said.

"I know, we're crazy at our age, but this neighborhood is a sad place now. We've hired Millie, my niece. She's off to the bank at the moment. Stay a while and meet her," Grace said.

"We're going to give her the business when we retire," Dan said.

"Does she know she has to wait a hundred years?" Anne asked with a smirk.

"Oh no dear, only fifty," Grace said. "We promised."

"How can we help?" Anne asked.

"That isn't necessary. With Millie's help we'll get it done."

"You agreed to let us paint or something," Paul said.

"I know. Thank you. We have permission to get in early. Cleaning day and painting tomorrow. You're more than welcome," Dan said.

~ * ~

"Thank you, love," Anne said when they were alone, "You didn't need to volunteer yourself."

"Hey, we're all friends I hope. Besides, it'll be fun. All that polishing has fixed my arm right up," Paul replied.

She smiled. He was right. Far more relaxed about going out now, she looked forward to this new event, one more in the path she was on. It was taking unexpected turns, this path, most of them quite pleasant. What would come next, a week from now, a month? A touch of excitement tickled her belly. Whatever came would be just fine.

~ * ~

Paul was pleased to help, to be included as if he were part of a family of friends. His injuries had healed nicely, but despite his optimism and all that polishing, his strength hadn't come back completely. He felt it if he used the arm too much, but he joined Dan and Millie in Providence each morning, wrapping, packing, filling cartons, loading his Toyota, Dan's van and the old truck. Furniture in the van and truck, boxes, lamps and assorted goods in the car.

By eleven or noon they'd load up and caravan together to Wickford. Unloading the vehicles, they'd leave the work of unpacking to Anne and Grace and make another run to Providence each afternoon. It took four days to empty the Providence shop, and the new shop remained chaotic and unorganized, with unpacking still undone, despite the best efforts of the two women. Paul would have junked a great deal of what they moved, but Dan insisted it all had to go.

"We're going to have a sale when we open," Dan said when he raised a question. "We'll make new people aware of the shop by holding it in Wickford."

Paul's arm and shoulder throbbed near the week's end, but both Dan and Grace soldiered on. Comfortable with the old man after all their work together, Paul commented on his endurance.

"Nice of you to say, but I'm beat too," Dan said.

"Why?"

"I know. Why are we doing this? It's Millie, see. The girl wouldn't be safe in the old neighborhood. We couldn't have her working there. I always worried about leaving Gracie alone."

The highlight of the week had nothing to do with the work. It came when the mailman appeared in the new shop for the second time. At five to noon, the new brass bell on the front door tinkled and he walked in carrying a handful of mail. Rushing to receive it, Millie upset a table, and smashed the ornate little china lamp so recently deposited on it by none other than herself.

The young mailman, Harry by name, dashed to her aid and stopped, apparently made quite awkward by the sudden nearness of her. There followed a polite exchange between the two, consisting of such brilliance as "Are you okay," "Oh yes," "You broke the lamp," "I know", "Will you have to pay for it?", "Oh no, my uncle will forgive me."

That last drew a snort from a watching Dan, but Grace shushed him with a soft punch to the arm.

Young Harry offered the envelopes he held with an eloquent, "I have to go now," which drew a blushing, "Thank you, bye," from Millie. He backed away, bumped another table, but caught it, narrowly missing a second disaster. With a red-faced, "Bye," he was gone.

The girl turned, noticed the watchers in the store, and said, "What?"

To which Dan said simply, "Nice young guy isn't he? Remind me to get some more insurance, Gracie."

It was an interplay unlike any Anne had ever seen. She squeezed Paul's arm. "Wasn't that adorable?"

"Pretty neat."

"I'm so glad you came to me that day. I'd never have been a part of this if you hadn't."

"You might have been here."

"I doubt it. This whole week has been so wonderful. I feel like a regular person. I love you, you know that?"

"I never would have guessed."

"Do you think they'll get married?"

"They need to start dating first."

"They will. You know what? I have an image for tonight," she said.

The statement was uniquely her own. She had said it before on two occasions when he'd interrupted to offer food after she painted for hours without pause.

"What is it?" he asked.

"I can't be sure until I paint it, Paul. It's just an image in my mind. Like an idea, but more."

"I don't get it."

"Wait 'til it's done. You'll see."

~ TWENTY-EIGHT ~

Barefoot in a bathrobe, he staggered to the kitchen to find her washing brushes. A spot of red paint on her nose, another above her right eye, were the only color in a tired face.

"You never came to bed. It's almost eight," he said.

"I told you I had an image."

"Is it done?"

"Go see."

Two canvases lay abandoned on the floor, and her smock lay in the corner, simply thrown there in a heap. The finished work sat on the easel. Larger than her usual paintings, his first impression was of a mass of red. Then he drew close enough to see more clearly and came to a halt.

Her creation was a far cry from the delicate rose beneath a fence she'd given him months ago. This was a rose in full bloom, filling the picture with dramatic detail. There was no suggestion of background, only the flower reaching out to gather him in. She had painted the heart of the image and the canvas seemed too small to hold its form.

"It looks like it's exploding off the painting."

"Bursting, not exploding," she said.

"Whatever. It's powerful!"

"You like it." She said it as fact, not a question.

"Of course. It's great."

"I'm going to bed. Would you call Graham and see what's going on with my painting? All that fuss he made and nothing's happened."

"What about this one? Should I tell him about it?"

"I suppose so. He probably won't like it."

"Why not?"

"It's not my usual style."

He looked at her, then at the painting. "I think it's the culmination of your style."

"Really? I suppose, in a way. I'm too tired to debate. I just want my bed."

He smiled. "You want some breakfast first?"

"Just sleep."

"Okay, I'll pick up in here."

"Those are no good, the ones on the floor, but don't throw them away. I'll reuse the stretchers."

"Get some sleep."

~ * ~

Betty called at eleven, inviting her to run. He was politely turning down the invitation when Anne appeared, awakened by the phone.

"Tell her to come here. I'll go," she said, stretching. Anne hadn't seen her friend in two weeks, but Paul insisted she'd do better to rest this morning. She laughed.

The phone rang again as he went around picking up the bedroom after she left.

"Miss Hoskins, please," said a hoarse male voice.

"Who's calling?"

"Jean Hoskins. Her mother."

"What? Who are you?"

"I'm calling for her mother."

"Her mother's dead," Paul said, and slammed down the phone.

It rang again.

"The lady isn't dead. She'd like to talk to her daughter," said the hoarse voice.

"Yeah right. Who are you?"

"Henry Molina. I'm calling from the O'Brien Clinic in Boston. Is Miss Hoskins there?"

"No. You, or her mother, have a lot of nerve."

"Look, just tell Miss Hoskins her mother would like to see her. Tell her to call. I'll give you the number."

"I don't believe you."

"Hey, how about a little help here?"

Paul heard a voice in the background, and the hoarse voice told someone okay and came back to him.

"Listen, ask her what Hannah expected to give her for a graduation present. The answer is Paris."

"Okay, so you know something about her. I don't know what you're up to, but it doesn't matter. Her mother isn't popular around here."

That brought silence and then whispering to the mysterious other, nothing but a mumble to Paul.

"Would you tell her Jean wants to apologize?" Suddenly the man was pleading. "Ask her to call, please?"

"I'll see what she says."

"Hold a minute will you?" said Mister Molina.

Paul waited, and then a new voice, sounding worn, but as raspy as the man came on the line.

"Sir?"

"The name is Breland."

"Mister Breland, I'm Jean. How is my daughter? Is she well?"

"Yes." What could he say to this ghost Anne thought she'd buried? Come see us some time? That wouldn't be welcomed. What would Anne want to do? "Are you in good health too?"

The woman ignored that. "Why won't you tell her I called?"

"I didn't say that."

"She still hates me then?"

"I'd say that's accurate."

"You must know about me."

"I do."

"Does she think I've drunk myself to death?"

"Yes."

"Then you really don't know that she won't see me, do you?"

He almost told her he was quite sure, but didn't have the heart.

The raspy voice continued. "Please tell her I'd like to speak to her. I'm tired now. Goodbye."

"Wait. Give me something of yourself, something to tell her."

"I haven't had a drink in thirty years. This is the O'Brien Alcoholism Clinic. I worked here, but I live here now. She can call anytime, or come. Here's Hank."

He thought there was a goodbye, but it was faint, distant. Not a retreat, she claimed she was tired. Then the man got on again, offering a phone number. Paul jotted it down.

He considered, then decided Anne should know. If she'd see her mother, it might do her good. The woman had to be telling the truth about the drinking. She'd be long dead if she wasn't. Anne would be shocked.

A little ceremony, a gentle prologue at lunch seemed a good idea. He called a local restaurant and requested two of the soup de jour to go, then jumped in the car and drove to town. He returned with the soup and a dozen pink roses, just in time to set the table and lay out lunch. He'd just sliced a loaf of fresh marbled rye bread and set it on the table when Anne called from the front door.

"Paul. We have company."

He moved to the hallway in time to see her follow a slightly taller, younger woman through the front door. Both wore shorts, Tee shirts, and running shoes.

The stranger gave him a small wave and said "Hi Paul."

He nodded, a bit nonplussed, and then remembered.

"You know Betty. I invited her for lunch."

"Sure. Nice to see you again. I'll set another place," he said, forcing enthusiasm.

"Oh! Roses. They're beautiful," Anne said, as she entered the kitchen.

Betty began to back away. "I think I'm intruding."

"No you don't. It's okay. We're pleased to have you here. Sit down," Paul said.

Anne repeated the invitation and gently pushed Betty toward a chair.

"If you insist, thank you." She gave Anne a look. "Don't ever get married. I can't remember the last time I got flowers, no less for lunch." She said it with a smile, but there was bitterness in the tone as well as the words.

"This is just a bribe," Paul said, as he set a third place at the table.

"Oh that's it, I'm leaving."

"Paul, don't tease."

"Sorry. What can I fix you Betty?"

"I'll just have a taste of soup, thanks. I have to watch my waistline."

That raised an eyebrow from Paul. If the woman was much thinner she'd be a matchstick as far as he could see.

"Really?"

"Bill doesn't like fat women."

Anne began a lecture then, on demanding husbands, Bill in particular, and the women were soon discussing the latest in Betty's marital troubles. Paul served and cleared as fast as propriety would allow, increasingly anxious to present his news. Not in Betty's presence, that he wouldn't do. Anne was in for a shock, best dealt with in private.

Lunch lasted an interminable hour and Betty finally departed, leaving Anne subdued.

"I wish we could help her. Bill is such a jerk."

"She obviously thinks he's running around," he said.

"She's afraid he's going to leave."

"Anne, I have something to tell you."

She laughed. "I know, you had plans for this afternoon. Flowers and that lovely lunch. I'm sorry I invited her, but you didn't warn me."

"Not that. I have news."

"Is it something bad? Why so serious?"

"I spoke to your mother."

Nothing. She didn't move, didn't make a sound. Her eyes were blank, locked on his.

"She wants to see you."

"It's a mistake. She can't be alive."

"No mistake. She stopped drinking."

"Where is she? How is she living?"

"In a Boston alcoholism clinic. She used to work there."

"She wants to see me?" she asked softly, finally showing some emotion, looking like she was in shock.

"She said we can go there anytime."

"To a drunk tank?"

"No, a clinic. It's where she lives, Anne. She doesn't sound very strong."

"I hate her."

"It might be good to go. You can tell her."

"Did you do this? Did you call her?"

"How could I? She called here. She wants to see you."

"No."

~ * ~

She wouldn't hear anything about her mother, couldn't believe Jean was alive. And sober? And cared enough to want to see her? None of it made sense. Or maybe she just didn't want to believe. She wouldn't talk to Paul about it at all, until they visited the Sinnises' shop on Thursday, where Millie's love life became the first subject of discussion.

"What's happening with that budding romance we saw the other day?" Paul asked.

"He's a goner," Dan said. "Yesterday he hung around a good fifteen minutes gawking at the girl. Grace had to send him off to deliver the rest of the mail."

Anne laughed, a rarity since hearing of her mother's continued existence. "Is this developing into something?"

"It is, it definitely is," Grace said.

"What about Claire? Will she have something to say about it?" asked Anne.

"Why would this be different? Her mother never approves of anything the girl does," Dan said.

"Claire is?" Paul asked.

"Claire is Grace's younger sister, Molly's mother, and a good-for-nothing who makes her daughter take care of her. Millie will have to stand up to her if she wants this young guy," Dan said.

"We heard from my mother," Anne said softly.

"She's alive?" Dan asked, blinking with surprise.

"Paul thinks so."

"My goodness. Where is she? What? Tell us," Grace cried.

"Paul knows it all. I'm going to get some coffee."

"There's a pot going in the back," Dan said.

"Thanks." With that one word, she left her baffled friends to await Paul's explanation.

He completed the picture, providing details of his conversation with Jean, and a summary of Anne's reactions.

"It's too quick," Grace said. "There's too much bad to discard easily."

"Why don't we talk to her, Gracie?" Dan said.

"Me, you mean. You two stay here."

"Bring us some of that coffee then, if you're going to be nasty."

"Dan, please, not now."

"Okay, good luck. Give her time though, right?"

"Paul, will you shut him up?"

Paul laughed. "You two. I never know when you're serious or mad."

"We're madly serious, that's all," Dan said, as Grace went off to follow Anne, "Or seriously mad, your choice."

"Is that mad as in crazy?"

"You got it. Seriously crazy, that's us."

Paul smiled, then sobered quickly. "I'm not sure Anne's mom has much time to wait for her."

"Too bad. She's the one who waited this long."

"I still think it would be good for them to meet. Not for her, for Anne."

Dan shrugged. "Whatever our girl wants."

~ * ~

Day three, without preamble, Anne said, "Call Boston. Tell her I'll come."

"What?" Paul asked. "Where did that come from?"

"Oh darn, I don't know. You think I should, and so does Grace."

"You're sure?"

"I can't let this pass without seeing if she's different."

~ TWENTY-NINE ~

She'd go to see her mother, would get to look at the ghosts of her past. She groaned. Oh darn, was she crazy?

Paul made the call, set up an immediate appointment, and hung up the phone.

Her stomach did a flip. Committed now, she sighed. "How did she sound?"

"Old, but okay."

"No, I mean how did she sound?"

"Gravel voice, sort of hoarse. Very clear though, knows what's going on."

"Mother had a sweet voice when she was sober."

"That was thirty years ago."

"Did she sound excited or anything?"

"She said three o'clock is fine. She's glad we're coming."

"Why?"

"Anne, I don't know. Maybe she's afraid you'll change your mind."

"I never made up my mind. This is your idea."

"You told me to call her. You don't have to go."

"I know. I have to see her, she's my mother." That sounded stupid, after so many years, but she didn't know what else to say.

Paul nodded. "Sure, okay. Should we get ready to go then?"

"I don't know why I should see her. She's a stranger, a monster."

He planted a kiss, sexless, loving, on her cheek. "But, she is your mother. We'll take my car."

She primped and fussed as if she were meeting royalty. She told herself she didn't need to impress, yet she wanted to, yes indeed. She wanted to show the drunk she'd done just fine without her. Lie. She wanted her mother to be proud of the life she'd made. How stupid. What did she care about Jean Hoskins?

She wondered then if Jean was primping to see her. What she was doing that very moment to meet her long abandoned daughter? Why Jean stopped calling so long ago. Would she have gone to see her without Paul's prodding?

He hadn't, not really, she had to admit that. He'd hugged her and said not a word and that was good, just the right thing. She didn't want advice, not now.

Getting to the city took forever, sitting there in the car, anticipating, speculating, and waiting. Paul seemed to take it all in stride. He drove as if he were going calling on Grace and Dan. She didn't like that, so she challenged him.

He laughed, as usual. "What will be, will be, that's all. There's nothing I can do about it."

"Suppose I want to bring her home?"

"Then we'll bring her home."

"I couldn't do that."

"Then we won't."

"Darn you, don't you understand?"

"What, that you're all upset right now? Yes."

"Well?"

He sighed and touched her arm, a gentle pat. "I can't help, love. This is your demon to deal with."

Of course, she knew that. Jean Hoskins was her mother, drunk or sober, back in her life again. The drunk had to apologize, no excuses. Crap, she was just struggling to go out again and now this. She should be celebrating and planning an excursion somewhere. Her mother better say she was sorry.

~ * ~

The man named Hank greeted them. Dissolute looking, gray of face and hair, Anne guessed he was about sixty. He insisted on knowing why they came, as though he had first claim to her mother, as if he had the right to approve before Anne could see her own mother.

"What business is that of yours?" Anne demanded.

"You have no claim to her. We do," he replied.

"Where do you get that? Her mother asked her to come. You did too," Paul said very brusquely.

Anne could have kissed him.

"You haven't seen her in how long? Thirty years? Forty? We see her every day."

"She's a drunk," Anne snapped, seething now.

"We all are here. She's dry, and a mother to everyone." Anne started to protest, but he continued. "I know, she was a lousy mother to you. She's been trying to make up for that as long as I've known her."

"Well, good for her."

He smiled then, sad faced. "I just want you to know we care about her. She's old and sick and we don't want her hurt."

"We have no intention of hurting her," Paul said.

Says who, Anne thought. The thought was a shock to her, but she hated the woman, so why not. She wouldn't hit Jean or anything, but her words would be honest, nice or not. And then she felt a lump, hard in her throat, and tears about to start. "I want to see her right away."

The man nodded and they followed him down a long hall to a door. He pushed it open and said very plainly, "Jeanie, she's here."

The room was a dormitory with a dozen beds, no two the same, and bare floors. An old woman had her back to Anne, at the edge of a rumpled bed in the corner, carefully arranging herself. Old and frail and gray were the first things Anne saw. And then the woman turned. She had a thin, long face like Hannah's, not the mother of Anne's memory.

"Hello Anne. I'm so glad you've come," the apparition said softly.

Her words seemed almost casually polite. Anne didn't know what she expected, but it wasn't that. The old woman reached out thin arms, wanting a hug, but Anne stopped at the foot of the bed and stared in silence. Her mother stepped toward her and reached out one hand. Cold and thin that hand, yet the touch on Anne's cheek was so soft and tender, unlike any childhood memory. Tears welled up and flooded down her cheeks. Jean gently pulled her daughter's head to her shoulder and stroked her.

"Anne, dear. Anne, dear daughter, I am so sorry. So, so sorry."

Anne heard Paul speak, indistinct words, and then her mother, strong, quite clear. "Please leave. I'd like to be alone."

Anne jerked back, wild with a sudden unknown dread. "What?"

"They were watching," Paul said.

"What?"

"My friends were at the door, being nosey. Your friend asked them to give us privacy, but they ignored him," Jean said.

"I thought you wanted me..."

"No dear, it was them. I'm so glad to see you. Do you still hate me? You can't, I suppose. You wouldn't have come if you did."

Anne would have answered that easily a week before, even this morning, but not now. Her mother had answered for her and she could sort out feelings later.

"What happened to you? You don't drink anymore? Tell me. How did you get here?"

"My money was gone, so the house went, and I came here for help. They dried me out and I took a job and never left."

"Who's Hank?" Paul asked.

"The assistant manager. My friend."

"Your friend?" Anne asked, wondering at her tone.

"He was more than that once upon a time, but just a friend now. He takes care of me." She smiled. "I was in charge of this facility for a long time. You didn't know that did you?"

Who cared. "You were horrible to me."

Jean patted her hand, as if Anne were still a child. "I know. I was a miserable mother and I am so sorry for that."

"Why? I was just a kid."

"I drank, Anne. It was the alcohol."

"That's an excuse. Why were you always drunk?"

"I hated my life. Hated your father and my mother, and couldn't deal with either of them. You were an easy target."

"That's another excuse. Grandma didn't do anything to you."

Jean shook her head. "Deliberately, no. I was the one who couldn't manage. Another daughter would have told her what for. I was afraid to."

Anne wanted to tell her off, but she had said the blame was hers. Why did it feel like she was blaming Hannah then?

"It was my fault, Anne. I was the coward. I had to face that before I could get better."

"You're telling me you did?"

"I wouldn't be here if I hadn't."

Anne groaned. An hour ago she hated this woman. "My Mother," she could have said with scorn, but now? "Why didn't you let me know what you were doing?"

"I wrote a few times. You never answered."

"You always lied to me. I threw them away."

"That's what I thought."

"You should have called."

"I did in the beginning, remember?"

"You were always drunk."

"I know, and you were always mad."

"Why didn't you call later? After you stopped drinking?"

"You wouldn't have believed me. You had to want to hear."

"I would have come."

"I didn't think you would. I guess that was another terrible mistake."

She said it so easily Anne wanted to hit her. Tears started instead and then she was in Jean's arms and they hugged and cried and Anne didn't know how long they stayed that way. When finally they separated, she sat, staring at the wrinkles in her mother's face.

Jean smiled and asked about her life and Paul, and she couldn't manage. "It's not over Momma. I hated you last week. This is too quick." Anne stood and Jean did too, but staggered against the bed.

"Are you all right?"

"Yes dear. I stood up too fast, that's all."

"I'm leaving now."

Her mother looked like she would cry. Anne shuddered with emotions still unclear, then almost cried too, but Jean worked that old face and steadied like a poker player.

"I'm glad you came today. I know I was terribly mean to you, though those days are a blur. I would hate me, I expect. Go then, but think it over. We can visit again soon if you want."

"If I want? What about you?"

"Dear, I'd keep you here if I could. I'll visit you tomorrow if you'll let me. I have to leave the choice to you."

The steadied face was gone, replaced with a smile, but Jean's eyes begged her for a pact.

She could only say goodbye.

Paul sat chatting with that obnoxious man when she returned to the office. Anne dragged him to the car.

"I thought you'd spend hours with her," he said.

"Never mind" Leaving had felt like a good idea, but second thoughts tore through her now. What she didn't need was Paul challenging her.

He slid into the car and sat there, quiet, waiting for Anne to speak. When she didn't, he finally said, "Well?"

"Shut up. I don't know why I let you drag me here."

"What? You two have a fight or something?"

"No, she was nice."

His face showed nothing but confusion.

"She's mean, a drunk. That's what she's supposed to be. It's like you stuck me in a washing machine and I'm twisting all around. Why didn't you hang up on her?"

"I thought you should know what happened to her," he said softly.

"I hate her and then she smiles and I want hugs and kisses. She said she loves me and she's sorry. How can I hate her? She loves me she said. What am I supposed to feel?"

"All of it I guess."

"No, I hate that. I have to know what I'm doing."

"Hank said it's been eating at her since they met."

"Who is that man?"

"He worships her. He said she's helped a lot of people in that place."

"Oh sure. My mother, the heroine? Loved by everybody? I should tell them how she was with me."

"Hank knew. Others might too. He said she's talked about it a lot."

"Probably boasting."

"Anne."

"Super Mom Jean. What about her daughter? Where was she then?"

"You still love her."

She cursed him, but sobs began to wrack her body.

"Should we go back?" he asked.

"No. I need a drink or something. Tomorrow."

"Okay."

~ * ~

They went back. She actually couldn't wait, wanted to see her mother, hear her voice, and feel Jean's tender fingers on her face again.

Hank greeted them and dragged them to his office. "Our fearless leader has waylaid your mother, Miss Hoskins. They won't be long."

"What do you mean, waylaid?" Paul asked.

"She's chewing her out. Jean ignored her instructions about not seeing a client anymore." He smiled. "Your mother tends to do things like that. She's helped more people than Miss Turgeon ever will. That's the woman's name."

"Is Mother in trouble?"

"Miss T. would like her out of here, but the staff would quit and picket the place if she tried to do that. She gives her a hard time instead."

"Jean seems to have a lot of friends," Paul said.

"She straightened us out, most of us."

"You too?" Anne asked.

He nodded, his sad eyes crinkling at the corners. "I owe her big time."

She wanted to ask why, but didn't. He was too special in her mother's life and she didn't need to know any more than that.

Hank smiled, as if he could read her mind. "She'll mention it if she wants to."

Her mother appeared, frail but grinning, quite untouched by Miss. T. apparently.

"Are you all right?" Anne asked.

"Hank told you? Oh yes. Nothing to it."

"He said you were in trouble."

"He exaggerates. I'm so glad to see you. Are you all right today?"

"Yes. I've decided I want to see you. That much I know."

Her mother nodded, smiled.

Anne went on, before courage abandoned her. "I don't know if I can forgive you, Momma. Not now, not right away. Maybe never."

"There's no reason why you should. I just want to see you, to talk, or touch, or have a hug. Is that all right with you?"

"That's good, I like that."

"Good. So, how should we start? Why don't you tell me about yourself."

"There's not much to say. I still live in the same house. I just met Paul."

"You never married?"

"No, I'm still Hoskins, Momma."

"You might have taken back your name. People do that sometimes. Do you like him?"

"I love him. He's wonderful."

"What did you do before you met him?"

She didn't want to answer. Her life was a waste. "I painted, that's all."

"She's a fantastic furniture restorer too," Paul added, all enthusiastic.

"What's wrong Anne? Is there something bad?"

"No. I just paint pictures and fix furniture."

"That sounds fine to me. Are you a good painter?"

"She does beautiful paintings. You should see her work," Paul said.

"I'd love to. I'd like to see your house too. I drove by sometimes, but couldn't see much through the trees."

"I hide, Mother. Not so much since Paul came, but I did all these years."

Her mother's face went sad, and she took Anne's hand. "I ruined your life. I'm so sorry."

Yesterday her apology wasn't enough. Today felt different, Anne felt different. "It's all right. I enjoy painting."

Jean sighed. "Does it blot out pain and loneliness?"

"Yes. Anyway, Paul takes me out and I'm starting to enjoy it now."

Jean turned to him. "I should get to know you, I suppose." She laughed and turned back to Anne. "He hasn't asked for my approval. Should we make him?"

"Mother! We're adults."

"So? What say you, Mister Breland?"

He laughed. "I do believe I must ask the fair lady first."

"Really? Why?"

"I don't know. It seems appropriate."

His eyes were twinkling. They liked each other; Anne could see it in their faces.

"A wise man," said Jean.

"What about your life? Who is this man Hank?" Anne asked.

"He was a lawyer once. Married, with children. Alcohol cost him everything."

"He said he owes you."

"He tried suicide. I saved him. We were lovers for a while."

"You said that yesterday. He's hardly older than me!"

"A few years actually. He needed a woman to hold him and love him, so I did."

"I can't believe this. After what Daddy did to you?"

"You knew he had someone else?"

"I suspected."

"Oh my, I didn't know that."

"I couldn't tell you."

She shook her head. "Anyway, I didn't have a lot of ego involved with Hank. It was a good thing to do, and I like him."

"Are you lovers now?"

"At my age?"

Of course. She looked frail enough to break if he touched her. But she answered very plainly.

"That was a while ago and it didn't last long. Well, I suppose I've slept with him occasionally since then."

"Mother, I can't believe this."

"I shock you, I suppose. We specialize in truth around here. I'm not the proper princess my mother thought she raised. Better though, I do believe. Maybe I've become the strong woman she wanted me to be after all."

"You just did what you thought was needed, Momma."

Jean laughed. "Not quite, dear. I wasn't entirely altruistic about the man. One thing I've learned is that you have to grab the brass ring when it goes by. You only get the one chance."

Anne considered that, trying to understand what her mother was referring to. Did that mean she loved Henry Molina once upon a time, or was she talking about something else? Jean turned to Paul and asked if he was divorced and Anne never asked her question.

Paul gave a little thumbnail of his life, explained about meeting Anne and what they did together and soon they were into that, and then Jean looked tired and said she needed to sleep.

Anne left reluctantly, only to find Hank waiting at the door.

"How did it go?" he asked.

"She's exhausted. She's so frail."

"This is a lot for her. She's not doing well."

"What's wrong with her?"

"Age and diabetic complications."

"Will she be all right?"

He stared as if she were crazy. "She's old, Miss Hoskins. You don't recover from that."

"Shouldn't she be in a nursing home?" Paul asked.

Hank looked at him and then at Anne and drew a deep breath. "I take her for kidney dialysis every couple of days, and someone is always here for her. No nursing home would care the way we do. You need to understand she's failing. This is where she wants to be, despite our grouchy boss."

"Doesn't that woman know about her?" Anne replied, irritated at his casualness, and that stupid woman he was referring to.

"I've told her to back off. Jean laughs at her, so there's not much I can do."

"Maybe I should talk with your boss."

"It's your mother you need to talk to, but I wouldn't hold my breath."

"She'd like to see Anne's home. We talked about it," Paul said.

"Tomorrow morning will work. She goes for dialysis at two, but if you come early?"

"We will," Anne said.

"She'll need to test her blood sugar and you need to know what to do if it goes low."

"Show us," Paul said.

~ * ~

Paul wore a, "See, wasn't I right?" grin the next morning as they dressed to pick up Jean.

"Excited?" he asked.

"Silly question. Of course."

"Worried?"

"No, should I be?"

"She's pretty sick."

"It's only for this morning. Hank told us what to do. I can do her blood tests."

"You're happy, more than I've ever seen you."

"She loves me, I know that now. Besides, she's become the woman I wanted for a mother. Even a little like my Grandma was. You know, sort of gruff and brave and smart. It's so wonderful to have her like this."

"What happened to your hate?"

"I don't know. I just want to enjoy her. We've lost so many years."

"I'm glad you found her. I'll get it," he said, as the phone rang.

She slipped into a pink blouse, half listening. Studying the blouse in the mirror, she hoped Jean would like it. It was more feminine than the one she'd worn yesterday, form fitting with a filly neck.

Paul's tone caught her ear, shock and disbelief, he lowered his voice as if he didn't want her to hear what he was saying.

"Oh crap. I'll tell her." He turned and it was in his face, something bad.

"What happened?"

"You should sit down."

He waited, but she didn't move, just stared at the sick expression on his face. "Who is it?" she whispered, thinking something had happened to Grace, or maybe Dan. "What happened?"

"Your mother. She passed. During the night."

"What does that mean?" she whispered, knowing.

"She died in her sleep."

Died. The word hit her like a hammer blow. It crushed her chest, and rattled her knees and she could barely stand.

"Why did you say that? People don't 'pass,' they die. Was that Hank?"

"Yes. He—"

"He's an idiot. Stupid, stupid, idiot."

He wrapped her in his arms and rocked her gently. "It's okay. It's okay."

"No. She can't die now."

She pulled away and took a step to somewhere, anywhere. This wasn't fair, not now. She circled the room blindly, seeking a chair. Paul pinned her in his arms, crooning condolences, and she screamed, "Let me go!" But her rage turned to sobs, and then the whimpers of her childhood came, and she was a baby in his arms. Thought shattered like smashed crystal, shards of memories and broken images flashing through her mind, and then there was nothing. A blank.

"Anne dear, wake up."

She came out of the dark and peered up at the face of Grace, bending over, concerned. "What are you doing here?"

"Paul called. I came right down."

"How long have I been sleeping?"

"Two hours. Are you all right?"

"He told you?"

"Yes dear. I'm so sorry you lost her like this. You had so little time."

"Two days, that was all. I wasted so many years. Just two days."

"Oh dear, don't say that. At least you had those."

"She was so sweet, not like when I was little."

"I'm glad. You'll have a nice memory of that."

"I want more than memories. Where's Dan?"

"Off at an estate sale. We expected to come later to meet her. He'll come soon."

"Grace, I was so bad. I had no desire to dust off memories. I even wished she had died and left me in my pleasant life."

"Paul said you loved seeing her again."

"I gave her ultimatums the first day."

"You had a bad history. Don't blame yourself. I can't imagine finding my mother hadn't died when I thought she did."

"I have to be responsible for the way I acted. She talked about facing truth to get well."

"You're always responsible. Too much sometimes. And my goodness, you're certainly well enough. Now, I want you to stop worrying yourself over it. I wish I'd met her. She sounds very nice."

"She talked about grabbing the brass ring. There were so many days and hours when I could have sought her out, or changed my life. I let it all go by."

"You didn't let Paul go."

"I know, but everything else..."

Grace patted her cheek, as she often had before, but it wasn't the same. Once consoling, today it marked her loss. Her mother's touch of yesterday remained a warm memory on her cheek.

"Don't cry dear. There are arrangements to be made. You have to tell her friend what you want to do."

She called Hank, thinking they'd have a simple family service. She and Paul, and Hank, perhaps Molly, and Dan and Grace. They would have met her mother today at Paul's suggestion. It had all been arranged.

They arrived in Boston to find the wake would be in a large funeral home procured by Hank.

"Why do we need such a big room?" Anne asked.

"Don't worry, it's gratis. The funeral director is one of her success stories. He owed her too."

A woman arrived, young, well dressed, and then a man, in glasses and clean but rumpled clothes, older. Others came, a man in a business suit, a middle-aged woman with two adolescents by her side. They all had a look she couldn't identify, calmness, perhaps an all too knowing of some secret truth. Most showed signs of dissipation. They came, some greeting each other, all greeting Hank.

"Who are all these people?" she whispered in his ear.

"Jean touched them. That's the nice way of saying she kicked us in the teeth until we woke up."

"There are so many."

"I told you. She helped a lot of people."

He introduced her and everyone wanted to talk, to tell what her mother had done for them. One woman asked if she and her mother had come to terms and she was shocked at the impertinence, but said yes.

The woman smiled. "That's really nice, I'm glad. She agonized over you, you know."

Others joined with comments of their own, and she turned to Hank at the first opportunity.

"How do they know all this? Did you tell them?"

"Your mother did. It helped us to know how much pain she had. If she could stay dry then we could too, see. That was the idea. She never said it just so, but we felt it."

She went silent and he added, "Don't blame her. She wouldn't have done it if she thought you'd ever be upset."

"There's no blame involved. It's just hard to hear it. For them she gave so much." That last she whispered to herself, but Hank gave her a strange look, as if he'd heard.

~ THIRTY ~

"You're awfully quiet. What's up?" Paul asked as they cruised south along I-95 with her mother's ashes in a dark gray urn on the floor of his car.

"I'm, I don't know, overwhelmed. All those people there. They all loved my mother."

"I think so," he said, giving her a quick look of concern.

"They did Paul. Why didn't she love me?"

"She did."

"When it was too late. I know, she was sorry, but it hurts, you know?" She shook herself and smiled at him. "I'll survive."

"I know. I love you. And I always will."

She patted his leg. "Thank you. It's so ironic. She's finally coming to my house and now she'll be there forever."

"Will you scatter her ashes?"

"I don't know. Maybe I'll bury the urn in the woods." She reached back to touch the gray pot with her stub. It was hard, some kind of stone, but had warmth somehow. "I blamed her for all the trouble in my life. Not only the accident. All those years when I was little and she was a mean drunk. I made all that a reason to do nothing with my life." Mulling over that thought, she sighed. "I think I might have hurt Mother by the way I favored my grandmother. Hannah must have known. I wonder if she did."

"Hey, you were a little kid and your grandmother was trying to protect you."

"I'm not so sure about that."

"You think the old lady had ulterior motives?"

"I don't know. She could be very severe, very harsh with Mother."

"Back then she needed that, right?"

"I suppose, but my poor mother had to see I preferred my grandma. No wonder she was always mad at me."

"Anne, you were a kid."

She sighed. "Not always, not later."

"She could have tried harder. You made peace. She was happy at the end."

"Small consolation that is."

"I think she got over it a long time ago. She was just glad to see you."

"She was so sweet," she whispered and touched her stub, as if discovering it for the first time. "What do I do now?"

"What do you mean?"

"I don't know where I am. She's come and gone so fast. My head is a mess."

"You're grieving. You'll get over it after a while."

"There's more. I'm going out now, but don't know where to go."

"It doesn't matter. You can go anywhere."

"Maybe, but how do I start? I mean, my mother just died. I can't go running off somewhere now."

"Why not?"

"I should be crying or something. You know, grieving."

"You don't have to cry to grieve. Just go along and see what happens. Never mind what you're supposed to do,"

A long sigh felt like it came from the depths of her soul, but she smiled. "All right. Let's do something new tomorrow."

"You name it! Anywhere you want to go."

She didn't respond. Brass rings Jean had spoken of, opportunity to be seized. Thirty odd years she hadn't even ridden the carousel.

"How about sailing? The boat will be hauled for the winter in two weeks, but we can get a day in. You'll have a great time."

"Tell me about it."

"We'll drive down tomorrow noon, after we do something with your mother's ashes. You'll be running the boat by yourself in an hour."

She should say she was excited, looking forward to it, but the words weren't there. Going on a sailboat left her empty, but no alternative took form.

"I want to bury the urn. Today, not tomorrow. Keep tomorrow for the sailing."

"I invited everyone for a small ceremony in the morning. We should say some words over her, or read something from the Bible."

"Why did you do that? You should have asked me."

"We can't just stick her in the ground."

She studied him for a moment, musing over what he was about. "You need a service don't you? To make it right."

He nodded. "Not to do the proper thing, if that's what you mean. I just think we should finish this. It needs a formal, final end. She won't know, but you need that."

She wasn't sure why that was important, but it didn't matter. "All right."

"Maybe you should say a few words too. Your mother would be pleased."

Mother would want to know what she planned to do with her life, what remained of it at least. "It's good she died."

"What?"

"Oh, I was thinking out loud. If she lived she would have seen what a fraud I am."

"Where are you getting that from?"

"It's true. Hiding is my best skill. I used to think I was happy and had a life others didn't know how to achieve. It was a myth. I hid, that was all."

"You did not. What about—?"

"Stop, please. I don't need advice or excuses. Opportunity lost is the story of my life and it was all my own doing. I'm the one who threw away my chances, not my mother."

"I'm just saying don't blame yourself."

"That isn't the issue. I'm too old for mountain climbing or anything like that, but there must be things I can still do."

"Well sure, of course. That's easy. I'll jot down some ideas."

"Like sailing and visiting your friends? Just let me make my own list, please."

"What's wrong with sailing?"

"Leave it be, will you? I functioned well enough before you came along."

"I know you did."

"You don't sound like it. You want to arrange everything for me."

"That's part of being together. We help each other."

"I don't think I help you with anything."

"Sure you do."

"What?"

"Crap, I don't remember. What difference does it make?"

"Why can't you honor the fact that I've always made my own decisions?"

"I do." He looked at her, tension in his face. "You don't believe that?"

She shrugged, sensing this wasn't going anywhere good. "I have a lot to consider right now."

"Take it easy. You're upset."

Grief clutched at her, anger at his glib answers, but she squished it. "I'm all right."

"You could fool me."

"I have a lot on my mind, that's all."

"Sure, you just lost your mom."

"I know, but I don't want to cry. Just leave it alone will you? She gave me a lot to think about."

"Like what?"

"Never mind, not now."

~ * ~

She relegated the book Paul was reading, and his shaving kit, to the bathroom, with a quiet, "Please, I need this space."

Jean's few possessions, presented by Hank at the memorial service, she spread out carefully atop the dresser. Faded photos; Mother and Father together, Jean and Hannah. One of Anne herself, at five or thereabouts, looking surly in a frilly dress. Jean and Father again, looking young and happy, as they might have been just before or after marriage. In the other photo Hannah's face looked stern and her daughter's stiff, somehow awkward and uncertain.

"You were beautiful Mother, did you know that? I don't think you did," she whispered.

There was a plain silver chain, a Timex watch with worn leather band, and a silver hand mirror, bent and cracked. She opened the dresser and pulled out the brush to match, from the set Hannah once owned.

"You must have cared, even in the bad days, to keep these things. I think you cared more than I did, Mother. I kept not a single picture, except the one of Hannah in the living room."

She slipped the chain around her neck, felt the cold metal settle into place above her breasts, and began to weep. Paul found her there and took her in his arms.

"I'm such a fool. We could have had so much."

"Never mind, you don't know that. She might have started drinking again if she was sure of you."

Anne shook her head against his chest, but he held tight, crooning in her ear, "Go ahead, it's okay, get it out."

~ * ~

The Sinnises' and Molly arrived. He'd thought Anne would like their company, but she was indifferent this morning. He read the Twenty-third Psalm and Anne made a little speech about how much she regretted not checking on her mom a long time ago and they each threw a clutch of dirt on the urn. Jean would reside just outside the front door, on the studio side of the patio. Molly picked flowers and Grace helped her stick each one in the soft ground, like brightly colored columns at the borders of a temple.

After the ceremony, Molly gave them all the latest news of she and Graham. They were getting serious, she said, and Paul wondered if Graham agreed with that. Dan asked if this one was going to last, sarcasm that earned him a scowl from Grace.

Molly just smiled. "We had a long talk yesterday on the way back from Boston. It's different this time."

"He was very kind at the Memorial Service," Anne said.

"He consoled you, I know. I mentioned that and he asked if I were jealous. 'No,' I said, 'should I be?' 'No,' he said. 'I just wondered if you care.' I mean, one minute I'm offering a compliment, and the next thing I know he's getting serious."

"What did you say?" asked Grace.

"I was flustered. Me, can you believe it? I knew exactly what he meant, but darned if I could answer."

"So, come on, get to the point," Dan said.

She gave him a smirk. "I told him it wasn't an easy question. He said it sure was, just a yes or a no, that's all."

"So you said maybe?" asked Dan, restraint disappearing again.

"In so many words, yes."

"And?" asked Grace.

"He said okay."

"That was all?" Dan said. He looked annoyed.

Paul suspected Molly's free and easy ways didn't sit well with the old man. He suppressed a smile. He still hadn't gotten an apology from her, or Graham, and let himself enjoy Dan's digs. Served Miss Molly right as far as he was concerned. She owed Anne an apology too and that annoyed him more than anything.

"He was smiling, Dan. He knew my mind. And you know what? We're different now."

"Where is he today?"

"Meeting with a critic from one of the Boston papers. I said he didn't need to come."

She looked to Anne for confirmation, but Anne had disappeared.

Paul figured she'd gone to the bathroom, but she didn't come back. Why he didn't know, unless Molly's chatter bothered her. There had hardly been a word said about Jean since the urn went into the ground. Or a word said about the Times article either.

He found Anne in the kitchen staring out the window.

"You okay?"

"I needed a cry."

"Sorry I invited them."

"It doesn't matter I'm just thinking."

~ * ~

Anne called Molly a few days later. "Does Graham still want my paintings?"

"You'll have to ask him," Molly replied, bitterness in her voice, obvious even to Anne.

"You sound funny."

"You'll have to ask him yourself. I don't know if he'll keep the gallery."

"What happened?"

"He's in New York with the little woman."

Anne bit her lip before she said something better left unsaid. Molly sounded quite upset, obviously having thought she and Graham were becoming a couple.

Not that she could do anything about their situation, but she hadn't heard from Molly since the memorial service. All because Molly hadn't apologized to Paul. She sighed, knowing she was being hard on Molly, who really deserved a little sympathy at the moment.

"Is Graham gone for good?"

"I don't know. His wife called and called, pretending to be talking about their divorce. I'm so brilliant I believed him."

"How long has he been gone?"

"Three days. He's been telling me he needs more time, claiming his wife wants to bankrupt him."

"Maybe that's true."

"Last night he said she wants to reconcile. I told him to have fun and hung up. He should die having fun."

"Maybe he's just mixed up. Like you were when you and Jim broke up."

"I never wanted to go back to Jim."

Anne ignored that and responded automatically, in the old way. "Come for dinner. We bought a grill and Paul's going to break it in tonight."

Molly hesitated. "It's practically November."

"He'll be in the garage."

"That would be awkward, wouldn't it?"

Anne hesitated. This wasn't the time to bring it up, but still frustrated with her friend, she plunged ahead. "Molly, it's time to put an end to this. Apologize and it will all be over. Paul won't be mad."

"Have you seen his paperwork? All the proof he claims he has?" Molly said, all trace of misery gone from her voice.

"I don't need to. He didn't do anything wrong."

"Anne, listen to me. You could be in danger."

"No. You're being totally unreasonable. If you think you're right, investigate on your own, and see if you can find some more dirt. Otherwise, just forget the whole thing."

Anne waited, but all she heard was silence.

"Well?"

"I did," Molly said softly.

"And?"

"Google didn't have anything. I'd have to hire a lawyer to search through court records."

"Well go ahead then. Do you need money?"

"That would be ridiculous. All you have to do is tell him you want to see his proof."

Anne gave her a sardonic laugh. "That's all? Just tell him I'm sorry I don't trust him? I want him to prove everything he told me? Isn't that a wonderful idea."

"He could be dangerous, Anne," Molly almost whispered.

Anne struggled to manage her temper. "Tell me. How much research have you done on Graham? I know you said there are millions of Graham's on Google, but what else have you done to find out if he's not a serial killer?"

"That's not the same. We already know Paul is...."

"I already know he isn't," Anne snapped.

The phone was shaking in her hand. Never had she had a conversation like this with Molly, but she was fed up with the whole business. Molly would apologize or else, that was all there was to it. She waited without speaking.

"I'll pass on dinner," Molly finally said.

"Molly," Anne said softly.

"No, you're probably right, but I can't deal with this right now. I'd rather stay home and stare at the TV and drink tonight. Maybe I'll dump Graham's stuff on the porch and leave it there until he comes for it."

"What will happen if he closes the gallery?"

"He has a lease, but that's his problem. I'm out of it."

"Good."

"What about your paintings? Do you want to keep selling them now?"

"I want to make painting a career."

"A career? What do you need that for?"

"A job then. I just need to do something with my life. Something meaningful."

"Don't get carried away. You've done all right for yourself so far."

"Oh sure. I have a houseful of paintings no one ever sees. Big whoop that is."

"So now you want Graham to sell them?"

"I don't know about him. He has that one painting, but I'm glad I held off giving him the rest." Anne paused. "Why don't you come for dinner tonight? Let's settle everything."

Molly laughed softly. "No thanks, we're both in a mess. Your head must be spinning after losing your mother and I'm no bargain at the moment either. Enjoy yourself with Paul. I'm going to shut up now and hang up and we'll worry about everything some other time."

~ THIRTY-ONE ~

She had *Jeopardy* on the screen and a beer in her hand when he called. "Molly? Are you okay?"

"Yes." What was this about? No way she would ask. "Where are you?"

"In the city. Listen, I'm sorry about this. I just wanted to be sure you're okay."

"Why? So you don't have to feel guilty?"

"Look, I know you're upset, but we said no commitments, right?"

"And that makes it okay?"

"I'm sorry, Molly."

Sorry, sorry, sorry—bull. He was so creative with that. She was about ready to let him have it again, but aborted an outburst for some silly reason.

"Listen, I've been through worse."

"Maybe, but still, this isn't easy. For you, I mean, for either of us. Take care of yourself?"

"I'm fine Graham. Don't worry."

Why did he call? Guilty, he wanted absolution? Of course. Why was she so stupid nice? 'I'm fine, don't worry.' Was that ever dumb. Down went her beer, and she wanted another. Nice, that was her calling card, except when it came to Paul Breland. Anne might be letting him off the hook, but he could drop dead for all she cared.

She opened another beer and sat back on the couch as a new thought hit her. If he didn't drop dead, Anne would probably marry him. Which would make for an awkward wedding, not to mention down the road a piece. She took a swig of beer and sighed.

Grace called in the a.m. They didn't talk that often, but she was all business, wanting a new house close to Wickford. She probably expected Molly wouldn't charge her a commission. Friends were friends, but she didn't work free. What the heck, she could work cheap. She grabbed her listing book and met Grace at the Wickford store.

Dan left Millie behind the register and joined them. They'd never seen eye to eye, she and Dan. He considered her a bit disreputable, she knew that well enough. He and Grace had been married a hundred years and he acted like she'd been married a hundred times. He was pleasant at the moment though, even pulling up an ancient chair for her so they could all look through the listings. Graham, they did not mention, it was just innocuous talk of business, and the houses in the book. When she mentioned Anne needed a place to sell her paintings, they volunteered the store without taking a breath.

"No problem. We can make wall space for a dozen or more," Dan said.

"Oh certainly, dear. She'll have to tell us how much to charge for them though," Grace said.

"Graham thought he could get about three thousand."

"We're not a fancy Newport gallery. She better figure something less," Dan said.

"I'm sure she'll appreciate it," Molly said.

"I thought your friend was going to sell them," Dan said.

"That fell through."

He gave Molly a hard, no, a serious look, but it was Grace who asked the question. "Has something happened dear? I thought he was your friend."

"He was."

Not another word about Graham, even though they had to have a million questions. They were polite, but she wasn't sure that was what she wanted. It would be nice to tell them what a louse Graham was, but then too, it might be nice if he called tonight. Stupid thought again. What good would that do?

"You're such a good friend to Anne," Grace said.

Molly didn't respond. Way out comment that was, they all knew that. Where was Grace going?

"She's worried about you." Here it was, she knew it. Anne had arranged all this.

"I'm okay, Grace. I'll have to tell her not to."

She wondered what Anne had in her head, getting them involved this time. In all her ups and downs, Anne was always there, but not like this, so much concerned. Maybe she'd come to understand the real hurt these days, what a person felt in real life. She probably had Paul to thank for that.

There was a message on the machine when she got home. Short and to the point, a hello, just wanted to say hello. He was original. Surprising, he didn't apologize again. She got another dinner invite from Anne and turned her down. She just wanted to be alone.

She told Anne about Dan's offer before she hung up.

"That's wonderful, thank you Molly."

"Thank them. It's their shop."

"I know, but you told them I need a place."

"Yes, well."

"Are you all right?"

"I'm okay. Listen, Graham's a jerk, but he knows art. Those paintings don't belong in an antique shop. You should deal with him yourself."

"You wouldn't mind?"

"Go ahead. As a matter of fact, I'll help. It's just business."

She'd hassle the man when he called, play on his guilt, that was what she'd do. Brilliant. She'd probably heard the last of him. Tough, then she'd call him if she had to.

"You sound better," Anne said.

"Yeah, I'm okay. Tell Grace not to worry."

"I'm sorry Molly. I just thought they might be good for you."

"Might be they were. Bye."

Determined not to drink as much as she had the night before, she struggled. There was just nothing to think about except Graham and her own dumb life, so she was on a second Sam Adams when the phone rang. It was the last call she'd get from New York, but she didn't know that when he started.

"Molly, how are you?"

"Just fine."

"Really? You're okay?"

"I said, I'm fine."

"You sound mad."

"What do you care? You have your wife back. What more do you want?"

"Molly."

"What? Just stop calling."

"Okay, but only if you promise me something."

"I'm not promising anything. I want a promise from you. I want you to show more of Anne's paintings. She wants to sell them all."

"Sure, but listen, please."

"I can't deal with this every night. Find your own absolution. Just leave me alone."

"Wait. Listen. This was a mistake. I'd like to come back, if you'll have me."

"You're kidding."

"No. I wasn't done here, Molly. I had to figure that out, for certain. Will you have me?"

She was reeling, two quick beers on top of dinner wine, and now this. Her answer should have been a big fat loud, "Get lost," but the words tumbling from her brain were very different, "I'm not going anywhere."

"Wait up for me."

~ THIRTY-TWO ~

Her workshop felt happy the next morning, with sunlight strong in the yard beyond the window and the door wide open to chill fall air. The space heater struggled to keep a bit of warmth in the room, but there was enough to let her work at least.

Louie's woodwork lay spread throughout the shop, resting on bits of wood that served as drying racks. She was cleaning a small brush she used for colors when Paul wandered in.

"You're certainly gung-ho this morning," he said.

"I thought I'd get an early start."

"What are you doing?"

"I just put on a red wash. What do you think?"

"I can't tell. You put the paint on so thin I can barely see it."

She smiled. "I know. It all looks brown to you. I just thought I'd ask."

"Brown with some black to give it grain. That I can see. That and the gleam you're getting with all the thin coats."

"That's the varnish in between."

"What's on the agenda today?"

"This. I'd like to finish and get it back to Dan."

"We need to talk. You've spent the last two days in here. I thought we'd licked your fear of going out."

She sighed and rubbed the brush against her arm, splaying out the bristles. "It just feels good to do this now. It occupies my mind." She waited for a response, but he kept silent. "There's too much to deal with Paul, too many changes too fast. Do you realize three weeks ago I went to a restaurant for the first time in forty years? Three weeks ago I thought my mother was dead and now I know she is? I practically watched her die."

"I know."

"I don't think you do. How long did it take you to deal with your wife's cancer? I'll bet you never knew what she felt."

"We shared all we could."

"That isn't the same as feeling it."

"I know, but I could never do that."

She stopped then and nodded, a gentle headshake. "You would have if you could, wouldn't you? I'm sorry. My mind is a mess right now."

"Okay, I get that, but don't overdo this chair business. Let's go for a walk or something. You need to relax occasionally."

"This is relaxing. It's all I want right now."

"You're not going to fall back into old habits are you?"

"Staying in? No, there's no chance of that. If Mother hadn't died, I'd be celebrating now. I was beginning to think about our future when you got that call from Hank Molina."

"She was like a bump in the road then?"

"A large one if you want to call it that. Like when Hannah died, or when I lost my hand."

He reached out and touched a finger to her cheek. "Hey, you hadn't seen her in years. You didn't even like her."

"Well, maybe, but she was my mom. I'll be all right, don't worry."

He grinned. "I'll take that as a promise."

"Never mind. Take it as very likely. I still have dreams you know."

"Oh? Such as?"

"This isn't the time for that."

"Why not?"

"I'm supposed to be grieving for my mother. How can I get excited about the future? New adventures should be fun to think about."

"Oh, we're looking for adventure now?"

"Don't tease. You should always have dreams."

"What does that mean? Are you going to spend the rest of your life looking for excitement?"

"Would that be so terrible?"

"It would get pretty tiring."

"Then I'll rest a while."

"I will too then."

She studied him. "Does that mean you won't stay with me if I go off around the world or whatever?"

"It means I'll stay home sometimes when you go."

She frowned. "We've never discussed marriage. We're considering the future, aren't we? Whether we'll stay together?"

"I don't regard that as an open question."

"You seemed to a minute ago."

"I may not do everything you do, but I won't leave. What about you?"

"I want to stay together, of course. I don't even know if I'll go anywhere, without you at least."

"You want to get married?"

"It's just a piece of paper."

"We're committed, that's what counts. Right?"

"Yes."

"You don't want a fancy wedding someday? White gown and all the trimmings?"

"Paul, I'm beyond that. You are too, I think."

"Yes. But we can promise ourselves to each other. I hereby commit myself to you, Anne Hoskins, for the rest of my days."

"That's silly. Oh, all right. I commit myself to you Paul Breland, for the rest of my days. You do have to kiss me at least."

~ * ~

She told Molly what they did the next day over lunch in Newport.

"Very romantic. Congratulations," Molly said, and then announced the return of Graham.

"I thought you were done with him."

"I have a feeling about him. This is going to work."

"You always say that. You aren't even happy this time."

"That's the funny thing. Normally, I'd be on Cloud Nine at this point, so this is good. I'm more realistic now."

"I hope so."

"He'll take your paintings by the way. The one you gave him hasn't sold, but he still thinks they're very good."

"Will he be in the gallery tomorrow if I go there?"

"He opens at nine. What brought this change of heart?"

"I want to make money, so it's like a job, or a career."

"Be nice to see some sold, won't it? You certainly have a bee in your bonnet lately. What else are you up to?"

"I've invited Paul's family for a visit. It's time I met them."

"Really? How many are there?"

"Fourteen, including Paul and me."

"Where will you put everyone?"

"On the second floor."

"You're kicking out the Linden's?"

"Molly stop, you know that was just a story."

"I wondered in the beginning. Your perfect family, inhabiting a second floor full of Victorian furnishings. When you first mentioned them, I thought you had boarders. Then when I found out they were imaginary I was afraid you were crazy."

"I'm sorry. You never said. I haven't played at that in years."

"I always wanted to ask this, but why did you?"

"I don't know. Maybe I was afraid to be alone, or just plain lonely. I always knew they were imaginary. Whatever, it doesn't matter."

"So now you're putting real people up there."

"For a few days. Paul and I started cleaning."

Molly studied her for a moment, then shook her head. Paul's name was still a sore point between them and Anne wondered if she was about to apologize.

"It must be a mess. He's not upset?" Molly said.

"That they'll be sleeping up there? We'll have it spic and span by tonight. He thinks they'll get a kick out of the Tiffany lamps and four poster beds."

Molly nodded and gave her a look out of the corner of her eye. "And what about Mister Breland? You married each other?"

"Not married. Committed to."

"Wouldn't you have liked a little more formality?"

"We can still marry officially, but I'm not impressed with the marriages I've seen."

"True. My track record ain't so great. Graham and I are just together too."

"Are you sure you're all right?"

"I am, definitely. Graham is like a warm blanket on a cold night. He makes me comfy."

"That's a terrible description for a lover."

"I like it. Love is like a blanket for the heart. Fireworks and flowers don't last. In the end it's comfort that counts."

"There must be more than that."

"Think on it. I need that warmth," Molly said with a smile.

"And I don't?"

"Once I would have said no, but now I'm not sure."

"Blankets can be heavy."

"Don't be negative. And one more thing? Tell Paul I'm sorry I accused him."

"You're apologizing?"

"Yes."

"You still need to tell him yourself."

~ THIRTY-THREE ~

On the second floor landing, Paul bent over the door, replacing the knob Anne had ignored the last twenty years.

"I'm surprised you never locked yourself in up here with this," he said when she returned.

"I don't come up that much."

"It'll get a lot of use this weekend. Helen called, at last. You've got yourself a full scale family visit coming."

"Everyone can make it?"

"They want to meet you. You'll get their full attention."

"That's to be expected I suppose."

"We could have done this one at a time, you know. It would have been easier."

"I'm ready for them."

More than that, she wanted this as it was, a single all-inclusive, complete family gathering, quickly over. She'd thought about facing them a few at a time, but the fear had eased quite a bit and wasn't driving her this time. Instead, she felt a certain urgency, as yet unidentified, not even clearly there.

"Yeah, it'll be fun. What did Molly have to say?"

She hesitated. Should she tell him Molly tried to apologize? He wasn't unhappy about the situation, so why bring it up? Molly needed to make her own apology to him.

"Graham is back."

"How'd that happen?"

"He asked."

"And she said yes?"

"She thinks everything is fine now, he'll stay for good."

"You sound skeptical."

"Molly always says that and it never happens that way. She survives though, and then she finds another guy and starts again."

"I wonder what price she pays when that happens." Paul said softly.

She didn't answer. She couldn't imagine herself in the same situation. Would she survive if Paul ever walked away?

He sent her an inquisitive glance, frowned into her silence, and asked about her paintings.

"Tomorrow," she said, "I'm going to take some to the gallery."

"What about these rooms? It's nowhere near clean up here yet."

"I'll help you when I'm done."

"I thought you said tomorrow."

"I have to choose the paintings to give him."

"I'll help." He rose to his feet.

"You finish here. I won't be long."

He stared after her. "Slow down woman. The gallery's not going anywhere."

"Ta, ta," she called over her shoulder.

"You need to wrap them in something," he called.

She stopped half way down the stairs. "Throw down some of that old bedding. I'll use that."

"It's pretty musty."

"It'll get a good airing by the time I'm done."

An hour later she returned. He was taking apart a window in the front room.

"What are you doing?"

"Fixing it. The darn thing won't open."

"Can't you open the other one?"

"It's stuck too."

"It needs new paint now. You've chipped the edges."

"We need fresh air up here. The place smells like a cave."

"It does not."

He turned to face her. "What is this? Why are we arguing? You mean to say the air up here is sweet and fresh?"

"No, but we could put a fan in the hall. You're ruining the window."

"I'll have it all fixed up before you know it. A little touch up and it'll be done"

She stared at him, and then nodded. "I'm sorry, go ahead. I'll wipe down the walls."

"What's eating you today?"

"I'm a little tense, that's all."

"My family, or giving paintings to Graham getting to you?"

"Probably both," she said, but there was something else.

Not Molly either. She knew that, but not with any sort of clarity. It was simply a tension rippling just below her skin.

~ * ~

She rushed him in the morning, anxious to get going.

"We have a million things to do. I want to get back so we can finish the cleaning."

"The windows are done, the place is almost all cleaned up. You still have another day before they come."

"We haven't done the first floor yet."

"Okay, so we have a little more to do. We'll be ready."

"I know. I have no idea what to say to Graham though, especially after talking to Molly yesterday. I don't know what to expect."

"He wants to represent you remember? You're doing him a favor."

"It's not that. I don't know how to be with him. I didn't tell you, but Molly tried to apologize. I don't know if Graham will though."

"She apologized?"

"I wouldn't let her. She has to tell you herself."

He grinned. "Good for you."

"So, what do we do about Graham?"

He shrugged. "Play it by ear. I don't much care what he does. Listen, today will be good. Don't worry."

"I know, I know."

"How's Mother today?"

"My mother? You think that's upsetting me?"

"Could be."

She stared at him, then nodded. "If she lived a little longer she'd have seen this. We'd have shared it."

"Yeah." He pointed upward. "But you know, I bet she's up there with your Grandma, telling her how great you are."

"Don't be silly," she said, but there was a touch of warmth in her heart.

She'd covered a dozen paintings with bedding and towels to transport them to the gallery. The selections were the ones she thought the best, but today it seemed others might do as well.

"Forget that," Paul said. "You'll drive yourself crazy. If you're going to be a professional, they'll all be sold sometime."

"I don't know what I'll do if no one likes them."

He reassured her again, and she squeezed his arm with a soft, "Thank you."

The gallery seemed far less glitzy than she remembered, even a touch elegant with more paintings on the walls and a few small rugs finally in place. The same paintings that hung near the door the day she first visited remained exactly as they were and she wondered if they were overpriced. Nice paintings, not exactly spectacular, but they served to draw attention. She wondered if Graham even tried to sell them.

He seemed less glitzy than usual too, greeting her with no more than a sedate smile. "Good to see you," he said. "I was afraid I'd seen the last of your work."

"What's with the painting she gave you before?" Paul asked.

"It's there, on the side wall. I've had one offer, but turned it down."

"Why?" asked Anne.

"The guy offered eighteen hundred, but he'll go higher. The man's been through the gallery twice since then, hoping I'll drop the price. Hey, let me help," said Graham, as Paul began to unwrap a painting.

"We have more in the car," Anne said.

"Excellent. One painting is a bit lonesome by itself. They do better in company. Our potential buyer will be quite unhappy when he returns."

"Why?"

"I'm going to raise the price of your first one by a thousand now. He'll be kicking himself."

"Can you do that? How much will it be?" Paul asked.

"Four thousand and I certainly can. If he matches the original price I might take pity, if he's nice about it."

Anne studied him, surprised by the remark. There was something different about Mister White, but she couldn't finger it exactly. He seemed subdued, not beaten, but far less pretentious. And he kept peeking at Paul, then turning away so he wouldn't have to meet his eyes. Was he trying to work up the courage to apologize, or to accuse him again? Anne sighed. This could not go on. Molly and her stupid Google search.

Graham kept them there to help decide how the paintings should be hung. He had space along the outside walls, but recommended the freestanding dividers in the center of the shop. Anne pointed out the sidewall had considerable open space in front of it.

"You'd get a good view of all of them at once," she said.

Graham laughed. "I've been saving that for something special. I guess you're it."

It took an hour to bring in the paintings and set them in place against the wall. Graham insisted they not be actually hung or sold until they'd been framed.

"It's a matter of pricing again," he said.

She moved slowly from one to another in a daze. This was real, her paintings on display. The work of her life. Her babies, her soul, and her heart, exposed for the entire world to see. She had an urge to take them home, to keep them safe.

Glancing around at others he had on display, she decided hers were as good as anything else he had. Maybe better than most. A surge of happiness thrilled her heart.

A young couple entered the gallery, likely in their late twenties, not poor from the look of them. They hovered over her canvases as Graham leaned the last one against the wall. The woman spoke earnestly to the man.

The man said softly, "It's beautiful. Let's make an offer."

The woman said something Anne couldn't hear and they began quietly discussing a bid.

Anne's heart began to pound. If only the painting had a frame.

"I love these," the woman said to Graham. "Who's this artist?"

He gave Anne a quick appraising look and then turned back to the woman. "She's local. This is the first of her work to go on the market," he replied, and Anne felt a burst of relief that he'd kept her out of the discussion.

"Buyers already?" Paul whispered at her elbow.

"Maybe. Let's go."

"Don't you want to find out what they'll do?"

"Graham said he won't sell anything without a frame. Come on," she said, dragging him away.

"He'll change that if they come up with the right money."

"I don't want to wait. Wave good bye."

Graham returned the wave, casual, satisfied, fully in charge. "Take care," he called.

~ THIRTY-FOUR ~

That afternoon they spent cleaning, and the next day as well. Second floor finished, Paul dug in on the first, wielding the new vacuum like a wild man. Anne's use of the quilts to wrap her paintings had shaken out a bit of dust, but they still seemed not quite clean. She soaked them in the bathtub and used sunlight as her dryer, spreading them over a rope strung between the house and the big maple in the front yard.

"We're really turning back the clock," she said.

"We'll qualify for one of those shows PBS used to run, the ones where people live like they did in the 1800's or during World War II."

"Thank you, no, I'll stay where I am. If I were to go somewhere, I'd want it to be real."

~ * ~

Helen and her family arrived a little after four on Friday, to a spic and span house, completed to Anne's satisfaction just thirty minutes earlier. After hurried showers, she'd joined Paul on the patio, a glass of wine in hand, to await the upcoming arrivals. She began fluffing cushions, pacing, rearranging chairs. He got to his feet and took her in his arms.

"Take it easy. They won't bite."

"I'm all right. I just get fidgety when I'm waiting for something to happen."

He kissed her, his lips hard on hers, his tongue probing.

She giggled. "Stop that. What would they think if they caught us?"

"We'll hear their cars on the gravel, no problem."

"If we don't get carried away," she said, pushing him aside. "And I hear a car."

She followed him out to the driveway just in time to see a young woman stepping out of a car, followed by a man who was obviously her husband. This had to be Helen and Frank because the young woman looked like Paul.

Paul introduced them. Helen and Frank, four year old Amelia, and a little one, year old Jean. Anne did a double take with the mention of that name, but it was Amelia who stole her heart.

"Mommy, I'm thirsty," the child announced.

"Would you like some juice?" Anne asked.

The question drew a quick nod and a smile from the little girl.

"Come see what we can find in the kitchen," Anne said, and Amelia followed her through the front door with barely a glance at her parents or grandfather

"Will you look at that," Helen said. "Your lady has a magic touch, Dad."

Paul beamed as he led the way to the kitchen. Anne poured drinks for everyone and asked him to show them to their room.

"Amelia can stay with me. We're best friends now, aren't we, Amelia?" Anne said.

Later, Paul tried to fuss over Amelia, but she clung to Anne like a cocklebur, following her everywhere. Anne brought out a set of watercolors and spent the afternoon on the floor with the child, creating art in quantity if not quality. It was the high point of Anne's weekend, or so it seemed it had to be.

Jane and her family arrived after dinner. Anne was introduced to husband Charlie, and the boys, Sam and Tommy. Eager hands dragged bags and boxes to the upstairs bedrooms. Tommy teased Amelia and she began chasing him around the yard, easily catching her older cousin, with his cooperation, of course. Scott, Maggie, and their girls arrived a few minutes later and their oldest girl, Libby, joined Amelia and Tommy.

The next three days left Anne breathless. The young grandchildren spread toys all over the living room and studio, while Jane's boys lived outdoors, exploring the fields and crossing the half-mile of brush behind the house to reach the beach.

Conversations were constant in every corner of the house, on subjects from sports, to cooking, kids, politics, and books. Anne's paintings received great admiration.

She settled into a warm and comfortable feeling with them, and delighted in their pleasure. It was all a big party and she had never seen a family like this one. Everyone took a turn at cooking and washing dishes, the men included. Bedrooms overflowed with suitcases and clothes, and chairs were in short supply. She marveled at Paul's stamina. Just a few hours in the chaos left her weary, but the love and warmth she received from all of them almost made her cry.

"When are they quiet?" she whispered over Saturday's dinner.

"Never when we're all together," he replied.

Saturday night the children toasted marshmallows while Charlie told stories. Sunday afternoon, with hands waving from car windows they all drove away. Anne waved slowly as the last car reached the street. Her arm dropped to her side and she hugged herself.

"It's so quiet when they all leave. I think I miss them."

"I always feel that way. One minute it's a mob scene, the next I'm alone. I'm glad you had fun."

"I loved having them. From now on, I'll join you when you visit."

"You're on woman. Every one of them before the end of the year. Thanksgiving and Christmas, too."

"They like me, I think. Right?"

He kissed her. "They gave you the Good Housekeeping Seal of Approval." He stopped then, and added, seriously, "You're permitted to replace their Mother, and that makes you very special."

"What do you mean?"

"Ellie never made it with them, but you have. Jane said it all."

"What?"

"I quote, 'Mom would be glad you found her.' That's quite an endorsement, don't you think?"

"What a nice thing to say."

He laughed. "You're one hundred percent family now."

She hugged him. "The real thing and wonderful too."

"Yeah, that's the way families are sometimes. They can be cranky though. Don't expect this every time you see them."

"Don't be negative. This was wonderful, an adventure almost."

"Almost? It doesn't measure up?"

"Adventures are different, not like families."

"I don't think you know what adventure is. Should I plan one for you?"

"We have a chair to finish first."

"That can wait a day or two. I'll set up a trip to New York."

"No, you'll have to go by yourself."

He laughed. "No way. Not without you."

Despite his dissent, she suggested a trip to see his friends while she continued the repairs on Louie. He demurred, but she ignored him and headed directly for the shop. Louie's rebuilt parts couldn't be stained, but Anne intended to obtain the same effect with paint. Each color she applied was thin, almost transparent, a blend with linseed oil to give a shine, and Japan drier to speed the work. She walked the floor, turning each leg in the light before choosing colors to use. One coat of paint and one of varnish, equally thin, went on each time.

She quit well after ten. Paul took a look and hinted she'd soon be done.

"Not nearly. The color and finish are a long way from being right."

"Are you sure I can't help?"

"It's fine art work now Paul. Maybe when it's time to reassemble it."

"How much longer will this take?"

"Two weeks, possibly a little less."

"I think I'll shoot home tomorrow then. It's lunch day for Ben and the guys."

She nodded. "They'll be glad to see you."

"I'd still like to take you to New York."

"When Louie's done. Have fun."

She almost asked him to bring back the records of his lawsuit so they could end the tension she felt with Molly, but didn't. No way did she want to upset him about that again. But she had a knot in her stomach and it was growing.

The work moved in fits and starts. Study what she'd already done, choose color for the next wash, apply and wait. Three hours later, and varnish could be applied. With caution, she'd wait longer between coats, but she wanted to finish and move on. Each hour's wait seemed interminable.

To Paul, the wood was brown, with flecks or streaks of black grain. To her the black alone had different tints, and the brown had a multitude of subtle tones. It would take time to capture all she saw, but she had exaggerated the effort needed in her mind.

It didn't matter. She put in sixteen hours that day, and welcomed Paul's call to say he'd stay the night. The second day she started early. Waiting between coats, bored, she called Graham.

He offered his usual encouragement, but no news of a sale. With the fifth varnish layer applied and drying, she called Molly.

"Hi," Molly said cheerily.

"Molly, what am I doing?" she asked without offering a reply.

"Asking me a dumb question, I guess. What else?"

"No, I mean what am I doing wrong?"

"What happened? Did it go so badly with his kids?"

"The visit? No, that was good. I'm just all mixed up again."

"Why?"

"I don't know. It just seems like my life is constantly in turmoil lately."

"You want to meet for lunch? One o'clock?

"I can't," Anne said. "I'm working. Pick up something and come here."

"Serious stuff, huh? You're really pushing this career business."

"It's Dan's chair, not a painting. I can't wait to get it done."

"I'll bring wine."

Molly arrived promptly at one, merlot and a Wendy's bag in hand. "I didn't have time for gourmet. What's going on?"

"I'm all fidgety. Nothing's right."

"Are you sure this family thing went okay?"

"Yes. I loved it and Paul was very pleased. That isn't it."

"Let me get this straight. The family thing went well. You're starting the career you want, selling paintings, and you have a guy you love. Life is a disaster though, right?"

"Don't be smart."

"Are you happy?"

"That isn't the point. I sent Paul away and I'm going crazy with this chair. I'm in a huge hurry."

"To do what?"

"The chair. Don't ask. I don't know why."

"Are you happy?"

"You already asked that. No, and yes. Come to the shop with me. I have to paint the chair again."

"Eat first, I hate cold burgers."

"Come on. We'll eat in there."

Molly grabbed the food and wine, followed her to the shop, and then sat munching fries as Anne prepared another wash of color, this time with a red tint.

"Your food is getting cold," she said.

"I need to get this done. I lost so much time while Paul's kids were here."

"How long has this been going on?"

"Since Mother died. I don't know, it's been starting slowly."

"Sneaking up on you, huh? Is there a big rush to go somewhere?"

"No."

"From then?"

"What?"

"From. If you're not rushing to somewhere, you must be rushing away from something. Or someone. Paul maybe?"

"That's silly. He's a dream."

Molly didn't respond.

"He's a dream, Molly. When are you going to apologize?"

"Soon."

"No, now. You're still holding onto that Times story aren't you? You have to let it go."

"Darn it Anne, we still haven't seen any proof that he's such a wonderful guy. He could take a knife to you or something any time."

Anne stared at her. "Do you really believe that?"

Molly groaned. "Your head is in the clouds. Somebody has to be the skeptic."

"My head is fine. You just won't admit you're wrong."

"Don't be an idiot."

Anne studied her face, forcing Molly to meet her eyes. "Don't make me choose between you."

Anne seethed with righteous indignation when she spoke. Molly was so stubborn. And such a busybody, stirring everything up for no reason. She hadn't done any Google searches on her Mister White. Paul wasn't a man who'd try to kill someone. Anybody could see that.

If only Molly would give up on this murder thing. Paul had explained everything, what more did she need? Anne sighed, her anger fading. Of course, Paul could show everybody the records to prove his innocence. That would shut Molly up. Oh right. But he'd feel as if, what, no one trusted him?

She was in a trap. If she left things as they were Paul and Molly would never get along, and if she told Paul she wanted to see his proof, things would never be the same with him.

It dawned on her that she had threatened her best friend. Don't make her choose? Yeah right, she had to. Unless Molly apologized, and Graham did too. Or Paul volunteered to show them his proof. She couldn't open her mouth without poisoning one relationship or the other.

Her agony eased as the day went on, and she ignored the dinner hour to varnish Louie once again. This time, when dry, she couldn't select a color for another wash. It seemed she'd finished far sooner than expected. She left the pieces as they were, doubting the final tones would be right, but unable to go on until the varnish had completely cured.

Frustration in full swing, she picked at the living room bookshelf for a read, and came away with travel books she'd collected over the years. The three she chose dealt with France, and two of them with Paris. She picked the older of the two and flipped pages randomly, trying to distract her brain.

Photos, white and black, with notations in Hannah's script, brought tears to her eyes. The book had been used to plan her graduation trip so many years ago.

Scanning faded pages for names of places, she started making notes. Mother's death was settled in her mind now. There would always be regrets, but they held no pain anymore. A small tremble took hold of her and warmth rushed through her body. She grabbed the newer Paris guide and paged through it, seeking those old names.

~ THIRTY-FIVE ~

Paul ran a hand over the gleaming surface of a chair leg. "This looks great. I guess your two weeks was a little pessimistic."

"I still have to reassemble it and finish the upholstery."

"You've been busy though."

"How was your trip?"

"The guys gave me a hard time for being away, but lunch was fun. I had dinner with Jane and Charlie and went to Tommy's soccer game this afternoon. They won in overtime."

"You sound like you enjoyed it."

"Yeah, I didn't realize how much I miss that stuff. I may go again next week. You want to come?"

"All right. I'd like to meet your friends."

"Hey, that's great. Ben's invited us for dinner. How's about we stay the night at my house?"

"All right. I..."

"You'll love Hazel. Ben too. This is great. You're sure?"

She laughed. "Be quiet for a minute, will you?"

"What?"

"I'm done Paul. I'm not mixed up anymore. I know what I want."

"Really? That's great. What?"

"Remember I said I wanted adventures? I do, and I can have them now. I want to travel, to go everywhere and see everything."

"What about Louie?"

"That won't take long. We can go to New York and Paris. The Boston art museums. Chicago, London, anywhere."

"All the art museums?" he asked, mock serious.

She sent him a coquette's grin. "Other things too, anywhere and everywhere."

"What about your paintings? Any news?"

"No."

"They'll sell soon."

"You sound like Graham. I'm about ready to make him cut the prices."

"I wouldn't. He knows his stuff."

"This isn't New York. People around here aren't that rich."

"Some are."

"I'll go to Paris and sell my paintings there."

"Sure, your grandma's favorite place. You'd probably be better off in New York though. That's do-able. We can check out New York and then spend an evening with Ben and Hazel."

"When?"

"Next week? He might invite Jack and Marty and their better halves too."

"That sounds like a party."

"The others don't have to be there."

"It doesn't matter."

"I'd like you to meet them all."

"That's fine."

"I'll tell Ben."

"Next week then. After that it's Paris and London and Washington."

"You'll need a passport."

"How long do you think it will take?"

"The passport? Weeks I think. You sound like you've caught your grandmother's wanderlust."

"Almost, yes. Dan's chair comes first of course, but once it's finished, I want to travel. And if Graham can't sell my paintings, I'll sell them somewhere else."

He stared at her in silence for a moment, a look of concern in his eyes.

"What?" she asked.

"You haven't mentioned Molly."

Her breath caught. She simply nodded.

"Trouble in River City?" he asked softly.

"No, what?" It was the perfect opportunity to tell him about the threat she'd made, to ask for his help, but she couldn't risk upsetting him.

Anne called Molly in the morning and made a date for lunch again, this time at Fletcher's. She couldn't let her horrible threat hang in the air without seeing if it still bothered Molly.

"Hey," Molly said when she slid into an empty seat with a grin on her face.

How wonderful, Molly looked relaxed and glad to see her. They could forget their argument for the moment at least, and talk about going to Paris with Paul.

"He's going to do all this world traveling with you?" Molly asked.

"Certainly, why not?"

"You're talking a pretty drastic change in his life."

"He's cautious that's all, conservative I guess you'd say. I want the moon, and he talks about going to New York, and seeing his friends. I mean, that's fine, but there are so many other things to do."

"So, tell him that."

"I will."

"Don't be mad if he backs off. It was only a few months ago you were stuck in the house, and now you want to travel? Where'd that come from?"

"I've wasted so many years, so many opportunities. And I don't have fifty years left to see different things. There has to be more than trips to Newport."

"Well, don't be petty with the man. It does you no good."

"Why would I be petty? Where did all this sudden wisdom come from?"

Molly laughed. "Interest on years of stupid choices. You should talk to Grace about this. She's the one who has it figured out."

"You always thought she and Dan were fuddy-duddies."

"I'm learning, painfully, but it's coming. You never see the two of them in a real fight, right?"

"What does that have to do with me?"

"What if Paul won't do everything you want to do now?"

"He will."

"He might not."

"Then we'll figure something out. I still want to do interesting things."

"Like what?"

"Fly an airplane, climb a mountain."

"That's all? You wouldn't like to run the Boston marathon maybe?"

Anne drew a deep breath. "No, it's really Paris. It's my entire focus right now. Don't ask why. I suppose I want it because I didn't go when I was a kid, but there's more I don't understand. I have this urge, this urgency, to go there."

"Just Paris? I thought you want to see the world."

"Oh, other places too, but mostly it's Paris."

"That's easy. A trip to Europe is nothing to panic about."

Recognition dawned with that comment, not a shock and yet it was, but Anne covered it well. "I'm afraid to tell him. You're the first to hear"

"You better call Grace. You need help."

"Why?"

"Listen to yourself, my friend. You've already told him you want to travel, and now you're afraid to tell the man you want to take one trip?"

"That isn't it."

"What then? You don't go to Paris or climb mountains every day. Most of life is flat routine stuff. He'll go with you."

She nearly said a trip was not the question, but Molly's quick reply cut her off. Now, a second time, she didn't make the point. "I won't be bound by that, Molly. I've had enough routine."

"Talk to Grace."

"I want your opinion."

"If he won't do one trip to Paris he's bad news. I'm sure he'll go. So, if he's not the problem, it's you. What's the big deal about a two week vacation?"

"I don't know," Anne lied.

"There's something you're not saying, something else, right?"

"I have to think."

"Really? It seems to me this is pretty clear, to you at least."

"I want to stay there a while."

"What's a while?"

"I don't know."

"More than a month?"

"Probably."

"Two months? Half a year?"

"Probably, yes."

"Now that's interesting. We're back to traveling the world."

"No, we're not."

"Same difference. The world, or Paris permanently. Either way his life's disrupted."

"I want to go alone, at least at the beginning."

"What in the world for?"

"To know I can."

"You better talk to Grace. You've got trouble girl."

~ THIRTY-SIX ~

The chat with Molly cleared her head on one thing, but she still didn't have all the answers. She'd go to Paris, but it was no two week vacation she wanted. It would be an indeterminate excursion into the past, and from there, the start of a new future. How could she explain to Paul, since she couldn't really explain it to herself. She'd have to be convincing though if she didn't want to lose him.

She had fussed about the color of the chair legs, thinking one more wash was needed. By the afternoon that thought died away and she bolted the first leg to the frame. Barring an accident, Louie would be finished in the morning.

One thing was clear. In Paris she'd stay in Montmarte, the place Hannah loved far more than any other. That was the place to start, and the rest would be a pilgrimage of sorts, to places Hannah had noted in the old guidebook, the ones made magical to her child's ear. The places she should have gone to as a teenager if Hannah had lived and she hadn't become a coward.

Paul could join her later. After all, she wanted that. Six months or more at least they'd stay. The house could be rented, and his as well, to pay the costs. Perhaps not his, if he didn't want to. A shiver coursed through her at the prospect, its source uncertain.

Paul asked about the lunch with Molly and she gave short answers, anxious to avoid discussion. Incomplete explanations seemed likely to bring only disaster at the moment. Paris could fulfill her childhood dreams and give her time to choose a path to the rest of her life. That much she was clear about.

"The chair will be done tomorrow. We can talk in the morning," she replied.

"You made up your mind then. About Paris."

"What? What makes you say that?"

"I've seen you with those guide books. That old one, with the writing all over it. That was Hannah's, right? You plan to go to Paris."

He said it flat, without emotion, and she nodded.

"Then what's the problem? You know I'll go with you."

"I want to stay a while. Six months at least."

"That's some vacation. Why not a year?"

"A year? Would you do that?"

"Six months is enough. Are you kidding?"

"Oh, of course, that's right."

"How about England? Let's go see where Hannah came from."

"No, I want to see Paris."

"We'll have time for both. England can be a short trip, just a couple of weeks."

"You really don't mind going for six months?"

"Actually, I can't see the point. I mean if we're going sightseeing in different places that's one thing, but six months in one city? You'll know every ant on the sidewalks by the time we come back."

She smiled at that, and turned away, confused suddenly. It had to be Paris, but why?

Paul replied with a frown on his face. "What are you doing? Each time we get into this you shut me out. It's like you have some secret I can't know. What's going on?"

"I'm not shutting you out. That's silly."

"We've talked about traveling, so what's the big deal? You read that guide to Paris only when I'm somewhere else in the house. That sure sounds secretive to me."

"I didn't mean it to be."

"Then what's going on?"

"I don't know Paul. It's just *Paris*. I feel like it's waiting for me, ever since I saw my mother. It's been waiting since I was young, before Hannah died. Her stories were always filled with romance and beauty and fun. Magical. It's that joy I want to feel, that childhood treasure to recapture."

"Okay, so what isn't clear? It sounds like you wanted that all your life."

"I didn't know that when I started. I mean, I did and didn't. I used to dream about it, but felt I'd never get there. Now I can do it, don't you see?"

He sighed, then smiled. "Okay, you have it resolved now. Just talk to me, will you? Don't keep secrets. I don't like it when you do that."

"I'm sorry. The only secret was that I was all mixed up," she lied.

"Let me help then. We're in this together, remember?"

"All right, no secrets." She said the words, but saying them almost choked her. She sighed and put a wrench to the bolt on Louie's second leg. He had to hear it sometime, best perhaps now. "Paul, there's more. I want to go by myself first."

"What for? You've already proven you can do anything."

"There's a lot I can't do."

"You know what I mean. What makes Paris different?"

"It just is."

"I see. You'll call me then, when you want me to come?"

"Of course."

"I can book my flight when I hear from you? Or should I book ahead, so I can come as soon as you call?" he said sarcastically.

"What does that mean?"

"I may have an affair while I wait. You won't mind will you?"

"You're being silly."

"You're so sure of me? That I won't cheat on you? What about you? What will you be doing all that time in Paris?"

"Paul, stop. This is ridiculous."

"Answer my question please."

"I told you. I want to prove to myself that I can do this trip alone. Like my grandmother did, and like my mother wanted to. It's the culmination of everything we've worked for. Why are you talking about affairs?"

"Like your mother wanted to? How do you know that?"

"I just think she did. Even if she didn't, she should have. That was why she drank. She never stood up for herself until she went away."

"When did she say all this?"

"It doesn't matter. She said she couldn't stand up to my grandmother. I think she would have been better off if she'd gone overseas like Hannah did. No one could have pushed her around then."

"Who's pushing you? Me for instance? Is that what you think?"

"I've been doing everything you tell me to."

"And I'm a dictator?"

"Please calm down. It's just that I like what I've learned these last few months and I want to feel really free."

"Who says you're not?"

"Me. I feel like I haven't finished what we started. That's the reason I want to start alone, the only reason. Can't you accept that?"

He turned to the window, silent, scowling.

"I want you with me. It's just a little time, like a vacation," she pleaded.

"You want your grandmother's life. To go off by yourself like she did," he growled.

"Only this once. Don't you see that going to a country where I don't know the language is a final proof for me? I'll never have to hide again after that."

He stared at her then and finally smiled a little smile. "Okay, okay. You'll find a reason to go no matter what I say. Can I have a date for when I'm supposed to join you?"

"I don't even know when I can leave yet."

~ THIRTY-SEVEN ~

Wednesday the bell tinkled on the door of the antique shop a little after ten as Anne and Paul walked in. Grace stood behind the register talking to Millie.

"Where's Dan?" Paul asked, in a stage whisper.

"In the basement. Good morning," Millie said.

"Give me a hand," he replied.

"He wants me down there. He'll be mad."

"Not for long," Anne said, happily grinning.

"Louie?" asked Grace, and got a nod from Anne. "Oh my. Never mind, I'll keep him occupied."

Louie was sitting in front of the counter when Dan appeared. "Gracie, we don't need an inventory. For Pete's sake, we just moved in here."

"We really should do one this morning."

"That's crazy. We..." He stopped before the large blanket covered mound beside the counter, a sly smile settling on his face. "What's this?"

"An old friend," Anne said.

"Take inventory, eh Gracie? Sneaky you are, that's what, every one of you. Is it really Louie?"

He reached for the blanket, but Millie shooed him away. "In a minute, Uncle Dan. We have to do this right."

"Are you kidding? Never mind fancy ceremonies. Let's have a look-see."

"Okay, but don't get too excited," Paul said. "Are you sure you're ready for this? You better sit down first."

"Never mind that baloney. I'll sit down when I can sit in my chair. Get on with it."

"Ta-da," Paul said with a grin, slowly lifting the blanket.

The old man stood transfixed as polished legs were revealed at a painfully slow pace, then the fabric-covered seat appeared, and at last, the remainder of the chair.

"I can't believe it, Gracie. Look at that! It's just like it was before!" Dan grabbed Paul's hand and pumped it up and down. "Thank you, thank you, thank you! Annie girl, give us a kiss. You are a genius! An absolute magician! Can I sit in it?"

"We haven't tried it, but you can. We put steel rods in the broken pieces," Anne said.

"You mean these are the original legs? They were splinters." He eased into the chair, gingerly settling weight on the seat, then looked up beaming. "Gracie, isn't this something? Come sit in it. Annie, you are unbelievable. You could do restorations for museums. No, forget that. I'll keep you busy right here. We have two new pieces waiting for you, right Millie?"

"She's going to France," Paul said.

Dan stared at him, then at Anne. "Really? To Paris?"

"Yes."

"That sounds like fun," said Millie.

"I never thought you'd go." Grace turned to Paul. "She told us if she ever went anywhere it would be Paris. Isn't that wonderful. Is it a honeymoon trip?"

"No, it would be for six months," Anne said.

"You don't seem very happy," Grace said, appraising Paul's expression.

"I'm okay."

"Six months?" asked Dan. "What about my furniture?"

"Really, Dan, don't tease. Isn't that something? We'll come and visit while you're there. Won't that be wonderful? Millie's ready to run the store, right dear?"

"I don't know about that, Aunt Grace."

Ignoring the girl's reply, Grace continued, "When are you going?"

"We're still talking about it," Paul said.

Dan studied him. "You ever been to Paris?"

"No."

Grace frowned. "Are you not going?"

"There's a lot to be resolved."

"Are you two breaking up?" Dan snapped.

"No," Anne said quickly.

"She's going alone, at least to start," Paul said.

"Are you going at all?" Millie asked.

"I don't know."

"I don't know what to say," Grace murmured, her voice almost a whisper.

"What's happening here? You're good people. You belong together," Dan snapped.

"Dan stop," Grace said, taking Paul's arm. "He's right you know. Don't let her go."

"I can't stop her."

"I didn't mean that. Go with her. You must. You absolutely must."

"It's her choice."

"It's been my dream, Grace, from when I was little. You know that," Anne said.

"Nothing is final," Paul said. He glanced at Anne. "We should leave now. Enjoy the chair."

Stunned, her stomach rolling as if she'd been kicked, Anne kissed Grace and followed him out the door.

~ THIRTY-EIGHT ~

"Thanks for that," she said, as they slid into the car. "You could have told me first."

"It just came out. I hadn't made up my mind."

"And you have now? You're not coming?"

"I don't think so. I'll be here when you get back."

"Suppose I don't?"

"Come back?"

"Yes."

He shook his head, looking annoyed at the threat. "Is this a new gambit?"

"I'm serious. If you won't come, maybe I'll stay there. Why should I come back?"

"Knock it off. This is no game. Six months is way too long."

"I'm not playing. I'll move there."

"Really? When were you going to tell me? When we got over there?"

"Sarcasm I do not need," she shouted, and turned away.

That was her mother's way, shrieking, shouting, with Father's slashing sarcasm in reply. She recalled the terror of those fights and how she'd sought safety in her bedroom with the door shut.

"What are we doing? Please, let's stop this now."

He was fuming, it was in his face. "What magic pill do you propose?"

"Let's just stop, all right? We can talk later."

"I don't see an answer. You're making the fight."

"No, please, don't say that. Won't you come with me a while? Three months?"

"One maybe, that's all."

"Please, two?"

He sighed. "Are you coming back?"

"Of course."

"Two then, okay."

He'd said it grudgingly, demanding concessions to cooperate, an angry bargain.

A sense of great foreboding fell on her, but she kept it to herself. What was happening? She should placate him, make this argument go away, but she couldn't stop, could not give up her dreams.

"Good, two months, then. The middle months."

He went silent, but gave a nod, a bare hint of one. It was all the affirmation he offered.

Apprehension grew, and she felt a rising bitterness in her heart. His love, it seemed, came down to haggling, dealing with a rug merchant.

"It's the newspaper article isn't it? You think I tried to kill my wife?" he said suddenly.

"What? No, not that."

"I'll bring you the papers. I'll show you copies of the checks I got from the lawsuits." His eyes looked stricken and she hated seeing that pain in his face.

"Paul, no, it's not you. I trust you."

He shook his head. "It's not over. There's something there. Is it Molly?"

She surrendered. It had to be said, had to come out in the open. "She keeps asking if I've seen the proof."

"Meddling."

"She worries. She wants me to be sure about you."

"And you're not?" he said, his voice without emotion.

"No, I mean yes, I am. She's the one who needs to believe. She keeps bringing it up"

He nodded. "Pressuring you. That's why you want to go away."

Her breath caught. This discussion needed to end right now. She had to calm herself, had to think. But she wouldn't give up, couldn't. Crossing her arms to stop the trembling, she said softly, "It's my childhood dream. You won't refuse me that will you?"

Anne stopped, recalling the excitement she'd felt the day Hannah announced the plan to visit Paris. That, and how devastated she'd been when Hannah had died so suddenly.

Agitated by the memory, she struggled to calm down. She had to decide, had to end the pitched battle going on in her head. Conscience, guilt and the overwhelming sense that she had to go to Paris or she'd never be the woman she could be. The woman Hannah had been, and her mother had become at the end. There was no choice involved.

~ * ~

Paul spent the day absorbing TV trash, while she wandered the house and property. Early evening found her in the workshop, fingering the small scrapers Dan had given her years before.

Paul's agreement to join her for two months gave her some solace despite their disagreements. His resistance had left her doubting whether she should actually go. That doubt had disappeared now. Some shop equipment had to be sold, but Dan's scrapers would go with her.

She'd find restoration work in Paris, and when paintings started to sell the income would be enough to live on comfortably. If not, then she'd use her savings to supplement. She'd lived on the income from her inheritance for many years and that alone had kept her. Finances were not the problem.

Paul's unhappiness haunted her. Words had to be found to show him her need, but she would go without him. Fingering the small round scraper they used so much on Louie, she headed for the living room. Paul was gone.

She found him in the kitchen, jacket on, at the outside door.

"I'm going for a walk," he said.

"Don't please. We have more to talk about."

A frown coursed his brow. "More? I thought we had a bargain?"

The word grated on her. "I want to live there. I need to."

"What? Permanently?"

"Yes."

"You knew that all along."

"No, yes, I don't know."

"That tops it."

"Don't be mad. I just realized it's important to me."

"Crap, what next? Should we move to East Africa? What other surprises do you have?"

"That's all. I promise. I've been all mixed up, but now it's clear."

"Clear and easy, right? All I have to do is sell my house and boat and car, and say bye-bye to my kids."

"That isn't necessary. We'll visit. We can rent the houses and keep one car."

"What about my kids?"

"Paul, you'll love it. You can buy a boat there and we'll fly back whenever you want to. Your family can visit Paris too. It will be wonderful for your grandchildren."

He shook his head. "That will cost a bundle. And it won't work."

"Why not? I want to see my friends, too. We'll maintain our contacts here. Your friends will start moving to Florida soon anyway."

"Says who? Ben and Marty will never leave New England."

"We don't have to spend all our time in Europe. It would be so exciting to live there. We'll become Left Bank bohemians." The smile she tried to offer met his frown and faded away.

"You're going to do this," he said, voice flat, hard-edged.

"You'll love it, I know you will."

"My life is here. I want to see my grandchildren grow up."

"We will. You don't see them every day, or even every month. We'll fly back. It'll be like going to California."

"That's too far to go. Why does it have to be permanent?"

"Because it's where I want to live. It's a major art center. It's central to the rest of Europe, and Hannah loved it and taught me to love it. I want to see and feel all the things she told me about."

"I don't like it. We could go for six months and then come back."

"To what? A house like the one I've lived in all my life? I'm done with country living. Paris is an exciting, exhilarating place. Hannah loved it and I will too."

"You're trying to live her life."

"It wouldn't be a bad idea. She had a good one." She paused, fighting back the anger raging in her belly, but he didn't speak. "I thought you were committed to us, to me. I don't think you are."

"Me? You're the one who wants to run away. What makes me wrong and you right?"

She stared at him. "It's not a question of right and wrong. I'm asking you to move with me. You're just refusing what I want and I don't know why."

His scowl seemed to ease a tiny bit. "Maybe I'll come for a couple of months to help you settle in."

"Are we back to bargaining again? You already agreed to that. I'll survive on my own. Come later, if you're not coming permanently."

"What difference does it make when I come?"

"You want it all your way. You leave me nothing for myself."

"What does that mean?"

"You think you're my caretaker. Let me guide you for a change. I don't need help anymore. I wear my prosthesis in public now."

"This is ridiculous," he said, and stood.

"What are you doing?"

"I can't deal with this."

She followed him to the bedroom and watched as he dragged out the duffel bag he'd moved in with. Tears threatened, and then couldn't be held in check. He tossed clothing into the bag, gave her a gruff, unfeeling peck, and walked out.

~ THIRTY-NINE ~

He should be there, making dinner, with NPR playing softly in the background. He wasn't a loud man, never rowdy, but she could always sense his presence. It had been a strange new feeling, knowing one was not alone. Little sounds, a door, a foot-fall or a word or two, they always told the tale, but there was more to it than that somehow. He might have been outdoors, painting the old windows, perhaps washing his car, making no sound audible inside. Yet, she'd know. It seemed that was the thing, the knowing. She felt comforted, warm and cozy with him nearby.

At any moment he might dash inside, calling, "I'm going to the hardware store. Want to come?"

Stillness reigned now and with it a difference, the empty silence, day long, ages long, absolute. Sweet quiet had held the house before. A creaky floorboard, the rattle of an old loose window, were all the sounds she'd heard, gifts of a friend that asked nothing but a bit of tending.

In recent months, her friend had been still, or so it seemed. Paul had drowned out such whispers, except in quiet moments, on the couch or patio, when she could melt into his arms. Today, a creak in the bones of the old house brought only awareness of his absence.

She called on Hannah for advice, but even she seemed a distant dream, their conversations a silly invention of another time. Mother Jean served no better. Real or imagined, it was Paul she wanted to hear from. He didn't call.

She should never have told him Molly wanted to see his proof. That had been a trap and she'd fallen right into it. There would always be doubt in his mind, not about Molly, but about her trust, her faith in him. A poisoned burr that would never go away. If that was why he wouldn't go to Paris, nothing she did would make a difference. She choked back a sob.

~ * ~

A day went by, then two, and she dialed his number. His recorded voice replied.

"This is the Breland residence. Leave a message."

"Please call me, Paul. We need to talk," she said. Another day she waited and left her plea, and then another. Each time the machine answered after four rings. The machine was resetting; he was listening. That was clear.

Frozen fish sticks having long since disappeared from the freezer, dinner became a can of soup, this night lentil. A pear and coffee for desert, she wanted nothing more. She carried a tray to the living room.

It seemed impossible this man who had urged her on, who wanted her to see the world, would now refuse her wish for Paris. She turned on the television. Sound was necessary, any kind, it didn't matter. Soup in hand, she moved room to room, seeking. There was only space, cavernous rooms, each one a chamber of silence. She entered, and stood, and waited. Nothing filled her heart, no joy, nor curiosity, no peace, no excitement.

She finished the soup and moved to the next room, then the next, and soon, knowing nothing else to do, she started again. He'd change his mind. Unless she was wrong about him, misunderstood him completely. Unless he didn't love her as she thought, unless all that, he would come. She simply needed to give him time to come around. Even Grace said that.

She left bits of gossip on his machine each day, enough to keep in touch.

"Molly came for lunch today. She said Graham has been wonderful since he came back from New York."

"Grace sends her regards. Millie and her mailman are dating hot and heavy. Grace says he's going to propose." Pain stabbed through her heart at the bittersweet thought. She wondered why she told him, thinking it unlikely he cared.

"Graham sold two of my paintings. At last. One went for five thousand dollars. I guess he was right about them." That news should have thrilled her, but somehow it didn't matter anymore.

"I'm going to rent my house out. I'll store some furniture and sell some too. Dan is going to run a tag sale from the house the week I leave. Won't you come up?"

She kept calling, sure he listened. No response seemed better than a negative. That much kept her at it, hoping something would break soon, he'd answer and say he would come, that he loved her still. It wouldn't help to be angry, not at all. There was no good in that.

He didn't respond. Doubt competed with manufactured certainty, disabling her resolve. It took three days to deliver a dozen paintings to Graham's gallery. The rest would go to Molly's house until the dozen sold, but they remained in her studio for the moment. The passport hadn't come, her flight had to be arranged, a million things demanded her attention, but she often found herself staring at the windows in those silent rooms, seeing only glass. She walked, without purpose or benefit, and walked again.

~ * ~

"So forget him. Find someone in Paris. If you want to that is. I don't recommend it though, not right off," Molly said.

"You of all people. Someone in Paris. That's stupid," Anne said, her tone harsh, belligerence released at last, in safety. "You at least should understand."

"I do, that's the trouble. You can't chase a man. Believe me, I know."

"Really? Since when?"

"Don't be nasty. You have to be the nectar of a flower. Bees come to you then."

"That's just wonderful advice! Yuck!"

"I know, I'm the original bee hunter. Look, it's hard, but don't let him get you down."

It was an unsatisfactory conversation, but no worse than the one with Grace. The older woman was her usual supportive, reassuring self, but Anne felt no better when their conversations ended.

Nothing changed. Each time Grace called she contrived to ask the status of Millie's romance and Grace gave positive reports. Anne took pleasure in the news, but it was a sad sweet joy. Millie and her boyfriend, happy together. A sweet but painful report.

Painting frustrated her. She had no furniture to restore, which was fine. Her once beloved garden seemed utterly unimportant. Early bedtime held a great attraction.

Then she'd had enough and left a different message.

"I'm leaving soon. Answer me, you jerk."

That produced a response. No plea this time, emotion not to his liking. She had felt and sounded sure, so sure of herself.

"How are you?" he asked.

"I've been better. You've been there all the time, haven't you?"

"I didn't want to talk. It would make it worse."

"Oh sure. Come with me, damn you."

"You know I can't."

"We'll visit."

"This is the same old argument. It won't work."

She sighed, "I'll be getting my passport soon."

"What does that mean? Are you moving right away?"

"I booked a studio apartment in the Luxemburg Gardens."

"Where's that?"

"In the middle of the city, off the Boulevard St. Michel. Why can't we work this out?"

"You've already decided everything."

~ * ~

He couldn't, wouldn't say what was in his mind. She didn't love him, not enough. It had needed only a day of brooding to produce that certainty. After all, she'd go off despite his objections, clear proof she didn't need him now. He'd helped her overcome her fear and this was his reward. She used him, just like Ellie did. That and more he'd dwelt on since he left her that day.

He'd met with friends, worked on his boat, and gone to lunch with Ben, seeking distraction.

"Something haywire in Rhode Island?" Ben asked more than once, but Paul just shrugged him off with a never mind, everything's okay or some such words.

Hope, that was his watchword, and the belief she'd turn contrite and change her mind. The whole idea of Paris was totally irrational. A childhood dream! She hadn't mentioned it before.

The possible implications of that thought included one too painful to contemplate. She simply wanted to escape from him, as Ellie had almost two years ago. The thought sat like a woodpecker hammering away, a needle buried in his soul.

"What's wrong with you?" she cried. "This is what we've worked for since you first took me out."

"What does that have to do with Paris?"

"I won't hide again."

"Who's hiding?"

"We won't abandon your family. I love them too."

"You could fool me. You're totally unreasonable," he growled.

"You've got to be kidding. Answer my question."

"I'll go along with something reasonable."

"But not Paris?"

"Not permanently."

"Well. Then I guess I know where I stand in your life." She spiked the words into the phone, then deposited it on the table with a bang.

~ * ~

Her anger cooled, but not to peace or pleasure. He was lost to her, that seemed certain. She'd compromise, accept a year or two commitment in lieu of a lifetime, but he had to care enough to make the offer.

The house had been her shackle. That was broken now, and love of Paul could not become another chain. The house was her own doing and she would not do that to herself again, no matter what the price.

"I'll grow to hate him if I abandon Paris," she said aloud. The thought drew a brief tear, and she tried to call Molly, had to leave a message on her machine.

She delivered the remainder of her paintings to Molly's spare bedroom until the ones Graham had were sold. Passport, tickets, packing, buying things occupied her as the days passed with no word from Paul. Because Dan had offered to run a tag sale for her at the house, she insisted on working in the shop to repay him.

"Why doesn't she put the effort into him? It's like she doesn't give a hoot, Gracie. She loves the guy, doesn't she?"

"Of course she does."

"Nuts. I don't get it."

"It's busyness. She's trying to keep the hurt away."

"Then why is she doing this?"

"The question is Paul. Why is he so obstinate?" Grace said.

"Two stubborn people in a battle of wills? Is that all that's going on?"

"I think for Anne it's more. She wants to make up for all the days she let go by."

~ FORTY ~

She stepped from the warm Ford and pulled her heavy winter coat tight against the late January chill. Surprising, it was colder here than in Rhode Island, or maybe she'd adjusted to the warm car. She tried the back door. It wasn't locked.

"Paul," she called, as she stepped into the kitchen. He didn't reply, but the television was going in the other room. She headed for it, calling his name.

"Who's there? Anne? How did you get here?" No hello, no kiss of greeting. She noted both without rancor. No surprise, it reflected her own mood.

"I drove. The car was fine."

"You're crazy. That old heap could have died on you anywhere."

"How are you?"

"I'm okay."

"The sink is full of dishes and you have a week's growth of beard. That's okay?" she said, touching a finger to his cheek.

"It's three days and I like it this way. What are you doing here?"

"I miss you."

"I guess you'll have to get used to that."

"Paul, we don't have to do this. Why won't you come with me?"

"My life is here. I told you that before."

"Yes, parked in front of the TV in the middle of the day."

"Every day isn't like this."

"The house is a mess, you're a mess, and everything is just fine," she said bitterly.

"Listen, I did okay before we met and I'll do okay after you leave."

She stared, heat rising in her face. "You think I'm trying to run your life? Is that what this is about?"

He turned back to the TV, and turned up the volume.

"Paul. Talk to me. Don't do this."

"What's the point?"

She snapped off the television. "You've made this into a trap. We need to talk if we're going to fix this, but you're not doing it and you won't let me do it."

She stopped, breathing hard, and waited. His glare was the only reply. "You want this your way, no matter what it costs," she said softly.

"That's you, not me," he said, tight-lipped and very still.

She sighed. There was no anger in it, only resignation. "You thought I was weak, that you could run my life for me. Was that the attraction? Why else would you go for a one-armed old maid recluse?"

He shook his head. "You're wrong. You're a lot more than that."

"Oh, I know that now. You forced me to take a look at myself and I learned." She paused, but he remained silent. "I thank you for that, but I still think you want to be in charge. I made a decision on my own and you can't stand that."

"It's not who made the decision. It's what the decision is. I told you my life is here. Family, friends, everything, but you expect me to abandon them!" He stood close, almost in her face.

"I never asked you to do that. You won't lose them in Paris any more than if you move to Rhode Island," she said, driving the words at him, wishing she could shove them into his brain.

"Crap!" he snapped, and waved her away.

"Things will be different if we're in Paris, but nothing has to end."

"Yes it will. Maybe not right away, but eventually."

"Like us?"

"No. We'll write and call and visit. Maybe you'll come back in a year or two."

"Is that what you're counting on? That I'll come back so you can rescue me again?"

"Of course not."

She gave a sardonic laugh. "You better hope not. If I came back that way, you wouldn't want to be with me. And if I did come back that way, it wouldn't be to you."

"Anne. Please, let's stop this. I don't want to fight."

"I agree. I love you, but you have to make a choice." She moved toward the door. "I'm leaving soon. I still have things to do at home." She left then, deliberately holding back a goodbye.

~ * ~

He found perverse pleasure in her attack. It confirmed opinions he'd nursed since Paris became an issue. He'd reached many conclusions, none of them happy. Her head was screwed up, that was the latest. If reason failed, then of course she didn't recognize the hurt she inflicted. Paris wasn't in the bargain either, not in the beginning. Women were totally irrational.

His opposition wasn't frivolous resistance to a decision she made, no way. He disowned that idea completely. He would not tolerate ultimatums, especially about leaving him.

He stared at the phone, yearning to call and tell her he loved her. Still, he didn't call, wanting it to come from her. Instead, he called Jane.

"What a nice surprise," she said. "You haven't called very much since you found the love of your life. How are you both?"

"Surviving."

"That doesn't sound very positive. What's wrong?"

"She's going to Paris."

"I gather you're not? I thought you two were inseparable. What happened?"

"Nothing. We'll visit back and forth. This isn't the end, just a modern relationship."

"Modern relationship! What have I missed?"

She kept at him, asking why he wouldn't go, pointing out he could learn French, had always liked languages.

"I'll be too far away from my grandchildren," he said without heart, tired of his own use of the excuse.

"You sound like a woman whose husband made a job move without consulting her. Thoroughly ticked," she said.

"Don't be smart. I'll see you."

He hung up, annoyed with himself for making the call. He didn't need her blasted approval. Why the hell did he call her? He turned on the TV, surfed three or four channels, then switched it off and stared at the blank screen.

He gave her love and got what in return? Paris! Go with her or else, no compromise, no discussion, no choice. And every time he accepted her terms she upped the ante. What was next?

Even if they resolved this, the future wasn't certain to his way of thinking. He remembered how small disagreements festered into harsh bitterness with Ellie. It was a mistake he would not willingly repeat. What point was there in going on with the whole business? She cared for him just about as much as Ellie had.

~ * ~

Unable to sleep, he rose by six for an early breakfast. A light powdery snow coated the ground, but the forecast was good. Good for flying. Would it be as good next week when she left? Stupid thought, what difference would that make?

If only the phone would ring and she'd be there, saying "It's all off."

The phone didn't ring. She'd have the movers coming to empty out the house in a day or two. Years ago Molly would have been with her to keep them in line, but maybe Anne would do that for herself now. He considered lunch at eleven, but decided it was too early to eat. Instead, he grabbed scotch from the liquor cabinet. Filling a glass with ice, and a good dollop of booze, he added water, walked to the window and stared out at his neighbor's house.

She stood on the back steps, using a broom to sweep away the snow. A couple of years younger than he was, attractive and divorced, she lived alone. He watched her vigorous clearing of the steps and walk. She entered the house, shaking snow off the broom before depositing it on the top step. She reminded him of Anne, all business and no wasted motion.

Other memories filled his head. The feel of Anne's body against his own in a simple hug and the joy of quiet moments in the woods or a glass of wine together. Her very presence in the house. And their time in bed. And she believed him about Carol's death. He picked up the folder he'd assembled for her, the papers that proved his innocence, the ones she'd never asked for. He should send it to Miss Molly just to shove the truth in her face. He groaned and dropped it on the table again. He was thinking like a spoiled child.

It seemed as if he should have an ache or a pain somewhere, but there was only emptiness, a pervasive blackness. Analyze it, label it, fix it and make it better, that he would have liked to do. He couldn't. The house was empty. Warmth didn't exist anymore. He had to find something to replace it. Some way to fill the gap.

His neighbor came out of her house again with a package in her arms. She struggled to open her car, deposited the package on the seat, and turned back to the house. Winter wind caught her long dark hair and curled it across her face. She saw him through the window and mimicked a shiver, pulling her collar around her face, then popping it open to reveal a grin. He waved.

"Pretty woman," he told the window. "She'd probably be happy to go to lunch. Nice too. That's what I need, no complications, just someone to have a good time with. When they define your life, it's trouble."

He paused. Odd words, define your life. He'd always worried about how Anne was doing. He worried when they went out. Crap, he reacted to her feelings, her wishes, her attitude. He swore. He hadn't thought of that. It was time to decide what he wanted for a change.

Staring at the neighbor's house, he recalled the windblown hair, the smile she gave him in the cold. His heart eased, the first time in many days. He picked up the phone, then stopped with it against his ear. The phone wouldn't do. He put the receiver down and went looking for his coat.

~ FORTY-ONE ~

Grace arrived first, driving the white van alone, in time for breakfast. She wished it were Paul in his Toyota. The maple and the oak had lost their leaves to winter cold and stark branches left the sky exposed. Bare trees and winter sky, it was a scene to store away in memory. She wondered how the trees would look in Paris.

Anne's offer of coffee drew an apology for being so early and a, "Thank you, I've already eaten." Grace had come for the music cabinet. Anne had offered it to Paul, with a message on his machine, but he hadn't replied.

It wasn't often Grace visited alone. The old couple was normally inseparable, yet this day Dan was absent.

"He said to apologize, but he couldn't take another goodbye," Grace said. "He was the worst grump I have ever seen after the tag sale."

"What? Why?"

"So he wouldn't cry, of course. It's not every day we say goodbye to our daughter. Even if you aren't really."

"Oh Grace."

The old woman wiped away a tear. "Forget that last part. It's not true. You really are you know. My daughter. Is that all right with you?"

Anne wrapped her arms around the plump body and got a big squeeze in return. Quick hugs and tears and kisses and then Anne abruptly turned to the business of the moment. She expected frequent travel to be common, and she knew Grace expected her back before long. After all, why else would one simply lease one's house? And besides they still had six days left before Anne left.

The business of the moment was the music cabinet still sitting in the hall. Once a symbol of joy, it could serve only as a painful reminder of better days.

"You keep it for your own," Anne said.

"I couldn't. You already gave us that wonderful old phonograph."

"Never mind that. You keep both of them."

"Dan plays it all the time, you know. He won't use your cylinders though. He had some from an estate sale."

She told her old friend to use the cylinders, they belonged to her now, but Grace just smiled. It was a pact of sorts. She was their girl and certain things remained unchanged, and always would. They agreed to disagree, for love, with love.

"Have you seen your friend Betty?"

"She stopped by during the tag sale, but I haven't seen her since."

"She seemed unhappy that day."

"You saw her? It's the divorce. Her husband left her." Betty talked incessantly of being abandoned by her man. The way she was feeling, the last thing Anne wanted was to hear about Betty's unhappiness, so she'd avoided her running partner lately. A final goodbye toward the end of the week was all she wanted.

She helped Grace load the cabinet into the van and they bid farewell for a second time. This one was less emotional than the day of the tag sale, but barely so. They had stayed the night, before the sale, Dan and Grace, to be there when the crowds arrived they said, but she knew it had been for moral support as well. So typical, so constant, their love for her. For the umpteenth time in recent weeks, her hard sought resolve wavered.

Molly arrived a few minutes after eleven-thirty. Many of Anne's possessions had been sold or were safely in the hands of Dan and Grace, but this was Molly's time to choose herself a gift or two. They had argued over this before, Anne wanting her to pick before anyone else, before things were sold, but Molly flat refused, telling Anne the things she wanted weren't likely to be chosen by anyone else. Anne wandered through the house with her, watching as she made her choices. Molly picked a tiny painting of a daisy Anne had done years ago and a pair of wine glasses the two of them had used so many times.

"They'll remind me of you whenever I look at them," Molly told her.

Anne hugged her and then returned to the kitchen where Molly had set out a Wendy's lunch. She also produced a bottle of wine and plastic glasses.

"We're not using my souvenirs," Molly said, and then went on. "I noticed your mother's ashes on the mantel. You dug her up."

"She's going with me." Anne stopped as if waiting for a comment.

"That's a little ironic don't you think. After all the years you hated her?"

"I suppose." Anne said, and then, "It's hard to leave. So many years, so many memories."

"I know. It's strange to think you won't be here for me to visit."

"Did you find me a tenant yet?"

"Yes. The young love birds you didn't like."

The young couple had irritated her. They had life all planned, she'd seen it in their attitudes. A child, a year or two in her house and then they'd buy a house of their own. No one had told them it might not work out that way. Or that even if it did they had no idea what would happen in another twenty years. She didn't want them living in her home, but it was too late now.

"Remember when I tried to help you paint the house?" asked Molly.

Anne smiled, "You were lucky you didn't get killed when you fell off the ladder."

"I'm lucky you didn't kill me. I got paint on your redwood table and the patio tiles."

"Only four or five."

"Yeah, and your beautiful boxwood that I fell on."

"Molly, stop. I'm going to miss you, you know. I'd love to have you in Paris to paint my apartment."

"I won't even know where you are."

"You have my address."

"That isn't the same. I can picture you here, or in Boston or New York. I've never been to Paris."

"Then come and get to know it with me."

"I thought you'd never ask."

Anne walked slowly into the studio, stood for a moment, then turned, tears trickling down her cheeks. Molly offered a hug, but she held up her arm as a barrier.

"I thought Paul would call."

"He's a jerk," Molly said.

"No. He's upset and doesn't know what to do about it."

"You're making excuses for him."

"That doesn't matter. He's not here."

"Maybe he'll come to the airport when you leave."

"He'll come here if he comes at all." Anne sighed.

"Does he know you'll be staying with me the next few days?"

"We haven't talked lately."

"I don't know what you're doing. I mean, I know this is a dream for you, but there must be some other way to go."

"I've tried. He won't come."

"Why not lie to him? Tell him you changed your mind, it's only for a month."

"That's no good."

"Why not? If you get him over there, you could stall and maybe he'd get used to it."

"Molly stop, please."

"Well, you're going to have an unhappy dream if you ask me," Molly said. "Will you ever get together again?"

"I hope so."

"What if you don't?"

"Let's open that wine," Anne said. Desperate to change the subject before she burst into tears, she set to work with the corkscrew.

Molly waited in subdued silence while she poured. With one cup full Anne paused, the bottle in midair.

"What?" asked Molly.

"I hear a car. He always races up the drive." Still clutching the bottle, she dashed to the door.

Certain it was Paul arriving, sure she knew why he'd come, she tore across the patio. Bursting through the hedge opening, she crashed head on into him. He stepped back, wearing a smile that brightened her heart, holding an envelope and a bottle of red wine in one hand and two glasses in the other.

"Hi beautiful. I thought maybe I'd buy you a drink."

Laughing, she held up her own bottle and waved it at him. "Molly got here first."

"She's here? Crap, I had big ideas."

"Really? What kind of ideas?" she said demurely.

The smile left his face, replaced by a look of sadness. "I've been an idiot about Paris. I want to go if you'll still have me."

"Idiots are welcome. And you really weren't an idiot."

A sweet smile returned to his face. "Thank you, but I was. A change of address is nothing compared to achieving the dream of a lifetime. I love you, Anne Hoskins."

His arms slipped around her as she leaned into his body. He brought the wine behind her neck, gently pulled her to him as his tongue sought her mouth. She nibbled sharply on the tip and let it enter.

"Well, well look who's here. Did I hear someone talking about idiots?" Molly asked, standing in the doorway.

Anne stumbled backwards as he gently nudged her into Molly. Her mouth still locked on his, she felt him fumbling to shove bottle, glasses, and envelope into Molly's hands, then she was in his arms, being carried into the house.

"You're supposed to save that for the wedding night," Molly said.

"What?" Paul asked.

"That threshold thing. You know."

"He's practicing," Anne said.

"He needs to," Molly said. "So, are you going with her?"

"As soon as I get my passport. That envelope is for you by the way."

"What is it?"

"Papers you've been wanting to see."

Anne pulled him down and planted another kiss fiercely on his lips.

"Hey Molly," he said with a grin. "How long will it take you to get lost?"

"Forget that. It's time for public celebrations. I'm calling Dan and Grace to join us. Maybe a few dozen other people too."

Anne laughed. "Don't you dare."

Molly gave them a happy smile and grabbed the open wine from Anne. "Behave yourselves for two more minutes and I'll pour."

With his arm on Anne's shoulder Paul surveyed the kitchen. "You moved some stuff out already. Are you shipping everything to Paris?"

"No. It's going to different places. To storage, to Dan and Grace, and some is coming with me."

Paul nodded and kissed her on the nose. "I assume you still have a bed?"

"That's in Paris already," Molly said, "She's staying with me until she leaves."

Anne gave her a loving smack on the arm. "Stop Molly. I still have a bed. It's here."

Paul took the glass Molly offered and hoisted it into the air. "To Paris."

Anne clinked her glass hard against his. "To Paris and to us," she added, trying to suppress a leering grin.

The happiness in Paul's eyes sent a warm and mushy wave through her heart. Obviously, his decision to join her was clear of doubts and recriminations. Nothing of his anger remained, only the joy of being with her danced in his eyes. This had started out to be a sad day with Molly holding her hand. At the moment, she couldn't wait for Molly to leave.

She downed her wine in three big gulps, hoping Molly would take the hint and do the same. She felt as giggly as she had in the beginning. Back when she first wanted to go to bed with Paul, when she felt like a schoolgirl teasing with a new boyfriend.

"You look like you're ready to jump him right now," Molly said, leering like the Cheshire Cat.

"You're so brilliant. Isn't she Paul?"

"Right. Pure genius."

"You have the whole day ahead of you. And tonight. I think we should be having some kind of intellectual discussion about now. Maybe about politics or religion," Molly said with great seriousness.

Paul laughed. "Do you still have a broom, Anne?"

"In the garage. There are two, I think."

"I'll get them. We'll sweep her out together."

Her eyes dancing, Molly finished her wine. "Never mind, I'm gone."

She kissed Anne and picked up Paul's envelope, then turned to face them again. "You guys should fight more often. You're hot enough to melt the chandelier." She turned as she reached the door. "I want to see you both again before you leave, so cool it by then please."

Anne slipped an arm inside of his as they stood watching her car disappear. "Thank you for bringing your proof."

"I figured we needed to calm her down for good on that subject." He kissed her. "She'll probably read everything as soon as she gets out of sight."

"Don't be mad. She just worries about me. Did you bring a suitcase?"

"Nope. I left in a hurry." He nibbled at her ear.

"Will you stay the night? You can wear the same clothes tomorrow."

He wrapped his arms around her, then tilted his head back and smiled into her eyes. "I should go back. I have to get started on my passport and sell the house and my boat."

"You're selling everything? Why?"

"Hey, if I'm going to live in Paris, why keep them? I figure we can charter a boat when we want to. Just think, we'll be able to sail the English Channel."

"Is that why you're coming with me? It took you long enough to figure that out," she teased.

"Yup. That was my one and only reason. Except of course, there was that bit about getting you into bed. That was a minor consideration, but I took it into account."

"You are so bad."

He swept her into his arms and started toward the house. "I know. Just terrible, that's me."

"Put me down. I can walk."

Instead, he put his lips to hers and gave her a very heated kiss. Tense excitement surged through her as he headed for the bedroom.

~ * ~

She lay quietly running her fingers slowly down his cheek when they were done. She didn't want to speak, didn't need to, simply felt so warm and wonderful beside him, knowing he would be there for the rest of the day, for all their days in Paris, forever. Warm happiness bubbled in her heart as a sense of joy and peaceful pleasure filled her very soul. Everything, simply everything, was right with the world.

As the clock neared six, he whispered in her ear. "You know I'm not twenty-one anymore. I need a little nourishment to keep me going."

"This wasn't nourishment enough?" she teased.

"I need a little of the kind that goes into the stomach."

"You're such a spoilsport."

He laughed. "And you are so hot. But I think it's time we ate and I went home. I need a little something left for when we get to Paris."

She slid off the bed, found a pair of slippers and put them on. "All right. I can probably find us something to eat."

He grinned. "We could go out."

"But then I'd have to put some clothes on wouldn't I?"

"Yeah, let's forget that idea."

The dinner preparations were a little haphazard as they played with each other in the kitchen. Eventually, despite her attempts to distract him, Paul made an improvised omelet with the little bit of food she still had on hand, eggs, hot dogs and frozen vegetables. Afterwards, Anne sent him her most seductive smile.

"Are you sure you don't want to stay the night?" she whispered.

"The sooner I get my passport, the sooner I can join you in Paris. Don't tempt me."

"One more time then?" she asked softly.

He grinned and kissed her. "How can I refuse?"

Laughing with the sheer pleasure surging through her heart, she began to pull him toward the bedroom.

An hour later she watched him dress, then stood, still naked, and buttoned the last two buttons of his shirt for him. He wrapped his arms around her and crushed her to his chest, then nibbled gently at her ear.

"If you keep doing that I'm going to attack you again," she whispered.

"Can't have that. You've already worn me out today."

She punched his arm. "You are so wimpy."

"Wimpy? Now that presents a challenge."

She shook her head, smiled, and touched his cheek. "If you're going home, I want you to stay awake in the car. No more funny business today."

His face went still, but his eyes were twinkling. He kissed her forehead, gently, softly. "I love you, Anne Hoskins."

"I love you, Paul Breland."

He smiled again. "You know, if I'm moving to Paris, I have one last demand."

"Which is?"

"You have to take my name."

She touched his chin and tapped it with her finger, realizing what he meant. "Why would I want to do that?"

He stared at her, then laughed. "Hey woman, it's the custom."

"I don't think so. Paris is known for lovers and mistresses."

"Yeah well, we shouldn't scandalize people. We have to make it legal."

"I suppose I might consider it," she said coyly.

He gave her a smack on the fanny. "As soon as I get there we'll buy the ring."

"Oh, you're talking about marriage?"

"Come on, you know I am."

"I had no idea," she teased. "I need a real proposal. Down on your knee and all that."

"Right now? Here?" he said, grinning at her like a kid.

She nodded.

He dropped to one knee in front of her and she thrilled, knowing what he was going to do.

"Will you say I do?" he asked and, without waiting for her answer, buried his face in the curly black hair of her center.

"Mmm," she moaned.

He backed away, looked up and caught her eye. "I take it that was a yes?"

"Do that again. Yes what?"

He laughed and stood to hug her. "It's time I hit the road. Put a robe on so you can walk me to the car. I want to get home while I'm still awake."

"Be careful Paul. Call me when you get there."

She watched his tail lights disappear down the driveway and hugged herself. Could it really be true?

They were going to Paris. She would have the love of her life and the dream of her childhood together.

"Hannah, I'm getting married and we're coming," she cried, feeling like she could burst with joy and pleasure.

They'd have romantic lunches at some of those famous sidewalk cafés. She'd buy new clothes, French clothes, maybe even something by a French designer. She hugged herself again and danced around the kitchen, imagining herself in Paul's arms at the top of the Eiffel Tower. She'd have to get someone to take their picture there so she could send it back to Molly.

They'd have to look at bigger apartments once they got there. The place she'd rented might not be big enough for the two of them. Maybe they'd buy a small house in the suburbs, or even in the city as long as they could get one with a yard. It didn't have to be a big yard. Just enough so they could have a garden.

And Paul's idea was so wonderful about the boat. Of course, they could rent one and sail the English Channel, or maybe even the Mediterranean.

She hurried inside to get out of the cold and put on her warm pajamas. Wrapping the robe around her again, she headed for the kitchen and began to clean up the dinner mess. She glanced at the clock. Paul had been gone twenty minutes and she was missing him already.

She started the dishwasher and picked up the phone. Punched in Molly’s number.

"Molly. I can't believe we're both going. And we’re getting married. Isn't it wonderful?"

"What are you doing talking to me? Is he asleep or something?"

"He went home. He has to get his passport straightened out and a whole bunch of other stuff done right away."

"You sound like you're delirious. Or are you drunk?"

"I'm drunk on happiness. We're going to sail in the English Channel someday."

She heard it then, outside the house. A car coming up the drive, the sound faint, as if it were moving slowly.

"Is he taking his boat with him?" Molly asked.

"Hold on, someone's coming."

Anne moved toward the front door with the portable phone at her ear. "I thought I heard a car."

"Paul? Maybe he forgot something?"

The sound outside stopped and Anne peered through the sidelight into the darkness of the patio. She flicked on the outside lights and looked again.

"Oh dear God, please no. Molly," she croaked.

~ FORTY-TWO ~

His heart was singing, almost literally it seemed, as he left the island and headed for Kingston. If it were not for the bloody passport he'd turn around and go back to her.

He'd been such an idiot, putting up an argument about Paris. Hurting her for all those days, and for no blasted reason at all except his stubborn pride or stupidity or whatever it was. He flicked on the radio and then turned it off, almost laughing with the warm knowledge that he needed nothing else but Anne. She'd been so happy all day, like a child with ten Christmases at once. He chuckled softly. She was wonderful. Wonderful, wonderful.

He reached the intersection at old Route 1. The light was red, but turned green as he approached. He pulled out to make the left he'd done so many times before.

~ * ~

Anne swung the door open before the man knocked. She simply stood there staring at him, an overwhelming wall of dread draining every ounce of strength from her soul.

"Anne Hoskins?" he asked.

She nodded silently, her hand on the doorknob, her stub against the frame.

"I'm Trooper DiLeo. Rhode Island State Police."

She nodded again, nausea roiling over her.

"I suggest we go inside and sit down, Ma'am," he said softly.

Why are you here? And so nice. I know what nice means. Go away, I don't want to talk to you. I don't want to see you in front of me like this, so quiet and so still.

But she didn't speak, simply turned, and led him into the kitchen.

Still gentle, he said softly, "You might want to sit down, Ma'am."

She took a seat, her breath not working right with the terror rising in her heart, the phone still in her hand. The kitchen seemed very dark for some reason. It had been so bright when Paul was making dinner.

"Do you know a Paul Breland?" the cop asked softly.

His badge glinted in the light against his gray uniform and the radio on his hip squawked briefly. A cop in her house. Being too nice to her. Why didn't he just go away? Not be there in front of her. Ever.

Her mind was playing tricks. She had worried sometimes, in the beginning, that love like theirs could never last. That it would end somehow in disaster. And now, this cop was here. Why didn't Paul call to tell her something was wrong? He'd had a fender bender or got a ticket or something. Why this cop?

"Yes," she whispered, and then, "where is he?"

"There's been an accident. He's on his way to Merritt Hospital by helicopter. Is there someone you can call to be with you?"

"That isn't the Newport hospital."

"It's in Providence, Ma'am." He hesitated and went on. "It has a burn unit."

Her mind was doing tricks. They only used helicopters when the person was really hurt. Badly hurt. There had to be questions she should ask, but she couldn't think, couldn't put words together in her head. A helicopter. A burn unit? Car accidents meant broken bones, that was all. A burn unit?

The cop reached out and took the phone from her hand. Someone was speaking very strangely, the voice tinny but sounding like the person was shouting. The cop put the phone to his ear.

"Hold on a minute," he said. "Who is this?"

Molly, she had forgotten about Molly.

"I'm Trooper DiLeo of the State Police. Are you a friend of Ms. Hoskins?" He paused and Anne could vaguely hear something coming from the phone. "Look, if you live nearby she really could use your help. There's been an accident."

He put the phone down and studied Anne. "Your friend will be here in a few minutes. I can stay until she comes if you'd like."

She stared at him. Was he asking a question? She got up from the chair and walked to the sink. She still hadn't washed the skillet Paul used to make the omelet. Jamming it into the sink with her stub, she grabbed the scrubber and went to work, grinding the scrubber into the nonstick surface as if it were coated with baked on food.

She was still scrubbing when Molly arrived ten minutes later. The cop took Molly by the arm and led her into the living room. Anne stared at the skillet, trying to decide if it was clean. She should get dressed, shouldn't she? Paul was hurt. He'd been in an accident. In his car, of course, it must have been in his car. He'd be all right. She'd go to the hospital and see him and he'd be better.

Molly entered the kitchen, alone. Anne stared at her, stared at the manufactured smile she had plastered on her face. Molly stepped forward and wrapped her in her arms. She pushed back and glared at Molly.

"What did he say? Is Paul all right?"

Molly touched her cheek gently. "There was a crash, and a fire. They're taking him to a burn unit in Providence."

"What's a burn unit?"

"Get dressed now. We'll go see him."

Anne shook her head. "He was in a fire? What happened?"

"We'll find out at the hospital. Get dressed. Where's your phone book? I have to call his daughter."

"It's bad, isn't it?" she whispered, as Molly pushed her toward the bedroom.

"I don't know. Put on something pretty so you look nice when he sees you."

"I don't... He likes that red sweater I had on today."

She had every intention of putting on the red sweater, but somehow she just couldn't move. Molly helped her dress.

"He'll be all right, Molly?" Anne asked, her voice barely above a whisper.

"Yes, hon, he will."

"How did the police come here? Why didn't they call his children?" Anne asked suddenly, the thought coming out of nowhere.

"I don't know. Maybe Paul gave them your name," Molly said crisply. "Now, can you put your shoes on? I have to call his daughter."

Anne's heart soared. Paul gave them her name? That had to be. The police would have no way of knowing about her if he hadn't. "I'll call. You don't know her. Her name is Jane."

Molly nodded and stepped back, watching her with careful concern in her eyes. "You finish getting ready. Let me take care of things like that."

~ * ~

She couldn't get her thoughts in order. Molly made the call to Jane and asked her to relay the news to her siblings. She threw a coat over Anne's shoulders and led her out to her car, then slid into the driver's seat and started down the driveway.

"Where are we going?" Anne asked.

"Providence. To the hospital."

"Where was the accident? In Kingston?"

"No, right here, by Route 1."

Anne grew silent for a moment and then whispered, "Are we going that way?"

Molly threw her a startled look and shook her head. "No, we'll go through Newport."

"Do you think he's badly hurt?"

"Honey, I don't know."

"He is, isn't he? They wouldn't have put him in a helicopter if he weren't."

"I don't know," Molly said again, much too quickly.

~ * ~

Molly parked and slipped out of the car. Anne didn't move until Molly opened the door and almost dragged her from the seat.

Numbly, she followed her friend to the lobby information kiosk, then stood to one side as Molly spoke to the man at the desk. Without another word, they started down a long corridor. People hurried by, busy with their problems, paying no attention. They turned into another corridor and then another and then another and Anne was lost.

But suddenly it was all real. Paul was here and he was burned and he was hurt. He must have spoken to the police, but they had used a helicopter to bring him here. She didn't want to see him. Didn't want to know how bad it was.

Molly stopped in front of a nurse's station. A young woman with red hair sat staring at a computer.

"Excuse me. Where's the burn unit?" Molly asked.

The young nurse looked up. "Are you here to see someone?"

"Paul Breland. They brought him in a little while ago."

The nurse consulted her computer. "They're working on him now. There's a lounge half way down that hall on the right. You can watch TV until someone comes for you."

"Is he all right?" Anne cried, fear like a vise crushing her chest.

The nurse glanced at her and sympathy flickered across her face. "It's too soon to know."

Anne's legs seemed to disappear and Molly's hands grabbed her. The nurse came around the desk and helped drag her to a chair.

It was bad, very bad. The knowledge sucked the breath out of Anne's body. She fell back in the chair, her heart clutching with pain and fear beyond endurance, beyond anything she'd ever known before. This could not be happening. Dear Paul. Her handsome wonderful Paul. No, no, oh please God no. Her world went dark.

Voices murmured around her. Indistinct, garbled, making no sense at all. Molly? And Paul's daughter, Jane? Talking about her. She opened her eyes and stared. And remembered where she was.

"You're awake. At last," Molly said.

Jane bent down and gave her an awkward hug. "Are you all right? We thought you'd never wake up."

She squeezed Jane's hand, drew in a deep breath, let it out in a sigh, and fought to keep tears from starting again. She caught sight of Charlie by Jane's side, and Scott behind them. The family was gathering.

"Have you heard anything? What time is it?"

"Eleven o'clock, and yes, the doctor talked to us," Jane said.

Molly took her hand and held it. "He has second and third degree burns. You won't be able to see him for a while."

Anne shuddered. Struggled to stop the surging in her heart. She had to be brave. For Paul. "Tell me. His face?"

Molly nodded. "Wherever he touched the seat there were no burns, but the fire was everywhere else."

"Why can't I see him?" she asked, not sure she wanted an answer, afraid not to ask.

"They have to clean the burns and make him stable. The biggest danger is infection," Jane said.

Anne stared at her. How could she be so calm? She squeezed Jane's hand and saw the red around her eyes and felt oddly better, knowing Jane shared her pain. And then another question hit her. The same one she had asked the nurse.

"Will he be all right?" she whispered.

Molly looked away and a searing pain ripped through her.

"They don't know," Jane answered softly.

Her belly heaved. She couldn't be sick now, not when Paul needed her. "They have to know. Why don't they?"

"It's the burns. It takes..." Jane started.

"He's going to be all right. He has to be. Why don't they..." Anne cried, but Molly crushed her face against her shoulder.

"There's nothing we can do here. Let's go home. We'll come back tomorrow," Molly said.

"No. I'm staying until he wakes up."

"Anne, please."

"He could die, Molly. Right? He might die? I won't go home."

~ FORTY-THREE ~

Someone had turned on the TV hanging from the wall in the corner of the waiting room. She ignored it and tried to get comfortable in one of the stiff vinyl covered chairs.

The new day dawned gray and rainy, but she barely noticed, didn't care. Charlie went to find coffee. He returned with cups for everyone along with plastic wrapped muffins.

People were all around her, Paul's family and her best friend, but she'd never felt so alone. He was probably a hundred feet away and they might as well be on separate planets. How could everyone chatter on like that? The only voice that mattered was Paul's.

She ached to hear his mellow tenor, telling her he loved her, saying he would go to Paris, teasing about making love. She changed the way she was curled into the green chair and tried to sleep. That was all she wanted if she couldn't have him. Just some quiet darkness to make it go away.

Someone entered the lounge and said something almost unintelligible and then left, but it was enough to catch her attention.

"Who was that?" she asked.

"Somebody. He was probably lost," Jane said.

She stared up at the clock. Again. The hands seemed engraved in place, but somehow it had gotten to be nine a. m. And still no word. She stood and stiffly hobbled toward the nurse's station.

"When can I see my husband?" she asked the blonde nurse typing at the computer.

"Who's that?"

"Paul Breland. He came in last night."

The woman shook her head. "Not for a while yet. He's in isolation and heavily medicated for pain. He wouldn't even know you're here."

"Can't I see him at least?"

The nurse sent her a sympathetic look. "They're still working on him. Treatment has to start right away. Besides, the risk of infection is very high right now so visitors aren't allowed until he's stabilized."

"Couldn't she stand outside his room and look in at him?" Molly asked, suddenly at Anne's side.

"I'll talk to the doctor, but it's not likely."

"We'll be in the lounge," Molly said. She slipped a hand around Anne's waist and gave a small tug.

"I'd like to see the doctor. I was asleep when he came in before," Anne said.

"She," the nurse said with a smile. "I'll tell her."

She let Molly guide her to the lounge and collapsed into a chair. Tired, she was so tired. She looked up at Molly and simply closed her eyes.

"Anne," Molly said, sounding like an angry mother.

"I'm not leaving." She shrugged down into the seat and tried to turn her mind off. If only she could talk to Paul, tell him how much she loved him. That would make him stronger.

She sat back in the chair and stared up at the ceiling, remembering the first time he made love to her. How nervous she'd been. How sweet he'd been, how gentle. Not like yesterday. They'd been so passionate together. Hot and cool and calm and wild, different every time. Naked from the middle of the day until he decided to go home. His skin touching hers, so smooth and firm and strong. His perfect skin. His body so warm and wonderful.

A tear rolled down her cheek, one and then another and she began to sob. It didn't matter if he had scars, nothing mattered except he had to live.

They wouldn't go to Paris. She'd stay with him until he was well again and wanted to travel. He'd have to stay in Rhode Island for treatment, whatever they would do to him. Paris didn't matter anymore. She wouldn't go, couldn't even think of it.

"Molly. You go home. I need you to cancel my flight and take care of my house," she said suddenly.

"There's plenty of time for that. You have most of the week yet."

She didn't have the week, not for that. She'd be at the hospital and they might as well get things settled. She sighed. Molly wasn't going to leave her alone, no matter what she said.

A woman entered the lounge. Jane embraced her before Anne realized who she was. Helen, his other daughter, just in from Chicago. Anne stood numbly to embrace her. They had met only that one time for the family vacation, but she should have known Helen after spending a few days with her. But who knew anything. Her mind was playing tricks on her.

"I caught the first flight I could get. The weather was terrible in Chicago," Helen said breathlessly.

"Well, you're here now so that's good," Jane said.

"How is he?"

"Not good. We're waiting for an update," Charlie said.

"What happened?" Helen asked with a glance at Anne.

"We don't have any details. Someone ran into him and there was a fire," Molly chimed in.

Helen stared at her with a puzzled look on her face, clearly wondering who she was.

"I'm Molly," Molly said. "You must be one of Paul's children. Helen, is it?"

Helen nodded and turned back to Jane. "Is he okay?"

Anne cringed as Jane shook her head and told her sister what they knew at the moment. She watched Helen collapse into a chair and begin to ask question after question. It wasn't hard to see that the young woman was reacting from nerves and anxiety, but it was like rubbing gravel across an open wound for Anne. She got up and started toward the hallway, looking for some quiet.

A woman wearing a white lab coat entered the lounge and stopped in front of her. She glanced around at the people in the room and then fixed her eyes on Anne.

"Are you his wife?"

Anne nodded. There was a gasp behind her from someone, but she paid no heed.

"I'm Doctor Clement," the woman said, "I'll be taking care of your husband today. The nurse said you wanted to talk to me."

Anne stared at her. The good doctor looked barely old enough to have graduated from college no less medical school.

"I... When can I see my husband?" That wasn't what she meant to ask. That wasn't the important thing. She almost sobbed.

"He's medicated right now. He wouldn't know you."

The woman hadn't answered her question. Terrified that there might be significance in that, Anne sucked in a deep breath, marshaling her courage.

"Is he going to be all right?"

It was the doctor's turn to stare. She looked as if the question had surprised her. Steepling her fingers in front of her face, she tried to adopt a dignified appearance.

"Burn cases are very difficult to predict. There's a high risk of infection. There's also great strain on the internal organs at a time like this."

Anne stared at her in silence, unable to make sense of what she'd just been told. Was Paul going to die?

"When can we see him?" Charlie suddenly boomed from behind her.

Dr. Clement looked up at him with a startled expression, then quickly composed herself. As if she were giving a lecture on the life of a fly, she answered, "Are you all family?"

"No, and we don't all need to see him," Molly snapped.

"He's in isolation. No one can see him at the moment. We do allow visitors when patients have been stabilized, but that won't be for a day or two yet."

Anne couldn't breathe. A tremor ran through her body and she began to shake.

"Last night they said he was seventy percent burned," Jane said in a tremulous voice.

The doctor nodded. "That's on the high side. His back and the back of his thighs are okay. He has second and third degree burns though, so that's pretty serious."

"What are his odds?" Charlie demanded.

The doctor gave him a hard look before her face softened. "I'd say about fifty-fifty. I'm sorry, but that's the best I can offer you."

"He'll have scars from the burns, right?" Jane asked suddenly.

"We'll do skin grafts and there are other techniques available nowadays."

"I don't want to hear this anymore," Anne whispered.

She covered her ears and bent down. It was too much-she couldn't bear it. Paul would be scarred and in pain if he even lived. Fifty-fifty? No, he'd get better.

Molly put a hand on her shoulder and pulled her tight against her hip. "When will you know more?"

"I'm sorry. It all depends on how he responds to treatment," the doctor said, sounding resigned. "And even then, it will just be his wife at first and then immediate blood relatives. How many of you are there?"

"He's not married," Helen snapped.

The doctor stared at her and then at Anne.

"They were married last week. By a justice of the peace," Molly said.

Anne looked up, devastated by Helen's outburst. She glanced at the doctor and saw the disbelief in her face. She gave the woman a half smile and waited for her reaction.

"I'm sorry, but if you're not legally his wife I can't let you in to see him," Dr. Clement said softly.

"For how long?" Molly demanded.

"For as long as he's in isolation. Perhaps a number of weeks."

Pain tearing through her heart, too upset to be angry, Anne stared at Helen, not really seeing the younger woman. They wouldn't let her see Paul. Didn't they understand he needed her to get through this?

"Great move, Helen. Just brilliant," Charlie growled.

"We're his family. We should be able to see him first. It's not right..."

"He doesn't need to see us. He needs Anne," Jane said quietly.

"I didn't mean she shouldn't see him. Just not first."

Molly choked back a snarl as Anne got to her feet.

"Don't fight please. Not now," Anne said softly. "Please."

"Let's get out of here. You need sleep," Molly said, still glaring at Helen.

Anne shook her head. She didn't know why, but she couldn't leave, not yet anyway. Paul's family would be given information about him. If she waited with them, she could hear what they heard. And maybe he'd know she was here, know she was waiting to hold him in her arms. Maybe he would feel her love, feel it through the doors, feel it through the walls, through the air somehow.

She knew she was wishing, knew she was being silly, couldn't stop herself from hoping. Didn't want to. All she wanted was to remember their day together yesterday and pretend it hadn't ended, pretend she was in bed with him, laughing, teasing, touching. She remembered pictures she'd seen of burn victims, remembered their shiny scars. Never could she touch his smooth skin again, feel his hard smooth body against hers. What would his face look like? It wouldn't matter. It couldn't; she just wouldn't let it.

"We'll get you in to see him, Anne," Jane said.

"How are you going to do that?" Molly demanded.

"She goes in or no one does," Scott said quietly. "He'll need visitors. They'll allow it if we insist."

Anne stared at Helen. The young woman looked shocked, and then sheepish. If she had more energy Anne would have told her off or something, but that was more than she could manage at the moment.

Catching her eye, Helen said quickly, "I didn't think. I'm just crazy right now." The pleading look in her eyes begged Anne for forgiveness.

Anne stared at her, unable to forgive, but unable to decide anything. Lost and confused, she turned to Molly.

"Come on. We're going home," Molly said again.

She couldn't resist. She'd lost Paul in all the upset. All her feelings for him, all her hope had evaporated in the shock and fear of the last few minutes. With a nod to Molly, she started toward the hall.

"We'll talk to the doctor," Jane said. "Don't worry."

Molly stopped and turned to face Jane. "Thanks. She'll be staying with me for a while. Here's my business card. Call my cell."

Anne kept going, knowing there was one more thing she wanted to do. Had to do, and could. She turned away from the nurse's station and stared into the depths of the burn unit.

Double doors barred her way. Two sets, one in front of the other. A prominent sign on each door read, "Do not enter. Isolation area."

The doors marked off a separate corridor of white walls and polished floors. A separate nurse's station stood halfway down the hall. The place seemed deserted.

It was like looking into a huge empty aquarium, at a world devoid of life, a world she could not enter. Where was everybody? She stopped in front of the double door and stared through the glass. There were buttons to push to open the doors, but she didn't touch them. Paul was in there somewhere, in one of the rooms, with doctors and nurses doing things to make him well again. Wasn't that what the doctor said? Her mind was in a muddle, she wasn't thinking right. But where was everybody?

As if someone had heard her, a person came out of a room, peeled off a white coat, and tossed it into a bin beside the wall. It was a woman, probably a nurse, and the woman walked down the hall and entered another room.

Her heart shuddered, seemed to stop, and then began to race. He was in there, on the other side of the double doors. Were they really working on him or was he alone? Someone should be with him. As long as he wasn't alone. He didn't like to be alone, not anymore. She'd have to tell them that before she left.

She ran her fingers along the glass of the door and stopped them in one place, not far from the edge. Paul. I'm here love. Feel me, I'm here.

She pressed her hand flat, palm tight to the glass, then added her stub, flat as she could make it, urging her love to him.

"Feel me Paul, I'm here. Be strong. Get better," she whispered.

A door opened at the near and of the hall. A nurse came out of a room and stopped to stare at her. Anne ignored him.

"I love you. I love you, love, get better."

The nurse seemed to understand what she was doing. He nodded.

Wanting to beg him to let her stay, afraid he'd chase her away, she nodded back.

He put his hand up, as if to stop her from trying to enter.

"I won't open the door," she mouthed at him, shaking her head.

He showed her a thumbs-up sign and began to remove his outer garments just as the other nurse had done.

Anne closed her eyes, not wanting to communicate in any way with him, wanting only to send love through the door and down the hall to Paul. If only she knew which room he was in. She watched the nurse take a seat at the desk in the hall and turned away. Molly stood beside her, waiting.

She followed Molly down the long confusing corridors and out to the parking lot. The day was cold with a light snow falling and the chill seemed to curl into her heart.

Once the heater got going her eyes began to droop with fatigue. A man appeared before her, reaching out to embrace her. A man without a face. He moved toward her, then stopped, arms still outstretched, but unmoving. She called his name. Not Paul, what was his name? He didn't move. Just waited. She called his name again, again not Paul. He turned away, or did he. His head remained the same, a blank, without hair in the back, without features in the front. She called again. Paul this time, Paul. He turned, or did he, and stood there arms outstretched, waiting. She had to take a step toward him. Many steps. She couldn't.

The sound of gravel under Molly's tires woke her.

"Are you okay?" Molly asked, her voice concerned. "You were having nightmares. I thought you were going to jerk the wheel out of my hands."

"I thought we were going to your house."

"Don't you want to get some clothes for tomorrow?"

Anne stared at the house. Her house with all its memories. Her house no more by the end of the week. She wasn't sure she even wanted to go inside. The bed was still unmade from their last lovemaking. The bottle of wine he'd brought stood empty on the kitchen counter, their glasses beside it with the touch of red resting in the bottom. She could avoid the kitchen, but not the bedroom.

"I don't want to go in," she said softly.

Molly said nothing for a moment, then opened her door and got out of the car. "I'll pack something for you then?"

Anne nodded, relief flooding over her for the moment. She could never go into this house again.

"You want that book you were reading?"

"No, just clothes, whatever's left."

Molly disappeared into the patio and Anne heard the front door open in the silent grayness of the day.

She slipped out of the car and stood, letting the light snowflakes fall on her face. There was no place to go, nothing to do. No one to wait for. Paul wasn't returning from his home today, bringing news about his passport and what he'd done about selling his house. Tight and frightening fear filled her heart. Would he be that faceless man of her dream? Would she be able to approach him without blanching? To kiss him and love him? A tear fell down her cheek and mingled with a snowflake and she brushed it away. With a shiver, she slid back into the car and sat, staring at the house, seeing nothing. Paul had to be all right. A few scars would be nothing in their lives.

"I brought everything that wasn't packed," Molly said, as they dragged Anne's big suitcase into Molly's house a short time later.

"I don't need anything fancy."

"When you see Paul you have to look your best," Molly said and hugged her. "Now, come into the kitchen and I'll make us a late breakfast. I don't know about you, but I'm hungry."

Anne followed her silently and stood unmoving near the white hutch that filled the corner opposite the sink. She stared through the glass doors at the delicate English teacups Molly collected. It seemed odd, but those cups represented something very special in Molly's life. They had talked about them before. Molly's men had come and gone and many things had changed over the years, but she'd had those cups since she was a teenager. Anne really never understood how they could be so significant in a person's life, but she knew Molly would be devastated if anything ever happened to them. Like Paul.

"Why don't you sit down?" Molly asked, as she broke eggs into a skillet.

"I've been sitting for hours."

"You're exhausted. You need to rest."

Anne didn't answer. How could she rest, not knowing. Molly's house was pretty, all decorated in frilly styles, with soft pinks and blues and white backgrounds everywhere. It was a comfortable house, normally. Anne began to pace the kitchen, trying to get her thoughts in order.

So much was in turmoil. Paris was out of the question now, she'd cancel her flight. The house was rented, the movers were coming, and her car was sold. She needed a paint brush in her hand, and a pallet beside her. Needed to splash paint on a canvas, to slash and smoosh colors around and up and down and sideways. And her equipment was in Paris.

"We need to get you a cell phone before you go back to the hospital," Molly said. "You'll need it to keep in touch with Paul's family and the doctors now."

"I was going to get one when I got to Paris."

"It's about time you joined the modern world. And, you'll need another car. It's too bad you sold yours already."

Sold it, but she hadn't made delivery yet. The man was coming to the house tomorrow to pick it up. She would have to meet him there, unless she stayed there instead of at Molly's tonight. That might be a good thing to do. She felt a sudden urge to walk in the woods again, to feel the warmth of nature even in the winter, to feel the silence. Maybe, just for a little while, she could do that tomorrow. If Paul was better.

"I'll rent a car until we go to Paris. We'll only need it until Paul's better."

Molly turned and gave her an odd look, then went back to flipping their eggs. "Okay. We'll do a few errands and then you're going to bed my friend." She set the eggs on the table and added a plate of buttered toast. "Now it's time to eat up."

"I need to find an apartment."

"We can break the lease on your house. You can stay there until Paul's better."

"No. I want to be in Providence so I can be near him."

Molly sent her an inquiring look and smiled. "I was worried about you. Guess I don't need to, huh?"

"I guess not," Anne said, but it was hard to breathe and she wasn't sure at all. Wasn't sure of anything at the moment.

~ * ~

They bought a cell phone, picked up a rental car, and an hour later Anne began unpacking her clothes in Molly's guest bedroom. Exhausted suddenly, she simply flopped across the bright quilted bedcover and fell asleep in the clothes she'd worn the night before.

The blessed stupor of sleep didn't last. Images filled her mind, that faceless man, Paul with a shiny scarred face, the skin red and white and purple, his eyes stark and protruding. She woke up with a start. Twenty minutes after four, the winter sun was setting. She had slept less than two hours. A shower, she needed a shower.

Calling Molly's name, she wandered into the kitchen, but the empty house did not respond. Molly must have thought she'd sleep longer. Graham would be home in another hour or so. Maybe Molly went out for groceries, or to meet him for some reason.

Anne found dry towels in the bathroom, and stripping, quickly showered, and put on fresh clothes. A pale blue turtleneck Paul liked, with a pair of tight jeans. He loved to tease her about the jeans. She remembered the first time he'd followed her around the woods beside the house, how she had been aware he was watching her butt as she walked. Back to the suitcase again, she searched for the skirt she'd worn that day. It wasn't there. The jeans would have to do. If he could move, he could pat her fanny and she knew he'd understand she'd chosen the jeans just for that reason.

She had to get back to Paul. Had to get out of Molly's house. Graham and Molly together, and her sharing their home for tonight would be too much. They'd be awkward together, lovers that they were, and so would she. She couldn't stay with them.

Picking up her new cell phone, she keyed in Grace's number at the store. Dan and Grace lived much closer to Providence and she was sure they wouldn't mind letting her use a bedroom for a few days.

Dan answered the phone with his usual gruff, "Old Folks Antiques, Dan here."

"Dan," she started and broke down.

"Annie? Hey, are you okay? Molly called us about Paul. We know, honey," he said gruffly.

She choked back a sob. "I need a place to stay for a few days. My house..."

"You got it. You at the hospital?"

"I'm at Molly's. I'm going to the hospital now."

"Front door will be open. I'll tell Gracie. Say hello to Paul when you talk to him. We'll see you later. "

With tears streaming down her face, she fumbled for the off button on the phone, not quite sure how to work it yet. Dan was such a dear. He had as much trouble talking to her as she did talking to him.

~ * ~

At the hospital, she navigated the maze of corridors on her own and found Helen sitting in the waiting room. She looked remarkably calm and self-possessed, but as she greeted Anne her voice broke.

"They keep saying they're working on him and there's no news yet," she said. "What kind of news are they waiting for?"

Anne started at the first thought that entered her mind. What news could there be, other than he was getting better? Why did they have to wait to report that? She nodded at Helen, touched her hand, and took a seat beside her.

"Jane and Charlie went to find a motel. Scott left about fifteen minutes ago. He seems to think this is going to go on a long time, so he went home to get some rest."

"What about you? Your job?"

"I told my boss I didn't know when I'd be back."

Jobs, careers, everybody had something important to do. They should be there for Paul. Just as he'd been there for her when her mother died.

"My mother-in-law is taking care of the kids while I'm gone," Helen said.

"Oh. That's good." She wasn't paying attention, but that was no surprise.

Her mind wandered. So much to think about. Making sure she was there to sell the man her old Ford, where was she going to live while Paul was in treatment, would they do skin grafts on his face, remembering the smile in his eyes when they went back to Fletcher's and she enjoyed herself so much. And would he be all right and how bad would the scars be. Remembering the wonderful things they'd done together. And wondering if they would do any of them again.

Paul didn't seem to care what people thought of him, but would he feel the same if he had scars they could see. Maybe they'd be lucky, and his face and hands would be all right. She wished she could see him. See how he looked. Hold him to her breast. Whisper in his ear and tell him she loved him

Another white-coated doctor entered the waiting room.

"Are you the Breland family?" she asked.

"Yes," Helen said quickly with a smile for Anne. "I'm his daughter and she's his wife. Helen and Anne."

The woman nodded. "I'm Tracy Gardner. I'm a counselor for Mister Breland and for you. Have you got a few minutes to talk to me right now?"

"Do you have news?" Anne asked, almost afraid to hear what the woman had to say. Was this the big moment they'd been waiting for? The time when there was news to impart?

"I can bring you up to date on Mister Breland's treatment, but I'm really here to tell you what to expect in the next few weeks."

Anne drew a deep breath of relief. "What?"

Tracy Gardner began then. She explained what the treatment was about, how it worked, what steps the doctors were following. She was reasonably good at keeping everything in plain language, but lapsed occasionally into medical terminology that left Anne confused.

Debrieding, necrotic tissue, the words made no sense at all, but she didn't really want to know what they actually meant. Two things were important, that was all. Would he live and would he be scarred.

Ms. Gardner began to describe the kind of pain he would suffer.

Anne's stomach lurched. Something had happened. It felt as if a door had slammed in her face and she was in a black hole with Paul, locked in forever, with nothing but frigid cold and darkness everywhere.

She strained to cry out to him, to let him know she loved him, to tell him everything would be all right.

Don't give up love, I love you, she screamed in her heart.

It's hard.

Had she heard him? Had he answered, or was that her imagination playing games?

I love you Paul. I love you so much.

She waited. There was no answer. A tear trickled down her cheek. She wiped it away, but another followed and she leaped to her feet. She would not cry. It did no good. Paul needed her strength. If he had heard her and answered, she couldn't let him know how frightened she was.

Ms. Gardener stared up at her. "Is something wrong?"

"Be still," she snapped. She needed quiet, needed the silence to send her love to Paul. Her hand began to tremble with the effort and she felt Helen squeeze gently. And then there was something else, a feeling, something very small that started growing, that began to spread throughout her body.

Something coming back?

Paul? What is it Paul?

I'm trying love.

She rushed to the glass doors. A nurse hustled out of one of the rooms at the far end of the corridor, dashed across the hall and returned with something in her hand. A doctor hurried after her.

Anne touched her hand to the glass. She jerked back, shocked by how cold it felt. Pressing her palm against it again, adding her stub, she pushed her love to Paul again. A sob rose from her belly. She wasn't helping, nothing she could do would stop what was happening. The glass was so cold. She sobbed, turned and stumbled back to the waiting room and sat down, back stiff, without looking at anyone. For the first time since her childhood she began to pray.

"What's wrong?" Helen demanded. "You look sick."

"Something's happening. In one of the rooms."

Helen leaped to her feet and rushed to the glass doors, then came dashing back. "I couldn't see anything. What's happening?"

"Doctors and nurses went into one of the rooms," Anne said, her voice breaking, trying not to say what was going through her head, what she knew was happening.

Helen stared at her. "They do that all the time. I've seen them do it."

Anne nodded. How could she tell his daughter? She'd know soon enough. They all would.

Helen shook her head and sat down, still staring at Anne.

A worried looking male doctor broke the silence in the room a few minutes later. Massive infection had set in.

Her precious love was gone.

~ FORTY-FOUR ~

She woke up to the brightness of a clear day, uncertain for a moment where she was. Then she knew. She was in Grace's house and Paul had died. How had she gotten there? Through the fog in her head it came clear, Grace and Dan had brought her home. Paul was dead. He was gone, for always and forever. He'd never come to her door again. Never hold her, never kiss her, never tell her he loved her. He was dead.

A shiver slid down her back. She crawled out of bed and searched for something to wear. And then noticed she was still wearing the turtleneck and jeans, and tears began and would not stop. Fumbling blindly through her suitcase, she found a blue skirt and white shirt, not Paul's favorite skirt, but what did it matter. She changed and stumbled into the bathroom.

Her hair was a straggly mess, her eyes sunken, wet, and red, but she grabbed a washcloth and began to wipe her face. It was good she hadn't gone in to see Paul. One look at her and he would have known he was doomed. She quickly ran a comb through her hair and teeth half brushed, she headed for Grace's kitchen. It was midday, sometime, and Grace was probably at the shop with Dan, but maybe she could find a bite, though she wasn't sure she could swallow.

The clock over the sink said two-forty-three. Grace stood leaning against the counter, slicing peeled potatoes. She turned as Anne entered, her face drawn but composed.

"Hello dear. How are you today?"

"Weary."

Grace nodded without a smile. "Are you hungry? I can make you something quickly."

"All right, thank you."

Anne sat down at the table and laid her head on her arms. The tiredness was heavy on her head, numbing and overwhelming.

"Did you come home early?" she asked.

Grace sent her a weak grin. "We didn't get home from the hospital until almost four-thirty. Dan and Millie are running the store today." She studied Anne for a moment and then said, "What are you going to do today?"

"What day is it? I've lost track."

"Tuesday."

Anne struggled to remember the things she had to deal with. Someone was coming to pick up the car, movers would be emptying out her house so the new people could move in. She was supposed to fly to Paris Friday. And there was the funeral.

Arrangements had to be made, or were his daughters doing that? They had talked during the wee hours, made some kind of plans, but she couldn't remember anything they'd said. Or, maybe, yes, there was something Jane mentioned.

Cremation. They wanted to do a cremation. With all the burns he suffered, they wanted to do more. Tears began again.

Grace abandoned the potatoes and wrapped Anne in her arms. "It's all right dear. Go ahead and cry."

"They want to cremate him," she sobbed. "After all he's been through."

"I thought Jane said that was what he wanted."

Anne groaned. Of course, Paul had said that, but that was before the fire, before he was so horribly burned. Before she had seen him so damaged. She had almost refused the doctor's invitation, but it wouldn't have been right if she walked away. It was important to know exactly what he'd been through, and so she went in to see him when they let her. She would never forget.

He wasn't Paul, not her Paul, not the way he looked in that horrible white room with all those metal things and pans and tubes and bottles and the bed. Not her Paul. No, no, no. She whimpered and Grace heard and wiped her face and it did no good at all. She sobbed and couldn't stop and it didn't matter and she cried until her eyes went dry. Grace put her back to bed.

~ * ~

Somehow, she made it through the next few days. Dan went to meet the man who'd bought her car and she didn't care. Grace went with her to deal with the movers. The things that remained in the house were going to different places and she had to be there to tell them what to take and what to leave. She forgot where everything was supposed to go and gave them arbitrary directions. What did it matter.

Before the end of the week she had to decide whether to go to Paris as scheduled. The decision required no thought. She couldn't go, not without Paul, and not without going to the memorial service for him. His children arranged that along with the cremation and she hated them for doing it.

Dan and Grace, Molly and Graham, even Betty and Millie drove down to his hometown and attended with her. She kept waiting for him, almost believing he would walk down the aisle of the church to sit beside her with that familiar easy grin on his face.

"Sorry I'm late," he would say. "The traffic was terrible." And then it hit her heart that she'd never hear his voice again. Molly threw an arm around her as she tried to choke back racking sobs.

~ * ~

"You should go to Paris like you planned," Molly said more than once.

She couldn't. She needed to hold on. There was very little left to her. The house was gone, the car, her daily routines. Her tools had been stored, her art supplies shipped to Paris well over a month ago. Still living in Grace's second floor bedroom, she didn't even have a place of her own. Or her Paul.

All she had were memories. It was the strangest thing. The memories started with Paul and ended with Paul. That first day he came to the house when he was injured. How frightened she'd been, but how excited too. And the day he came back with Jane and she saw the look in his eyes, and had known he'd come back again. How could she have thought to go to Paris without him? What a fool she'd been. All those days lost, all that time wasted in stubborn, foolish hurt and anger.

She held tight to the memories, played them in her mind, wanting him to be alive forever. But they came each time with a terrible ache in her heart and that awful weight in her chest. Three weeks went by, then four. She couldn't read, couldn't concentrate, stared blindly at the TV. Rarely did she leave the bedroom, except to help Grace with cleaning or cooking. Grace's home felt comfortable, much as her own had been before Paul first arrived. Calm, and still, and safe. Except when the tears came and she thought her heart would break.

She began to fidget. She woke up as she often did before, in the wee hours of the morning, an idea in her head, ready to splash paint on canvas. Except she had no canvas and no paints, and the ideas drifted into a gray haze of weary oblivion.

She began to walk the neighborhood near Grace's house, blind to the sights and sounds around her, her artist's eye seared shut against the pain. If she were to paint, her palette would be black and fire, hurt and pain.

Dan dragged her to the shop and she worked with him and talked to customers, but they were not enough. She recalled the day they brought Louie back to Dan; the way Paul had teased him and her old friend's delight when they took the blanket cover off the chair.

"You're living in the past," Molly said one day.

"What else do I have? Paul is gone."

"You had a life before you met him. You have to start living again."

"Says who?" Anne snapped, regretting the words even as she spoke.

Molly took her face in her hands. "Listen to me. You're moping around like a zombie. Everything is negative. It's time to get off your butt and move."

"You have no idea..." Anne started, ready for a fight.

"Yes I do. I never felt quite the kind of hurt you're in, but don't forget I've had guys walk out on me. I hurt then too."

"It's not the same."

"Yeah well, one thing is. You beat me over the head until I stopped feeling sorry for myself. And now my friend, I'm about to do the same to you."

"I'll feel sorry all I want."

"Paul would be ticked, you know? You're right back to the way you lived before he came along."

Molly's words slapped her in the face. Anne stared at her, her brain trying to strike back, to defend herself, her heart too staggered to snap out an answer.

Molly nodded, seeing Anne's reaction. "So, you're about to face the world again. Think of me as Paul's replacement. Starting now. Let's get drunk."

They did that day and Molly was as good as her word. She badgered and pushed. Demanded Anne book a flight to Paris. And then, a week later a letter arrived from the Paris rental agent.

"Madame;

I am informed that you have not paid the most recent monthly fee. Were you not to arrive on 12 January? I am informed that no one has seen you. If you do not respond by post in the next two weeks your lease will be canceled."

She crumpled the paper and threw it on the kitchen table with a tear threatening to run down her cheek. She was so emotional over everything. It was ridiculous.

"What's that?" Grace asked.

"A letter from Paris. They're going to cancel the lease on my apartment."

Grace picked up the crinkled paper and spread it out to read. "Oh, you'd better send them some money then."

Anne stared at her. She almost asked why she should, but knew without an explanation exactly what Grace had in mind.

"I'm not going."

"Paul would be disappointed. He'd be horrified to think you wouldn't go now."

It was almost the same accusation Molly had made. She raised an eyebrow at her friend, angry bile rising in her throat.

"That's dirty."

Grace shrugged. "He wanted you to have your dream."

"I wanted to go there with him."

"Not in the beginning. Remember? Somebody I know was determined to go alone if she had to."

Anne bit her tongue rather than start a fight. Her emotions were on edge, but if she didn't keep quiet she'd regret it. First Molly and then Grace and of course, Grace was right. Paul would want her to go.

Jane drove up to see her, bringing a portion of Paul's ashes, if she wanted them, in a tiny urn. She thought to put it on the mantle, but it was Grace's mantle not her own, so she put it on the nightstand in her bedroom.

She sent the rent money to Paris and told herself it was a waste and she was stupid, but she did it. And she looked at the urn, and stared at it and one day he spoke to her. It was as if he did, Paul did, and he told her how disappointed he was that she wasn't getting out after all the work they'd done together. Told her there was nothing left for her with the house and car gone and all her precious things in storage somewhere. Told her to buy a ticket and get on a plane. She told him he couldn't tell her that, he was dead, and she burst into tears again.

Her life was on hold. She was still renting a car, but rarely used it and spent her time in her bedroom, or walking the streets, or occasionally helping out in the shop, partly to repay Dan and Grace for their hospitality, and partly to occupy her mind. She was numb when she wasn't crying and it didn't matter at all. But it bothered her that Paul would have been disappointed. A lot.

She looked at the apartment ads in the newspaper, but couldn't bring herself to call about the ones that sounded good. Dan asked her to take on another restoration project and offered her a corner of the shop to work in. Bringing a piece of furniture back to life struck her as a sacrilege and she turned him down. It had been three months since Paul died and she was feeling sorry for herself. Grieving was one thing, self-pity something else. Something had to change. She bought a new prosthesis and went shopping for thank you gifts for her best friends.

~ * ~

Three days later Anne was sitting in the boarding area at Logan Airport waiting for a flight, feeling like a boat adrift in a storm. She was done with self-pity. Maybe not with grief, but that she would deal with.

Molly and Dan and Grace had come to bid her goodbye and her emotions were dangerously explosive. Graham had come with them, but he was only a business contact. She really didn't give a darn about him.

She took out a small package of tissues and used one to pat her eyes. Returning the tissues to her purse, she glanced up to find a man watching her from a seat across the aisle. He smiled and nodded, his thick black hair tossing slightly with the movement. He looked to be about her age, perhaps a little younger. The smile he sent her was sweet and included his dark eyes. She ignored him.

She had a book to read and resolutely turned it open, determined to lose herself in its pages.

"Mademoiselle?"

She started, and looked up to find the man almost leaning over her. "What?"

"I'm sorry, but you seem upset. May I help in some way?" he said in a heavy French accent.

"No thank you. I'm fine."

"You are off to France for a vacation?"

Anne sighed. He was trying to pick her up? A fifty-four year old woman with a prosthesis? And then Paul's voice came to her with his familiar words. You are so beautiful. So lovely and so brave. Be brave now, my love.

She started. It was in her head, she was imagining again. How silly she was. Don't make a fool of yourself now, be calm.

She studied the stranger. A good looking man despite that sharp nose he had. A pleasant face, probably in his late forties or so, a few streaks of gray in that black hair she hadn't noticed at first. He might have a high opinion of himself, but he didn't color the hair at least. She could be polite if nothing else.

"Actually, I'm moving to Paris. I have an apartment there."

"Have you been there before?"

"This is my first time."

"You go alone?" he asked, sounding thoroughly amazed.

"I'm meeting my cousin. He'll be at the airport when I arrive," she lied.

"Ah, that is good." He glanced down at her ring-less hand. "There is no husband?"

Despite herself, her breasts heaved as a sob almost ripped from her body.

The stranger noticed. "I am sorry Madame. I did not know."

"Never mind. I'm fine."

He leaned back and seemed to consider her, then offered his hand. "I am Giles Bombardier. Paris is my home."

Very deliberately, she reached out her prosthesis instead of the right hand. He shook it as if it were the most natural thing to do and nodded at it.

"You have been injured badly. I am sorry."

"It's fine." She wasn't sure what she felt for a moment. His words had been relaxed and natural, not the least bit awkward.

He smiled at her then, and she heard it again. A voice in her head. He's a good man. Tell him your name.

"I'm Anne Hoskins," she whispered.

Paul, are you talking to me? He was urging her on? Was she imagining again, like she did sometimes with Hannah? Like she did before? He's a good man. There it was again, clearly Paul's voice.

"Anne. That is a very pretty name," Giles said, offering a gentle smile. "I wonder. Perhaps you would like a guide? Until you learn your way about the city? I know the best places to buy your groceries."

A soft stroke of warmth whispered in her heart.

She smiled.

~ END ~

About the Author:

A Blanket for Her Heart is RC Bonitz's second book. He has been writing for sixteen years and has more to come. He is a member of the Romance Writers of America and the Connecticut chapter of RWA.

A father of five children; he lives in Connecticut with his wife, just down the road a piece from Long Island Sound. Many years a sailor, he has retired to a canoe and fishing rod. And his computer. You can contact him via his blog at http://www.rcbonitz.com

Made in the USA
Charleston, SC
16 April 2012